ALEXANDER FULLERTON

Look to the Wolves

WARNER BOOKS

A *Warner* Book

First published in Great Britain in 1992
by Little, Brown and Company
This edition published by Warner Books in 1993

A CIP catalogue record for this book
is available from the British Library.

ISBN 0 7515 0399 1

Printed in England by Clays Ltd, St Ives plc

Warner Books
A Division of
Little, Brown and Company (UK) Limited
165 Great Dover Street
London SE1 4YA

LOOK TO THE WOLVES

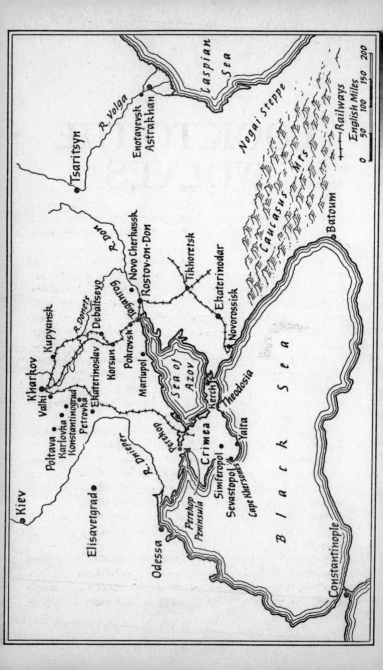

Kiev

Elisavetgrad

Poltava
Karlovka
Konstantinograd
Petrovka

Kharkov
Valki

Ekaterinoslav

Kupyansk

R. Donets

Debaltsevo

Korsun

R. Dnieper

Perekop
Peninsula

Odessa

Pokrovsk
Mariupol

Sea of
Azov

Crimea
Simferopol
Sevastopol
Cape Khersones

Yalta

Kerch

Theodosia

Novo Cherkassk
Rostov-on-Don
Taganrog

R. Don

Tsaritsyn

R. Volga

Enotayevsk
Astrakhan

Caspian
Sea

Nogai Steppe

Tikhoretsk

Ekaterinodar

Novorossisk

Caucasus Mts

Batoum

Black Sea

Constantinople

Railways
English Miles
0 50 100 150 200

1

When the racket of machine-gun fire jarred him out of sleep his waking reaction was to push his hand under the pillow to his Webley pistol: now he was on his back, listening intently, holding the weapon on his chest outside the bedclothes.

Lying still, listening — to unbroken silence — and noting that dawn's beginnings were visible in the gap between the curtains. So — four-thirty, roughly. Dismissing the thought that the shooting could have been part of some dream: there'd only been that one blast, perhaps half a dozen rounds, but the barking of the gun still reverberated, echoed ... And there was no mystery as to who'd have done the shooting — unless of course some person or persons unknown had caught Kotter's man napping, if that had *not* been the Lewis gun which Kotter and his cronies had set up in the hotel foyer, its muzzle trained day and night on the street door.

If that was the case — if Kotter's henchman had been the victim — intruders might now be on their way upstairs. He moved the other arm out into the cold — this thought having sparked action that was overdue — to jerk the top round from the pistol's magazine into its chamber. Then he was still again: listening, with the arm back in cover.

Not that one could think of *oneself* as sufficiently important to be a target. At least, one hadn't — up to this minute ...

Nonsense, anyway. There probably wasn't a single Red who even knew of one's existence. Or would give a damn. But there were plenty of others in the hotel who'd surely qualify as enemies of the revolution. As many as fifty or sixty of them, all former Tsarists, now refugees and awaiting — begging, in some cases — sea transport westward. Having in most cases to grease French palms before they'd get their names added to the waiting-lists.

To the Reds, of course, the slaughter of such people could be virtually an end in itself. And the Crimea was swarming with Red infiltrators and sympathizers, only waiting for their time to come. As Kotter and his henchmen were well aware.

Go down, take a look?

He — Bob Cowan — slid out of the warm bed and shrugged his naval greatcoat on over his pyjamas. No need to switch the light on: the coat had been in easy reach, spread on the bed for extra warmth. Here at Sevastopol you had the benefit of the Black Sea's tempering influence, but this was still December, with a Russian winter blanketing that vast hinterland to the north.

And everything going to hell again. White armies, who'd been riding high a few months ago, reeling back, the Bolshevik counter-attack gaining momentum on all fronts.

And *she* was out there somewhere . . .

He jerked the curtains open, to let in the dawn's grey light. Too high and sheer, up on this second floor, to see down into the street from the closed window. No sound penetrating, meanwhile. If a patrol had heard the shooting — and surely one would have, there'd have to have been one within, say, half a mile — they must have turned deaf ears. Military policing here was shared by the French and the Greeks, but it was mainly French, and they tended not to risk their own necks or over-exert themselves when they didn't have to.

So — cause and effect — you could say there was good reason for the existence of Kotter and his team of vigilantes. The plain fact was that the French were useless. The Russians — the Volunteer Army — loathed them.

He buttoned his coat, pushed size ten feet into old tennis-shoes that served as slippers, and the gun into his right-hand pocket. It was a Webley and Scott .455 automatic, advertised by its makers as possessing 'Greater Smashing and Stopping Power than any other Automatic on the Market', and it had been issued to him by Colonel Temple, Royal Marines, the naval intelligence officer in Constantinople.

At the door, now. Turning its squeaky handle as quietly as possible using his left hand, the right one in his pocket on the pistol.

'Hah! Commander!'

Short, tubby, dressing-gown sash pulled in tight round his paunch, sparse ginger hair fringing a round, white crown: former middle-ranking diplomat, name of — Nyeporojhnii. Pompous little man, liked to air his French although he knew Bob's Russian was as fluent as his English. The Nyeporojhniis' bedroom door was ajar behind him: that camel-like wife listening to every word or move, of course ... 'What d'you think's happening, my dear Commander — all that shooting?'

A nod: 'On my way down to find out.'

'Ah. Well. If *you're* going down, I won't—'

'No.' Bob told him, 'Go back to bed, if I were you.' He started down the stairs. These people seemed to regard him as their protector — despite the fact the Crimean port and the Black Sea coast to the west of it was in French mandate. It spoke well for the reputation of the Royal Navy, perhaps. And there was a British cruiser and a destroyer in the anchorage, as well as the French battleship *Jean Bart* and the Greek armoured cruiser *Averov*. People in dressing-gowns or overcoats were milling around on the landing below, and there was a murmur of low voices; and the Ukrainian girl, Aksana Lyashkova, was climbing the stairs towards him. Her room was on this top floor, next to the Nyeporojhniis'. She was in her mid-twenties, very attractive — more of a Georgian look than Ukrainian, one might have thought. In colouring, for sure: big, dark eyes slightly aslant, café-crème complexion ... Addressing him now: 'Commander — really, it's too frightful! There's a man dead down there, shot down just like a dog! Right here in the hotel, if you please!'

'My dear young lady.' Nyeporojhnii, smirking down at her over the bannister. 'Don't distress yourself. Those fellows know what they're about, you know. Anyway, the Commander's on his way down, don't worry your pretty head, he'll—'

'Commander.' She was ignoring Nyeporojhnii. Her quilted dressing-gown clung rather bulkily, unflatteringly: her figure was in fact — Bob had noticed, a couple of times — sensational. 'If you could spare a minute — oh, perhaps not now, *this* minute, but—'

'I do rather want to get down there.' She had his left hand in both of hers now; the small, caressing movements she was giving to it might have been only symptoms of anxiety, a sort of fiddling. But her closeness to him, and the soft hands, the heady perfume had an effect, all right ... He frowned: 'Perhaps in the morning.'

'*Thank* you, Commander ...'

'Excuse me.' Her hands released him but her eyes and scent followed him down to the next landing. Nyeporojhnii's wife summoning her husband back into their room, meanwhile, calling the little man to heel. The Lyashkova girl was probably a spy, Ashmore had said in the notes he'd left by way of a very skimpy handover to Bob. And having on top of that seen her strolling arm-in-arm with a particularly obnoxious Frenchman, one had dutifully stayed clear.

Until now.

But — even if Ashmore's guess was wrong — in this snake-pit it would be lunacy...

Ashmore — Lieutenant, Royal Navy — had been gone by the time Bob had arrived here, a week ago, and those notes had been the only briefing that he'd had. Not that he'd come to take over the man's job, in any case, he'd been sent here to concentrate on one specific task. He'd been on his way, taking passage from Constantinople in the destroyer *Terrapin*, when Ashmore had been summoned to Novorossisk by the Rear Admiral 3rd Cruiser Squadron, who was currently visiting that port with his flag in HMS *Centaur*. So Bob had found himself a stranger in a strange town with another man's job on his hands and not much idea of how to set about it.

He had the hang of it now though, more or less. The job was to maintain a list of persons entitled to passages out of Russia in British ships, and allocate any available berths to them in such ships as called. One had also to beat off French attempts to extend their own system of bribes into the British operation. That was the basic, routine function. But realistically, you were in a last-ditch situation. There'd be no more refugees arriving, unless they came by sea — from Novorossisk or elsewhere in the Caucasus, for instance — because the Crimea was by now isolated. There was heavy fighting around Perekop, the narrow isthmus that was the land-bridge to and from Taurida and the Ukraine, and no certainty at all that the Whites would hold out there; while the eastern flank — the Kerch peninsula and the north and west coasts of the Sea of Azov — was being held only with help from the Royal Navy's guns. Evacuation, therefore — although one wouldn't so much as whisper the word, here in the Kist Hotel — was a contingency for which one had to be prepared.

His own special brief, which had been given to him by Colonel Temple, RM in Constantinople, had to do — for heaven's sake — with governesses.

He'd thought Temple had been pulling his leg, when the subject had first come up; but it was nothing but the truth — when he came to think of it, casting his mind back to his own childhood here in Russia — that before the war there'd been many British women employed as such, both in St Petersburg — where he, Bob, had been brought up — and along the coast eastward from here, the sun-baked Yalta coastal strip where so many well-to-do Russian families had summer residences. Palaces, even. British governesses, nannies and nursemaids had been more or less standard furnishings in pre-war days, and quite a number of them had stayed on. Now there was some urgency — had been pressure from London, apparently, in recent weeks — some of the families demanding that their daughters should be found and shipped home — and some — two, to be precise — had failed to respond.

'Excuse me.'

'Oh — Commander—'

'Countess. Forgive me, but — I'll be back presently. Please, excuse me ...'

Like hens clucking, and a few nervous old roosters strutting around the fringes. Poor devils ... He went on down the last flight of stairs. Maroon carpet, threadbare patches here and there, brass fittings on mahogany. Above him as he came on down a few residents hung around or craned over to see what might transpire, but he could also hear doors clicking shut as others drifted back into their rooms, satisfied presumably that no assassin had got in.

But maybe one had tried?

That one.

Sprawled on the carpet, just inside the door. White face with blood all over it, watery brown eyes open, fur hat still in place and a shard of glass hanging from a deep gash in the cheek. This was where the visible blood was coming from; the glass was a splinter from the top half of the street door, which had shattered.

Civilian overcoat, leather-trimmed and fur-collared. Boots heavily muddied. A revolver — a Russian Nagant — lay on the carpet close to the outflung right arm.

'See, we're not here just for our own amusement, Commander!'

Kotter himself. A big man — about Bob's own height and weight — in Imperial Army uniform, greatcoat with shoulder-boards, breeches and boots, fur *shapka* adding a few inches to his height. The Armenian hotel manager looked like a dwarf beside him, and behind them both the one-eyed Grusjenko was sitting on what they called the duty officer's chair, close to the stove and behind the Lewis gun. The chair was gilt, with spindly legs and red velvet upholstery.

A gesture towards the body: 'Proof of the pudding — wouldn't you say?'

Grusjenko chuckled, juggling spent cartridge-cases in one palm and looking delighted with himself. He'd lost the eye in the fighting around Kiev, in February – this year, 1919, just ten months ago — and he wore a patch over the empty socket. The Bolsheviks had taken Kiev. That was when the French had begun to think about evacuating Odessa, which they'd done in April with very little advance warning, leaving thousands to be murdered, entire families committing suicide on the quays as the ships pulled out.

The manager began 'If you gentlemen will excuse me now—'

'Did you telephone the Monsieurs?'

'Not yet, Captain—'

'Do it. Get this removed, for God's sake!'

'At once. At once …'

'Does anyone know who this is — or was?' Bob looked from Grusjenko to Kotter, as the manager withdrew. 'Or what he was after?'

'Burst in with that pistol in his fist.' Kotter's face was squarish, heavy-jowelled. Dark with stubble, now. He stood with a list to port, his weight on the stick he always carried. He'd taken a shell-fragment in his knee, and that leg didn't bend. When he walked, he swung it out in a half-circle. Nodding down towards the Nagant: 'It's fully loaded. Wasn't calling in to pass the time of day, was he?' He swung round to Grusjenko: 'Didn't have time to ask him for his papers — eh?'

'Certainly did not!'

'Which, however —' Kotter showed Bob — 'here, see for yourself. Name's Lapin — Alexis Lapin. Transport driver and interpreter, it says there.'

Bob gazed down at the soiled, creased document. Taking care, as the name Lapin struck home, not to react or give any sign of recognizing it. But Alexis Lapin was the name Colonel Temple had given him, the name of the man who'd been supposed to contact him here. In fact one hadn't expected him to show up quite this soon. Temple, in Constantinople, had asked an individual by name of Reilly — Captain Sidney Reilly, who had a British passport and fluent, unaccented English but had been

born an Odessan Jew — to put out enquiries as to the
whereabouts of the two missing women. Governesses,
nannies, whatever they'd been. Only two, because all the
others had either come forward when invited to do so,
presenting themselves for passages home to Britain, or
had been found and brought out. There'd been about two
dozen of them, initially. It was known that the missing girls
had volunteered as nurses or nursing aides: which for Bob came
close to the bone, since *she* had also gone back to nursing.

At least, she'd expressed an intention of doing so. In the
same letter in which she'd broken it to him that she'd
married Count Nicholas Solovyev.

Which made her none of his — Bob's — business, now.
As he was having constantly to remind himself. At every
time of waking from sleep, for instance, it was a reality to
be faced, accepted.

But the governesses — those two had been at the
hospital in Simferopol as trainees, they'd gone off on leave
and never reported back. The hospital people had made
enquiries, found no trace of them and assumed they'd
deserted, run away home to England.

He handed the dead man's papers back to Kotter. 'Anything else on him?'

'Nothing. Take a look, if you like.'

The linings of Lapin's pockets had all been pulled out,
as proof of their emptiness. Or to save the searcher
looking twice. Not that this was any kind of proof that
there'd been nothing to find in the first place. Nor for that
matter that the whereabouts of a pair of British governesses — *if* Lapin had discovered anything about them —
need have been any major part of his preoccupations or
endeavours. Captain Reilly wasn't employed by Temple or
by British naval intelligence, more likely he was either
freelance or Secret Service, or conceivably both; but he
had contacts everywhere and he'd told Temple he'd entrust
the investigation to a certain Alexis Lapin, with instructions to transmit anything he discovered about any of the
women directly to Lieutenant-Commander Cowan at the
Hotel Kist, Sevastopol.

And here he was.

Icy draft ... Glancing at its cause, the shattered upper part of the swing door, he was surprised he hadn't heard the glass breaking. Except that — well, from two floors up: and those bedroom doors were solid, heavy timber. The noise of the gun was a different matter, you'd hear that through concrete. He stooped, carefully removed the sliver of glass from Lapin's unshaven cheek. The flow of blood from that small wound had more or less stopped, but on the dead man's torso patches were darkening and slowly expanding in the fabric of the coat.

Kotter asked him, '*You* never saw him before, I suppose?'

Glancing up: allowing surprise to show, at the question that hardly deserved an answer. Kotter's slits of eyes shifting to the body, then back to him ... 'Or heard the name?'

He straightened up, dusting the skirts of his greatcoat. 'Should I have?'

Kotter studying him, the expression on his heavy face saying *You tell me* ... Nobody trusting anyone at all: and usually with good reason. Bob wondered whether Lapin had, as Grusjenko had alleged, burst in with the revolver in his hand, or whether he might only have made an abrupt, noisy entry and Grusjenko's finger tightened on the trigger — in reaction to sudden fright — as his single eye blinked open. Then they'd have dropped the Nagant where it lay now. Otherwise, wouldn't it have been more natural to have picked it up and taken the shells out of it, rather than have left the stage set as it was?

He thought it would have been. Nobody in his right mind left loaded guns lying around. When you'd been used to handling guns, that sort of thing was more or less instinctive.

They might even have had some reason of their own for killing Lapin. Knowing these people, you couldn't discount it as a possibility. Climbing the stairs slowly, putting his feet at the edges of each tread where the timber creaked less; he didn't want to be intercepted again and bombarded with their unanswerable questions. Besides, they could sleep late if they wanted to, and he couldn't. He had a problem now; and the answer to it was to get up early and out to the cruiser, *Caledonian*, whose captain was currently the senior British naval officer here, and arrange for the despatch of a signal to Constantinople to let Temple know that Reilly's man had turned up dead.

Reilly would transfer the enquiry to one of his other contacts, no doubt. He'd need to know about Lapin anyway, they'd surely have more irons in the fire together than this one of Temple's. Sidney Reilly was a fairly bizarre character, himself. But presumably he was on the right side, could be trusted. Making him, if this was the case, more or less unique. But that was for Temple's judgement, not one's own.

All the bedroom doors on the first landing were shut, and stayed shut as he padded past them. Climbing again: hoping to God he wasn't in for another session of French small-talk with Nyeporojhnii. But their door was shut too, and the wide landing was empty. Thanks to the Ukrainian girl, he thought: Madame Nyep wasn't giving hubby any rope when *that* one was on the loose.

Her door was shut too. Really shut — not just pulled-to, as for a moment he'd thought it might be.

Wishful thinking ... But — coming to earth and practicalities, as he shut his own door quietly — it was about five now: so two hours' sleep, then a quick wash and shave, and if he was down there to connect with the cruiser's first boat inshore he'd be on board in time to cadge a decent breakfast.

2

'Tell me, Cowan.' In *Caledonian*'s wardroom her navigator, a lieutenant-commander by name of Hackett, had nodded off over his after-lunch coffee, had actually been snoring at one stage; now he'd stirred, was blinking across at Bob from the depths of the Admiralty-issue, horsehair-stuffed armchair. 'About these young ladies — governesses, you said ...'

It was three days since the encyphered signal had been tapped out to Constantinople. Bob was spending as much time as possible on board — including nights, sleeping in the captain's sea-cabin, a sort of tin dog-kennel in the bridge superstructure which wasn't used when the ship was in harbour and had been offered to him as an alternative to the hazards of the Kist. And this was the best place to be; as a matter of routine the ship's telegraphists were keeping round-the-clock listening watch, sooner or later Colonel Temple had to come up with *some* reaction to the report of the courier's death, and it would save time and trouble if one was on the spot to get it.

If there was to be an answer. If this wasn't a dead-end ...

'Cowan?'

He'd been scanning a two-months-old copy of the *Morning Post*. References in its pages to Britain's involvement in this civil war included reports of military withdrawal from Archangel and Murmansk, and of 47 Squadron RAF's spectacular performance in support of General Wrangel's advance through Tsarytsin to Kamyshin. There was also coverage of the Prince of Wales' tour of Canada and the United States, and a somewhat ambiguously-phrased review of Lady Astor's chances of becoming Britain's first woman Member of Parliament. Having finished this, Bob lowered the paper and focused on the navigating officer's pale face and puffy eyes.

'Sorry ... What about them?'

'Well. Suppose the monkey who got shot the other night had managed to reach you with whatever information he was bringing—'

'Might not have had any. I don't know, but I think he may have been coming to Sevastopol anyway.'

'Do you know where from?'

Thumbing tobacco into a pipe, he shook his head. 'Not the foggiest.'

'Well. Couldn't be from any great distance, could it? Seeing that nobody can get in or out of the Crimea, as things stand at present?'

'I honestly don't know. But a man of his kind — may well have had a foot in both camps. Spies and so on do manage to come and go, don't they?'

'Ah. Ah, well ... Those Johnnies at the Kist *might* have had reasons of their own for shooting him.'

'It's possible.'

'Yes. Yes ... What thrilling times we live in, don't we?' Hackett yawned. He'd been to a party in the Australian destroyer *Yarra* the previous night. 'Anyway — I know curiosity killed the cat, but — what I'm really asking, I suppose, is if he'd got to you and told you where the girls are, what would you have done about it?'

Striking a match. Then — between huffs — 'Depends.'

'On what?'

'On what he had to tell us, of course.' Hackett wasn't too bright, he thought — even allowing for a touch of thick head. He glanced round, down the length of the rectangular wardroom with its low, white-enamelled deck-head, chairs and sofas at this end and dining-table at the other. Almost emptied now, as the ship's afternoon routine got under way. He looked back at the navigator: 'Where they are, and in what circumstances — and whether they'd come away voluntarily. There's nothing we could do about it, incidentally, if they didn't want to.'

It was a reasonably good bet, he thought, that they'd be somewhere in the Crimea, and most likely on this coast. Between say Poros and Theodosia, probably. At least, if they'd had any choice in the matter. They'd hardly be on the wrong side of the mountains, in biting winds and driving snow, if they'd had the option of that sheltered, sunshine coast. Another guess was that there might be a man or men involved. But not necessarily: a military nurse's training would be no joy-ride, and these were young girls — in their twenties, Temple had said — who were used to soft living. They might have volunteered as nurses without much forethought, even in total mis-conception of what they'd be getting into, and been appalled at the realities.

Hackett said, checking the time, 'Anyway, you've come all the way from Constantinople, just on the assumption you'll find them here?'

'Hope, I'd say, more than assumption. But why not? Unless they're dead or someone's spirited them away, they must be — well, I mean, it should be within our powers to find them. And they're British citizens, you know, they're entitled to our protection. What's more — and this is a very big factor, obviously — you know as well as I do that we may have to pull out of here at short notice and quite soon. Eh?'

'Well — yes, that *is* a point ...'

'Isn't it, just ... And imagine — if the worst did come to the worst, and we hadn't done whatever we could to find them?'

'H'm ...' Hackett frowned, staring at his own out-stretched legs, well-boned halfboots gleaming like patent leather. 'I do take the point. But — if you'd allow me to say this — I suppose it's part of what rather puzzles me — an officer of your seniority, sent all this way just for — well, for instance, couldn't Ashmore have taken care of it?'

'You're raising more than one point there. One, Ashmore has his hands full — most of the time — and this might well entail chasing off somewhere — along the coast, or — God forbid — up to Simferopol, for instance. Ashmore couldn't do that, his job's *here*. Incidentally, I hear he's on his way back … But point two, my seniority — they only gave me the half-stripe a few months ago, and as a bribe at that. I was in at the start, straight out of P & O, so I'm entitled to discharge now any time I want. But we're short of Russian-speakers, and as it happens I'm in no hurry to get back to civvy street, so I allowed myself to be — persuaded.'

'In right from the beginning, you say—'

'August '14. A minesweeper to start with, then destroyers. Dover Patrol, and the Harwich flotilla.'

He knew what Hackett's puzzle was: that he, Bob, looked older than he was. He was twenty-eight, but Hackett probably saw him as a man well into his thirties; Hackett himself being nearer forty — half bald and with a stomach on him. He'd obviously have been passed-over for promotion to commander years ago; and wouldn't ever make it now, having failed to do so even with four years of war to help him.

Hence the addiction to gin. There were a lot of Hacketts in the Navy, especially in battleships and cruisers.

'What'll you do, when you do take your bowler? Back to the old P & O?'

'No. I've other plans. But that's the whole story — I was persuaded to stay on, I was in the Caspian flotilla at the time but by then we were pulling out, having done what we went there for, and — cutting it short, I wound up in Constantinople as a sort of odd-jobs man. Dogsbody to Colonel Temple, Staff Officer (Intelligence). And when this business of the governesses came up — well, there I was … Make sense to you now, does it?'

Colonel Temple had decided Bob was the ideal man to deal with it: effectively, to take this particular problem off his own back. Bob could see him now: the lean, tanned face, bristling black-and-grey moustache, blue eyes gleaming with enthusiasm as he explained, 'Not just because you're bilingual, Cowan. Thing is, when we know where these females are, someone's going to have to go and fetch 'em — by the scruffs of their necks, if necessary! And you've already proved yourself over that sort of country — what?'

Bob had glanced down, at the littered desk between them. Knowing what the man was talking about, of course. Temple meanwhile prompting, 'A hundred miles behind enemy lines — up the Volga?'

He'd nodded. 'But only sort of by accident, sir. We'd put our man ashore, then the boat came to grief — I was stuck there, stuck with *him*, so—' He paused, shook his head. 'It became largely a matter of survival.'

'Well, it may interest you to know that I've seen a copy of SNO Caspian's report on that exploit of yours. You and Count Thingummy — yes, I remember that bit. Your CMB hit a mine, didn't it? But everything beyond that was entirely due to your personal efforts — to what I call guts and gumption. Eh? You brought out that fellow's sister with you — and another young woman — some princess, was it?'

Nadia. Who'd now married 'Count Thingummy' — Nicholas Solovyev. Which was the real reason Bob had agreed to stay on out here, instead of taking his discharge as he could have done.

Not that staying on could change anything. But it was how you felt, not how you reasoned. When he had to go home he'd go, but for the time being he didn't have to, and he felt better staying than he would have done if he'd turned his back and walked away.

He hadn't said anything to Temple about Nadia and her new sister-in-law having gone back to nursing, although at the time of that conversation there'd seemed to be some element of coincidence. In fact there was no real parallel between two young English girls who'd failed to stay the course and Nadia and Irina who'd worked together in a military hospital before he, Bob, had known of their existence and who might by now be virtually anywhere in south Russia. Simferopol — the base hospital where these

other girls had been in training — was a possibility; but
they might be with Wrangel's army, or on the Don front
where Sidorin commanded, or with Mai-Maievsky's
Volunteers. She — and Irina — might have gone (or tried
to be posted) wherever Nikki Solovyev had been going;
Nadia had written, in that part of her long, anguished
letter, *So with Nikki leaving at once for the Front I cannot
remain here. Irina is of the same mind, and we are going
together. The reasons — my own, anyway — are similar to
those which I have been trying so hard to explain to you in
the foregoing pages; that I am very conscious of being
Russian through and through, to the last drop of my blood,
and just as Nikki would be broken in his heart and spirit if I
had held myself back from his long-held expectation that I
would marry him, I would be in torture if I had to wait in
safety and simply lazing time away while he and others
work and fight and face death in defence of everything that
I too love and value.*

*Indeed, some foretaste of this was forced on me in April
when her Majesty the Dowager Empress Maria Feodorovna
embarked in your battleship HMS* Marlborough *at Sevastopol for passage to Constantinople and — Maria Feodorovna herself — to Malta. As you will remember, we came
here to join her entourage at Kharaks, in accordance with
the invitation which she had extended to Irina and Nikki's
mother; you will remember that Maria Ivanovna had been
Lady in Waiting to the Empress. So we were with them all
at the time and went to the harbour to see them leave and
wave our farewells as that huge ship departed. There was
Maria Feodorovna herself, also the Grand Duchess Xenia
and her family, the Grand Dukes Nicholas and Peter with
their wives and children, and Prince Youssoupov — the
slayer of Rasputin — and his wife. And a few others also. I
can tell you, strictly between ourselves my dear, dear Bob,
that seeing them all depart the soil of Russia, possibly for
ever, I was asking myself how* could *they — whether in their
place one might not feel even that death would be preferable. And from this point of recollection, you see, I ask
myself whether if I had kept to the understanding which I*

had shared with you that we would eventually be reunited in your country and spend the remainder of our lives there, whether it would have been fair to you, knowing that however perfect our life might have been in every other way there would have been times when I should have felt myself to be a traitress, and through my own guilt and sadness made you miserable too.

There were nine pages of it altogether, in her angular Cyrillic script, by far the longest letter he'd had from her. Several of its paragraphs were repetitious, in what had clearly been a desperate anxiety to make her feelings clear to him.

There was a two o'clock boat into the dockyard, and he went in it, telling the officer of the watch that he wouldn't be out of the ship for long. He needed to collect some gear from the Kist, and to check that there were no emergencies in Ashmore's office, which was a small room on the hotel's ground floor. When it was locked up, messages were left with the manager or pushed under the door. In fact the next British ship scheduled to call at Sevastopol on her way west after off-loading war supplies at Novorossisk wasn't due for at least a week, and Ashmore would be back before that, in plenty of time to settle any problems.

The swing door's top section had been covered with a sheet of plywood, and the vigilante behind the Lewis gun this afternoon was a former Imperial Army cavalryman, completely bald but with a heavy white moustache. Bob had forgotten his name, but remembered his claim to have served in the legendary *Dikaya Divizia* — the Wild Division, a formation of Caucasians said to have been led originally by the Tsar's brother, in which all ranks had taken an oath either to kill or be killed.

Bob nodded to him. 'Good day, Captain.'

'Major!'

'Oh — of course. Forgive me.'

'Been away, Commander, have you?'

'Well.' A gesture, towards the anchorage. 'Yes ...'

The manager had no messages. Nor — he said, in

answer to Bob's enquiry — had anyone learnt anything about the late Alexis Lapin. A shrug: 'An assassin, evidently ...' One might guess that no further questions would be asked — let alone answered. But everything seemed to be in order in the poky little office — in which all Bob had been doing anyway was keeping the paperwork sorted into one pile that might call for action and another — a larger one — that didn't.

He had to pass through the foyer again *en route* to the stairs, and the old cavalryman stopped him.

'Should have mentioned. The young lady's been asking for you. Where you'd got to, when were you coming back.'

'Young lady?'

Knowing damn well ...

'The one who hangs round the Frenchman's neck. Isn't her name Lyashkova?'

'Oh — *that* one.'

'And now you've been warned.'

He smiled at the old man. 'Yes. Thank you, Major.'

Passing her door, he wondered what she'd want with him. Because while it would have been very nice to have thought of her interest in him as personal — kindled perhaps by her having noticed his interest in *her* the other night — caution or realism told him this was unlikely, that there'd surely be some much less romantic, less self-flattering explanation.

Although — when, so to speak, the chips were down, would one accept the risk, swallow the bait?

Yes. Probably. Here and now — *yes*.

He opened his own door, went in and pushed it shut behind him. Quite noisily. If she was in her room, he thought she'd have heard.

Meanwhile — looking around — nothing in here seemed to have been touched. Although it probably wouldn't have been done so clumsily as to be obvious ... But it would be surprising if someone hadn't had a snoop round, on the off-chance of finding some item of interest — interest to themselves, or saleable to others. It was simply a matter of recognizing how things and people were, in this place and present circumstances. Aksana Lyashkova, for one — if she did have some interest in him, and had known the coast was clear ...

So work it out. What kind of interest might it be?

To start with, there was the French angle. That individual — her friend whom the old man downstairs had mentioned — that fellow made a lot of money out of the refugees, not just accepting bribes but unashamedly insisting on being paid before he'd add a name to the waiting-list for a berth in a French ship. And nowadays there were more British ships than French in transit westward; so if his lady-friend could get herself into a position from which she could exert persuasion on the British Naval Liaison Officer to release berths in Red Ensign ships to French-sponsored refugees, obviously he'd be doing a lot more business.

An extra dividend — with a strong appeal to a Frenchman, of course — would be to leave the British looking like bribe-takers.

But why in any case would she be working for or with this Frog?

Standing near the window, with a shirt in one hand and socks in the other, forcing the grey-matter into action — albeit in unfamiliar territory — he decided that a better, more fundamental question would be why, if as Ashmore contended she was a spy, she'd have come to Sevastopol in the first place.

Well, she was Ukrainian. That had to be the clue: an excellent one, making the rest quite easy. There was a Ukrainian separatist movement, a Ukrainian nationalist army led by a man called Simon Petlyura. His troops had been threatening Odessa not long ago, had only been driven off by Denikin's Volunteers supported by French naval bombardment. Petlyura's army was still very much in being, a 'third force' opposed to both the Bolsheviks and the Whites, and one might guess that (*a*) if Ashmore was right the Lyashkova girl was more likely to be spying for Petlyura than for anyone else, (*b*) Petlyura might well be seeking some kind of accommodation from the French.

At the very least, information about their intentions in the Ukraine, where they'd been heavily involved — still were, in the Odessa-Kherson region.

Then as to her interest in so to speak one's own person — well, as most naval activity on this Black Sea coast at the present time was not French but British, it might well occur to her to cast her net a little wider. Especially if she thought she had her sights on a sitting duck?

Having perhaps already tried it on Ashmore, and found him too tough a nut to crack?

Not so flattering. And distinctly possible. He frowned, fastening the canvas holdall into which he'd packed the things he needed. He picked it up, opened the door — quietly, this time — and went quickly down the stairs.

He'd been ashore less than an hour, and had the luck when he got down to the landing steps to find the cruiser's launch there, loading cases of wine that had come by lorry from Massandra. The launch's crewmen were stacking the cases in the boat's forepart, under the supervision of the wardroom messman, Mr Rogers.

'Not *all* for the wardroom, sir, this isn't. The Tokai there, that's the skipper's.' The little man smacked his lips. '*Lovely* drop, is that Tokai.'

'Yes.' Bob nodded. 'I remember.'

Rogers glanced at him oddly. But he didn't bother to explain that his father had introduced him to Crimean Tokai when he'd been still a young boy. Bob's father, Alexander Cowan, had been only a boy himself when he'd arrived in Russia — at Kronstadt, near what had then been called St Petersburg and was now Petrograd. He'd arrived as a stowaway, in rags and without a word of Russian, but by the time of Bob's birth in 1891 he'd built up a thriving business — import and export, shipping and marine insurance.

The old man was dead now. He'd drowned, last year, when taking passage home from Archangel to Rosyth in the cruiser *Splendid.* From 1914 onwards he'd been attached to the British embassy in Petrograd, with responsibility for the reception and documentation at this end of Allied war supplies to Russia, and they'd sent him home last year for medical reasons. 'Getting a bit of trouble from the old ticker,' he'd written to Bob before embarking in HMS *Splendid*: she'd gone down either to a mine or a torpedo, taking Alexander Cowan with her.

Bob and his father had been very close. All the more so perhaps because Bob's Russian mother, who'd been less than half the old man's age and the pride and passion of his life, had died in giving birth to a stillborn second child, when Bob had been just nine.

He'd been a marvellous man and a wonderful father. Great character, enormous heart. Bob knew that if he ever came halfway to measuring up to that man, he wouldn't have done badly.

A touch on his elbow: 'Ready, sir?'

Mr Rogers — waking him out of his thoughts, drawing his attention to the fact they were just coming alongside *Caledonian*'s gangway. Deep in recollection of his father, all of it sparked by mention of that wine, he'd had no awareness of embarking or of the short trip across the grey, slightly loppy anchorage. Now the coxswain had put his engine astern, and a moment later the launch bumped gently against the gangway's slatted lower platform, bowman and sternsheetman neatly taking hold with their boathooks.

'Thank you, Cox'n.' A side-boy — quarterdeck messenger — came nipping down to take the holdall; Bob went up the gangway, saluting as he stepped aboard. The officer of the watch, a young lieutenant, told him as he too saluted, 'Captain Fellows would like to see you, sir. As soon as you got back, he said.'

'Very good.' Spirits rising sharply: Colonel Temple must have come up with something — at last. 'Thank you ... Could my case be put in the Captain's sea-cabin?'

'Of course.' A glance at the side-boy. 'Bellamy—'

'Aye aye, sir!'

Down one deck, now, by way of a hatch set under the jutting barrel of the six-inch gun, and then right aft.

Thinking there might be some truth in the old saying that a watched pot never boiled: better to turn your back on it, as he'd just done by going ashore. Rattling down the steel ladder and turning aft on the main deck, feeling a lot brighter suddenly, heartened by the prospect of getting a move on now ... He acknowledged the Royal Marine sentry's salute, knocked on the cuddy door, heard Captain Andrew Fellows' loud 'Come in!'

As he entered the cabin he removed his cap, pushed it under his arm. 'Wanted to see me, sir?'

'Yes, Cowan.' *Caledonian*'s skipper was a heavily-built man with a reddish face and ginger hair. 'Yes, indeed. Look, take a pew.' Hospitable wave of the hand towards a chintz-covered armchair: there were three, and a settee, also a desk in the starboard after corner to which he'd gone now, to extract a sheet of pink signal-pad from a folder.

'This came in cypher, of course. They've only just un-ravelled it. It's what you've been waiting for — but I'm damned if I can see what you or anyone else can do about it. Eh?'

Bob took it from him, and accepted the invitation to sit down. Seeing at a glance that the message was from SO (I) Constantinople, addressed to *Caledonian* for BNLO Sevastopol.

INFORMATION RECEIVED IS THAT VOLUNTEER NURSING AIDES KATHERINE REID AND MARY PILKINGTON WERE SERVING IN LETUCHKA NO. 7 REPEAT SEVEN ON THE KHARKOV FRONT AS RECENTLY AS LAST WEEK NOVEMBER. CONFIRMATION NOW UNOBTAINABLE OWING TO SEVERANCE OF COMMUNICATIONS WITH THAT FRONT. INDICATIONS ARE KHARKOV OUTFLANKED BY BOLSHEVIK FORCES, VOLUNTEER ARMY STILL HOLDING TWO DAYS AGO BUT WITHDRAWAL AND GENERAL RETREAT PROBABLY INEVITABLE. ONLY ACCESS FOR PURPOSES OF ANY RESCUE MISSION PRESUMABLY RAIL FROM NOVOROSSISK VIA ROSTOV, BUT DISTANCE AND TIME FACTORS SEEM TO MAKE SUCH ATTEMPT FUTILE. IT

SHOULD ALSO BE NOTED THAT BRITISH MILITARY
MISSIONS ON THE DON HAVE BEEN ORDERED TO
WITHDRAW TO EKATERINODAR IN READINESS FOR
EVACUATION THROUGH NOVOROSSISK. UNLESS INFOR-
MATION AVAILABLE TO YOU LOCALLY SUGGESTS ANY
VIABLE ALTERNATIVE YOUR RETURN HERE BY FIRST
AVAILABLE SAILING IS THEREFORE AUTHORIZED.
TIME OF ORIGIN …

A *letuchka* was a mobile field hospital. Literally, 'flying
column'. But how on earth, he wondered, could those girls
who'd allegedly deserted from their nurses' training at the
Simferopol base hospital have turned up in a front-line
unit?

Deserting *to* the Front?

He met Captain Fellows' quizzical stare. 'Not too good,
sir.'

'I'd say that might be something of an understatement,
Cowan.'

'Except that we've seen it before more than once —
advances petering out, other side pull themselves
together—'

'What I've heard referred to as the Seesaw Syndrome.
Yes. With Tsarytsin as the most dramatic example,
perhaps. Wangel taking the place, then driven out, re-
occupying it the very next day. But that was thanks to the
RAF and two or three British-manned tanks. And look at
what else your Colonel Temple's telling us — that we're
evacuating, for God's sake!' He shook his head. 'What
he's really saying, Cowan, is there's a complete rout developing. And between you and me, much as I hate to say
this, I wouldn't want any daughter of *mine* to be where
those young women are.'

Bob looked down at the signal again. Wondering
whether the last line but one, that 'Unless information
available to you locally' line, might not have been
Colonel Temple's paraphrasing of *Cowan, can't you for
God's sake see some way to save their skins*?

He let out a long breath as he looked up. 'May I take a
little time over this, sir?'

'Time?' Fellows looked surprised. 'Well — I suppose ...
Time to do what, though?'

'Well — might there be any maps on board, sir? Shore-
side maps, as distinct from charts?'

'There's a *Times* atlas, at any rate. Hackett keeps it in
his cabin, I think. Oh, you could try Meyrick — Captain of
Marines, he *may* have something ... What's in your mind?'

'I'd like to see where that railway runs, sir — the line
from Novorossisk through Rostov. It must turn up
northward there, I suppose. But I hardly know what we're
talking about, at the moment. And as Colonel Temple
does query whether there may be ways or means ...'

'Look into it, certainly. But don't take longer than you
have to. And — Cowan. Better keep this business about
withdrawal of the missions under your hat, eh?'

Captain Meyrick RM had a few Russian military maps
which he'd scrounged here and there, but none that helped
with these present researches. Bob went on to find
Hackett, the navigating officer, who did have a *Times*
atlas. Although the scale was very small, on a plate
covering the whole of southern Russia it showed that the
railway line to Kharkov, running west from Rostov, turned
inland from the coast at a place called Taganrog.

The atlas gave no indication, of course, but one knew
that most of the Sea of Azov was extremely shallow. Royal
Navy monitors and two Russian barges with six-inch guns
were deployed more or less permanently along the
western seaboard to prevent Bolshevik infiltration of the
Crimea from that direction, and British destroyers had
also been operating there, their orders being to destroy all
vessels transporting Bolshevik troops or capable of being
used as transports. In the course of this, Bob remembered
from a recent intelligence report, *Parthian* and *Forester*
had both been hit by gunfire from the shore. They'd
suffered no casualties or serious damage, and had
continued their patrols — at a safer range from the coast
— but the incident was indicative of the presence and
strength of Red infiltrators.

The main problem would be navigational, anyway. Especially inside the Gulf of Taganrog. Unless the Russians had had dredgers working in recent years, which seemed unlikely.

Hackett asked him — from the bunk, where he'd started in a sitting position but was now prone with his eyes shut — 'Solved your problem, have you, Cowan?'

Bob glanced round at him. Thinking — in reference to their earlier conversation — that if curiosity didn't kill this cat, Plymouth gin and bitters might well do so, in the long run. He told him, 'Hardly. Oh, I do have the answer to one question.' Back at the map again ... 'The problem we're left with, though, is first how to locate and then physically to extract our governesses from somewhere up *here*—' he'd put a finger on Kharkov, at the same tilting the heavy atlas so Hackett could see it, if he could manage to raise his head — 'where the front is said to be crumbling, Bolshy breakthrough imminent if not already achieved.'

'Good God. For "needles in haystacks" read "needles in *burning* bloody haystacks" ...'

It wasn't a bad analogy. And in the light of all the known facts of the situation, the answer to Temple's query was surely that it was too damn late to do anything at all ... Hackett asked him — going so far as to sit up, then sliding his legs off the bunk — 'What are you contemplating — putting some kind of rescue party ashore, in that gulf?'

'Not so much contemplating as — well, investigating possibility of ... But that's the railway to Kharkov, and if one had to get up that way it'd be a lot better to be landed at Taganrog than to start right down here at Novorossisk, having then to chug all the way up to Rostov. A couple of hundred miles — and if you know anything about Russian trains, at any rate in present conditions ...'

'I can imagine. But whether anything that floats *could* get in to Taganrog—'

'That's the next question. Exactly. Perhaps we can have a look at the chart?'

'Of course. But I can tell you now it'd be a deuce of a tricky job, getting in there. Except perhaps in a CMB. Which we don't have, of course. Unless you could have one shipped up from Batoum?'

A CMB was a coastal motorboat: very fast, and drawing only a couple of feet of water. Bob shook his head. 'Time wouldn't allow, would it? Even if they'd spare us one. Chartroom, please?'

'Right. Right.' Hackett preceded him out into the cabin flat. 'This is what you were talking to our tame leather-neck about, was it? Landing party at Taganrog?'

He was jumping to the conclusion that any landing party would be composed of Royal Marines. A fairly natural assumption, perhaps — if one completely mis-understood the situation and the requirements. Bob wondered whether Colonel Temple might have studied maps and/or charts and pondered this very problem, and perhaps concluded that Taganrog would be inaccessible. But he certainly wouldn't have been thinking of anything like putting a platoon of Royal Marines ashore. He'd have had in mind a one-man infiltration, the one man being — for God's sake — Lieutenant-Commander Robert Cowan, RNR. Merely because said Robert Cowan had done something of very broadly the same kind on that one previous occasion — in totally different circumstances — and had the luck to get away with it.

Should have had the sense, he thought, to put in for discharge. Might have been home by now — resting on what might be termed one's laurels. Facing, no doubt, all sorts of new problems — but none of *this* kind.

Simple solution, anyway. Take Temple's last sentence at its face value: YOUR RETURN HERE BY FIRST AVAILABLE SAILING IS THEREFORE AUTHORIZED …

Why *not* snatch at it?

Meanwhile he hadn't answered the navigator, who, undeterred, added over his shoulder as he went up the first of several ladders into the bridge superstructure, 'Come to think of it, a man who might help you, Cowan — straight from the horse's mouth, so to speak — is *Terrapin*'s captain. Fellow by the name of Everard.'

'I know him, as it happens. I took passage in *Terrapin* from the Bosporus. But is he coming here?'

'Came in early this afternoon. She's alongside the oiler there. Or was — maybe at anchor now. Surprised you didn't see her when you came off from shore, you'd have passed within a couple of cables' lengths of her. Anyway, she's just come from patrol in the Sea of Azov, Everard should be up to date on — oh, not the Taganrog gulf, I dare say, but he'd have a much better idea than you or I ...'

So all right: he'd pick Everard's brains. As long as he could get hold of him, if *Terrapin* wasn't leaving as soon as she'd refuelled ... Here and now, anyway — in *Caledonian*'s chartroom — Hackett was leafing through the currently-in-use chart folio. Extracting first *The Euxine or Black Sea*, chart 2214, flipping it on the table where Bob opened it.

Not bad ... But Hackett was pulling out another. 'Here — this is the one you want. However you pronounce *that* ...'

Azovskoe More: the Sea of Azov. The Taganrog Gulf alone occupied as much space as the whole Azov Sea did on the other. He checked quickly and saw that soundings were shown in feet, not fathoms as on the smaller-scale chart; then that off Taganrog itself depths varied between six and nine feet.

More than ample for a CMB, but a destroyer would need a minimum of twelve feet, two fathoms. And the nearest to the town — a railway town, for sure, the chart showed the line looping in from the east and curving away northward — the nearest point at which you'd have that much water would be about four miles offshore.

'Haven't been any recent corrections, that I can see.'

Hackett frowned, resenting the suggestion that he might have been lax in his duties as navigator. 'If there had been, Cowan, they'd be on it.'

'Wouldn't doubt it. All I'm thinking is there could have been silting, less water than it shows, even.'

Because the mouths of the river Don were only a dozen miles south-east from Taganrog, and the Donets about ten miles due east. Close in to those river mouths were sandbanks with no depths of water shown at all, only the warning *Banks extended seaward.*

So say *five* miles offshore. Then land by seaboat. If anyone'll take you there in the first place, which they probably will not ... But in any case — he caught himself up on this as he straightened from the chart — wouldn't the best outcome be to find it was *not* a practical proposition?

From one's own point of view — yes. But from those two girls': and their families' at home ...

He asked Hackett, 'Any idea how long *Terrapin* will be here?'

'Only for the night.' Lieutenant Nick Everard, Royal Navy, answered that question in his day-cabin on board the destroyer about half an hour later. By this time *Terrapin* was at anchor, having completed fuelling and left the oiler. He told Bob, 'Sailing 0800 tomorrow — for the Bosporus, *en route* to Marmara to join the anti-gunrunning patrol there.' He frowned, added half to himself, 'Not for very long, I hope ...'

Everard was about four years younger than Bob. In fact he looked surprisingly youthful to have command of a modern destroyer. But the ribbons of the DSO and DSC on his shoulder went some way to explaining it: and he looked hard, fit, with a hint of obstinacy behind present affability. His only response to Bob's rather diffident comment on those medals, during the journey here from Constantinople, had been to mutter that he'd been lucky — 'in the right places at the right time, as they say ...'

He asked now, 'Why? Want to come along with us?'

Bob nodded. 'Might take you up on that. If — well, what I've come to ask you about—'

'You'd be welcome.' Everard glanced at the time: he was due on board *Caledonian* at six, having proposed 'making his number' — in other words paying a duty visit to Captain Fellows, the senior naval officer in the port —

earlier than that, and in reply getting an RPC — *Request the Pleasure of your Company* — for 1800. It was just after 1730 now. He nodded to Bob. '*Are* very welcome ... You've come to ask me something? Sit down, ask away ... Like a drink?'

'No, thank you. But — when you brought me here, I think I told you that I was being sent to dig out some missing governesses?'

'Why, so you did!' A wide grin ... 'And have you found 'em?'

'Not exactly. First thing was I had to wait for some mysterious character who was supposed to be bringing me the information we needed; and he came, all right, but when he arrived they shot him dead. However—'

'Who did? The governesses?'

Bob laughed too ... 'No. But — listen, just for the moment ... Thing is, we do now know where the girls are — or where they were very recently. Up near Kharkov — four hundred miles inland, roughly — with a mobile front-line hospital. They're working as nurses now, you see. And — here's the worst of it — the front's given way, or anyway it can't hold much longer. Bolshies have outflanked Kharkov — we have this from Constantinople by signal this afternoon. So—'

'Your governesses are — not well placed.'

'Putting it mildly — they certainly are not. In fact it may be too late, even now. But it's supposed to be my job to get them out — *if* there's any hope of doing so.' He paused, holding Everard's hard stare. 'The obvious answer's to get up there by train — the line from Novorossisk via Rostov was mentioned. But that's the devil of a long flog — *days* of it, time we haven't got. So I've been looking at an atlas and a chart or two, and it struck me—'

'Taganrog?'

He smiled, at the destroyer man's quickness. 'Exactly. *Exactly* what I've come to ask your advice on — since you've just come from the Azov, and you'd know as well as anyone ... D'you think it's a viable proposition — to get in there, get ashore?'

3

Three-thirty, roughly. Dark, and cold, *Terrapin* moving to the long, low swells while her cable came clanking in, the regular metallic crashes as each iron link banged in over the hawse seemingly loud enough in the night-time quiet to have everyone else in the anchorage awake and cursing. Then it stopped: you heard the sea's jostling, the creaks and groans of the ship's structure as she pitched, the wind's thrum in and around her mast and superstructure, and above all that chant-like cry from the fo'c'sl — 'Cable's up-and-down, sir!'

Meaning that all the slack had been dragged inboard now, so that the next few turns of the steam capstan would break the anchor out of Sevastopol's black mud. Everard, one of several figures in a group in the bridge's forepart, said quietly 'Weigh', and his first lieutenant, Harrison, leant over to shout that order down to the cable party. Torchlight flickering down there, and the steady clanking starting up again. Bob Cowan, at the back of the bridge out of the others' way, aimed borrowed glasses at *Caledonian*'s three-quarter profile some three cables' lengths away on the bow. He'd seen movement on the bigger ship's quarterdeck, and found a group now static in a glow of light spilled between an open screen-door and the rear of the after six-inch gunhouse.

Captain Fellows might well be one of them, he guessed. Waiting with his middle-watch quarterdeck staff to see the destroyer leave. Slipping out like a thief in the night ... In daylight there'd have been a ritual of salutes exchanged as they passed: the shrill of a bosun's call from *Terrapin*, a bugle-call in answer from the cruiser. But none of that now, and no signals of farewell either. Farewells, hand-shakes and 'Good lucks' had been finished with half an hour ago.

'Anchor's aweigh, sir!'

Everard said, 'Slow ahead together. Come fifteen degrees to port.'

'Slow ahead together, sir.' Mackeson, the chief quarter-master, was on the wheel and voicepipe. 'Fifteen degrees to port. South eighty-five west, sir.'

Clang of engineroom telegraphs: then the first trembling in her steel frames as the propellers turned. The night air was like a serrated knife: Bob turned up the collar of his greatcoat. Conscious not only of the cold but also of a sense of unreality: that it could all have happened — at least, *started* — this fast, almost instan-taneously with the conception of the idea and its tentative broaching first to Everard and then to Fellows.

To be honest — with oneself, at least — the feeling wasn't only of unreality. It was also of fright. And recog-nition that whatever came of this he'd deserve it, would have no-one to blame for it but himself. Although it might also be true to say that he had not either consciously or deliberately put himself in this situation: he'd put an idea forward, that was all, raised a possibility. Then — *snap*, trap closing — closed.

Another hail from the cable party, down there where it would be even colder — ice-cold spray, most likely, in the wind lashing over that dark, wet fo'c'sl — a cry of 'Clear anchor!' telling Everard that they could now see the anchor itself in their torch-beam and that there were no cables or wires fouling it. *Caledonian* meanwhile looming closer to starboard, a long black cut-out with only that pool of radiance on her quarterdeck and her anchor-lights with haloes around them in the freezing salt-damp air. Everard's voice again: 'Half ahead together. Steer west. Pilot — take over, please.'

'Pilot' meaning the navigating lieutenant, Johnny Cruickshank — tall, thin, slightly stooped, doubtless from long hours bent over charts and binnacles; and caustically

humorous in his observations, especially on the Service
and the foibles of its senior officers ... One knew all these
people, of course, from the few days spent in their ship on
passage from the Bosporus — at which time, he recalled,
his expectation had been to spend just a week or two in
the Crimea and then return in some other ship with the
ex-governesses.

The recollection reminded him of Captain Fellows'
question an hour or so ago: 'Happy with this business are
you, Cowan? Think you'll pull it off all right?'

He'd hesitated: having no easy answer ... To a similar
challenge from Everard — earlier, in *Terrapin*'s chartroom
— he'd told him, 'I talk Russian, and I know Russians.
Well, I *am* one — half, anyway ... And I'm a big lad, I can
look after myself ...' Everard had laughed: '*Bet* you can!'
Laughing with a kind of happy enthusiasm which at first
Bob had welcomed but then found rather puzzling. Right
from the start Everard had seemed to jump at the chance
of making this trip: almost as if there was some personal
satisfaction in it for him. It was puzzling because you'd
have thought that having just come from the Azov and
about a week of semi-sleepless nights he and his ship's
company would have been looking forward to at least one
restful night in harbour.

To that question from Fellows, though, Bob had only
been able to mutter something to the effect that he
thought finding the two women might not be as difficult as
one had imagined at first sight of the problem. To get
there in time was the crucial thing: but there couldn't be
more than two or three mobile field hospitals, and military
units must surely be kept informed of their whereabouts.
So as long as the front was holding, or at least as long as
the Volunteer Army were conducting a more or less
orderly retreat, not in complete rout — well, with a
modicum of good luck ... He'd shrugged, and Fellows had
sat there blinking at him as if he thought this fellow
Cowan was something special. Or something *peculiar*,
might be closer to it ...

In fact, the issue was simple. These two girls would

probably never see their families again if one did nothing, but conceivably *might* if one had a shot at finding them. And having been given the job, that was it, all there was to it.

Everard's motivation might have been similar, and as simple. He was a fairly straightforward sort of man, Bob thought.

They'd done the preliminary chart-work together on board *Terrapin* before *Caledonian*'s motorboat had come for them. Then, having arrived on board the cruiser — Everard as a commanding officer having the honour of being piped aboard — Bob had hung back, or rather hung *around*, until Fellows had sent word that he should join them.

The choice of drinks on offer was absolutely standard. Gin and water, pink gin, or gin with a dash of lime. Bob had asked for gin and water, and the captain's steward had poured it for him and then withdrawn to the pantry.

'Well now, Cowan. Everard here tells me you want him to take you into the Gulf of Taganrog. Eh?'

He'd nodded. 'I went over to ask him whether he thought the approaches to Taganrog might be navigable. Having given thought to Colonel Temple's signal — an alternative to getting on a train at Novorossisk. The next question of course is whether there'd be any ship going that way — which of course there is not ...'

'*Stuart* and *Mistral* are due in here about noon tomorrow, as it happens.'

'Tomorrow.' He'd nodded — without enthusiasm. 'Only thing is — time's so short ... If I'm to go at all — with the situation as one reads it between the lines of that signal?'

'If I could explain this, sir.' Everard had chipped in. 'We've done our homework — times, speeds and distances. Two essentials being — well, first the urgency, and second is that despite navigational hazards — shoal water for one, and there's ice now too, certainly at the top end — fact remains, I'd sooner not arrive in daylight. It's narrow, in places, and there's a strong Bolshevik infestation along the north shore. You never know where they are, places change hands almost daily. It could endanger us, could also endanger my passenger when he lands. Can't be sure how close to Taganrog itself we can land him, you see. And I'd like to be out of the narrows before daylight, too. What it comes down to is that if we were going at all I'd want to start well before dawn.'

'*Tonight*?'

'Yes, sir. Well — early morning. That's to allow for a fifteen-knot passage most of the way and a few hours at twenty knots at later stages. One has to think about fuel consumption, of course, and I'd propose refuelling in Theodosia when I come out of the Azov on completion. Then I'd sail directly from Theodosia to the Bosporus, *en route* Marmara.'

Fellows had screwed his eyes up, making calculations . . .

'So if this diversion were to be authorized, you'd reckon to be roughly three days adrift on present schedule. Am I right?'

'Sooner say four days, sir. Maximum five — but yes, probably four. That's allowing for possible unforeseen delays. In Theodosia, for instance — might reckon to spend a night there.'

'Very well.' Fellows had nodded. 'We'll draft a signal, Cowan, to your Colonel Temple.' He reached, touched a bellpush, gestured to the steward when he appeared to refill the glasses . . . 'Points to be made are that in the light of the information which he's supplied you're proposing to get on a train at Taganrog if you can be landed there, that the only ship immediately available, if she can be spared for it — etcetera . . .' He nodded to his steward. 'Thank you, Collins.' Back to Bob: 'It'll be in Temple's lap, then, up to him to twist whichever arms need twisting. Look, you draft it — use my desk there . . .'

The answer, approving the mission, came just before 0300, and at the same time Everard received his own orders directly from Rear Admiral, Black Sea. *Terrapin* had been kept meanwhile with steam up, at immediate notice for sea; within minutes of the signals being decoded

'Special Sea Dutymen' was being piped and Bob was boarding her from *Caledonian*'s motorboat. About forty minutes ago, that had been; now they were almost out of Sevastopol's long, rather narrow harbour, with North Point abaft the beam to starboard, the open mouth of Quarantine Bay discernible as a gap in the shoreline to port, and a faint aura of light over the town itself back on that quarter. *Terrapin* working up to fifteen knots, heeling as Cruickshank brought her round to a course of south 67 west, for a run of about six miles — half an hour, roughly — to the point off Cape Khersones where they'd alter to south-east.

'Wishing you hadn't started this, Cowan?'

Everard — a dark shape materializing from the front part of the bridge, reaching to a flag-locker for support as with his ship's beam exposed to the north-wester now her roll became more violent. Bob shouted back, over the racket of wind and sea and the ship throwing herself about, 'Not yet. Later, dare say I will.'

'What Britain does for her governesses, eh?' A bark of laughter, and a hand on Bob's elbow as he pushed past to the ladder. 'Get your head down, if I were you.'

He had the use of Cruickshank's cabin — back aft, one of four that opened on to the wardroom flat. The navigator would be catnapping, he'd said, on the padded bench in his chartroom right below the bridge. But for Bob not even a catnap was coming easily. Conversations from recent hours replayed almost audibly in his brain, and behind them was the continuing doubt as to how much sense there could be in making this trip at all. Whether there'd be any trains passing through Taganrog, for instance.

But of course there would be — when a front was under threat you didn't suspend supplies to it, you reinforced it, for God's sake! Denikin would probably be sending up everything he had to spare. And there'd be ammunition trains, rations, surely...

A question from Captain Fellows — 'What thoughts

d'you have as regards extricating yourself — or yourselves, if you do find these silly girls?' — was much less easy to dismiss. Bob and Everard had touched on the subject earlier, Everard pointing out that there'd be no question of a pick-up from Taganrog at any later stage. He'd be putting Bob ashore at some time after midnight, this coming night, and aiming to be on his way out of the Gulf by 0300 at the latest, so as to be out of those dangerous narrows before daylight. Foreseeable dangers being Bolshevik artillery at close range from the shore, navigational hazards from shallow patches not all of which would be accurately charted, and a possibility of mines in the channels between those patches. Everard's job as he saw it was to land Bob as close to Taganrog as possible, then get his ship away quickly; and as a withdrawal of all British forces was seen as imminent there couldn't be much prospect of a later pick-up — even if there was any way to set one up, which there probably would not be.

Bob had told Fellows, 'Only way will be through Novorossisk, sir, I imagine. Train again — join up with some military mission on *their* way out, perhaps.'

'Yes. Yes ...'

The cruiser captain frowning thoughtfully, fingertips feeling the late-night stubble on his jaw. 'One — er — complication you should perhaps be aware of, Cowan, is — well, in Novorossisk one hears it's of epidemic proportions now and getting worse, and of course any greatly increased influx of refugees can only make it *much* worse —' glancing at Everard, then back to Bob — 'I'm talking about this damn typhus. You may not know it, but — you do know Ashmore was supposed to be going there, at the admiral's behest, just before you arrived—'

'Yes, I—'

'He was diverted to Batoum — *Mistral* was, he took passage in her. The admiral thought it prudent to change the venue of that conference — which incidentally was to assess the numbers potentially eligible for evacuation, and the ports to be used for it and so forth ... And — look, this is confidential, both of you, not the sort of thing we'd want broadcast, but a steamer full of refugees from Novorossisk, the SS *Panama*, is currently anchored off Malta, they won't let her berth.' A grimace. 'Typhus. Riddled with it. She'll be sent back here, no option. Black Sea *somewhere* — God knows where ... Anyway —' Fellows had shrugged — 'as well to bear it in mind, Cowan. Not that there'd be anything one could *do*, but—'

'No ...'

Not a damn thing; and no way one could take any consideration of it into one's plans. 'Plans' in any case being rather a grand term for one's present notions of (*a*) getting ashore, (*b*) boarding a possibly non-existent northbound train, (*c*) arriving somewhere or other behind the Kharkov front and asking about *letuchki* — about one particular *letuchka* that had two British women on its staff — and (*d*) getting out again, somehow or other, with them in tow.

Some *plan*.

Novorossisk, incidentally, would be icing up before long, Fellows had pointed out. Just to add — Everard's comment, afterwards — to the joys of spring ...

Terrapin had begun to roll harder: she was pitching as well but the roll was savage suddenly. He had a knee against the ship's side and his feet jammed against the bunk's leeboard, left hand hooked over the mattress's edge. Enormous thumping crashes meanwhile, hundreds of tons of salt water hurling itself time after time against thin steel plating inches from his head, the steel trembling from the impacts, the ship's whole framework loud with it. She'd be under helm, he guessed, turning around Cape Khersones, getting the worst of it for a few minutes but this wouldn't last; once her stern was into the northwester there'd be a lot less roll, a lot more pitch. He could visualize it up there, breaking seas sheeting over from the quarter then from right astern, the bridge watchkeepers having a drier time of it then but having to cope with the danger of the ship being pooped — big seas rolling over her from astern, even perhaps flooding down into the wardroom flat if the screen-door up there wasn't shut and

clipped, or if a heavy one caught someone on his way out
or in. Another hazard was of the destroyer's screws racing
if the stern rose so steeply that they came out of water —
the danger of stripped shaft-bearings, so you'd need to
keep the revs down.

Their worry. He told himself, *Make do with your own.*

For instance — Fellows' voice again ...

'It's the finale now — you realize? We've withdrawn
from Murmansk and Archangel, and we're out of Vladi-
vostok as far as dry land's concerned. Italians and Frogs
have pulled out too. Last situation report was the Ameri-
cans were following suit — railwaymen as well as troops
they'd shipped in there, did you know? Anyway, they were
getting 'em out as much to avoid problems with the Japan-
ese as with the Bolshies. Japs seem to be hanging on, and
the Czech Legion's still on that railway of course ... But
by and large, certainly as far as we British are concerned,
intervention's been a flop. Oh, your Caspian campaign
fulfilled its purpose, but there's nowhere else you could
say the same of. Except — well, yes, I'm wrong, from a
purely naval point of view the Baltic's a very different
story.' Looking at Bob, Fellows had cocked an eyebrow:
'Meant to ask you this before, Cowan: are you any rela-
tion of *Walter* Cowan?'

'Afraid not, sir.'

Walter Cowan being the rear-admiral who was very
effectively commanding a Royal Navy cruiser squadron —
plus submarines and CMBs — in the Baltic, defending the
Estonians', Latvians' and Lithuanians' newly-gained
independence against Bolshevik as well as residual
German forces. *That* was justified intervention, all right,
and much to the Royal Navy's credit.

'A Cowan of another ilk, eh?'

'You could say so.'

With knobs on. Considering that Bob's grandfather had
been a trawlerman, and his father a stowaway Scottish
urchin turned trader. Very successful trader: self-made,
and as rough-grained as he was generous and warm-
hearted. About as fine a character as ever lived, Bob

thought — meeting Captain Fellows' interested gaze and knowing that behind that entirely friendly interest the cruiser captain would be thinking to himself *No — of course not. Of course not . . .*

Alexander Cowan, the former runaway from an impoverished Scottish home, had died a rich man with a prospering investment company based in Glasgow, and he'd left the business lock, stock and barrel to his son Robert Cowan, formerly an officer in the Mercantile Marine and now Lieutenant-Commander, RNR, who instead of hotfooting it home to Scotland to take up the reins of his inheritance was at this point committing himself to—

Well — shifting in the bunk, relaxing tensed muscles as the rolling became less violent — committing himself, he thought, to God alone knew what.

When he woke it was after eight o'clock and the ship's motion was gentle, rhythmic, a slow waltz compared to the wild fandango she'd been dancing a few hours earlier. She'd be in the shelter of the Crimean coastal mountain range, of course, and she'd have the benefit of it for most of the afternoon. Visualizing the chart, and the work he and Everard had done on it last evening, he knew they'd be on a course of about ENE and a dozen miles offshore, would have passed Balaclava and made two more course alterations while he'd been in dreamland, would now have Yalta somewhere abaft the beam with the white smudge of its sea-fronting villas and palaces possibly still in sight.

Yalta, which he and Temple had thought might be a likely place to find the two governesses; and where at an earlier time — before he'd received her letter — he'd daydreamed of reunion with Nadia. He'd enjoyed visions of the two of them on that warm, sunny coast with its palms, flowers, fruit and wine, an ideal setting for the kind of romantic dalliance there'd been no time or opportunity for earlier. At other times he'd been rather depressingly aware that the daydream was pure escapism, near-certainty being that he wouldn't set eyes on her again until they met in Britain, probably in Scotland and in Glasgow at that — of all places. The picture in his mind then had been of wet streets, driving sleet, shabby grey house-fronts, and local suspicions instantly aroused by a foreign accent — let alone by her title of Princess. Although one might have kept that quiet ... But there'd also been the fear that she might hate it, soon wish she'd never come: while he'd be tied to the business, stuck there at least as long as it took to get the hang of things then reorganize and get new developments under way. No option — a future to be established, inheritance to be justified ...

Whereas *now*, of course, it seemed extraordinary that these had been the areas of concern, that the possibility of *never seeing her again anywhere at all* had never occurred to him for a moment. Despite all the horrors and the chaos, the absence of any kind of certainty or security: as if their joint destiny had been something on another plane, untouchable.

One lived, and learned. Or *if* one lived, one learned ...

Might Nadia — he wondered this while he was shaving, balancing himself against the ship's pitching while he scraped at the dark stubble on his rather wide, blunt jaw — might she feature in his decision to go inland in search of these other women?

He didn't think so. In fact, was *sure* not. All right, so they were working as nurses, as she was — or as she'd intended doing when she'd written that letter — and natur-ally enough she was still quite often in his mind, so it was hardly surprising if thoughts of them and of her sometimes overlapped. But there was certainly no thought in his mind of trying to find *her*. In fact he wouldn't want to; and doing so by chance — such a chance being extremely remote anyway — would be an embarrassment. She'd made her choice, she was now the wife of Nicholas Solovyev — end of story. While this business of the gover-nesses was simply a duty that had been imposed on one — so impersonal that at this moment he couldn't even recall their names.

Thinking hard, as he wiped suds and stubble off his

razor. Annoyed with himself for the lapse of memory ...

Getting there, finally. Katherine Reid, and Mary Pilkington.

'Silly girls,' Captain Fellows had called them. Because they were making this nuisance of themselves, of course, causing so much trouble. But thinking about them now — the little that one knew of them — well, they'd had the initiative to volunteer as military nursing aides at a time when the risks were obvious — and the need for nurses and doctors probably acute — and then they'd managed somehow to cut short their training and get themselves to where the fighting was going on ... Dressing himself — hurrying now, encouraged by a mouth-watering aroma of frying bacon, doubtless from the wardroom galley — he wondered, *Silly* girls?

Everard handed Bob his binoculars, and gestured shoreward.

'Theodosia — Gulf of. The town's on the left edge there. Lighthouse on the point, then another to the left of that, and between them that must be *Benbow* in the anchorage. Something Bay, that is, long Russian name, trip off *your* tongue I dare say ...'

Focusing ... The battleship was a grey miniature inside an encircling arm of land. Bob said, 'Not much of a place to be when the wind's in the south, is it?'

'But the wind isn't in the south. Would hardly ever be, this time of year. South-west's all right, in any case.' Leaning over the bridge's port side, over the splinter-mattresses that were lashed around it, he added, 'Far as we're concerned, we'll be round the next corner, off the town itself. That's where the oiler-berth is.'

It was mid-forenoon now, and they were still in the lee of the coastal range although the mountains were much lower and sparser behind this Gulf of Theodosia, with gaps between them like missing teeth. Everard told him, glancing round first to check that McKendrick, the gunnery lieutenant and currently officer of the watch, was out of earshot, 'Matter of fact, there are some friends of mine ashore there.' Nodding towards the town ...'Long shot, but I don't suppose you'd ever have known an extremely good-looking girl by name of Ilyana Dherjorakova?'

'Can't say I have.'

'Countess. She's holed-up there with some friends. They trekked all the way from St Petersburg, via God knows where, went through the most frightful experiences. Brave as — well, I don't know what.'

Bob nodded grimly — thinking of Nadia and the Solovyev family, *their* ordeal by terror. 'I can imagine. It's incredible what they've survived, a lot of them ... Waiting for a passage out, is she?'

'Well.' A pause: hesitating ... Then: 'According to bloody regulations, she's not entitled. As you know, only Volunteer Army dependents and one or two other categories can get on the list, and she lost both her parents almost before it started, poor kid, can't claim to be *anyone*'s dependent.'

'Rotten luck.' He frowned. 'But surely—'

'Keep a secret, can you?'

He gave him back the glasses. 'I hope so.'

Another glance round ... Then, low-voiced, 'I'm going to marry her. Tomorrow.'

'You mean — this fuelling call—'

'Exactly. And as my wife, she'll be entitled to a passage to Constantinople — which is where we'll be going, so she'll come with us. See? She'll probably be stuck there for a while, but — *safe*, d'you see. Believe me, I'm damn grateful to you. I was worried stiff, until you came along — well, you can imagine, being ordered straight to the Marmara, no way to get back for her, and a general evacuation imminent — or it could be, I was trying to convince myself it couldn't, but — Lord, just *imagine*—'

'This may be — well, too personal a question, but — is saving her life the primary reason — motive—'

'No, it damn well is *not*!'

'I'm sorry.' He shook his head: his own expression conciliatory — in contrast to taut anger in the other ...

Like some large, placid hound facing a furious bull terrier ... He explained, 'Only the way you were putting it — entitlement to a passage, so forth—'

'Ah — well ...' A shrug: anger fading as quickly as it had flared. 'My fault — I'm sorry ... Fact is, though, it's — well, very much the opposite, you see, it's absolutely — what's the phrase — *the real thing*. Only more so, *very* much more—'

'Captain, sir!'

Granger, pointing ... 'Ship fine on the bow there, sir.'

'Excuse me.' Everard moved to the front of the bridge. 'Expecting to meet *Kornilov*, weren't we?'

Kornilov was a White Russian cruiser, based normally at Kerch. If this was her there'd no doubt be an exchange of polite signals, presently. Bob leant with his shoulder against a nest of voicepipes, thinking about what Everard had just told him: reflecting (*a*) that now one knew why the destroyer man had been so ready, even eager, to make this trip, and (*b*) that he himself might similarly have married Nadia – *if* he'd been quicker off the mark, and more determined, had had some of Everard's qualities of — what, decisiveness? Ruthlessness, even?

Although it wasn't easy to see how he could have managed it. Except by getting himself some Black Sea appointment while the Caspian show was still in progress — which his CO at that time, the Commodore of the Caspian Flotilla, would surely have refused to countenance.

But wouldn't an Everard in that situation — 'the real thing', as he'd called it, and which undoubtedly it had been, at least as far as *he* was concerned — wouldn't an Everard still have swung it, one way or another?

Everard was coming back to him now, while a signalman was uncovering the lamp on the starboard side and another was at the flag-locker further aft, whisking out *Terrapin*'s pendant numbers to have them ready for hoisting as identification. Bob murmured, 'In advance — and with regrets that I shan't be able to attend the ceremony — congratulations.'

'Thank you.' The younger man's smile was warm. 'And for making it possible in the first place, my heartfelt thanks, and hers.'

'Will *Benbow*'s padre be doing the job?'

'No fear!' He looked appalled at the suggestion. 'Red tape and brass hats? My God, *no*! No, Ilyana's got a Russian Orthodox priest lined up, we'll be doing it ashore.'

'You won't ask for anyone's permission — your Captain (D) or—'

'Indeed I won't … Pressure of time and circumstances as justification. Oh, I expect I'll get rapped over the knuckles. May even be deemed to have incurred their Lordships' displeasure. Believe it or not, I've achieved that distinction before — once or twice. And I'm no worse off for it … Anyway — my life and hers, isn't it, not their bloody Lordships' …'

Shortly before 2pm, *Terrapin* was coming up to the Kerch-Yenikale Strait, the bottleneck entrance to the Sea of Azov. Course was altered to NE, cutting the corner past Cape Takil, then to NNW, then due north. At this point, where the channel became very narrow, a seaman with a lead and line installed himself at the top of the fo'c'sl-break ladder on the starboard side — just below the bridge — and began taking and reporting soundings. Engine revolutions had been cut, but not by all that much, considering the navigational hazards as depicted on the chart — and confirmed by the leadsman singing out at this moment 'A quarter less two, sir!' Telling them in that high wail that there were only one and three-quarter fathoms of water, ten and a half feet, within a yard or two of the ship's side as she rushed on past the point where the lead had touched bottom: and *Terrapin* drew only inches less than *twelve* feet. Cruickshank was stooped mantis-like over the binnacle, Everard leaning sideways from his wooden seat in the starboard forward corner, directly above the leadsman — who had his lead on the move again, three or four pendulum-like swings parallel to the ship's side, demonstrating expert control in keeping it exactly parallel and each swing a little higher than the last until he let it go, the twelve-pound lead flying out ahead, describing a parabolic arc before splashing in, the line's slack coming magically up into his hands then while the tautness below them changed fast from the long slant to vertical and he leant outward, peering down to read the mark that was nearest above water-level at that instant: 'And a half, *one!*'

Nine feet ...

Well, they'd been through here several times recently, knew the channel and the margins of safety. They were professionals — as he was himself, for God's sake, feeling as the thought occurred to him not only that natural empathy with them but also a surge of envy. This being his own proper environment as much as it was theirs: while the job he'd been given made him an outsider to it, made him in their eyes some different kind of animal.

A 'cloak-and-dagger merchant' was what they'd call him. And he was nothing of the sort — neither by inclination nor aptitude. He was a seaman, nothing else, had nothing whatsoever in common with the Sidney Reillys of this world — or, for God's sake, with any Alexis Lapins, until very recently of this world ... For one thing, he didn't have that kind of brain. Recalling for instance the effort it had taken to sort out that Ukrainian girl's likely ulterior motives: hadn't Ashmore, probably — and wouldn't this quick-witted Everard character, for that matter — have seen the answers straight off the bat?

'Ah. Here you are ...'

Harriman, the destroyer's first lieutenant: short, thick arms propelling him off the steel ladder into the rear end of the bridge. 'Thought you might've had your head down. Won't be getting much sleep tonight, sir, will you? Or many square meals after you land, either — which is the subject for discussion now, if it's not inconvenient. The matter of what you'd like to take ashore with you in the way of rations. Sandwiches, for instance? If so — well, corned dog — beef — cheese ...'

Like planning a picnic. But he'd have plenty of room in the holdall that he was taking, and food might not be plentiful or easy to come by, wherever he was going. Harriman — having settled the sandwich question, more or less — suggested a bottle of gin to wash them down. Bob declined this offer, but accepted the loan of a flask which would be filled with whisky.

'Let's see — what else ... How about fruit? Crimean oranges, if you've room for some?'

Everard came aft to join them. At the binnacle, Cruickshank was settling the ship on a course of North 20 East and ordering revolutions for twenty knots. Out of the shelter of the straits now, the northwester was making itself felt again; she was rolling as well as pitching, dipping her bow into it and flinging the stuff back green and white as her speed built up. Everard said, 'So far so good. Four hours now roughly, to the entrance of the gulf ... Tell me — what do you do for a train ticket when you get there — or don't you need one?'

'I have a pass that takes me anywhere.' He added, 'Theoretically.'

'Theoretically?'

'Other than regions where the Bolsheviks preside.'

'Ah. Quite.' Blinking at him ... 'And money?'

'Plenty of that. Not that one's going shopping ... Food, of course, once I've eaten the rations you're very kindly providing — and especially when it comes to getting out, the long haul down to Novorossisk — and three mouths to feed by then, touch wood.'

'That's a point.' Everard put a hand on his arm. 'Subject of your exit — I was having a thought or two. If the Bolshies got into Novorossisk first, for instance. After all, if we're pulling out — as we well may be — doubtless to resounding cheers from the tub-thumpers back home who think we should never have gone *in* ... Look, come down to the chart for a minute, let me show you?'

'Gladly ... Although if the Reds did get there first—'

Harriman cut in, 'Excuse me, sir. Just one thing more.' He asked Bob: 'Do you have a pistol of your own?

Because if you haven't, it mightn't be a bad idea—'

'Webley and Scott .455 automatic — for better or for worse ... And before you ask, I've two boxes of shells for it. Thanks for the thought, anyway.'

He yelled to Everard, on their way down to the chart-room — having to grab for handholds, now, the way she was tossing herself around — 'You and your people are really nursemaiding me!'

'Well,' Everard laughed, lurching into the chartroom. 'Only until you find your own governesses. *Their* job, then. But look here, now...'

Chartwork: alternatives to Novorossisk for evacuation purposes. Although there were *no* alternatives, realistic-ally. If things got to such a stage that Novorossisk ceased to be useable, that would be *it* — curtains. At least, you'd be well and truly stuck ... But it was good of Everard to be giving this much thought to one's future wellbeing, and there was no harm in joining him in a bit of wishful-thinking.

4

'Steady as you go ...'
'Steady, sir. North three degrees east, sir.'
'Steer that.'

Cruickshank straightened from the binnacle — at least, straightened to his customary stoop — having put *Terrapin* on the last leg of her approach to Taganrog. Getting towards midnight: she'd been in the gulf for about four hours, steering ENE at a steady twenty knots, but more recently the speed had been cut to ten and now, having made the course alteration, he was ducking to the pipe again to reduce that by half again. Reducing windflow too, as the revs came off her; but the wind was over the bow now instead of on the beam and there was enough ice in it to make your eyes run. The sea was low, choppy, white-streaked, and the night was pitch-black, heavy cloud hiding whatever moon there might have been.

'That you, Cowan?'

Everard: hunched on his seat, binoculars at his eyes ... How he'd sensed one's arrival in the bridge was a mystery: unless Cruickshank had muttered something. He might have: he'd peered around, a second earlier, and with the glow from the binnacle the bridge wasn't entirely dark. But otherwise all eyes, watering or not, were strained into the surrounding darkness, primarily for other ships but also for floating mines. There was a westerly drift in this gulf, no doubt created by the influx of rivers at its eastern end, and it was thought that mines which had been spotted and destroyed in the Sea of Azov might well have been floated out from Bolshevik-held settlements on the northern shore.

Bob had moved up behind Everard. 'Not far to go now?'

'Half an hour, thereabouts. *You* ready to go?'

'Well —' making a weak joke of it — 'having come all this way ...'

A grunt. Then: 'Pilot, let's have some soundings.'

There'd been plenty of water under her for the past eighty miles or so, steaming right down the middle with the land roughly ten miles on either hand, but as she crept northward now there'd be a gradual shelving to start with and then, almost for sure, shallower patches. You could virtually have fixed your position by soundings, if you could have relied on them being as shown on the chart; as things were now you couldn't quite do that, but the general trend would be pretty well as shown. With luck *Terrapin* might get to within about three miles of the town and still have twelve feet under her when she stopped to send the boat away; she'd be due south of the point, then, and there'd be a rock — he'd forgotten its name — about halfway in, three thousand yards offshore. It had to be born in mind both as a navigational aid and as something to look out for — rather than bump into ...

The closer one could get in, the better, especially as they were going to land him in the whaler, under oars. There'd been a discussion about this earlier in the evening, and Mr Wilberforce, the commissioned engineer, had been adamant that the motorboat's engine wasn't to be trusted over any distance.

Harriman had agreed. 'Damn thing cokes up, drop of a hat. Wouldn't make for a very happy situation, would it?'

The motorboat's engine was of the kind that had to be started on petrol, then changed over to run on paraffin as soon as the vaporizer was hot enough to do its job on the heavier fuel. It was the vaporizer that clogged up, 'Monkey' Wilberforce had explained, more than the sparking plug, the basic fault in his view lying with the variable quality of the paraffin. There were motorboats in the fleet now that had engines which ran entirely on petrol, but they were still hard to come by, the Admiralty objecting to (a) petrol engines' higher cost, (b) the hazards involved in storing petrol in HM ships.

Wilberforce had slapped the wardroom table with one large, creased hand; the other hand been wrapped around an enamel mug of near-black tea. He had enormous hands on unusually long arms, which presumably explained his nickname. 'So it's beef an' brawn as'll best put ye on the beach tonight, sir ...'

The leadsman's voice rose hoarsely out of the darkness to starboard: 'Deep four, sir!'

A 'deep' was a point on the leadline at which there was no mark. At three there'd be three strips of leather, and at fifteen a piece of white bunting; on this sounding the leadsman would have seen the flash of white cloth about a fathom above the waterline. His alternative if marks weren't visible in the dark — the blue bunting probably would not be, nor for instance would the ten-fathom mark, which was a piece of leather with a hole in it — was to go by whatever he found closest to his hand and allow for the distance between hand and waterline. But fourteen fathoms was dead right, matched the charted depth exactly. Everard had commented, 'Right on the nose, Pilot, eh?' And now to Bob, inconsequentially: 'I hope for your sake there *are* some trains running.'

'Got it all in your head, Sub, have you?'

Everard asked the question of Granger, Lounge-Lizard Larry, who was to be in charge of the boat. It was a few minutes past midnight: very soon the destroyer's engines would be stopped and she'd drift to a halt in two fathoms of water, just *under* three miles from the port of Taganrog. Slightly better, therefore, than they'd hoped for. Everard's intention was to drop an anchor then, but to get the whaler away first, cutting delays to a minimum.

They were in the chartroom: he, Granger and Bob. Bob wearing uniform with a white rollneck sweater under his reefer jacket, folded-down leather seaboots with oiled-wool seaboot stockings in them, and his greatcoat over it all.

Granger had nodded to that question, and was now repeating the bare bones of his orders. A course of north twenty west to be made good, but an estimated westward drift of about half a mile in the time the trip inshore was expected to take, course to steer thus north five west.

The calculations were Cruickshank's. Bob was less certain of what seemed to him to be an unsafe assumption, but he'd queried it earlier and been politely overruled, so now — being only a passenger here — he kept his mouth shut.

Granger concluded, 'And if I see the Cherry-packer thing I'll know I've come too far east.'

The rock's name on the chart was *Chyerypakha.* Everard told him, 'You'd be on your way to missing the landfall altogether.'

'Yes. Hard a-port, then. But if the Pilot's right about this westward set—,'

'And if you steer a straight course and your compass isn't deflected by *that* damn thing ...' Everard pointed at the .45 revolver holstered inside the sub-lieutenant's oilskins, which were unbuttoned and hanging open. Granger had the boat compass with him too — a portable brass binnacle with a carrying handle on top and a lockable gymbal ring. It was locked now, of course, for transport, and the interior oil-lamp which would illuminate the compass card wasn't lit yet.

He'd nodded. 'I'll stow it well clear, sir.'

'And your course back to the ship?'

'Reverse of inshore course. Making good south twenty east, steering something like south thirty-five east. But depending on how I've found it on the way in, of course. And with your searchlight for a mark.'

'We'll expose the beam sixty minutes after you leave us.'

'But — if we happened to make the inshore leg faster than expected, sir—'

'All right. Forty-five minutes after you leave.'

'Aye aye, sir. Thank you.'

The searchlight, carbon-burning, was above and just abaft the bridge. By shining it vertically upwards into the clouds the whaler would have about as good a mark as one could hope for — might even have it in sight right from the point of departure from shore. Without something of the sort, a destroyer was a very small object to locate, in the dark and at the end of a three-mile pull on a dark night in a wind-lashed sea — literally *in* that sea, as they would be in a 27-foot open boat; and an outcome that Everard would dread was to have his boat lost and searching blindly for them, when he needed to get *Terrapin* out of the gulf before dawn.

There was sleet in the wind now. A foretaste, no doubt, of conditions one could expect ashore. Back in the bridge — Granger having gone down to the boat — Everard said 'Remains only to wish you luck, Cowan. I do, most sincerely, and I'll look forward to good news of you. If you feel like it, drop me a line?'

'Yes — I will. When I can ... And I'm very grateful to you. Oh, and your great occasion tomorrow — *every* happiness, and—'

The leadsman's hail: 'And a quarter, two!'

Cruickshank's bent frame swivelling: 'Stop engines, sir?'

'I'll say goodbye and good luck then, sir ...'

With one foot and both hands on the eight-inch mesh netting that slanted up from deck-level to the griping-spar, Bob glanced back at the first lieutenant's oilskinned bulk — wet oilskins gleaming in light shed from the galley. The others — whaler's crew and Granger — were already up there in the boat, and he'd passed his canvas holdall up to one of them. He nodded to Harriman: 'Thanks — for all your help.' Climbing then, while the boat-lowering party of half a dozen men, three to each fall, stood ready, waiting for Harriman's orders. Bob swung à booted leg over the spar, rested his weight on it while he got the other one over and then slid into the boat. The coxswain, a sharp-faced Irish leading seaman by the name of Hayes, put out a hand to steady him.

'Thanks.' Suppressing the urge to protest that he wasn't *that* much of a bloody passenger: but clumsy enough in the heavy boots as he ducked under the fore-and-after and dumped himself in the sternsheets beside Granger. 'My bag somewhere, Sub?'

'Under the stern thwart, sir.'

'Ah—'

Harriman's voice, from the iron deck: 'Slip the gripes. Turns for lowering.'

Gripes were bands of rope matting, like girths, which held a seaboat immovably against the horizontal griping-spar. Their shackles were being knocked off now, so they'd swing loose and free the boat for lowering. It was to be lowered almost right into the water, much as you'd do in harbour, not dropped from a height of several feet as was more usual with a seaboat and at sea.

Harriman's growl again: 'Start the falls!' The boat jerked, dropping an inch or two as the hemp ropes were allowed to creep around the staghorns. Then — having checked that there'd be no hangups — 'Lower away!', and the descent began, forward and after falls carefully in step so that the boat went down on an even keel, while its tendency to sway fore and aft was countered by the crew leaning their weight on crossed lifelines. Procedures that were entirely familiar, part and parcel of the home-from-home which one was on the point of leaving: as was Everard's having turned his ship to provide a lee on this port side, shelter for the launching.

'Vast lowering!'

The order came from overhead, distant-sounding. The falls jerked to a stop. Hanging this low the ship's rolling was a danger; some of the crewmen had unshipped their stretchers — the wooden bars that took the pressure of their feet when they were rowing — and were using them to fend off from the vertical steel side. And now Harriman's voice again — 'Out pins!' His face was a pale blur up there as he leant over between the davits, watching to see the order carried out, bowman and stroke oarsman removing steel cotter-pins from the disengaging gear — the big hooks on which the boat was hanging — while the coxswain, Hayes, stood by the steel-wire fore-and-after which linked the hooks and was now keeping tension on them. Until now they'd been locked shut by those pins. Robinson's Disengaging Gear, this assembly was called, and Bob had learnt all its mysteries in his cradle. Well, not cradle, exactly. Cradle days and early boyhood years had been spent in Russia — in St Petersburg — and instruction in elementary seamanship hadn't begun until he'd been thirteen and a cadet in the Merchant Navy training ship, an ancient hulk moored in the Thames. But still — a long, long time ago ... Hayes had called up to Harriman, 'Pins out, sir ...'

'Slip!'

Hayes' job. When he let-go the fore-and-after, both hooks would release and the boat would drop into the sea. It would drop only a foot or two on this occasion, but even now the knack of it was to drop with a wave right under her, not up-ended or into a trough. A matter of fine judgement, when the ship was travelling at any speed, but as things were now — *Terrapin* lying stopped, and with the sea as low as it was — and anyway with no time for dithering—

Now ...

The heavy timber boat fell, crashing in. Crewmen already getting their oars out, blades up on the gunwales, three on the starboard side and two to port: the imbalance would be corrected by a small amount of rudder. Hayes was in fact applying a lot of rudder right at this moment, so that the boat would sheer out from the ship's side.

'Give way, starboard ...'

Then when they were clear — lifting to a swell as they left the ship's close shelter and the driving sleet made itself felt again — 'Give way together!'

Another wave burst in a sheet of something like ice-bullets as the crew put their weight on the oars and the boat began to forge ahead, lifting and rocking as the black ridges ran under, a mound ahead exploding to sheet back vivid white as her stem drove in. Oilskinned and sou'westered crewmen adjusting their positions on the thwarts, getting settled, into the rhythm of it but inter-

rupted by Hayes again — 'Easy, starboard!' Voice pitched
high, to be heard over all the surrounding noise — wind,
sea, thumping of oars' looms in the metal crutches. Star-
board-side oars missed a stroke or two while he brought
her round, at a safe distance from the destroyer's plunging
bow. Granger meanwhile crouching over his compass,
which was glowing internally now, a pale radiance visible
in the little window in its brass casing. He'd set it down on
the boat's centreline just abaft the stretcher against which
the stroke oarsman's feet were jammed. Hayes calling,
'Together now. All together, lads ...' The boat lifting to a
wave and for a few seconds lying almost on her side —
wind gusting from behind the oarsmen's left shoulders as
she battered round into it, spray in it in sporadic bursts
that thickened the continuous, horizontally-flying sleet.
Tilting over that wave, angling down in a long surge
forward then checking with the next one foaming white
around her stem and boiling aft, the boat's timbers
juddering but five oars biting all together into solid water
to drive her on. From *Terrapin*'s bridge the sea hadn't
looked like much — it wasn't, from up there — but down
here, at closer quarters — well, this was the reality. No joy-
ride, exactly, but with no kind of agony in it either — no
surprise either, you were only reminded of what you'd
have expected anyway if you'd given it any forethought.
And adjusting now to conditions as they were, Granger
was moving the compass, re-positioning it between
himself and the coxswain.

'North five degrees west. There — as you go now ...
Uh?'

'North five west — aye, sir!'

The compass was the only guide. You couldn't tell a
helmsman how to steer when there was no mark of any
sort to steer by, nothing ahead except darkness and the
heave of black water. Granger unbuckling his webbing
belt with the pistol in its holster, then passing it to Bob —
to put distance between the metal and the compass
needle, as advised earlier on by Everard. Thinking of
whom — Bob was stowing the bundle under the thwart

with his own gear and Granger's binoculars which in these conditions were useless, when from the darkness astern came the metallic clatter of *Terrapin* letting-go an anchor.

Sitting upright in the whaler's stern with his eyes narrowed against sleet and salt, Bob did his best to keep a lookout. Granger might well have been doing the same — some of the time, anyway — but he'd also be preoccupied with the course, ensuring that Hayes stayed close to it — the lubber's line wavering more or less equally each side of it, no question of actually staying on the mark. And no other pair of eyes was free for looking-out.

Thoughts wandering, meanwhile. At this moment, to Nadia.

Connection being the boat, recollection of his last sight of her?

As if one needed any explanation, for God's sake ... But it had been a motorboat, otherwise not unlike this one. Beamier, for sure, but a ship's boat, no great difference, and it had been transferring her and the Solovyevs to a former Russian merchant ship, the *Slava*, which at that time had been flying the White Ensign. He'd relived the scene a hundred times, had it now clearly in his mind's eye: heaving, greenish sea, *Slava*'s tall-funnelled profile in the background, and the boat bouncing its way across the gap with that huddle of passengers in its stern. Nadia's taller figure distinctive with her mop of dark hair flying in the wind, Nick Solovyev between her and his fair-haired sister. Solovyev had had an arm round each of them, while in Nadia's left palm — unless she'd slipped it inside her dress by that time, but she'd still had it hidden in her hand when she'd gone down the ladder — in that hand, the folded sheet of signal-pad on which he'd scrawled an address where she could get in touch with him if — no, *when* — she'd got herself to Britain.

And neither of the Solovyevs having the slightest notion that anything of the sort had been going on.

He thought self-mockingly, *He who laughs last ...*

Out there in the dark, a flare of white. Gone: then back

again ... Broken water — where there was no damn reason—

Rock?

Straining his eyes ...

Then he'd got it. Lost it again immediately, but *had had* it, beyond doubt, recognized—

'Sub — boat of some kind — fine on the port bow, crossing left to right—'

'Oars!'

Rowing ceased instantly. Oars' blades parallel to the water, men's bodies hunched forward, all eyes on their coxswain, waiting.

'God — *yes* ...'

Hayes called softly, 'Port side only, one stroke!'

To keep the boat's head into the wind, which meant also pointing at whatever this craft was that was cutting a white track through black water, steering east across the whaler's bow, roughly fifty yards ahead.

May not see us — if we're lucky ...

'Heads down, lads.'

They *were* down. Hayes again: 'Barty — one stroke, now ...'

'*Two* boats. See?'

'Yes. Yes, you're right, sir ... But — could be friendly, just as likely as—'

'Best play it safe, Sub.'

'Yes ... Sir, my pistol—'

He didn't want to take his eyes off those craft, as he'd have had to do in the course of delving under the thwart for Granger's revolver. Which please God there'd be no use for anyway. Even less than there'd be for the glasses; their front lenses would be plastered before you'd even got them to your eyes.

He slid his hand into the greatcoat's pocket all the same, touched his own pistol. Strictly for reassurance: no kind of expectation ...

'One stroke, Barty!'

There were hamlets and fishing villages on small indentations and coves along the gulf's northern shore, and several of them had been in Bolshevik hands in recent weeks. Some would be *now.* Temporary bases of a kind a mine-sowing operation might be run from, for instance. And quite a large place further west, right at the entrance to the gulf, small town called Mariupol that even had a single branch-line of the railway connecting to it — and deep water, so access from the sea would pose no problems — Mariupol had changed hands three times in a month. Which was why he and Everard — and Hackett, the cruiser's navigator, before that — had rejected it as a possible landing place. That railway line would be highly insecure, in any case — even if it was still intact. But from there or any of the coastal villages these boats could have come.

Carrying what? Mines — a raiding party — supplies to Bolshevik partisans?

They were launches, was all one could say for sure. The second of them passing ahead now — a low, dark shape that wouldn't have been detectable at all if it hadn't been for the fringe of white around its stem. But — it was *audibly* detectable, suddenly, a mutter of diesel propulsion coming softly but clearly on the wind. And that smell — diesel exhaust, for sure. Hadn't either heard or smelt the first one: had been too startled at that stage, perhaps, hadn't settled to it . . .

Granger was right, of course, they could be friendly. Whites engaged in some clandestine operation or patrolling to intercept some expected Bolshevik intrusion.

But wouldn't they have been keeping a better lookout, then?

Seconds crawling by. Thinking, *Better safe than sorry, anyway.* Bearing in mind the local tendency to let rip and answer no questions afterwards: as demonstrated so recently by the one-eyed Grusjenko, giggling behind that gun . . .

'Port side — one stroke, lads!'

Bob spoke for the first time in several minutes: 'Reckon we've seen the last of them. Agree, Sub?'

'Yes . . . But — crikey, good thing you had your eyes peeled, sir!'

'May as well push on, uh?'

They'd been lying stopped for something like ten minutes. So if Cruickshank had been right about the half-knot tidal set, the boat would have been carried westward about one sixth of a thousand yards — for a round figure, say 150 yards.

It wasn't worth mentioning, he decided — having thought it over as they got under way again. Navigation wasn't going to be all that accurate tonight in any case, and adjusting for this would — if he was right — only be compounding Cruickshank's error. He still believed that the seasonal factor — rivers iced-up, their outflow thus either reduced or stopped completely — should have been taken into account. In other words, that there'd be no such current. And when after a few more minutes he sighted the rock he knew he'd been right. Not that any great feat of genius had been involved ...

The rock was dead ahead, if anything a degree or two to port. Breaking seas were spouting vertically as they smashed across it: undoubtedly a rock, not anything that floated.

'Sub — rock, right ahead — cable's length—'

'Oars!' Hayes hadn't waited for an order. Bob finished, to Granger, 'Come thirty degrees to port, if I were you.'

Helm over ... 'Cherry-packer?'

'No other, is there?'

'Give way, starboard ...'

To help her round. The three starboard oars swung forward, dipped raggedly ... Granger shouted, 'Must have reckoned a bit wrong somewhere — strength of the set, or—'

'Yes.'

The sub-lieutenant hadn't been present when Bob and Cruickshank had had their disagreement. But remembering Everard's later comment — 'You'd be missing your landfall altogether' — well, they *would* have. As it had turned out, all was well, but if Cruickshank's estimate had been of a whole knot, say — which wouldn't have been all that much more serious a misjudgement — in this low visibility they'd have seen neither that rock nor the point of land, they'd have gone plugging on and finished up plain lost.

Hayes peered into the compass. 'North thirty west, sir?'

'Steer thirty-five west.' Granger yelled at Bob. 'Bit of a dog's leg, I'm afraid. Sorry, sir.'

'Not your fault.' Shouting across the wind ... 'Take it into account going back though, won't you? Assume there's no set, your course will be — what, south twenty east?'

The wind was from over the starboard bow, on this new course, but within about ten minutes there was much less of it and less movement on the sea. Getting into some shelter from the land, of course — and the oarsmen's job a lot easier for it. The so-called Cherry-packer, he remembered, was about 1,500 yards offshore; so now, slanting in as they were after that alteration, you could reckon on having about a mile to go.

If there were any lights on the Taganrog shoreline, in fact, they ought to be visible pretty soon. Searching for some, he used a semi-frozen fingertip to wipe salt out of his eyes. Thinking that the pull back to the ship, with the wind astern, would be a much quicker trip than this had been. Not only the wind — they'd be steering the correct course, instead of two sides of a triangle — and in the final stages they'd have *Terrapin*'s searchlight to guide them in. All adding up to the conclusion that young Everard, owing no thanks to his navigating officer, instead of having to waste the pre-dawn hours searching for this whaler would stand a good chance of getting to the church on time.

Lucky beggar.

Or was he? He certainly *thought* he was. And he'd resented the suggestion that he might be marrying his countess primarily to save her neck. But what about *her* motives?

Everard wouldn't have any doubts at all. Being in love, and therefore blind ... But suppose she was not anything like in love. Only in fear. Being trapped there, and knowing how Bolsheviks treated people of her kind when they got their hands on them ... Could anyone blame her if she'd snatched at the one and only chance? In fact — wouldn't you be ready to marry her yourself, without any element or even pretence of love, if the alternative was leaving her to *that*?

Remembering the scene in a country house at a place called Enotayevsk, ancestral home of the Solovyevs. A line of ropes dangling from the gallery, their lower ends dark and stiff with human blood: and Nadia, for God's sake—

Granger's shout pulled him out of it: 'Lights to starboard, sir!'

Half-rising — one hand grasping the gunwale as insurance, the other shielding his eyes against the wet ... Seeing them at once — three pinpoints of light, flickery like stars on a night with hazy cloud. And above, beyond them, a vague lightening in the sky — dome-shaped, reflection of a town's lights and fires in the low, oppressive overhead. Taganrog, like Sevastopol, evidently had generators that still functioned.

Sitting again, he could still see the lights. A line of them — they'd be along the waterfront, of course.

'Steer for the middle, Sub. Until we see what's what.'

There'd be some kind of challenge soon. With things as they were, Bolshevik pressure and infiltration, the quays would hardly be left unguarded. This place with its railway yards on such a strategically important route — main access route to the Caucasus, no less — would be a prime target for the Reds.

The whaler was on course for those lights. Water almost calm, making the rowing a lot easier. Well, you were in a bay, of sorts. The five crewmen were working in perfect unison, regatta-style, the stroke precisely synchronized and the oarsmen's elbows — in the time-worn pulling instructors' idiom — 'polishing their ribs' ... Sleet still heavy, though, maybe more so than it had been. It would be the sleet that had created the flickering effect — which was already a thing of the past, the lights' glow now steady although weak enough. Seven or eight of them: and — he realized what he'd been staring at — in silhouette against the right-hand section, the skeletal outline of a dockside crane.

Programme, now — now that one might begin to think further than the coastline ... One, get ashore — preferably without being shot at. Two, get through the town to the railway station. Then — well, trust to luck ... But the railway junction and yards were shown clearly on the chart as being on the town's north side, inland of the built-up area and about two miles from the docks.

'*Hey—*'

Incredibly white light, as it were jumping out of the darkness — flaring out, a white beam growing out across ruffled, still white-streaked water, the beam scything round towards them then seeming to intensify as it settled on the boat and held it.

So they were on their toes all right, ashore there. Next thing — any moment — they'd open fire.

And why not — in their shoes? Why take chances?

'Keep going. Keep going ...'

He stood up, feet well apart for balance, spread both arms up above his head — gesture of surrender, peaceful intentions, whatever — then on second thoughts took off his cap and began to wave it. Balancing to the whaler's plunging motion, and completely blinded — Hayes meanwhile growling encouragement to his crew, the oars sweeping steadily to and fro, spray from the lifting blades flying like drops of silver in the searchlight's beam; he was hoping to God they didn't have any Grusjenkos here.

5

Terrapin lay head to wind, tugging at her chain cable, the blanket of sleet enclosing her and restricting visibility range to no more than a hundred years. Nick Everard — on the bridge at this moment, while his navigator and first lieutenant had their heads down — reluctantly admitted to himself that it was quite a bit thicker than it had been, and was glad he'd thought of using the searchlight as a beacon. Not yet: he didn't want to advertise his ship's position to all and sundry before he had to. But there was no doubt of it, this muck was coming down a lot faster than it had been when the whaler had pushed off into it, and even with the searchlight to help him young Granger had better be steering pretty fine.

One knew, from personal experience, how tricky it could be, finding one's ship from a small boat in foul weather. At Scapa, this had been, in thick fog, when he'd been a midshipman in charge of a battleship's steam picket-boat, with a five- or six-mile journey across the Flow to the anchored dreadnought — which he'd hated, loathing everything about the Navy at that stage, and had loathed even more after he'd made a hash of finding her and then been physically beaten and put 'under report' for what the ship's commander had called 'sheer bloody-minded incompetence'.

Jutland had changed everything. Hundreds of times since that last day of May and first of June 1916, he'd thanked God for Jutland.

'Closing in on us, sir.' McKendrick — gunnery officer, Australian-born and still sounding like it — had come to stand beside him. 'Wouldn't you say?'

He grunted. Not much wanting to say anything at all about it, at this stage.

'Boat'll be about inshore by now, I suppose.'

'Well. Hardly ...' Moving to the binnacle, stooping to use its light to check the time by his pocket-watch, but glancing sideways as some newcomer arrived in the bridge.

'Captain, sir?'

'Why aren't you asleep, Pilot?'

'I was, sir — until this cypher came in.' Cruickshank was signals officer as well as navigator. 'PO telegraphist saw fit to have me shaken to decode it. Net result being ...'

He'd broken off to yawn.

'*Being?*'

Impatience sprang from sudden dread — of an emergency of some kind, orders to proceed elsewhere than to Theodosia ... Cruickshank muttering, 'It's by no means *good* news, sir ...' Bent double now, close to the binnacle's glow, stooped over like that not only to get close to the light but also to keep the signal dry. Everard told him — having to control the impatience — 'Look, that's no good. Bring it down to the chartroom.'

Thinking, on the way down one level — all right, *not good* news ... But Cruickshank didn't know the underlying purpose of the Theodosia call. Nobody did — not even Harriman, who was going to be Best Man, if the Orthodox ritual called for one. And being thus unaware of the vital importance of putting in there, why should Cruickshank see a diversion from it as 'not good'?

So — something else — please God ...

Switching on the chart-table light, he snatched the sheet of signal-paper from this constantly yawning navigator, and leant over under the light to read it.

TERRAPIN FOR LT.CDR.COWAN: FROM SO(I) CONSTANTINOPLE

KHARKOV FRONT HAS BEEN OVERRUN, VOLUNTEER ARMY ATTEMPTING WITHDRAWAL BUT UNDER THREAT OF ENCIRCLEMENT BY RED CAVALRY. IN

THESE HIGHLY ADVERSE CIRCUMSTANCES THE
CHANCES OF SUCCEEDING IN YOUR MISSION ARE
SEEN AS INCOMMENSURATE WITH RISK. YOUR ORDERS
ARE THEREFORE CANCELLED AND YOU ARE TO
REMAIN IN *TERRAPIN* FOR PASSAGE TO CONSTAN-
TINOPLE.

He put the flimsy pink sheet down on the chart, asked
himself as much as Cruickshank, 'What the blazes am I
supposed to do about *that*?'

'They can't have known our programme, sir ... I
suppose *Caledonian*—'

'Yes. Temple must've ...' His voice tailed off. It was a
fact that he'd deliberately left his timetable rather open
when drafting the signal which Captain Fellows had sent
to Constantinople, so as to leave himself as much latitude
as possible. Partly with the Theodosia call in mind.
Although Temple would have made his own calculations,
surely ... There again, one could imagine the SO(I)
bunging out this signal within minutes of receiving that
intelligence — just on the off-chance of getting it through
in time.

'Anyway —' Cruickshank had re-read the message, put
it down again — 'there's no way we could get him back
now. Well, obviously ... But in the strategic sense it's
rather frightening news, sir — wouldn't you say?'

'Disastrous' might have been a better adjective. It
signalled, as likely as not, the beginning of the end of the
counter-revolution. Further proof, incidentally, of how
well that fellow Trotsky had transformed his Red Army,
which a year ago had been a hopeless rabble, into an
effective fighting force. While by and large the Whites,
despite heady interludes of glory, had never been anything
but a rabble. Poor devils ...

Cowan, though: whether there'd be any point in sending
someone after him in the hope of catching him before he
got on a train: whether the chances of doing *that* might be
regarded as 'commensurate with risk' ...

Send McKendrick, perhaps. Put a fresh crew in the
whaler when it got back ...

No. Too damn late. There was no guessing how long it
might be before it did get back, then that long trip again —
and in deteriorating conditions. Not to mention the
certainty of *Terrapin* being stuck in this gulf until well
after daylight: which was unacceptable. So — no question
— you had to leave Cowan to take his chances.

Having already decided to leave his governesses to take
theirs. But that had been Staff Officer (Intelligence)
Constantinople's decision, thank God, not one's own.

He glanced at his watch. Remembering Cowan telling
him, 'I'm a big lad, I can look after myself'.

The devil, he could: he'd bloody *have* to ... But another
recollection, sparked by images thrown into his mind by
Temple's signal, thoughts of defeat and evacuation, as of
the scene at Odessa last April when the French were
pulling out. He'd been there in *Terrapin*, had packed as
many refugees into her as she could carry without turning
turtle, and brought them to Sevastopol; but he knew that
as long as he lived the visual memories of that day and
night would haunt him: jetties still crowded with doomed
men, women and children as the ships drew off, full well
beyond their capacity — and British sailors, seasoned by
years of war, in tears as they handled the ropes and wires.

Novorossisk, he thought, might before long see a replay
of those scenes. Sevastopol, too. And — Theodosia. This
was no nightmare, either, no product of exhaustion or
fevered imagination: it was reality, even *probability*...

'Sir?'

Back to earth: to Cruickshank waiting with a pencil
poised.

'Ah. Yes ...' He checked the time again, then dictated:
'To SO(I) Constantinople, from *Terrapin*. Your — what —
ever time of origin's on his signal — received at — the time
it came in. Fullstop. Regretfully have to submit that
Lieutenant-Commander Cowan landed at Taganrog at —
the time the whaler left the ship. Encypher that now, but
it's not to go out until Granger's back and we know
Cowan did land. Understood?'

'Aye aye, sir.' Still scribbling: hearing Everard mutter to

himself as he started back up to the bridge, 'Better light ourselves up, meanwhile.'

'Oh, crikey, I'm *damn* sorry you've had this wait, sir!'

Some sort of motor had pulled up outside the shed, there'd been a shout in pidgin-Russian of 'Keep her running — *dva minuta!*' and now this boyish, pink-faced lieutenant — Bob focused on the cap-badge identifying it as that of the Royal Fusiliers — had come bursting in, pushing past the Russian sentry at the door, while the other Russian got to his feet. Bob stood up too — there were only two chairs, on which he and the older of his two guards had been sitting with the coal-burning brazier between them.

'You *are* Commander Cowan — sir?'

He admitted it.

'Tinsdale, sir. From our military mission.' He'd halted, snapped off one of those quivery military salutes, and was now ready to shake hands. Pink-faced, blue-eyed, fair hair visible under the edges of the cap. Rather large ears ... 'I'm *frightfully* sorry you've been stuck here such an age, sir. Fact is, we were told you'd be arriving sometime around dawn. So I'd turned in, and—'

'You had a signal about me?'

'Landline from Novorossisk. Communications aren't all that marvellous at the moment, but from Rostov and Novorossisk the lines are still open — and just as well — but ...'

Rattling on ... Bob concluding that Fellows — no, Temple, presumably — must have sent a message to be relayed from one of the ships at Novorossisk, without having done his homework properly. In point of fact there was no harm done, he hadn't expected to have anyone here to meet him anyway ... Tinsdale, still on the subject of telephones and telegraphs, was saying that there was no communications link at all from here northward. Kharkov, in particular, was as dead as a doornail. Might seem a bit ominous — what? Then, no doubt remembering that Kharkov was where this fellow wanted to go, he added that the telegraph lines up that way had been out of action several times before but had always returned to working order when someone eventually got round to doing something about it, so with any luck the present disruption mightn't last long either.

A bit of a blabbermouth, this Tinsdale. Bob asked him, 'Are there still trains passing through here northwards?'

'Oh lord, yes. And you want to get away as soon as possible, we're told. So I've got transport here, and — well, unless you'd care to come along to our Mess for a meal first—'

'I'd sooner get on a train.'

'Sure? Despite this long wait — for which I really do apologize—'

'Not your fault at all. But no — thank you all the same.'

'Right you are then, sir ... Although I should mention there's no way of knowing in advance when a train's coming, or leaving, or—'

'Only by being there when it does come. Shall we go?'

'After you, sir — please ...'

A Russian officer and half a dozen riflemen had met the whaler at the steps where Granger had put his boat alongside. There'd been several rifles pointing at him as he climbed the slippery stone steps, and others had been aimed down into the boat. Clumping his way up, one hand hefting the canvas holdall with his gear and food in it and the other resting on the pistol in his pocket, he'd been looking for red armbands or sashes amongst the reception committee. But it was all right — Taganrog was still in White hands, and after he'd shown the officer his papers and explained where he'd come from and what for, there'd been a considerable relaxation. Granger had been allowed to set off on his return journey to the ship, Bob had been ushered into this office at the end of a cargo-shed, which they were using as a guardroom, and the officer had gone off to telephone the British Military Mission, also to warn his own people about those launches heading up the gulf.

That had been about an hour ago. He'd been left here with the two soldiers guarding him — ensuring that he stayed put, effectively, but according to the officer their purpose had been to ensure his safety until his own people came for him — 'own people' as represented now by this lieutenant of the Royal Fusiliers.

The car was an old Ford with a flapping canvas hood and a bearded Russian driver in a fur cap, ground-length coat and for some reason goggles. As they moved off, Tinsdale asked Bob, 'Is it actually Kharkov you're making for?'

'The Kharkov region. I'll know better when I get there.'

'I see ... And you're confident you *will* get there?'

Bob looked at him, through icy darkness. The Ford wasn't anything like sleet-proof. It was grinding rather slowly through a typical docks area, bumping over rail-lines and pot-holes and weaving between the really deep ones.

'You mean because things aren't too good on that front at present.'

'Might be nearer the truth to say they're bloody awful, sir. At least, according to — well, can't say there's been any hundred-per cent reliable intelligence, this last day or two, but — well, for the last week — two or three weeks, I suppose—'

'What's the latest you've heard?'

'Well — nothing specific, really. Rather startling numbers of dead and wounded — that kind of thing. But — rumour, none of it's confirmed. Only thing is, it does rather fit into the picture we've been getting for quite a while now — Volunteer Army hanging on by the skin of its teeth, you might say ... Oh, one thing — we've moved a Flight of 47 Squadron — RAF you know, intrepid birdmen with their Sopwith Camels? — they've been transferred to that front, passed through day before yesterday, as it happens.'

'Well — that could make a *lot* of difference!'

'Might stiffen a few sinews, that's true, sir ... And incidentally, General Holman's gone up there, too. So I suppose it can't be all *that* unsafe.' He began to laugh, then checked himself, added, 'Joke. Sorry, sir. Actually Holman's rather a good egg.'

'Commands the military missions — am I right?'

'Commands all of us in south Russia. Instructors and advisors mostly — as you'll know, sir. Holman took over earlier in the year from old Biggs.' Grinning ... 'My God, *there*'s a character ...'

'What's Holman doing? Tour of inspection?'

'I suppose — up to a point ... But — well, the *assumption* is that his tour's not unconnected with plans for us all to be pulled out pretty soon.'

Silence, now — except for the Ford's thumping, rattling progress. There was a military guard-post ahead of them, as the driver negotiated a corner and the wheels began to thrum on cobbles. He drove with the awkward, jerky movements of a beginner: slowing even further, to no more than walking-pace. Making sure of being able to stop at the guard-post, perhaps. Bob meanwhile with food for thought, weighing up those two apparently contradictory items of information. The general was said to be touring his various missions in preparation for a withdrawal, but the transfer of a Royal Air Force unit to the threatened front certainly didn't suggest passive acceptance of defeat. General Holman — it would be his responsibility and decision, presumably — would hardly be risking those pilots and their machines unless there was at least some reasonable prospect of the Volunteers holding on.

In fact one might guess the intention would be to get the offensive on the move again. Not that one knew a damn thing about the Army — or the Air Force, for that matter ...

They'd stopped at the guard-post. A sergeant peered in at them, then called to another man to raise the barrier, and both saluted as the Ford lurched on through — at a snail's pace — and swung left.

Tinsdale cleared his throat.

'We don't see much of the Navy in these parts, sir. Quite a novelty, in fact.'

'Be even more so at Kharkov, I imagine.'

'Lord, yes ...' He added, after a pause: 'May I ask — if

it's not a State secret — what kind of duty takes you that far inland?'

'If I told you, you might not believe it.'

'Oh, I *swear*—'

'I'm looking for a brace of English governesses.'

'Er —' another clearance of the throat — 'you said — governesses?'

'Nurses now — in one of the Volunteers' mobile field hospitals. *Letuchki*, as they're called ... You talk some Russian, do you?'

'Well — darned little, I'm afraid—'

'*Letuchka* number seven, anyway. These girls were employed as governesses in the Crimea, joined up as nursing aides and now their families in Britain want them found and sent home. As others have been, but this pair seemed to have disappeared — and — well, there you are.'

'Yes. I see ... Well, good heavens ...'

The motor was now trundling along a narrow street, tall house-fronts on both sides, lights here and there haloed in the sleet. This was certainly better than walking, as he'd assumed he'd be doing.

'How far now?'

'Oh — a mile, or thereabouts ... I was thinking — I very much *hope* there'll be a train through in the next few hours, but—'

'Don't worry.' He added, 'Long as there's somewhere warm where I can wait.'

At the extremity of the headlights' beams a shadow — a man, the white of his face visible for a second and then averted — ran stooping across the road — joining two others on that corner ... The car's feeble lights on the three of them now, one with an arm up to shield his eyes as he turned — all three, stumbling, as if in panic — into a doorway — no, alleyway, there ... Passing it now; pitch-black, empty. Tinsdale, who'd been peering out, wiping at the glass to see better, muttering angrily 'Like rats — damn *rats* ...' then: 'These governesses, sir — what I find puzzling is why would they give a job like this to — well, to a naval commander, for heaven's sake?'

'It's a long story.'

Which he didn't much want to tell. But he gave him the gist of it — being on the staff of SO(I) at the Bosporus, the assumption that the girls would be somewhere on the Crimean coast, and now this second stage ... 'Matter of one thing leading to another, really.'

'Yes. Yes, I see ... And the imperative now — obviously, the urgency is to get hold of them — get them *out* — before the roof falls in.'

'The what?'

'I mean while the front still holds. Because once it cracks — well, my God—'

'If it's going to crack — yes. But if we're reinforcing now, there's no such immediate ...' He paused, leaning forward to stare over the driver's shoulder across a sleet-swept open square ... 'Arrived, have we?'

From the outside the station was palatial, incongruously so in the run-down area of devastated-looking railway yards through which they'd been passing in the last few minutes. A show-piece façade: one could imagine an official opening, twenty or thirty years ago perhaps, by some bewhiskered and bemedalled representative of the Tsar, applauding crowds around this great arched entrance with its pillars, and the dome above it. Dim lighting now, deep shadows across a cobbled forecourt where the car drew up — like something at its last gasp just managing to drag itself this far ... And a voice, strident through the icy darkness — from a far corner of the square where a small mob of soldiers was being addressed by an individual standing on some kind of platform — farm-cart probably. It was obviously a political harangue. Tinsdale muttered as he got out, 'Bloody agitators ...'

'Morale not too high, hereabouts?'

'Rock-bottom. The rumours don't help. When things were going well, the swine were anti-Bolshevik to a man.' He stooped to the driver's window, told him in Russian, 'Wait here.'

'For how long?'

In English — explosively — 'Until I come back, damn it!'

Bob cut in: 'Only a few minutes. I won't delay your lieutenant.'

The dark eyes held his. Then he'd nodded. 'Very well, Excellency.'

Tinsdale grumbled, as they went in together under the arch, 'You're lucky, having the language. Bloody frustrating, otherwise.'

'Must be.' Pausing, looking around at the virtually deserted station. As gloomy and unwelcoming as any other railway station in the small hours of a miserably cold, wet night. Some benches were occupied by slumbering military-looking bodies, but there was very little movement, certainly nobody hurrying anywhere — possible implication being that there were no trains either coming or going. He told the younger man, 'You've been very helpful. No need to hang around now, though. I'll get on a train, all right — *when* there is one.' A group of soldiers slouched past, a bottle going from hand to hand between them. Cropped heads, thin white faces, threadbare brown greatcoats, rifles, blanket-rolls ... Tinsdale said, watching them with a look of contempt on his face, 'I'd rather see you on your way, sir. Or at the very least find a waiting-room that has a fire in it.'

'Very decent of you, but — oh, look there ...'

A lot better than any waiting-room — at any rate to an optimist — was the fact there was a train standing at the farthest platform. Or at least part of a train: from here he could only see the tail-end of it, three or four box-cars. He thought, *All right, even that — if it's going the right way ...*

And if it had an engine attached to it, somewhere. Which it had — as indicated a second later by a rush of escaping steam — from that direction, vaguely, but out of sight, around the pillared corner that hid all the rest of it. Getting the smell of it too — steam, coal, oil, whatever, that worldwide railway reek ... 'Come on.' He began to trot — clumping awkwardly in the sea-boots. Knowing it was probably *not* about to leave — probably just goods cars being shunted — and that even if it was, it was as likely to be bound for Rostov, Ekaterinodar and Novorossisk as for the north. But also that if it steamed out now without him and it *was* the Kharkov train — well, you'd deserve all the frozen hours of waiting for the next one. Worse than that — infinitely worse — was an echo of Tinsdale's phrase, *before the roof falls in.* It had annoyed him when he'd heard it, but in fact it was an entirely valid observation ... He'd almost collided at the corner with two women, cloaked and hooded, one of them quite pretty and the other less visible but not ceasing her chatter as they both shrank back against a pillar and the two men lumbered by, Bob calling an apology. Then, rounding the corner, the whole length of the train was in view, another gush of steam belching up — suggesting imminence of departure. There was a crowd up there, too — or it looked from here like a crowd — filling that end of the platform, so if there were any passenger coaches that was where they'd be.

Warning himself as he ran that whether there were or were not, whatever kind of a train this was it wouldn't be going the way he wanted ...

He passed a corporal embracing a rotund, red-faced girl, the soldier's arms reaching barely halfway round her. And two other soldiers nearby — older men, bearded, leaning against a box-car, staring. He shouted 'Kharkov? This train for Kharkov?' One took the pipe out of his mouth and laughed, bawled some answer in a heavy country dialect which Bob couldn't make out, but the tone was derisive and the final words had been — decoding the meaning as they pounded on — *If Kharkov's still there!*

'Catch any of that?' Over his shoulder to Tinsdale, who panted, 'God, no!' It seemed less than promising: he knew he'd be walking back this way in a minute, winded and feeling like a damn fool ... But — *there* now — emerging from what was in fact only a sprinkling of people near the platform's top end, abreast the engine more or less — was what looked like an official of the railway.

It was, too. Short, squat, middle-aged, heavily moustached, in a tall, peaked cap and black coat, with a whistle on a brass chain as badge of office.

Slowing to a walk ... 'Station Master?'

'Excellency?'

'This train' — he was short of breath, but not as chronically as Tinsdale — 'going to Kharkov, by any chance?'

Blue-eyed stare, at Bob's naval cap and insignia of rank: then he'd put a finger to the peak of his own cap.

'Yes, Excellency. Passenger carriages up there.' Magisterial wave of one hand towards the engine: as far as Bob was concerned that hand could have had a magic wand in it. *Marvellous* — almost too marvellous to believe ... Here where they were standing was a flat-car with a tarpaulin-covered load on it, then a closed-in box-car, and beyond that, where this fellow was pointing, the passenger coaches.

'Only two carriages, Excellencies — and fourth class, I regret to say — but there's an adequacy of vacant berths. And the stoves are lit, you may be sure ... May I see your Excellencies' papers — a *propusk*, d'you have?'

'Yes. Here.' *Propusk* meaning a travel pass. 'Train just leaving, is it?'

'Oh *no*, sir ...' Glancing at Tinsdale — who pointed at himself and shook his head: 'I — not travel' — then turning back to Bob ... 'Regrettably, Excellency, this one won't be leaving for — oh, at least one hour, perhaps two. There are some — problems.' The blue eyes shifted, private anxieties showing through ... A shrug, then: 'Telegraphs not working, that's—'

'Needn't have run.' Tinsdale, rather irritatingly stating the obvious. He added, 'But what luck, eh — what *amazingly* good luck?'

'Thanks to you.' Bob handed the man his pass. 'I'd expected to have to hoof it. Might've got here by about first light — *if* I'd found the way, mind you.'

'*Angliskii* ...'

'*Britanskii — da.*'

Steam hissed deafeningly. For a train that wasn't going to leave for an hour or two, they were wasting an awful lot of it. The official, carefully refolding Bob's travel document and handing it back to him, waited until he could make himself heard, then enquired — with the strained air of a man forcing himself to be jocular, rising above adverse circumstances — 'No battleship in your baggage, sir?'

He managed a smile. 'Not this trip. Why?'

'Forgive me.' Jerking a thumb back towards the flat-car and its tarpaulin-covered cargo. 'My feeble sense of humour, Excellency. We have aviators on board — and they bring their flying machines, so I thought — well, a naval gentleman, now …' The insecurity was in his eyes again: even a slight tremor in his voice.

As well there might be. If – or *when* — the Bolsheviks took over here, he'd last — what, ten minutes?

He found them — the aviators — in the nearer of the two carriages. Stopping abruptly — surprised at finding them so quickly — in the doorway of a compartment in the middle of the coach where he'd just climbed in … Ignoring Tinsdale's shout from the platform — Tinsdale wishing him good luck for the third time, for God's sake — and already appreciating the warmth as he stood looking in at these two men in khaki breeches, brown boots, sweaters under their military tunics, revolvers in holsters on their Sam Brownes. One was a major — neat moustache, eyebrows raised over brown eyes at this moment narrowed, speculative — and the other a captain, a smaller man with glossy black hair, bluish-black jaw, deepset blue eyes. This one nodded, after a brief inspection: '*Zdrastye.*' Then in English — he might have heard Tinsdale's final shout from the platform — 'Or should I have said —' he put on a stagey voice — '*do* come in, old fellow?'

'Well, hold on there, Jim.' The major, cutting in … 'You know the goddamn rules, don't you?'

'Ah — sorry …'

'Indeed, you should be.' This major sounded American. A slimly-built man, wide-shouldered, who'd be tall if or when he stood up. About Bob's own age: with medal ribbons that included a DSO and an MC with a bar to it. And the younger man had an MC … The major telling him, 'No offence, sir, but this is Royal Air Force accommodation — exclusive, all that sort of rot ... Grand Dukes and commissars may be admitted but only through personal introduction. You're not a commissar, by any chance?'

'No.'

'Well — Grand Duke?'

The captain said, 'Could've sworn you were a Russki, anyhow.' Lilting intonation — Welsh ... 'That get-up — Navy, is it?'

'Right.'

'Royal, or Merchant?'

'Royal. My name's Cowan — Lieutenant-Commander. Levels with major, in case you didn't know. But far be it from me to break your silly bloody rules, so—'

'Shouldn't take any notice of 'em, sir, if I were you. I'm Davies. This Canuck here's Sam Scott. Welcome aboard, sir.'

'What are rules for, I ask you.' The major looked sad as he shook his hand. 'No standards left, that's the trouble.'

'Canadian?'

A nod ... 'One of those damned Colonials, don't you know ... What's the Navy doing on a train to God knows where?'

'Kharkov — taking two days, I'm told.'

'Wouldn't count on it. Odds aren't all that favourable. Time'll tell, that's about the one thing you *can* be sure of ... Come on in, sit down. The other Grand Dukes got out here, that's how it happens we have all this space.' He looked at the small, dark captain. 'Never know, Jim, he may have something to drink in that bag.'

'Navy drinks rum — right?'

'Well.' Bob dumped his bag on the wooden seat, as the Welshman swung his booted legs down to make room. The tiers of planks that made berths above this one had been removed, as had those on the opposite side above the major, but on the third side, across from the doorless entrance, they were still in place. Three top bunks, anyway: there'd be a stove at each end of the carriage, the custom being that male passengers kept them stoked and burning — they could be cooked on as well — and since heat rises, to be trapped under the wood-lined ceiling, the top bunks would be warm while passengers in the bottom ones stood a good chance of freezing solid. So three in here — if there were no others coming — would be perfectly all right ... Sitting, he removed his cap, blew melted sleet off its peak and badge, and confirmed, 'Rum — yes. Sailors get a daily issue. Hellish strong stuff, comes from the West Indies in barrels. If I'd thought, I'd have brought one with me.'

'You mean you *didn't*?'

'Always forget *something* when you pack.'

'It's unforgivable, you know. I mean, what the hell are we fighting for?'

He shrugged. 'Two days should be about long enough to debate that question.'

'Two *minutes* is all I need.' Scott, the major, shook his head. 'Open and shut case, see, far as I'm concerned.'

'So what's—'

'Please.' Davies begged him, 'Don't ask. You get a different answer every time and on a bad day it can take bloody hours, man.'

'I'll tell you anyway.' The brown eyes held Bob's. 'I enjoy it — that's why. So much so that when they tell me to stop I don't know what the *hell* I'll do.'

'He's not talking about women, either.'

'I did wonder.'

'But that's the short answer he's given you. You're lucky. Scary thing is it's the true one too, he means it. Scary for me, see, I fly with him, often as not. Puts *my* life on the line ... Well, it's a fact he knows his business maybe better than any man alive — certainly better than a lot who are *not* alive—'

'Be a pal and shut up, Jim?'

'I'm merely trying to explain—'

'Glad to have you with us, Cowan. Two more days in this train, a little variety in the company won't come amiss.'

'Been on it some time, have you?'

'Well — let's see ... We entrained at Kotluban — if you know where that is?'

'Tsarytsin area.'

'Flying range of Tsarytsin, sure ... But we were operating way up from there, you know. Kamyshin—'

'I know. We heard you did great things up there.'

'Had our moments. Well, don't we all ... But from Kotluban, seven whole days down to Rostov. Seven *days* — imagine it? Cooped up with this damn Welshman? Believe me, Cowan, it's going to be a pleasure to have your company. Incidentally, were you about to tell us how come you *are* here?'

'I suppose I'd better get it over with.'

'Bad as *that*?'

'Only that I seem to be answering the same question all the time.' He took a breath. 'Would you believe I'm looking for two girls?'

Davies muttered, '*Two* girls.' He looked at Scott, and shrugged. 'They do spend long periods at sea, of course.'

'Any particular two girls?'

'You won't believe this.'

'Try us.'

'Governesses?'

'Oh, my God ...'

'Hold it, Jim. Go on now, Cowan. Say, you're not Irish, are you?'

'No. Why?'

'Just your talk seems a little — wild. Governesses ... What sort of naval man are you, anyway?'

'Off the subject, rather, but — all right. I was Merchant Navy until '14, then in small ships. Mostly destroyers. But I talk Russian — my mother was Russian. I was born here — St Petersburg, Petrograd — so when this Intervention business started, and they needed interpreters and suchlike — here I am.'

'In pursuit of governesses.'

'I was with the Caspian Flotilla until a few months ago.'

'*Were* you, now. We were based at Petrovsk, for a while.

Shooting up Bolshy convoys on Old Mother Volga.'

Davies slapped his knee: 'Talk about turkey-shoots. Golly, did those ammo barges burn!'

'I'll bet.' Thinking for a moment of mentioning his own experiences on the Volga. But — better not. Much better let them tell *their* stories ... 'Look — I'm starving, and I've some sandwiches here — plenty, if you'd like to join me?'

'Kind of you, but — thanks all the same.' Davies shook his head too. 'So happens we're well fixed for rations. Leading Airman Pickerell — next door here — knocks up a damn good breakfast, I can tell you.'

'You've a team with you, then?'

'One leading airman, one airman, two mechanics. Anyway, you can mess with us, Cowan, and welcome.'

'Very good of you. And all the more reason you should try one of these sandwiches. Courtesy of the wardroom mess of HMS *Terrapin* — destroyer, I landed from her by seaboat a couple of hours ago.' He was unbuckling the holdall: thinking how extraordinarily abrupt — and total — the transition had been. *Terrapin*, then the whaler, then the well-meaning but slightly ridiculous Tinsdale, and now—

Thoughts checked abruptly ... 'Hey — tell you *what*—'

Instead of the flask they'd agreed on, Harriman had put in a full bottle of malt whisky. Bob held it up. 'This is better than rum, now...'

Scott handed Bob's tobacco-pouch back to him. 'Thanks. Navy 'baccy, eh?'

'Ship's stores.' He nodded towards his holdall. 'Large tin of it in there. But — you were saying?'

'Yeah. Well — with the reorganization, I was looking after C Flight, the crowd that's being shipped home now. That's done with, and now I'm to command A Flight, which is to follow B up this way. Jim and I constitute the advance party, the rest of 'em join us after B Flight's established some kind of a base for us all — wherever. Kharkov, say.'

'Let's say wherever.' Davies asked Bob, 'Would you

believe there are eight brand-new DH9s still in their crates on that quay at Novorossisk? Just bloody *sitting* there?'

'DH9s being — bombers?'

'Right.'

'But you fly Sopwith Camels — fighters.'

'Fly either. These are Camels we have with us, yes.'

'Can't General Holman get anything done about those others?'

'Oh, he's been trying. So has our mission there. But it's not *our* affair, technically, those machines are intended for Deniken's people, not for us. We're still only instructors, you know, officially. Believe *that* or not ... And if Denikin's crowd choose to leave the British taxpayers' gift lying idle — not only planes, either, field guns, ammunition, even a tank or two—'

'Spilt milk, Jim. None of it'll *ever* get off that dockside, now. Unless of course the Reds get to it.'

'Bloody hell!' Davies scowled at him over the tin mug from which he'd been sipping his tot of malt. They'd agreed to ration it, try to make the bottle last two days. 'If you believe *that* — hell, what are we on this train for? I mean, why should we even go through the bloody motions?'

'Holman's offering our services to Mai-Maievsky on the off-chance we might stop the rot. It's touch-and-go, he knows that, he'll make a fast appraisal and either we'll get stuck in or we'll come right out.' Scott looked at Bob, shook his head. 'Should've been there last week. Last month.'

Davies put his mug down on the bench. 'So what's the Royal Navy's view of the situation?'

'As far as I know it, when I left Sevastopol not much more than twenty-four hours ago, all anyone knew was it was — well, in the balance. For instance, we reckoned there'd be time for me to come up this way through Taganrog, but not if I'd had to get on a train from Novorossisk.'

'You could say *that* again.' The major sat back. 'But you see, Jim — writing's on the wall — huh?'

'Maybe, but — no, what the Commander just said implies we have a few days' grace — doesn't it? *At least* a few days. So if we get there quick enough — eh?'

Bob nodded. 'Our people — Naval Intelligence at Constantinople, that is — can't have known anything about your squadron being moved in. At least I don't think they did. So it's an entirely new factor. And — obviously you know more about it than I do, but surely General Holman must believe there's at least a chance?' He saw that Scott was looking dubious. 'What I'm getting at is that putting you in there *might* be all it'd take. On the Tsarytsin front, for instance, you really won the battle for them, didn't you?'

'Won *some*. At Tsarytsin, to be truthful, it was the tanks that really swung it. Initially, that is. But —' Scott grimaced — 'lines of supply so damn stretched, no re-inforcement or regrouping, lousy communications — ask me, Denikin's whole strategy's been asinine.' Leaning forward, peering out: 'Jim, much as I hate to break bad news to you, looks like we're about to be dragged away from this earthly paradise. How about checking the guys are all aboard?'

6

Breakfast was fried eggs on black bread with corned-beef hash, and they'd about finished it when Sam Scott returned to the subject of the governesses, asking Bob whether he'd remembered yet what their names were. Last night, or rather earlier this morning, when he'd explained the background of his mission he'd had to skip that detail, and the two pilots had amused themselves by speculating on the problems likely to arise from his loss of memory. Scott had suggested he might best approach them with such opening words as 'Miss Livingstone, I presume?', the Welshman then pointing out that this wouldn't wash because he didn't have a pith helmet.

'Well — a Grand Duke wouldn't, would he?'

Bob said now, putting his empty plate aside and reaching for the mug of tea, 'Tell you in a second. Just have to galvanize the brain. Excellent breakfast, by the way.'

Grim, frozen landscape. It wasn't sleeting or snowing but that was about as much as you could say in its favour. White, flat, featureless: disorientating, you could imagine, for anyone out there in it, but even from here depressing — if you'd let it be, or dwelt on the thought that a time might well come when you *would* be out there, *in* it ... Now at least you were being carried through it in comfort and quite fast: although there was a puzzle in that area too — why, when anyone could see and feel that the train was moving at certainly not less than twenty miles an hour and probably nearer thirty, it should take two days to cover the 250 miles between Taganrog and Kharkov.

It was Tinsdale, of course, who'd said it would take two

days. On the platform, last night — this morning . . .

'Well? Brain galvanic yet?'

'Mary Pilkington, and Katherine Reid.'

'Good.' Davies nodded. 'I'll take Mary.'

Sam Scott repeated, gazing upward with his eyes half closed, 'Mary Pilkington and Katherine Reid . . . Has a nice rhythm to it, don't you think? So let's concoct some verse. That's your first line. What rhymes with Reid?'

Davies began, 'Need, heed, feed — breed —' He held up a forefinger: 'that's it: *Decided it was time to breed.* How's that?'

'Brilliant.'

Scott agreed: 'Keep working at it.'

'Major.' Bob put his tea-mug down on the plate. 'If we could talk seriously for a minute—'

'Might manage that. While junior there galvanizes *his* brains . . .'

'Yes. Well — idea I had, I was thinking about it before I turned out this morning. Something you said last night when I told you these women were nurses in a *letuchka* and asked you whether you'd ever come across one. You said you'd seen one at close quarters when they took a bullet out of a friend's back, but several from the air.'

'Sure.' The smile was an encouragement. 'I noticed you blinked when I told you that.'

'You know what's in my mind, then.'

'Of course. And why not? That is, in *principle* why not. How we find the situation when we get where we're going, where and when we deploy and set up shop and what we have to do — that's something else.'

Davies nodded. 'A whole *lot* of else.'

'But a *letuchka*'s easy to spot from the air, is it?'

'Darned great red crosses on their tents. Sure, the whole idea is the crosses should be clearly visible.'

'And when they're on the move?'

'Oh.' A shrug. 'Can't rightly say. Don't recall ever seeing one. But if there's any danger of getting shot-up they'd be damn silly *not* to make 'emselves recognizable, wouldn't they? They use horse-drawn carts, and — yeah, you can bet at least the ambulance carts 'd have red crosses on 'em.'

'D'you think you *might* be able to help me?'

'Well — as I say—'

'But —' he hesitated. Feeling a little diffident about pushing his luck this far, but still having to ... 'Conceivably, whatever missions they're on, pilots could be asked to keep an eye out, then give me the locations?'

'It's — conceivable. But it wouldn't be my decision, see. CO's a guy by name Ray Collishaw. Lieutenant-Colonel. Canadian, same as me. *Hell* of a good man ... Point two, if the action's as hectic as it may be nobody'll have eyes for farm-carts, not even if they're *smothered* in red crosses.'

'Ah.' Nodding, fingering the stubble on his jaw. He hadn't shaved yet, none of them had. Hot water was going to be available when the cooking was all done. 'Yes, I appreciate that ... But — well, forgive me for — you know, pressing the point a bit. Fact is that finding these women isn't likely to be at all easy — that's putting it mildly — and that kind of help from you might — well, it could save their lives, apart from making my job a lot less difficult.'

Davies suggested, 'Try it on the CO, Sam, eh?'

'Count on it, I will. But you know, Cowan — Jim and I horse around a lot, but the sober truth is this whole deployment's pretty much a gamble. As I'm sure you realize. We may be a lot too late — may be turned right around, Holman may tell us get the hell out, *quick*. Or we could be in it up to our necks right from the first minute. In which case—'

'I know.'

'Well. Long as you do.'

He nodded. Knowing, in fact, nothing. But thinking about it and trying to visualize the scene as it might be up there, and finding it beyond the reach of his imagination. Having no idea of the terrain, or military operations, battlefield or near-battlefield conditions. Where one might even *start* ...

'By the way, Cowan —' Scott's quiet voice broke into thoughts that came to only one conclusion — that he *had* to have the flyers' help — 'last night, or more accurately some unseemly hour this morning — was I dreaming, or did you tell me in my sleep there was some kind of ruction on the line?'

'No, there was. You woke up, and I told you. But precisely what was going on — ask me another ...'

At the junction two miles out of Taganrog, where one set of lines continued eastward to Rostov-on-Don and the other, their own route, branched away northward, there'd been a train stopped about a hundred yards on the far side of the points, with a mob around it. He'd been in the act of turning in, having made himself a sort of pallet on the bunk-boards out of blankets supplied by the RAF contingent. The pilots had already got their heads down, having had no such preparations to make and being more practised at it anyway, and hadn't stirred when the train began to judder as its brakes jammed on, but Bob had hung down to the window to see whatever might be visible. The train had slowed quite a lot by then but it wasn't stopping — driver having second thoughts, perhaps, but it was continuing around the wide curve of track — circling to the left, the north, at this much reduced speed and with the engine noisily venting surplus steam. It had been too dark and the windows too fogged up as well as dirty and sleet-streaked on the outside to see clearly, but he'd had the impression there were passengers trying to leave that stopped train and others — soldiers, he'd imagined — forcing them back on board. Although where they'd have gone or wanted to go or why, when there was nothing in the entire surrounding snowscape except a signal-box on stilts and as far as he'd been able to make out two other buildings, one with a long spill of light leaking across the snow and the other probably a barn, was hard to guess. It had been gone from sight then anyway — less than a minute, probably, from start to finish — sliding away to the right as this train straightened itself out into the long haul northward.

He described the scene to Scott and Davies. His view of
it at the time had been so indistinct that it seemed dream-
like now in his own recollection of it; hardly surprising
that Scott, who'd been less than half awake when he'd
blurted, 'Wha's up, wha'sa matter?' had thought he might
have dreamed it.

'Told me all that, did you?'

'Tried to, but you flaked out again.'

'That train would've come from Rostov — uh?'

'Engine was at this end — yes ... Mind you, it could
have been the other way about — people trying to board,
others holding them off. Though why it should've stopped
in the first place ...'

Davies said, 'Local custom's to put stuff on the line.
Rocks, carts ... That's what they did to us, on our way
south to Tikhoretsk.'

'Bolsheviks did?'

'Hard to say who, for sure. Another time we had
horsemen riding along beside the train taking pot shots at
us. Like bloody Redskins.' He pointed with his head.
'Made my Canuck friend here feel quite homesick. But
Bolshies or plain brigands — countryside's crawling with
both, up that way.'

'So what happened?'

'Oh, we drove 'em off, cleared the line, got on with it.
And the horsemen got more than they'd bargained for,
sheered off pretty damn quick, I can tell you. We had a
crowd of troops on board, mind you, as well as a box-car
with loopholes and a sheet-iron lining.'

'Sheet steel.' Scott corrected him. 'Sheet iron's useless.'

'I didn't see loopholes in any box-car on *this* train.'

'Because there aren't any.' The major added, 'Our boys
have rifles, though, and we have our side-arms.' He patted
the revolver on his belt. 'Soldiers in the other carriage,
too. Recruits, by the look of 'em, but they might be *some*
use, if it came to the push.'

'Wouldn't you think they'd put one of those box-cars on
every train, though?'

'Wouldn't come amiss. The real kosher armoured trains,

though, they're by far the best deterrent. Troops, machine-
guns, light artillery even. But they can't be everywhere and
some of 'em are on the fronts. The Reds have 'em too, of
course. But the *big* factor — apart from morale being
lousy and desertions commonplace, even right in the
middle of a battle — the underlying problem is that
Denikin's great masterstroke — flat-out for Moscow, hell
for leather and paying no heed to any damn thing except
miles of advance *per diem* — well, you leave every kind of
riff-raff loose in your rear. Where we were, coming down
through that Don Cossack territory — like Jim said, woods
are stiff with 'em.'

'And here?'

'That I don't know.'

'Will soon, perhaps.'

'Can't see any reason it should be different. But a point
worth bearing in mind, Cowan, is whether they're just
marauders or they're Reds — or both — they're likely to be
hungry, even starving, short of ammo, and as often as not
very badly led, so they don't have much idea what they're
at. So, as long as a few of us keep our heads and shoot
straight ... You armed, by the way?'

He brought out the Webley automatic, took the clip out
and ejected the single round from the breech. Davies then
examined it and passed it on to the major, who did the
same. 'Long as it doesn't jam. With these things jamming
can be a problem, you know.'

'So I'm told.'

'Favour a plain, ordinary revolver myself. Much less
likely to lock solid just when you're up against it.'

'*What* a happy thought.' He took the pistol back and
reloaded it. Scott asked, 'Weren't still awake when we
passed through Pokrovsk, were you?'

'No. Would we have stopped there?'

'Don't know, that's what I wondered. We'll need to get
fuel and water before Debaltsevo, I'd imagine. Hang on —
I've a map here, someplace ...'

Bob sat with his eyes on the passing landscape. The train

was on an upgrade at this point, and there was a scattering of silver birch that grew denser into the distance. The other two — the major first — were in the shaving queue, each in turn spending ten minutes or so at the basin at the end of the carriage, stopping first at the stove to dip out a jugful of hot water. He'd been offered the guest's privilege of going first, but he'd declined, having decided to let his beard grow. Looking ahead a day or two, you could anticipate circumstances in which shaving would not be possible. No hot breakfasts either ... Might hope to enjoy such luxuries for two or three days more — *if* the squadron let him stay with them while they located the *letuchki* for him — but after that — well, there it *was*, outside the window: thousands of square miles of snow. And a beard did tend to keep the face warmer than bare skin did.

All right, so there'd still be trains running. Touch wood ... But the *letuchka* wouldn't necessarily be anywhere near any railway line, you'd have to get the girls *to* a train.

If they'd agree to leave. That was yet another bridge that couldn't be crossed until you got to it.

Scott was back, having scraped his whiskers off.

'I left you a *little* water, Jim.'

Davies had seemed to be dozing, in recent minutes. He looked up now, and smiled. 'I've got lines three and four. Want to hear 'em?'

Scott groaned, as he stowed his gear away. 'You been treated to a recitation, Cowan?'

'No. He's been waiting for his full audience, I imagine.'

Davies stood up, bowed, cleared his throat politely.

'Lines one and two, you will recall, run as follows: *Mary Pilkington and Katherine Reid/ Decided it was time to breed* ... Uh? Now we continue: *So with a bit of help from Jim—/ Not Sam, these girls would want no truck with him—*'

'Go and shave, you bloody Welshman.'

'Commander — while I'm gone, think up a last line for me?'

'I think I'd sooner leave it to your own rare talent.'

'You're right there, anyhow. It *is* a rare talent.'

Scott muttered, 'Rarer the better.' He added, when Davies had gone off for his shave. 'Finest Camel pilot in the squadron, is Jim Davies.'

'Really?'

Gazing out at the passing scenery. At least there was something to look at now. The birches had been closing in, thickening into what might loosely be called a forest — although at this moment the silver-patched trunks seemed to be levitating upwards out of the picture as the train thundered into a cutting. Nothing to see, then, except the close white blankness of the snowbank with a rock or tree-root protruding here and there. He looked back at Scott, who was telling him, 'Except we're no longer a squadron. We were, we were 47 Squadron, but now with one flight being sent home — and only volunteers staying on — incidentally, every man-jack of us is here by his own choice — they're calling us "A" Detachment RAF.' He shrugged. 'What's in a name . . .'

'Quite a lot, I'd have thought — when you've made yourselves famous as 47 Squadron. Even I'd heard of you . . . I wanted to ask you, by the way — personal question, if you don't mind — when you said you so much enjoyed what you're doing — did you mean it? You and Davies were talking a lot of tommy-rot at the time, so—'

'Relieves the strain a little, talking tommy-rot.'

'Of course.'

'Right. Well, *sure* I meant it.' Glancing at him. 'Don't you enjoy what you do?'

'Not to that extent. Certainly wouldn't if I thought I had to go on doing it for ever. But you dread the thought of having to pack it in one day. What's the attraction — the flying or the fighting?'

'Both. Flying's enjoyable enough, but just for its own sake I guess I'd find it a little tame, now. Been a long war, you know. Like a lot of us I was on the Western Front before this. Take Ray Collishaw, for instance — his score of downed Germans was sixty-eight.' He shook his head. 'A lot of dead ones, eh? And that's about the crux of it, I guess — being better at it than the other guy.'

'And if you come up against one who's better than you?'

'Then I'm either very lucky or I'm dead.' He nodded. 'I've *been* very lucky, a few times.' The brown eyes held his. 'It can be damned exciting — you know?'

'I can imagine.'

'You ever kill a man? I mean — personal, close up?'

Bob hesitated before admitting it. Recognizing that in just about any other situation or conversation he'd have given an evasive answer. He nodded. 'Matter of fact, yes, I have.'

'That surprises me. I'd thought of naval action as being — you know, impersonal. Ships miles apart, and so forth. Never experiencing — as we do, often enough — that face-to-face mutual understanding that one of you's going to kill the other.'

'Well, you're right, that's mostly how it is at sea. My experience of the other kind — not quite as you describe it, not as — well, open and above-board — took place on dry land. At a place called Enotayevsk, on the Volga.'

'Enotayevsk. I don't believe I—'

'Hundred miles north of Astrakhan. Hey — we're slowing ...'

'Damn *right*!'

More than just slowing. A roar of steam being released, then the steam itself, like cloud flying — and the same juddering he'd felt in the small hours of the morning, the driver braking and the engine fighting the momentum of all the cars' weight jarring up behind it and the ripple-effect to and fro, jarring impacts right back down the line. Then — like an explosion from up front ... If they'd been standing, they'd have been knocked down. Davies was, on his way back from shaving, and there were crashes all through the carriage's six compartments as the train smashed into — through — whatever, that tremendous impact, the sensation of being flung back and the one-word thought — sickening, doom-laden — *Derailed* ...

Rocking ... Echoes of that recent conversation, Davies telling him *Local custom's to put stuff on the line* ...

Still *on* the rails, though. Apparently ... Still rolling. Illusion? Out here, a snowstorm — blizzard, snow flying horizontally and thick, totally obscuring as the train — unbelievably, in these first moments of recovery — began to pick up speed. And after a few seconds you'd got used to the idea, accepting the evidence that whatever had just happened you'd come through it. In as much bewilderment as relief: plus a touch of embarrassment at having wondered, ten seconds earlier, how many of them even badly led could be held off for how long by four rifles and three pistols in the hands of men who were already half-stunned. Hearing Scott's voice ask quietly, 'What in hell did we hit then?' — and the answer in a shout from somewhere farther down the carriage — where they couldn't by even the remotest possibility have heard him —'Snowdrift! Bloody *snowdrift*!'

Bob's own voice, then: 'Of course. *That*'s what ...'

The storm outside was clearing. The train still in the cutting, with banks of snow near-vertical on each side, but you could see those banks again now whereas just seconds ago you couldn't. Scott shaking his head, muttering, 'Sure, that's what it must've been.' Pointing at the window: 'All that stuff flying. What d'you know. Must've smacked right in ...'

'Stone the bald-arsed crows.' Davies — leaning in the doorway with one hand to his head, blood seeping between its fingers, the other clutching his razor, shaving-brush, soap, and towel. 'Can't turn my back for a minute, can I? What were you *doing*, Sam?'

'Damn fool.' Scott frowned at him. 'Cut your head? Hell, I'd better see if any of the boys got hurt ...' On his feet, peering briefly at the Welshman's head. 'I'll look to that in a minute.'

'Look to it myself. Cracked it on some damn inanimate object along there.' Davies sidled in and sat down. 'Mind you — half a minute sooner, might've cut my bloody throat ... Commander — I was doing some composing, along there. What rhymes with Canuck?'

The major turned quickly, in the doorway. 'Cowan — don't you tell him ...'

*

At about noon the train stopped at a place called Korsun to fill up with logs and water. It was only a small village, a single street of timber shacks, with the station and a branch line presumably serving some other agricultural centre. There was a crowd of country people on the platform, mostly women and children and grandparents; they weren't interested in this train, could only have been waiting for one that would take them south. Not the most propitious of omens: nor was the presence of soldiers on duty on the platform. Bob and the RAF men had gone up to the front of the engine to see if there'd been any damage done — there had not — and by the time they were back at their carriage a lot of the young recruits from the train had disembarked to cluster round the older men — firing questions at them, like schooolkids round their seniors in some playground — and an officer, an elderly lieutenant wearing a Provost Marshal's brassard, was calling to an NCO to break it up.

Then the *poruchik* turned back to the station master, with whom he'd been chatting, and they heard him say 'Seems Budyonny's in charge up there now. Of course it's just another rumour, but—'

Pausing, glancing at the foreigners as they passed: stiffening slightly as his eyes fell on the major's crowns. Scott had passed him by that time, so the Russian had saved himself the trouble of saluting. Bob murmured '*Dobrii dyen*', but if there was any reply he didn't hear it. There was a lot of noise around them by then, and Scott had yelled at Davies, glancing round to see where he was, 'Hear that famous name?'

'Did he say the beggar's on *this* front now?'

'Isn't that what he said, Cowan?'

'He said the *rumour* is Budyonny's taken over.'

'Know who Budyonny is, do you?'

'Of course. Bolshevik general.'

'Cavalryman. And he's good. Although some of our guys did some of his a lot of *no* good, up north of

Tsarytsin a couple of months back. He had his main force in a gorge, smaller group out in the open as bait, and Shkuro's Wolves — Cossacks from the Kuban, you'll have heard of them? Well, they were about to fall for this dodge, reckoning the bait was all they had to contend with. Lucky for them our guys spotted the Reds in the gorge and went down and hit 'em. Goddamn slaughter. Eight hundred horsemen didn't come out of it. Five Camels did that, just *five ...*'

Davies said, 'Come to think of it, Comrade Budyonny'd likely have it in for us, wouldn't he ...? What's this, then?'

A peasant woman was offering him a skinned rabbit. Davies frowned, looking down at the proffered carcass. Then he'd bent down, put his nose closer to it, and winced. Straightening: 'You're surely not serious, *Babushka ...*'

Scott was getting back into the carriage. Bob strolled on alone, down the length of the narrow, crowded platform, passing between groups of young soldiers and observing that they looked very much like the ones he and Tinsdale had seen at Taganrog. Same thin white faces, shaven or near-shaven heads, poor physique and shabby equipment. Some of it might have been dead men's gear, he guessed. Poor devils ... He was face to face with one of them suddenly: a tall boy, broomstick-thin, nervous but intelligent eyes scanning the gold-lace stripes on the naval greatcoat's shoulders. Mouth half open — as if about to put some question, and Bob half inclined to stop and explain himself *without* being asked ... He didn't — or he'd hesitated for too long — and the boy had shied away by that time. What he realized then he *should* have done would have been to clap him on the shoulder and tell him something like *Cheer up, lad — the RAF's in it now, they'll stop the bastards ...*

The scared white faces were still in his mind's eye as the train pulled out of Korsun. He wished he hadn't held back from offering that kid some slight encouragement — when he and his friends obviously weren't getting any from any other source. Even if it was only whistling in the dark, it couldn't have done any harm to give them something to hope for — to smile about in their sleep tonight, instead of crying for their mothers.

If they'd been his own people, he would have. They weren't, so he'd minded his own business. That was what it came down to. Even though the truth was they were *half* his people, anyway.

He thought, *The hell with it* ... Gazing out at the passing bleakness, a distant edge of forest like a heavy black line scored between white and grey. More snow, probably, in that dark-grey sky. He thought — about the boy-soldiers — *Getting paternal, in my old age* ... Turning his head, focusing on the major, who was also studying the landscape. Brown eyes hooded, and an unlit pipe between his teeth. Bob's mind went back to the conversation they'd been engaged in shortly before they'd run into that snow-drift, and hadn't finished — which seemed to apply to most of the conversations they'd had so far on this train ... He said quietly — not wanting to wake Davies, who'd had his head back and his eyes shut since they'd started — 'Scott — there *is* strain, eh?'

Scott looked at him. The Welshman's eyes opened too.

'What are you talking about?'

'When we were on the subject of tomfoolery — you said it relieved the strain.'

'So?'

Bob waited, and after a moment's thought the major nodded. 'Well — of *course* there is. Would you expect there wouldn't be?'

'But you also claim to enjoy every minute of it.'

'Claim, hell — I *do*! Look — if there's no strain, where's the excitement? Or the satisfaction in winning out, for God's sake?' He shook his head impatiently. 'Now see here. As a change from going on about what *I* do —' he paused, pushed back his sleeve to check the time, murmured, 'Lunch, soon. Goat cheese, Pickerell tells me ... By the way, did Jim tell you some woman tried to sell him a rabbit that died a year ago?'

'I saw it. *Slight* exaggeration.'

'I don't know. For *him* to've noticed ... But — what I was saying — you have a story to regale us with now, don't you?'

'Story?'

'What's the place you mentioned — on the Volga?'

'Oh. Enotayevsk.'

'That's the one. Tell us all about it. Come on. It's called singing for your supper.'

He'd told them the story, before and during the meal. Now he was semi-dozing and the other two were flat out, up on their shelves. Full of black bread and goat cheese, washed down with strong, sweet tea.

Scott had commented, when Bob had finished his yarn — describing his last sight of Nadia and the Solovyevs being transferred by boat from one ship to another in mid-Caspian — 'And you got back on your own to — what's the place called — Krasnovodsk?'

'Right.'

'Pretty damn good going, I'd say.'

'Well, I did have a lot of luck.'

'Hell with *that*. Man makes his own breaks, mostly. I suppose having that exploit on your record is why you landed your present job — right?'

'Had something to do with it, anyway.'

'Moral in that, somewhere ... But what news of those people since? Did you hear from Solovyev?'

'I heard he'd married Nadia.'

'*Well*...'

'Heard it from her, actually. He was on his way back to rejoin the Volunteer Army by then. But anyway — that's the story — complete, and as they say unabridged.'

'Deuce of a yarn, at that.'

The Welshman nodded. 'Bloody hell...'

Bob reflected now, while the train rumbled on towards Debaltsevo, that this had been the first time he'd spoken Nadia's name aloud — in any personal context, anyway — since those events of a year ago. The dully informative

nature of the statement and the flatly unemotional tone of
voice in which he'd made it echoed over and over in his
mind, adapting itself as he dozed off to the rhythm of the
train's wheels — *heard he'd married Nadia, heard he'd
married Nadia* ...

Scott's voice broke through: 'Not married, Cowan, are
you?'

'What?' Surfacing: with Nadia still in his mind ... 'Oh.
No, I'm not. Are you — either of you?'

Davies had shaken his head, pretending to shiver. Scott
said, 'Damn near was. Back in '14. *Damn* near thing.' He
shifted on the seat, yawning. 'Taught me a lesson. You
think something's a calamity, later you get to see it was the
best thing could've happened.'

It was dark when they reached Debaltsevo, too dark to see
much detail, only that it was bigger than the other places
they'd been through. There was a long wait outside the
station before they finally got in, and when they did there
were soldiers on the platform to prevent anyone disembarking. Scott had just discovered this — he was on the
step of the carriage arguing with a corporal — when a
lanky, red-faced captain, the stars on his shoulder-boards
only scratched on in blue crayon, arrived at the double,
panting apologies and introducing himself as a liaison
officer from the staff of General Mai-Maievsky. He had a
lot to say, but what it boiled down to was that the Volunteer lines north of Kharkov had been broken — two days
ago, apparently — and there was fighting now in the town
itself. The men and machines of 'A' Detachment RAF,
still on their train, were stopped at Kupyansk — about
seventy-five miles this side of Kharkov — which was itself
in danger of encirclement by Red cavalry. In fact
Kupyansk should be all right for a day or two, but—

'Is General Holman at Kupyansk too?'

'General Holman?' The Russian turned his hands
palms-up. 'I don't know this general ...'

'So what else, Captain?'

'Tonight your train has to stay here, unfortunately. Only

hospital trains coming through, tonight. There have been heavy casualties, you see — and while there is a chance to get them out—'

'Of course. But in the morning—'

'Then you can continue, sir.'

'To Kupyansk?'

'Well — yes, I think ...'

'If Budyonny hasn't got it cut off by then, eh?' He looked round at the others. 'That could make for some *real* problems.'

7

Mid-morning, clattering northward ... They'd been woken in the first light of dawn by what they'd taken to be the train's departure, but the movement had been only a shunting operation, the removal of certain box-cars which some higher authority must have decided wouldn't be needed on that broken Kharkov front. This probably made sense, since retreating (or routed) armies as often as not left most of their material behind in any case. But within about two seconds of having his eyes open Scott had seemed to go crazy: yelling at Davies, both of them pulling greatcoats and boots over their underwear and tearing out, leaping down on to snow-covered cinders in the icy dawn and rushing back along the train, Scott bellowing like — Davies' description afterwards — a bull moose ... His anxiety had been that some of the RAF box-cars might be detached and left behind. There were two full of petrol in drums and one loaded with ammunition, bombs, engine spares and other equipment, Davies had explained — he being the first to return, winded but laughing to himself, imitating the major's antics and bull-like roars as he'd gone pounding along the train checking the markings on each wagon.

Eventually he'd come back, scowling at the Welshman. 'What's so funny, you damn fool? Lot of use we'd be up there without gas — eh? Imagine how tickled Collishaw'd be if we showed up without it?'

Bob had asked whether the main party hadn't had any with them.

'Course they have. But we need every pint and more. Could be no supplies locally at all. Eh?' Glaring at Davies again. 'The way things are right now? Christ, you know how these people organize themselves even when it's going *well*. How many train-loads d'you reckon they'll be sending after us — suppose we deploy from this what's-it-called place, how many flying hours'd we have?'

'You have a point, Sam.'

'Damn right I have!'

'But you'll feel better when you've had some breakfast.'

They'd finished the whisky last night. And Bob had drunk a silent toast to Nick Everard — who by about that time, he'd guessed, would have been ashore in Theodosia getting married to his countess. Before that, though, he'd gone with the liaison captain to find the local medical team — all that were left of the staff of a base hospital which had now been evacuated — to ask whether anyone knew anything about the present location of *Letuchka* number seven. There'd been only one doctor, who with two Estonian nurses had been left to render any necessary assistance with the hospital trains on their way through from Kharkov and Kupyansk, and all he'd known about *Letuchka Syem* was that it wasn't one of theirs — that it was not one of the *letuchki* that had been sending wounded soldiers back to Debaltsevo. This was the system, apparently — the mobile hospitals patched up lightly-wounded men and returned them to the front, and sent cases that were more serious but which had some chance of surviving the journey in open carts back to their own base hospitals. The doctor's guess was that a number seven would most likely be — or have been — somewhere to the west or northwest, and they'd have despatched their wounded to the hospital in Ekaterinoslav. Or — *possibly* — to Kupyansk.

So one might get more positive guidance in Kupyansk.

Touch wood. Ekaterinoslav was about 150 miles west. If that was the area in which the *letuchka* was operating, getting to it would be even more of a problem than he'd anticipated.

Might even — he thought, with Budyonny's cavalry in mind —be impossible.

Just on the off-chance, he'd tried the girls' names on the Estonian nurses. But he might as well have talked Chinese to them. He'd hesitated then, with yet another name in mind and the Estonians' round blue eyes shifting uncertainly between him and the weary little doctor ... Asking himself then, *Why? When she's none of your damn business? What's the point, for God's sake?*

In any case, she was probably in Simferopol. In comparative safety — for the time being. And as the wife of an officer in the Volunteer Army, who could also claim to have worked with the Royal Navy in the Caspian, she'd be entitled to be evacuated in a British ship. *If* there was a ship available — and a berth in it: and if either she had Nikolai Solovyev with her, or she was prepared to leave without him.

Which, being Nadia, having committed herself to him she probably would *not* be.

The liaison captain had escorted him back to the train — there was a curfew in force, passengers in transit were forbidden to disembark, and the sentries who were posted around the station had been given *carte blanche* to shoot if in doubt. Bolsheviks hid themselves away like bloody rats, the captain had explained, crept out of their holes at times like this to commit acts of sabotage and murder. The railway was of course a prime target.

'Rats in the ascendancy, rather, at the moment?'

'At this moment — yes. But — we haven't given up, you know. And with the arrival now of your flying machines — well ...'

'Still on their train at Kupyansk, you said. Is Kupyansk really about to be cut off?'

'They could hold out there, you see. Giving our own formations time to rally and regroup.'

'Let's pray you're right ... But tell me, Captain — this is a long shot, but — d'you know a Captain Count Nikolai Solovyev, by any chance?'

He didn't. He was sure there was no Count Solovyev on Mai-Maievsky's staff. Nor in any of the immediately subordinate commands.

'But here we are now, Commander . . .'

Scott and Davies had surprised him with the warmth of their welcome. They hadn't liked to help themselves to the whisky in his absence.

Four or five hospital trains had passed through Debaltsevo during the night, and this was another now puffing south-ward. Passing in a blur of thickly falling snow, the two trains were only a few feet apart, the southbound one's newly-painted red crosses discernible even through fogged windows. Then — gone, with the snow whirling in its slip-stream.

Five trains, say. How many wounded in each?

And — quite a different thought — how many nurses?

But also — attempting a double-take — had those been *people*, not freight, on the roofs of the box-cars?

He said, 'My nurse girls could have been in that.'

'Do they have nurses in those trains?'

'I don't know. Wouldn't you suppose they would?'

Not the happiest of thoughts, either. Nurses Pilkington and Reid *en route* to Novorossisk — getting *out*, while Robert Cowan travelled north — *in* — in search of them . . . Then — tangentially — the image shaping in his mind wasn't of English nurses but of a tall, dark girl — her soft dark hair would doubtless have been trimmed short if she had to wear some sort of nurse's headgear — tall, dark, rather pale-skinned, with wide-apart grey eyes and a wide, full mouth. He was picturing her exactly as he'd known her and dreamed of her — except she'd have cut her hair — seeing her now, this minute, in that other train, making her way along the corridor between compartments crowded with soldiers in bandages, bloodstained uniforms: that long-legged, long-waisted, supple figure, swaying to the motion of the train: and in close-up then as she paused at a compartment doorway: that look of calm, compassionate appraisal which he remembered so very, *very* clearly . . .

But — in point of fact — she was far more likely to be at Simferopol. It was the obvious place because when she'd written that letter she'd still been in the Crimea, and because when she'd worked with Irina in Moscow she'd been employed mainly on secretarial duties. She'd had experience of such work, having spent the first years of the war helping her father in the administration of his vast estates, and secretarial skills had been what that hospital had needed. Administration would still be her most valuable contribution, therefore, and it seemed likely that they'd have retained her in some kind of headquarters job, rather than have sent her off into the wilds. Which of course was why he'd dreaded the prospect of having to go up to Simferopol, from Sevastopol. Just a few days ago, for God's sake: it felt like a month ... But the thought of having to start his enquiries at the military hospital there, where the Misses Reid and Pilkington had done their training — as much of it as they *had* done — and quite possibly finding himself face to face with Nadia, having to mumble something like *No, it's not you I've come for ...*

The hell it wouldn't have been. Once he'd set eyes on her again. And maybe — just *maybe* — for her, too ...

'Jim.' Scott spoke for the first time in half an hour. 'When we get to whatever this damn place is called—'

'Kupyansk?'

'If the Flight's still there, and if this lot's going on through — God knows, but it's possible — what you and I have to see to like greased lightning is getting our wagons uncoupled and tagged on to the others.'

The Welshman nodded. 'Although I'd imagine if they're still there they'd have unloaded by this time.'

'Not if the place looks like being cut off, you dolt.'

'More so, I'd have thought. Wouldn't you want to get a few of the crates into the air?'

'Maybe. Take a look-see ... And — maybe gain some time, at that ... Sure. But *then* — my guess is we'll pull out — bloody quick, too, while we still can.'

'So why would they be sitting there now, even?'

'Waiting for *us*?'

'Pull out, you say?' Bob asked him. 'D'you mean back to where you came from?'

'I mean out of Russia. By way of Novorossisk and your gallant boys in blue. Finish.'

'The finish you said you personally can't even contemplate.'

'Well.' A shrug. 'Has to come sometime. For me, later the better, that's all.'

'Would've been nice to have seen our crowd winning first, wouldn't it?' Davies added, 'In point of fact — almost better not to've joined in at all, than get all their hopes up then duck out when it's beginning to go bad.'

'Say *that* again.' Scott nodded. 'Bloody politicians. Sixes and sevens and all a-dither. Like us being only instructors, then we can fight. Army must *not* fight, mind you — but they send in tanks, and if the British don't drive them who in hell can? I tell you, Cowan, makes me bloody puke. How is it with the Navy?'

'Confused. At the moment we're allowed to protect the Kerch Peninsula and the Crimean ports. But as you say, the politicians, back home—'

'Sam,' Davies suggested, 'why not take our discharge here in Russia, then sign on to fly for Denikin?'

Scott grimaced. 'On a hiding to nothing, pal. Too few, and — hell, you know how they are. Bloody heroic now and then, but short of everything that matters — including what's rotting on the quaysides — and three-quarters of 'em only half trained. Whereas the Bolsheviks are finally getting themselves into passably good shape — and they've a whole lot of machines the Huns left behind. Not to mention a few Huns flying for them.'

'Germans flying for the Red Air Force?'

'Sure. Run into 'em a few times, haven't we, Jim?' He nodded to Bob. 'Fokkers, Albatrosses, Spads, all kinds. All right, a lot don't count for much, we knock 'em down like bloody pigeons, but then you get a couple really well handled, and — bet your sweet life, those are no Red Air Force pilots.'

'Mercenaries . . .'

'That's one word for the bastards. I know some shorter ones.'

'Might there be mercenary work — somewhere or other — that'd solve *your* problem?'

'None I can think of that I'd touch.'

'Oh?'

'Christ.' The stare continuing ... 'Would *you* want to risk you neck — and kill guys, your neck or theirs — in aid of something you didn't give a damn for?'

'*I* wouldn't. But from what you were saying before, I'd have thought—'

'You'd have thought wrong.'

He nodded. 'Glad to hear it.'

'Hmm.' Scott took his pipe out of a pocket, blew through it, delved in another pocket for tobacco. 'I'm my own worst enemy. Except for Jim here, of course.'

Towards mid-morning they passed a big crowd of refugees trekking south parallel to the line of the tracks. Infantry with horse-drawn carts among them, and groups of horsemen in the lead and on the flanks. The train had been climbing for most of the past two hours, mostly through forest, and since then they'd been crossing featureless snow-covered plain, and although the snow had stopped falling when they'd been about halfway up to the plateau, up here with not even a tree to focus on it was like staring into a white infinity, no way to be sure you were seeing ten miles or ten yards. Then suddenly — maybe one had been half asleep — these survivors, if it wasn't begging too many questions to call them that, seeming to fill the landscape. They were following the line of a road which hadn't been visible until now, and over-flowing it, spreading over the slightly higher ground on both sides. The horsemen might have been riding as escorts, or were just cavalry lucky enough still to have horses under them; and the carts might have been full of wounded or — women, probably, children ... But not even one of them, mounted or on foot, had so much as turned a head to glance at the train as it passed.

No energy to waste. You could read it in the bent backs, figures around the carts dragging at those horses' heads,

and the saddle-horses on the column's flanks floundering
in snow that was sometimes stirrup-deep as the riders
urged them on. No spare energy, and no *interest* — in anything outside their own single-minded, urgent progress.

Then the whole crowd of them had passed, leaving a
flattened, brownish swathe across the snow. Bob thinking
yet again — with a greatly increased sense of urgency of
his own — that he'd *have* to have these pilots' help.

Davies growled, 'Not very jolly, is it?'

'More coming.' Scott, from his seat beside the window,
nodded in the direction the train was travelling. Then —
frowning round at the others — 'Why haven't we seen
anything like this until now?'

'Because their line of march coincides with the railway
tracks here. And didn't before.' He thought it was fairly
obvious. 'We were slanting in from the south-east before,
weren't we?'

Scott was looking slightly dazed. He'd turned back to
the window now: shaking his head, as if he was trying to
convince himself *No, I'm not seeing this . . .*

'This' being the reality of defeat. When you actually saw
it was the moment in which it became real. Out there —
now — men, and women, obviously — struggling to get
away, save their lives. *There* — within shouting distance, if
it hadn't been for steamed-up glass and the train's racket
. . . But nothing less than that: if anything, a little more,
because torture and rape would come into it too, invariably did — as every one of those struggling creatures —
there, in your sight this minute — knew for sure.

This next crowd of them was bigger, and nearly all on
foot. If there'd been five hundred in the first column, there
were probably a thousand or more in this one. Each
succeeding group of course would profit to some extent
from those who'd gone before them, flattening and
compressing the snow and leaving drifts and depressions
clear to see and avoid. Until fresh falls came: which would
happen before long. But there was also a lot to be said for
frozen ground that was too iron-hard to be churned into
mud.

He thought, *One* small mercy...

But — on one's own, for God's sake: with say a hundred and fifty miles of this kind of thing between here and Ekaterinoslav — even *without* the Red cavalry who were said to be on their way ... What could one man alone hope to achieve?

Davies gestured: 'This other side too, now.'

'Christ ...'

'Bear up, Cowan. Your girls *could* have been on one of those trains, you know.'

Scott, having so to speak recovered his own mental breath, seemed to have become a mind-reader. Either that, Bob thought, or he showed his emotions in his face much more than he'd ever realized.

He agreed: 'They could have been. Could indeed.'

'In which case —' Scott nodded at the scene outside — 'putting yourself into *that* predicament wouldn't be doing them or anyone else a mite of good, would it?'

'No, but ...'

Tongue-tied, for the moment. Staring out at it — at them ... He'd been about to answer that he wasn't planning on becoming one more in any horde of refugees, had stopped short because the statement wouldn't have made sense. It was what one *would* be doing. The mere fact of being Robert Cowan and dressed in naval uniform, instead of Ivan Ivanovich in the Russian brownish khaki, would make no odds whatever. You *would* be one of them — one of thousands, but entirely on your own, and only there in the crazy hope of finding two girls who might already have got away in any case.

'You see —' Davies was addressing Bob but looking to Scott for agreement too — 'if the dear General is ordering us out of here, there's no reason at all we shouldn't retain the pleasure of your company. I mean —' he waved one hand at distant, ant-like figures spread across the snow-scape — 'doesn't look like we'll be staying, does it? And since your young ladies may be revelling in the pleasures of Taganrog by now — heaven's sake, man—'

'He's talking sense — for once. You'd be an ass not to

stay with us, Cowan.' Scott assured him, 'And you'd be entirely welcome.'

'Getting close, perhaps.'

Davies, pointing at where a branch line joined this track from the west. Then a signal-box; and other lines curved away beyond it. Scott agreed: 'Can't be much longer now, I'd guess.' He glanced at Bob. 'You'll stay with us, will you?'

He still hadn't decided. For half an hour he'd been switching from one point of view to the other. Knowing that what the flyers were suggesting made good sense, and tempted to accept both the reasoning and the invitation: even with the feeling he'd be a damn fool if he didn't. But then, having come all this way — and having diverted one of His Majesty's ships in the process — the idea of giving up now, admitting that the whole exercise had been futile — and just at the moment of arrival ...

Arrival *where*, for God's sake? Except at the back end of nowhere ... And not necessarily within a hundred miles of those girls. And when the whole idea — his own, as discussed with Captain Fellows and submitted to Colonel Temple by signal, had been to get in and out, bringing the girls out with him, *before* the front gave way. It had been Temple's assumption, too, as expressed in his first signal — that if it wasn't a viable proposition to get them out before the Bolsheviks broke through, there'd be no question even of starting. Hence what might be termed the Taganrog-Everard solution.

So — on that basis ...

Frowning, gazing out at the whitish blur of snowbound steppe ... There were no refugee columns in sight now. So they probably hadn't been coming from or through Kupy-ansk. Otherwise they'd have been thicker on the ground than before, surely, as one came closer to the place. Davies had suggested that they'd know as well or better than anyone about the encircling cavalry movement that was said to be in progress: they'd have started from the Kharkov region — seventy-five, eighty miles north of here

— and they'd simply be swarming south, desperate to be out of the trap before it closed on them.

'And if I'm right, how clever does that make *us*?'

Scott had looked at him, shaken his head, and gone back to talking about B Flight; he was still doing so, sporadically, having started in response to questions which Bob had put to him and then found himself barely listening to the answers, his thoughts being directed elsewhere at least half the time. Asking himself, for instance, if the Misses Pilkington and Reid had needed rescuing *before* the front collapsed, how you could justify turning your back on them *now*?

How would you explain it to their parents?

Scott's voice broke in again: 'Kinkead's the guy who shot up Budyonny's cavalry near Tsarytsin. He was leading the team that did that, I mean. Marcus Kinkead: B Flight commander.'

'But surely Collishaw—'

'Guy's not bloody listening.' Scott sighed. 'Cowan — *old man*—'

'Sorry. You said—'

'Ray Collishaw commands the whole Detachment. Squadron, as it was. Three Flights, now down to two. The one we expect to find here at Kupyansk is B Flight, Kinkead's. A Flight — to follow, *if* it does, seems unlikely now — is mine. And our boss is Ray Collishaw. Kinkead and I are both majors, Ray's a lieutenant-colonel. Is that clearer, now?'

'Of course. Sorry . . .'

He'd asked, to start with, about other personalities whom he might be meeting, and Scott had named and described a few. Several were Canadians. A number of the younger men had the new RAF ranks — Flying Officers, Observer Officers, and so forth — and the more senior ones' present military ranks were going to be changed before long, Scott had said. Neither he nor Davies were very happy about this, but appreciated that a new Service — the RAF had come into existence last year, absorbing both the RFC and RNAS — needed such outward and visible signs of its own separate identity.

Scott had also told of some flying incidents — none featuring himself, all of them about his brother-officers' exploits, and invariably to their credit. Bob asked him now, 'How many Germans did you say Collishaw shot down?'

'Sixty-eight. Not bad, eh?'

'How about you?'

'Me?'

'What was your Western Front score?'

'Oh — God knows. I've no memory for that sort of thing.' He raised his voice to drown Davies' attempt to interrupt. 'But you see, when Ray was first in France—'

'Fifty-seven, Sam.' Davies had had to shout. He nodded to Bob. 'As he knows damn well. Fifty-seven.'

'Anything you want to know, Cowan, ask this fellow here.' Scott stared coldly at his friend. 'He's the source of all knowledge. Least, he *thinks* he is.'

'Hah!' Davies pushed himself up. 'At bloody last ...'

The outskirts of Kupyansk were in sight ahead and on that side. And on this side, simultaneously, more railway tracks and then a broad expanse of rails, engine-sheds or workshops, warehouses or whatever, stacks of coal and timber, all snow-coated. The train's whistle shrieked; the pounding rhythm of the wheels was already slowing.

'Scott, listen.' Bob knocked his pipe out against his heel. 'Before I decide on anything I need to find the local military hospital, to ask about that *lektuchka*. And you'll have your hands full anyway. So I'll see you later. On the other train — if it's still here?'

'*If* — sure ...'

'I'm saying it *is*. Who'll give me five to one?'

Davies had the window down, icy blast pouring in and his head and shoulders out: Scott muttering 'Don't touch it — bloody Welshman only bets on certainties' ... Davies pulled his head back in: eyes streaming, mopping them: 'Here to meet us — see?' Pointing: 'See old Monkey there?' He was laughing and yelling at them as the train crawled in, hissing to a halt. Bob saw several RAF uniforms and men waving, shouting back at Davies; Scott bawled, 'Pickerell! All out here! D'you hear me? All *out*!' He turned, as the train jolted to a stop: 'Fine — what you just said. But stick around a minute, so you'll know what's cooking?'

He had a fair idea already. One bright spot from his own point of view was that on the platform across the rails on this other side two stretcher-bearers were pushing into a doorway which as it swung shut showed a large red cross painted on it. But the other thing was the reason the reception party had been so easy to spot — simply that they had the platform to themselves. Clustering at the carriage steps now, Davies with them, all yelling at once, exchanging news — while Pickerell and the other airmen, unable to use the door, could only pile gear in the corridor. But apart from this small group of RAF the only people on the platform were some C3-type-looking soldiers who were being mustered up front beside the engine and its tender. Conscripts — like those now disembarking from the other carriage — taking over from railwaymen who'd presumably joined the migration southward.

8

The doctor was short, thickset; like Bob, he hadn't shaved for a day or two and by the look of the blood-stained once-white coat didn't have anyone to do his laundry. He'd glanced at Bob's identification; scowled as he pushed it back across the table: 'So what d'you want?'

This had been the ticket-seller's office, was now the doctor's and also by the look of it his operating theatre. Through the ticket window you could see patients lying wrapped in their greatcoats in the stone-floored hall. There was a brazier in there, and it was warm enough except when the swing doors were opened.

Bob told him, 'I need to find *Letuchka syem*. It has two English nurses in it. I've been sent to get them.'

'You have, have you ... What for?'

'Orders. And their parents—'

'Does it occur to you we need all the nurses *we* can get?'

'I'm sure you do. However—'

'Are they juveniles?'

'Doctor — their ages are not important. Parents can still worry. Anyway, they're British citizens and—'

'I have two orderlies out there. No nurses at all.' He belched. 'And you come here telling me—'

'Not telling. Asking. I need to find them, that's all. It'll be up to them whether they leave òr stay. But in any case, isn't it about finished, on this front?'

'*Here*, it's finished. Elsewhere — well, God knows. Or cares, probably ... Anyway, what's the odds, what am *I* here for, Christ's sake?' He glanced at the ticket window.

'For *them*, you'll say. And you'll be right — to the extent that thanks to my superhuman efforts about one in three of 'em may live. Don't ask me what they'll live *for*...'

He'd checked himself. It was obvious that he was slightly drunk. That frown, for instance, might accompany some difficulty in focusing. Now he'd nodded. 'All right. Got a map with you?'

'Afraid not.'

Stupid. Should have borrowed Scott's...

'Wouldn't help much if you had. *Letuchka syem* wasn't one of ours. They'd've come under *Otriad* eleven — feeding back to the base hospital at Ekaterinoslav, that means. I was in *Letuchka* seventeen myself, as it happens. Disbanded, I'm sole survivor, but this is where we sent our wounded, see. Not this place — in the town, just back of here, it's empty now. Good thing too, bloody sewer ... There's typhus around, did you know? Well, there is ... Anyway — what I was saying, or about to say — my *Letuchka syemnadtsat* was up in the Volchansk-Shebekino section. You couldn't get much closer to the front than that. Not without getting your head blown off — which some did ... But I'd guess — *guess*, mark you — number seven might now be in the region of — oh, let's say Karlovka, Petrovka, Konstantinograd. South-west of Kharkov, see. It's a good bet, can't be *far* out, because I happen to know they *were* up at Bogodukhov. That I do *know. Letuchka* number four replaced them there. The doctor in number four was a mate of mine, I met him in Kharkov on his way through. For what *that* information's worth — bugger-all, I dare say ... Listen — that triangle — Karlovka, Petrovka, Konstantingrad — on the railway from Poltava south-eastward — right? Obvious way to go. Even though the line's probably been blown up by now — and when it's repaired it'll be the Reds using it, you can bet on *that* ... They blow up the lines, otherwise the swine'll come steaming through in their armoured trains. Which means, of course, there are damn few trains — if any — still to the north of us now. They've been packing 'em full and sending 'em south in bloody droves, so there can't be much rolling-stock left for however many more there may be. Flat feet, or carts if they're lucky. You're right, my job's about done, here.'

He'd certainly had a few drinks, Bob thought. Although the belligerence seemed to have faded. And he'd got what he came for — a lot more than he'd thought he would, a minute or two ago.

'I'm grateful for this help, doctor. Very kind of you. Those place-names again, where you think—'

'Not *think*. Guessing … Because they'd have been near Valki when the order went out to start withdrawing — from Army Command, incidentally, that would have been, not from Ekaterinoslav — and they'd have shifted down that way because it's — well, it's the obvious bloody way to go, that's all. *And* for the railway from Poltava — which as I say is likely to have been cut by now, but they wouldn't know it … Another thing is — see, it's all very well saying pack up, sod off out of it — but when you're in this line of work and you're inundated with these poor bloody animals with their intestines hanging out, limbs half-severed and/or festering—'

He'd checked. 'D'you understand me?'

'Yes. And as I said, I'm most grateful for your — advice … Another possibility, though — when you send off a hospital train, would you have a nurse or two on board?'

'*Should. Should* have a doctor. Or two. But — well, God's sake, exactly what I *told* you—'

'I was only wondering — if all the *letuchki* had had orders to pull back — or pull *out*—'

'Back. When a retreat's in progress — obviously—'

'What I'm getting at is if *Letuchka syem* is where you think and trains are still moving on that line—'

'Your nurses might've been sent out with them.'

'Exactly.'

'They might too. *If* the doctor in charge decided he could spare 'em. Meaning as likely as not he'd happily be rid of 'em. But — as I was trying to convey to you — when you have a real fuckup like this is — like it *was*, right *here* — streams of 'em, place like a bloody slaughterhouse —

well, you wouldn't just hop on a damn train, for God's sake!'

'But if the *letuchka* had been ordered out—'

'*Back*. I just told you this — didn't I? Anyway — out of immediate danger — being blown up, taken prisoner, caught in artillery barrages ... To be any use, hospitals have to be where they can work — close enough to the action for men to get there or be brought there, but—'

'Yes. I see ...'

'*Yes, I see* ...' Less imitative of Bob's tone than parodying it. Belligerency — contempt, it sounded like — returning. He shook his head: maybe aware of it coming on ... Small hands — none too clean — flat on the table to push himself up. 'Work to do. Go find your damn English nurses ...'

Until he could check the drunken doctor's information on a map, there was no certainty it was going to help much. It *was* information — better than the vacuum he'd been working in up to now — but whether or not he could use it — well, distances were the main thing, and where the railways ran. He had a presentiment that the map wasn't going to make anything look easy.

On the other platform they were preparing to take the four RAF freight cars off this train in order to transfer them to B Flight's, which was on the far side of the marshalling yard. An RAF sergeant with a handlebar moustache and a squint told him this; the sergeant was there to make sure they detached the right wagons — three box-cars of stores and one flat-car with the two Sopwith Camels on it — and Scott had instructed him also to look out for Commander Cowan and direct him to the other train.

'Ramp at the end of the platform, sir. Cross the line there, and you'll see a gate in the fence. Our train's on the west side where the big shed is. Using that as a hangar, see. Then there's waste ground the other side, nice an' level for takeoffs and landing. Very 'andy, you might say.'

'Right. Thank you, sergeant.'

'We'll be all right now, then, sir.'

One eye met Bob's. Lips twitching slightly under cover of his moustache.

'Now we got the navy 'ere, I mean.'

'Ah. Well, we heard you were in a bit of a spot . . .'

A complication which he hadn't heard of until this moment was that the RAF train had no engine. On the night of their arrival, apparently, it had been stolen. Collishaw, the Detachment's CO, had got on another train that had passed through next morning *en route* to Kharkov — or possibly only as far as Chuguyev, about half the distance — either to find the engine and have it returned or to reach General Holman, who'd come up here a day ahead of the Detachment on his way to confer with General Mai-Maievsky. Subject of the conference, of course, being whether or not to commit the RAF to action.

The position was in fact more serious than the sergeant's light-hearted manner had suggested it might be. He'd given Bob the gist of it, and details were filled in by Sam Scott a few minutes later. Scott had been looking out for him, came to meet him as he crossed the marshalling yard, and gave him the basics of the situation in about one minute flat. Budyonny's cavalry were thought to be not more than forty-eight hours away — but possibly less — B Flight's personnel — about ninety men in all — had been issued with rifles, and a 24-hour guard was being maintained with a system of Very light warnings from posts outside the town.

'Stuck here, you see. Can't move without an engine — *and* orders of some kind.'

'What about using your aircraft to spot the cavalry before it gets here? Bomb them, or—'

'Might come to that. Might well. Mind you, they've only off-loaded two Camels and a DH9A so far. Over there — see, where—'

'Your sergeant told me. Using that big shed as a hangar.'

'Right. And Marcus Kinkead with Tommy Burns-

Thompson did a recce over the Red lines yesterday. Brought their Camels back full of holes — ground fire, rifles and machine-guns. So, as we have no authority to conduct offensive operations here, we're all grounded now. Pending Ray Collishaw's return that is. But of course, if it came to the worst — or best, depending on how you look at it — couldn't just bloody well sit and take it, could we ...' He grabbed Bob's arm. 'Come on over, anyhow, meet the boys. There's lunch, too, you'll be glad to hear. Hey — I should've asked, did you get anything on your nurse-girls?'

'Yes, but —' he didn't move: needing to have it clear before they joined the others — 'does this mean there'll be no air-search for the *letuchka*?'

'Couldn't say. Have to work on it, Cowan. If you *did* get something?'

Marcus Kinkead was a British edition of Sam Scott. More precise and serious in his manner — which in the circumstances was hardly surprising — but otherwise very much the same type. Bob shook hands with him, then with a whole crowd of others: 'Tommy' Burns-Thompson — a captain with the ribbon of the DFC on his tunic — and two other Camel pilots — Daley and Fulford — before abandoning the effort to memorize names, as another dozen beribboned pilots crowded into the compartment, bringing with them a stream of jokes all on the theme of the Royal Navy steaming to their rescue. Hadn't he brought a tug with him? *That*'s what we want, a bloody tug!

After a while Kinkead drove most of them out, so that he, Bob and Scott had room to eat lunch, which was a beef stew out of cans. They had plenty of canned food with them, Kinkead mentioned; if they were besieged here they could hold out for weeks, as far as rations were concerned. Water might become a problem ... Scott said, nodding towards Bob, 'This splendid fellow arrived with a bottle of single malt in his bag. Davies and I didn't have a doubt of him, from that moment on.'

'Clever of you, Cowan.' Kinkead nodded approval. 'Same principle as a missionary bringing coloured beads to cannibals. What?' He added, 'You've come to rescue a brace of ex-governesses, Scott tells me.'

'And I have a lead now on where their field hospital may be.' He pointed over towards the station. 'Saw the quack there. He was in a *letuchka* himself not long ago, and — well, cutting a long story short, he knows where number seven was at that time, and made a deduction as to where it probably is now.' He asked Scott, 'Got your map handy?'

'Here.' Kinkead had his with him, and unfolded it. 'Mind you, that quack as you call him is not the most reliable of informants.'

'I know what you mean. Poor devil.'

'But you believe him on this, do you? All right. Long as he was making sense. What do I look for?'

'Railway line running south-east from Poltava?'

'That's — some way . . .'

'And south-west of Kharkov — places called Konstantinograd, Petrovka and Karlovka.'

'Got 'em — all three. Sou'-sou'-west of Kharkov. Petrovka's not on that railway. Other two are, though.' He glanced up. 'And your *letuchka*?'

'Somewhere in that area — according to our friend. How far, roughly?'

'At a guess, a hundred miles. But hang on . . .'

He used the stem of his pipe, measuring from the tip of the mouthpiece and marking the distance along it with his thumbnail, then applying it to the scale at the bottom of the map.

'Yes. A hundred miles, near enough. That's to Konstantinograd, which is roughly the mid-point. Here, see for yourself.'

Bob turned it so Scott could also study it. Accepting, meanwhile, the offer of a mug of coffee. Aware of how vague his information was — the geographical location by the drunken doctor for one thing, and even if one could rely on that, whether the *letuchka* or individual members of its staff would still be in the field at all.

He glanced up at Kinkead. 'Scott said you're not doing any flying at the moment.'

'I was telling him — 'Scott was filling his pipe — 'that you and Tommy ran into some unpleasantness over the Red lines.'

'We did indeed.' Kinkead nodded. 'But the crucial thing is no decision's been taken about involving ourselves here. I rather doubt we will, tell you the truth. My guess is that when Ray gets back we'll be loading those three crates back on, and — skedaddling.'

'If you have an engine to skedaddle you by then.'

'Well — we *must* have, Sam!'

'Hope springs eternal ... But meanwhile, since we're stuck here — and it's a good cause, I'd say — would it be beyond the bounds of permissibility to use the Nine for a recce of that area?'

'Oh, Lord ...' He'd frowned. Explaining, then — 'I only had that crate made ready in case the General might want to be taken up. To see the lie of the land — if there's still any question at all of deploying, when he gets back. And as you know, it's the only Nine we have with us. Brought it for exactly that sort of contingency. *And* Holman knows about it. So—'

'He's not here now. Highly unlikely to be here before tomorrow. Wouldn't you agree?'

'Lap of the Gods, old man. But in any case—'

'I'd gladly fly it, Marcus.' Scott held a match to the bowl of his pipe. Sucking ... 'If you had no objection.'

He had the pipe going. Kinkead watching him, saying nothing. Showing nothing, either. He had the sort of face and manner that tended not to. Scott added, dropping the match-end on his plate, 'Hundred miles. Say fifty, fifty-five minutes. Half an hour over the target area. Say two and a half hours total, there and back. Probably less. So — if I take off within the next hour, say, I'm back on the ground here before dark, easy.' He paused. Then: 'What d'you say, old bean?'

'I — really don't know, Sam.'

Scott pointed the pipe-stem at him. 'Not talking about any kind of offensive action, you know. I can't see why you'd object, tell you the truth. Doubt if Ray would, if he was with us. Matter of accommodating the Navy here — and maybe saving two young girls' skins?'

'That's partly what bothers me.' Kinkead looked at Bob. 'Suppose we did find your *letuchka* for you. Then you'd want to get to wherever it is, wouldn't you? There's no rail link from here towards Poltava, you know. You'd have to go right down to Debaltsevo, to start with. All very well if you had a week or so in hand — and if the *letuchka* remained rooted to that spot, waiting for you — and if there are trains running west from Debaltsevo by that time — or even *now*, for that matter ... *And*, mind you, if the Reds aren't between you and the other place by then. If I was General Budyonny I'd have their guts for garters if they weren't, I can tell you ... Look at the map, you'll see what I mean.'

He'd turned it around again. Bob knowing before he even glanced at it that he was right. What he'd half expected in the first place: and the conclusion so obvious it didn't need putting into words — if you couldn't get there, get *to* them, why bother to locate them?

There was a pinch of salt in the wound, too. If he was right about the Bolshevik cavalry — as he probably was — and those girls still *were* there ...

Sickening.

'Cowan.' Scott broke the silence. 'Have you ever — er — been up?'

'Up?' Staring back at him. 'God's sake — no ...'

Scott explained to Kinkead, 'I'd take him along, see. Don't need an observer — *he*'ll observe for me. If we find his *letuchka* I'll put down as close as I can get. He'll then hoof it, tell the young ladies, "They want you home, kindly take the next train to Novorossisk." Give 'em each a hug and a kiss, back to the crate, we take off — and that's it. All right with you, Marcus?'

'You'll have been on the ground hour or two. That's *after* you've found it. Doubling the duration you were talking about to start with.'

'Not necessarily, at all!'

'You could write your message and drop it to them — if
the *letuchka*'s there. Give 'em that instruction and say if
Miss H and Miss Y are present and will comply with this,
please wave a — I don't know—'

'Pair of bloomers.'

Kinkead's tight-lipped smile ... 'Right. Please wave a
pair of red bloomers.'

'*Red*?'

'Oh—'

'Say pink. *All* young girls nowadays wear—'

Bob cut in: 'I'd much sooner be landed, so I could talk
to them. Couldn't you leave me, come back in the
morning?'

Scott shook his head. 'By morning, things could be very
different — here *and* there.'

Kinkead agreed. 'Rule *that* out, definitely.'

Scott's eyes smiled. Catching the implication — as Bob
did — that the rest of it was clearly *not* ruled out. He
checked the time on his wristwatch. 'Chances are we'll
find ground flat enough to land on quite close to them.
They wouldn't've set up shop on some bloody mountain
peak, would they. *Ten minutes* on the ground, Marcus.' He
added to Bob, 'We've all put crates down on just about
every kind of terrain you can imagine. Sometimes because
we've had no option — engines conked out, that sort of
thing. It's what we have big wheels for. Anyhow — what
d'you say, Marcus, old top?'

'Suppose after you take off we get Ray back — and an
engine — with orders to head south while the going's
good. If we had to wait two or three hours for you—'

'In anything like those circumstances, *don't* wait.'

'The way I see it —' Kinkead spoke slowly, as if thinking
his thoughts aloud — 'trying to see it objectively, mind
you, as an outsider would, or in retrospect — it seems to
me that to take that risk on the off-chance of contacting
two young ladies who may or may not—'

'Excuse me.' Bob cut in again. 'I should have explained

— this isn't just some jaunt I dreamed up on my own. You may not have realized — for instance, they sent me from Sevastopol to Taganrog in a destroyer — it was due to sail for the Bosporus, and the naval staff turned it around just so I'd have a chance of getting up here in time by landing at Taganrog. Naval staff meaning Rear-Admiral (Black Sea). Then again, my immediate chief is the Staff Officer (Intelligence) to C-in-C Mediterranean — Admiral Gough-Calthorpe. I think even your General Holman's subordinate to him. But in any case the strings are being pulled in London. So one gathered … But having got this far now, unless I have *your* help — well, as you just pointed out, I can't get any farther.'

'What d'you say *now*, Marcus?'

Kinkead took a long breath … 'I suppose — taking your word for all that, Cowan — well, naturally, goes without saying — and if you'll swear to be back on the ground here before dark, Sam—'

'Good man. *Damn* good.' Scott nodded to him, then looked at Bob. 'Your first flight, by God …' He checked the time again. 'Need to look slippy now, don't we. Can we have that crate fuelled right away, please?'

The bomber had been rolled out on to the waste ground beside the marshalling yard — a section of fencing having been removed for access and a pole set up with a wind-sock on it. Mechanics were checking over the machine's engine and filling its tank with petrol. It looked about twice the size of the stubby, blunt-nosed Camel that stood near it. Both were lashed down against the wind, with ropes secured to iron pegs that must have been sledge-hammered into the frozen ground. They were both biplanes, of course, the DH9 particularly high-winged, taller than he'd expected — with massive-looking struts, two pairs each side, as well as shorter ones in the middle rooted on the fuselage. About thirty feet long, he guessed: and the wing-span nearer fifty.

The original De Havilland 9s had been under-powered, Scott had told him. These 9a's had been re-designed at the

Westland Aircraft Works in Somerset, their fuselages strengthened to take a more powerful, American-made engine called a Liberty.

'You'll fly as you're dressed now, will you? Except you'll wear a helmet ... Want to know how to use that Lewis gun, in case of need?'

'Think we *might* have need?'

'Who knows ... Get up there, I'll show you.'

He'd been in the cockpit already, trying it out for size, while he'd been waiting for Scott to change into his flying gear. Meanwhile subduing a kind of disbelief that this could possibly be happening — while watching ground-staff patching bullet-holes in that Camel, and the start of the fuelling of this so-called Nine. He'd also chatted to the airmen, with the aim of filling in some of the huge gaps in his own awareness of what was going on. Learning for instance that the reason this trip had to be made in the DH9 wasn't only that a Camel was a single-seater, but that the fighter's range was extremely limited. A leading airman by name of Jamieson had told him, 'Can't 'ardly cross the bloody road in them things.'

'But they're very successful fighters, aren't they?'

'The best, sir. Nothing to touch 'em, in a dogfight. Long as the pilot knows 'is onions, that is. They kill learners, them buggers do. Kill 'em in bloody droves.'

At least, he wasn't going in a Camel. He climbed up into the DH9's cockpit, and slid in, bulky in his greatcoat. There were two cockpits, of course, the pilot's in front and this rear one for the observer. The pilot had a forward-firing Vickers machine-gun on the port side of the fuse-lage, while the observer had this Lewis behind him.

Scott told him from the step, leaning over, 'Called a Scarff ring, this mounting. So — unclamp the gun now — that's the way. Swings nice and easy, see. And elevate — depress ... Ever fire a Lewis?'

'Oh, yes. A few times.'

'Fine, I don't need to teach you. We'll have a full pan on it, and a spare. You'll notice, though, it's impossible to train it where you might shoot the tail off — or me in the back of the head, for that matter.'

'Could make for a problem when it came to landing.'

'You can see that, can you? Didn't make you a Commissar for nothing, did they … But don't worry, we won't be going near any front lines, like those boys did.' A nod towards the Camel; then he reached into the cockpit. 'Helmet. Communications tubes attached, see. This one's to your ears, and this your voice-tube — leads to *my* ears. Now, when you want to point out something on the ground — or in the air, for that matter — do it by clock-face reference. Nose of the crate being twelve o'clock.'

'Right.'

'One other thing I have to bother you with — apart from the navigation, the flight-plan we'll go over in a minute — it's important you should know the start-up routine. See, if we do land, back of beyond there, you're going to have to swing the prop for me. So … Simple enough — I'm in my cockpit there, and the first thing is to have the carburettor full of gas. We call it "sucking in" and we do it by winding the prop around. I check the switch is off, throttle's shut, and you — you're on the ground there — you give the prop five or six complete turns. That floods the carb. Then, I set my throttle — just a mite above "slow idle" — and you feel for compression and report "Contact", I switch on and call back to you "Contact", and you give the prop a good hard swing. There's a way to do it without getting your head knocked off.'

'Ah.'

'We'll show you, don't worry. But — suppose the engine doesn't fire. Sometimes doesn't, on the first swing. What we do is — well, if the engine's cold like it is now, we go through the sucking-in routine a second time, then try again. Should fire then, all right. But if it's warm — as it will be, after an hour or more's flying — I call out "Still on", you get the compression — yell "Contact" — and again I repeat "Contact" — and you swing again.'

'All right.'

'I'll have them demonstrate the swinging technique.

Then you can do it on your own, start us up when we're ready ... But now come on down, we'll take a look at where we're going.'

'Right. But —' he hesitated. Then: 'Look, there is one thing ...'

The major had begun climbing down; he stopped now.

'I'd have raised this before — before we left Kinkead. I didn't want to — you know, push my luck, as it were. Or look gift-horses in the mouth.'

'We don't have a lot of time to waste, you know.'

'No. Sorry. Thing is, having to tell these girls to get on a train, and so on. When you came up with this idea — well, the answer to the insuperable problem, marvellous ... But — second thoughts — there may not *be* a train. A lot of the lines will have been blown up, for instance — so that doctor said. So what I'm really telling 'em is "Start walking" — all right, to some place within their reach where I could meet them, perhaps, but—'

'Where is this getting us right now, Cowan?'

'Well — I'm supposed to be bringing them back, damn it!'

'So you meet 'em, *bring* 'em back.'

'We couldn't possibly squeeze them in with us?'

'Not on your damn life, we couldn't!'

'Not one in with me and the other with you?'

'Are you crazy?'

'Well — ignorant. But—'

'Listen.' Scott checked the time, then looked to see that the fuelling was still in progress. They were wheeling the steel drums out on a hand-trolley and over the rough, snow-packed ground; it wasn't happening very quickly. 'I'll tell you — when we were flying from Kotluban, one of these Nines did make it back with two extra guys on board. One crate had been shot down — up on the Volga, this was — the other landed, picked that crew up. There were Reds on the ground, and our boys were using their Lewis to keep 'em at a distance — the other machine got hit too, on its way down, but it got back into the air — *just*, by luck they had room for a long run — with two guys in the rear cockpit and one riding up front here — on top, between those centre struts, one hand to hold on with and the thumb of the other one plugging a bullet-hole in the gas tank. But — see, this was a real emergency — and what's more, if any of 'em had been your size —' he shook his head. 'Oh, and it was a short flight home, mind you — not a hundred bloody miles!'

He nodded. 'All right. Sorry.'

'Look at the map now, shall we?'

Back on the ground, he spread it on the aircraft's lower wing, and Bob joined him, crouching in over it between the two pairs of struts.

'First we'll be flying over this high ground west of us.' He glanced up, nodding towards what looked more like cloud. 'Heading west-sou'-west — all the way — and on that course we'll have say fifteen miles of the plateau under us. Then it falls away — *here* — to low-lying plain — steppe — and after maybe another fifteen miles we'll be over the Donets river. Here ... Then — well, twenty-five miles, roughly — when we're about due south of Kharkov, see — we cross the north-south railway line and the Orel river right close to it. Should be easy to make out — long as this clear weather holds. I'll be flying at five thousand, by the way — or thereabouts, depending on the cloud-base. Saying prayers we don't get more snow before dark, incidentally. If we do —' he grimaced — 'nothing to sweat over, just — you know, better without it ... Anyhow — here's Petrovka, smack on our line of flight. No railway or river, but it must be on a road of some kind, and once we're there we're over the triangle you want to search. Still heading west-sou'-west — brings us to Konstantinograd, which *is* on a railway track. That's, say, fifteen miles after Petrovka. Or if we've gone over Petrovka and not seen it, about fifty after crossing the Donets back here. Making sense to you, this far?'

'Can one use a map up there?'

'Sure. If you need to. Now, at Konstantinograd, we'll make a turn to starboard, follow the railway west-nor'-west to Karlovka. Twenty, twenty-five miles, and that'll be the farthest end of the triangle. If we haven't struck lucky by then we'll come around to east, fly across the middle. But listen, I do have to set myself a deadline, leave us time to get back here before dark, with some allowance for a weather change. When the time comes to turn for home I'll tell you — and I don't care how any red crosses you may have in sight. Understood?'

'Of course.'

Behind them, the leading airman told Scott, 'She's ready when you are, sir.'

'I'm ready now, Jamieson.' He put a hand on Bob's shoulder. 'But I want you to show Commander Cowan here how to swing a prop. Then we'll let him do it on his own.'

A crowd had gathered to see them off. Kinkead calling up to Scott, 'If you sight any Budyonny-type formations anywhere near, Sam, come straight back and tell us?'

Scott raised a gloved thumb. Bob was standing by at the front of the machine; Jim Davies had shouted to him, 'Making you do all the work, is he, Cowan?'

He'd called back, 'Most of it.'

'Give my love to Mary, will you?'

'Only if she's the ugly one.'

'My God, d'you hear *that*?'

Kinkead shouted, 'Hope you find 'em, Cowan.'

'Thanks. And thanks for—'

'On your marks, sir ...' Jamieson, his instructor, was standing close behind him and keeping an eye on Scott. They'd already done the so-called 'sucking-in'. Bob put both his gloved hands on one of the blades, moved the propellor round until he could feel the compression work against it.

He swallowed. Then: 'Contact!'

Scott drawled back, 'Contact ...'

Davies won a laugh with his shout of 'Anchor's aweigh!' just as Bob sent the propellor whirling: having placed his feet very carefully, so as to be sure of standing clear. His hands pulled back off the blade as off something white-hot as the engine fired. There'd be a few minutes of warm-up time, they'd told him — all the time he'd need to climb up and settle in, pull the helmet on and fasten its studs, say his prayers ... But the colder the conditions, the longer the warm-up. Engine just purring, meanwhile, and Scott's growl hollow-sounding through the tube: 'Nice work, Cowan. You'll make an airman yet.'

'Hell I will ...'

Several more minutes passed: then a grunt of 'She'll do', and a roar of sound as Scott opened his throttle and the machine bumped forward. It would be very bumpy until they picked up speed, he'd warned. They were waving from the touchline: must have been about fifty of them there. The airmen had rifles slung on their shoulders. This take-off would amount to at least *something* happening in a day when they had nothing to do except sit or stand around and place bets as to who'd arrive first — Collishaw, Holman or Budyonny.

He hoped there would *not* be any sight of approaching Bolsheviks. Also that the *letuchka* would be there and they'd find it, and that it would be the right one and have the girls still in it. Although for their sake it would be better if they were already in Novorossisk, or on their way. Whether or not one actually brought them out — he'd realized when he'd been talking to Scott — was of no importance; *having* them out was what mattered, not ways and means — or the personal achievement.

Speed building: and much smoother now, wheels only skimming the crests of the uneven ground, instead of hammering. Then suddenly no bumps at all — none of that bone-shaking vibration — total contrast ... Lifting: the machine's nose tilting upward, and — his head over the edge, looking down — the ground already some considerable distance below and receding fast. The Camel looked like a toy down there; the headless train, too, could have been a Hornby product. Midgets were straggling back towards it through the gap in the fence, although a few still stood there with their heads back, staring up.

'How's it feel, Cowan?'

'God, it's — I don't know, it's—'

'Words fail you, huh?' The wings tilted as he began to bring the machine round to the course of west-south-west. Canadian voice coming again through the flexible, metal-bound communication tube: 'Don't see any cavalry, do you?'

'Don't see much at all.'

'Well, try identifying features on the ground. Takes practice. Goggles need getting used to, too. If the *letuchka*'s there it's going to be up to you to spot it, see.'

'Right.'

'Won't be this much shindy, once we level out.'

Bewildering. Could *not* be happening. But *was*. Over the high ground that was shown brown on the map; and the railway tracks which led westward at this point were right below them. Leading slightly to the right, a five- or ten-degree divergence which suggested that Scott had her pretty well on course now. Still climbing, over the snow-bound Ukraine.

9

Just minutes ago Scott had told him through the tube, 'Getting close to the deadline' — deadline meaning turn for home, finish — and with that threatening-looking sky in the east you couldn't have blamed him if he'd cut it even shorter. Thank God, he hadn't. Bob had his head over the side in a rush of wind like steel flails, making sure before he spoke that he wasn't suffering from an attack of red crosses before the eyes.

Back astern there — unless you'd put it down to blurred goggles and wishful thinking . . .

But those *were* red crosses.

'Scott. Seven o'clock. Red crosses on tents. See that bridge over the river? Between that and the railway line.'

Silence — inside the helmet. Outside, a roaring that could have been the sound of the world spinning on its axis . . . Then inside the cocoon, Scott's growled answer to that unvoiced question: 'Must be stone blind . . .'

'Can you get down there?'

'Let's take a look. But — why not . . .'

Wings tilting against low grey cloud, nose up but the machine beginning to drop down from four thousand feet, a part-closing of the throttle achieving this, engine-note a lower rumble but the wind screaming in struts and wires while the ground down there swivelled, confusing sense of direction — sense of reality even — and his brain warned him that either it wouldn't be the right *letuchka* or the governess girls would have left it a week ago. The ground's re-alignment slowed and rested. The tents with the red crosses on them were several miles away but on this other side now, and beyond them was the curve of ice-bound river with its bridge — tiny, from this distance — and the snow-rutted road which you could only see or imagine you could see — because you knew it was there, and because otherwise the bridge *wouldn't* be — leading from it to some kind of railway crossing. Scott was easing his stick back, opening his throttle again as he levelled out at about two thousand feet and applied right rudder — putting the scarlet pinpoints of crosses out of sight for a few seconds before they reappeared on the left side.

Mary Pilkington, Katherine Reid?

Scott's mutter — a response to telepathic communication, maybe — 'Guess it's them, all right.'

'Certainly it's a *letuchka*, but—'

'Two to one on. Right area, huh? But we flew over just about here before, damn it. How come—'

'A bit to the north, surely.'

'Not all *that*—' He'd stopped. 'Hold on. Farmstead or somesuch at three o'clock. See? *See?*'

A big farmstead — or small hamlet — down on the right, with woods encircling it to the west and north. Something like six or seven miles from the *letuchka* — and there was a lot of activity around it. Men running — to horses, a swirling herd of them in a yard between the buildings: the picture began to revolve as the port wings dipped and the nose angled downwards. Scott's growl: 'Too close to your friends for comfort. If they're what they look like.' His head was out to the left — the side the Vickers gun was fixed — while he brought her down to about fifteen hundred feet. Or less: *much* less, probably. And still diving. Below them men were still converging on that yard where the horses were charging around as if they thought they were in a circus ring ... Now, surprisingly, rifles popping — small puffs drew the eye to them, and that meant bullets coming, reminded one of how flimsy this structure was. Not, surely, that one would be in range of them — yet ... Except that Scott was jamming on rudder to jink his machine away: as proof that he hadn't done it any too soon, a bullet ripped through the fabric of the lower wing. More of them doubtless singing past —

but in the space of those few seconds that was the one you noticed. He'd side-slipped, was now in a tight, climbing turn to starboard, with a revolving bird's-eye view down there astern of — God knew what, but there must have been twelve or fifteen horses and at least that many men.

Reversing the turn. Banking left. A snipe might have admired the last half-minute's jinking.

'Budyonny scouts, I'd guess.'

'What's our height now?'

'Huh?' A pause, then the double-take: 'Oh. Four hundred. We *were* at two-fifty ... Scouting troop, for sure.' The wings were levelling. 'Listen. I'm putting some distance behind us, then I'll follow contours around and set down beside the *letuchka*. Then, you'd better move twice as quick as you thought you would.'

They'd have seen the RAF markings before they'd opened fire. So there was no doubt which side they were on. Probably no Red Air Force in these skies anyway. But so damn close to the *letuchka*: he wondered whether either knew of the other's presence. Or whether that crowd would respect the red cross. It would depend on the individual commander, he guessed, but the Bolsheviks weren't exactly famous for their respect of international conventions.

With some distance behind him — *some* — Scott was easing her down closer to the ground again. From about five hundred feet, say, steadily losing height, and bumping a little, now. There were trees off to the left, a long straggle of them extending from the thickly-wooded area to the north of the farmstead. They seemed to be more or less in profile. So you were at treetop height. Circling right. *Bloody* low ... Nothing to do but shut your mind to it, cling to blind faith in the man up front — who presumably knew what he was doing. But guessing at it — well — a circular route, more or less, to the *letuchka*: and staying this low because if he'd been much higher the rifle-happy Bolsheviks might have seen the 'plane when it went down again, wondered what for and ridden out to have a look. Instead of just passing out of their sight at low level.

That would be it, near enough ... Searching for the *le-tuchka* now. Imagining Nurses Reid and Pilkington seeing the roundels on the wings and hugging each other, jumping up and down with excitement ...

Except that it was distinctly possible that they weren't even within two hundred miles — and perhaps better if they weren't, with cavalry scouts so close and the presence of that small troop surely presaging the arrival of larger forces; and when one's own feeble contribution was going to be *Start walking, girls* ...

'Cowan, you hearing me?'

'Yes—'

Flying over trees now, the trees seeming to topple over in swathes as the 'plane raced over them. Scott explaining, 'Holding this course to the railway tracks, see, then I'll turn up that side of 'em and put her down on the far side of the road. Should be all right for take-off from there, after you've had your two minutes flat with 'em.'

He grunted. Deliberately not rising to that. Looking down over the side as the last of the trees flashed back astern. Skimming low over level, snow-covered steppe-land now with a line of telegraph posts marking the railway line ahead at right-angles across this line of flight. Nose lifting, and Scott's mutter inside the helmet, 'Should've brought a bomb-load. Put those characters to rights if we had bombs.' Low-voiced, quite possibly talking to himself: it sounded like it, that kind of mutter. At something like two hundred feet now, with the railway just ahead, starboard rudder coming on and the parallel steel lines beginning to swivel anti-clockwise. Scott continuing his soliloquy: 'Thought I'd have no use for 'em. Save weight. Can't always guess right. Damn shame though.' Still on about bombs: and he'd probably been explaining himself to his passenger, not to himself. Bob guessing — reading between the lines — that if he'd had his load of bombs he could have used them because that would have amounted to obliteration, whereas shooting-up a few men and/or horses would only have stirred up the hornets' nest.

The railway tracks were steadying from their swing — like some huge compass needle settling, down there on the right.

'Here we go.'

Nose up — surprisingly. But engine-sound right down, as he throttled back and the ground swam up towards them. Bob couldn't see the tents, but they had to be somewhere close ahead.

'Hold tight.'

'Bet your life.'

'May be a little rough ...'

He'd pulled his stick back, the wheels touched, then the engine roared as he opened up for taxi-ing. Tremendous jolting. Mud, ice and stones flying back. Bob keeping his head down, but still managing to look out: catching a glimpse of a red cross on dirty-looking canvas, then — surprisingly, one more surprise in a whole succession of them — a horse rearing with a man hanging on to its head, his boots well clear of the ground. Other figures here and there appeared and disappeared like snapshots while a silly little jingle ran repetitively through his mind to the drumbeat rhythm of the wheels' slowing and lessening impact on ridged, hard-frozen ground: *Mary Pilkington, Katherine Reid* ...

'All right, back there?'

'Scott, listen. I *must* have time to talk to these people. Even if it's not the right bunch, they may know where—'

'Just don't *waste* time. Helmets off now.'

The engine's last rumbles had ceased, and the machine itself came to rest. Flat, dismal-looking surroundings abruptly static: telegraph posts starkly black receding into grey, frozen distance. He'd wrenched his helmet off and was turning to look back towards the tents when a male voice called in Russian, 'Are you all right?' The man who'd shouted was loping towards the aeroplane. Bob waved, then he had a leg over the side, probing with the toe of his boot for the first of two cut-away steps. Scott, also in the process of dismounting, told him, 'I'll take your place there at the Lewis.'

On the ground, in a shambling trot to meet the man from the *letuchka*, he thought about this and realized his replacement by Scott must be a routine precaution. There'd be sense in it, probably, not to risk being taken by surprise. If the *letuchka* were full of Bolsheviks, for instance: or if those horsemen, or others like them—

'*Royal Air Force?*'

Russian-accented English. A wide-faced, square-built man of about — forty, perhaps. Grey-black moustache, grey also at the temples and a sprinkling of it in the stubble on his cheeks. Cavalry boots showed under the skirts of his overcoat, on the outside of which he wore a revolver on a belt with a diagonal shoulder-strap to take its weight. Fur *shapka* pulled low on the broad forehead, over wide but slightly slitted eyes. No insignia either of rank or unit. A doctor? But they didn't go armed, surely. He didn't have the look of one, anyway. He looked — behind that rather formal manner — as hard as nails.

Bob had told him, in answer to that question, 'Actually, Royal Navy.'

A cold, hard stare ... 'You've come here to make jokes?'

'My name is Cowan — Lieutenant-Commander, Royal Naval Reserve. I'm only a passenger — but yes, it's an RAF machine.'

'I beg your pardon, Commander. Schelokov. Boris Vasil'ich Schelokov.' He bowed slightly. He was a few inches shorter than Bob. 'May I ask what—'

'May *I* ask first, is this *Letuchka syem*?'

'It is — as it happens — but—'

'Are there two English nurses here?'

'Oh. You've come for *them*.' He swung round as another male called from the direction of the tents — a man standing slightly apart from others who'd gathered there — 'Boris Vasil'ich, what's it about?'

'Just one moment.' He told Bob, 'That's the doctor. Come — please ... But listen, are you aware there are Bolshevik cavalry in this area?'

'We know it *now*, all right. They shot at us — when we

flew over a farmstead nine or ten versts from here. Is there more than one group of them?'

'I couldn't say. We only know of them from a man who came in yesterday. He'd seen them from some wood where he was hiding for several days, he said. But this has decided us to get out — while the going's good, as they say. Could be a good time to take your English girls, at that ... Intending to fly off with them, are you?'

'Can't, unfortunately. No room. Best thing would be if they could get to Debaltsevo — where I could meet them and take them on. Perhaps *you* could take them that far ... Are *you* a doctor?'

'No — just a hanger-on. Soldier, of sorts. Had the rank of major — acting colonel once, for three days — but since then I've served as private, corporal and sergeant.' He shrugged. 'Take your choice.'

'I'll settle for major.'

'As you wish. A private soldier has better chances of survival, though, these days.'

'Yes. I suppose ... But — second question — have there been any trains through on this line?'

'One — a few days ago. We put our wounded on it. It seemed natural to assume there'd be others, but so far—' he shook his head — 'No such luck. We're preparing now to set off with the carts, making for Ekaterinoslav ... Where did you fly from?'

'Kupyansk. An hour's flight, bit less.'

'Merciful God — just *one hour* ... And are there trains on the line south from there?'

'At the moment. At least there've been quite a few hospital trains, in the last few days.'

They were face to face with this other man now: a stooped figure, in the obligatory heavy overcoat and fur hat, only a triangle of very pale, black-stubbled face visible between the turned-up peaks of the coat's collar. Schclokov introduced him and then the others, as they closed in to the waiting group: 'Doctor Aleksei Markov — who's lucky to be alive. He had typhus. Our matron and the *sestritsi* whom you want to take away pulled him through it ... Doctor — and ladies — this is Commander — Kaun, did you say?'

'Cowan. Robert Aleksandr'ich Cowan.' He'd shaken the doctor's hand. Schelokov continuing with introductions: 'Our matron — *Mamasha* — Liza Sokolova.' A tall woman, wisps of grey hair visible, deepset brown eyes: Bob held her long, bony hand for a moment. Then another nurse, also middle-aged, whom they all called Annushka; and finally the two English girls — one rather small and the other larger, both shapeless in bulky army greatcoats, Schelokov introduced the little one first: 'This is Katya. And this, Maria ... Ah — Maria Peel-king-ton. And Katya is Ridd.'

'Reid.'

'*Tochno.* Exactly.' Half-smiling as he looked at her. Avuncular: or a regard that might have reflected the thought *If only I were ten years younger* ... There'd been a touch of sadness a minute ago, too, in that *whom you want to take away* ... 'Commander Cowan is of the *Britanskii Korolyevskii Flot,* ladies.'

'*Navy?*'

Katya glanced at her friend. 'What did you *think* that uniform was, silly?'

Laughing ... She was rather pretty, from as much as one could see. Dark hair, and very light blue eyes; and a small, well-shaped nose ... He explained to her and the other girl, in English, 'I'm in a staff job, based at Constantinople. I talk Russian so I'm the man they send out on errands. And you see, your parents have been — er — making enquiries—'

'Making a great hullabaloo, d'you mean?'

Smiling: and Mary was laughing, displaying rather large teeth. Hazel eyes, turned-up nose with freckles on it: one could well imagine her as a children's nanny. He nodded: 'I dare say. They're worried for you, anyway, want you home. But we thought you were in the Crimea, and I was sent to Sevastopol to winkle you out, and — well, cutting it short the RAF very kindly offered to fly me over here to see if we could spot you. Snags being (a) that the RAF

detachment is sitting on a train at Kupyansk and may pull
out at any moment — Red cavalry supposed to be
encircling the place within a day or so, we're told — and
(b) this aeroplane only has room for the pilot in his
cockpit and me in the other. What it all boils down to is
the best solution would be for you to get yourselves to
Debaltsevo.'

'Debaltsevo.' Katya frowned. 'We've been rather hoping
to get on *some* train — all of us — but—'

'Major Schelokov just told me.'

'Not one single train on this line since — oh, four or five
days ago.' Mary Pilkington seemed to have taken over. 'In
any case — well, until the last few days — we've been
concentrating on getting Doctor Markov back on his feet.
But also — *mostly*, I suppose — waiting for — oh, I should
have mentioned, we did at least get our patients away on
that one train, which was *something*, to say the least — but
we've been *hoping*—'

Katya cut in again — they would have set up the
letuchka in Karlovka, except for 'this typhus thing' ...
Typhus in Karlovka, or Dr Markov's — it wasn't clear,
didn't matter — but because of it they'd established themselves here in the open, had put up a spare tent every
morning right on the railway crossing with its red cross
clearly visible to the driver of any approaching train ...
'Then yesterday this wounded artilleryman — he had a
shell-splinter in his knee, Doctor Markov got it out for
him — no anaesthetic, if you please, and the very last drop
of our peroxide — anyway, he told us he'd been in hiding
in the woods up there and he's seen Bolshevik cavalry
detachments several times. And sooner or later you can
bet they'd find *us*. So we've decided — that's to say Doctor
Markov and the Major decided — we'll start trekking
towards Ekaterinoslav, rather than wait longer in the hope
of a train. We've started packing up, in fact.'

'Except for this one man you've no patients now?'

'Two. That one and a boy who didn't want to go on the
train — screamed blue murder, so we kept him. He's just
— shellshocked ... But just as well we got all the rest

away, we've really nothing left — no drugs, not even sterile dressings or iodine or—'

He asked the doctor, 'Why Ekaterinoslav?'

'Because it's our base. Base hospital, this division's headquarters.'

'But wouldn't you agree that with the Poltava flank turned — as it must be, or damn soon *will* be, now they've broken through at Kharkov—'

'You think the direction of Debaltsevo would be better?'

'Yes, I do. I know it's a long haul, but there still might be a train and you might get on it. It's the direct route to Rostov, too, and on to Novorossisk — which is now the only port available for embarkation, evacuation to the Crimea for instance. And the area's still in White hands, after all. But also — I was just saying, to these girls — I could get down from Kupyansk to Debaltsevo to meet them. In fact from there I might be able to organize a train — if I knew you were coming down along this line?'

Schelokov murmured, 'Man's talking sense.'

'You'll be travelling in your own carts, I gather.' Looking past the groups of tents he could see three carts and three hobbled horses; also some person dragging a tarpaulin cover off one of the carts. He nodded in that direction: 'Who's that?'

'The Tartar driver.' Schelokov told him, 'The *letuchka* had two, but we sent one off with another cart loaded with wounded some time ago. *I*'m second coachman now.'

'So — three men and four women. Plus the two wounded.' He was looking at the carts. Thinking of the distance they had to cover, and of Budyonny's encircling cavalry, and this small party protected only by one able-bodied though middle-aged male: the doctor being still convalescent, and the Tartar not counting for all that much, in terms of dependability.

'And you have that *fourgon* and — two *dvukolki*?'

'Yes.' Schelokov nodded. 'I see the question in your mind. The answer is that one of these young ladies will also drive. They can take it in turn, in fact. They've had some practice, they're both competent. And when he's stronger I imagine that Doctor Markov—'

'Oh, I'm strong enough right now!'

'No, doctor, you are *not*.' The matron turned to Bob. 'I think it should be explained that we've had another reason for waiting here, namely the hope that *Letuchka* number four would be withdrawing in this direction and we could join up together. The reason for this in the first place being that soon after we got here Dr Markov became ill, and it was the course *he* urged on me. Before he became incoherent, and in the full expectation that he would die, he foresaw our predicament — a *letuchka* without a doctor, and in all this chaos and confusion ... If we could join up with *Letuchka chetiri* — who'd replaced us at Bogodukhov in the front line when we were moved back to Valki, we'd been with them several days and we'd all come to know each other — well, it seemed a very good solution. Although in the event it hasn't happened. Nobody knows *what*'s been happening, up there ...'

Checking the time ... 'But you had reason to believe they'd have been falling back this way.'

'You see, during the time we were at Valki we lost contact with our base at Ekaterinoslav. Supplies then came to us from the Army in Kharkov: orders too, and in this instance they sent a young man on horseback to tell us to retreat again, and that again *Letuchka* number four would take our place. Orders had been sent to them as well, at Bogodukhov. As well they *might* have — the way things were going by then ... So, we moved — with our carts packed to their brims, taking every wounded man who had some chance. Including some whom Boris Vasil'-ich had brought to us.' She glanced at Schelokov. 'He'd come just before this — fortunately with his own trans-port. Otherwise—'

The doctor put in quietly. '*Letuchki* have been obliged to abandon their wounded before this, Liza Pavlovna.'

'The point I'm making is that we did *not*.'

'Except for the hopeless cases.'

'Yes. I *said* that. Although if *Letuchka chetiri* weren't too long in getting there after we left—'

'They'd have had graves to dig, as well as latrines.' He shrugged. 'At least the wolves couldn't have got at them, this time. Our dear friends and colleagues, the wolves ...'

'I think you should rest, doctor. Go inside, lie down. You're *not* strong yet — not by a long chalk — and we'll be travelling all night, remember.'

He'd turned away. Muttering, 'I can sleep in the cart.'

'Annushka.' The matron signalled with her head, and the other nurse nodded, went over to the doctor and took his arm, murmuring to him. The matron called, 'Please, Aleksei Mikhail'ich. For *all* our sakes.' She looked back at Bob. 'I only want you to understand why we've waited here this long. In case the question should be asked — you'd be in a position to explain ... At first it was for our own benefit — the prospect of having no doctor — but more recently it's been very much more our concern for *them*. What state they might be in when they *did* get here — or they could be prisoners, even, or — well, God help them ...'

'Yes.' He nodded. 'God help them.'

What she was really expressing, he realized, was her own sense of guilt in having to start out tonight without this other team. She was saying *God help them because we can't, now* ... While in his own mind another question nudged the surface — out of this concept of prevailing chaos, groups of people lost ... 'I don't suppose — by any chance — not in that *letuchka* but in any other, or for that matter in your hospital at Ekaterinoslav — you wouldn't I suppose have known someone—'

He let the question fade. The Tartar had come over to Dr Markov with some long complaint or argument; Schelokov had stepped in there now, but the matron had been visibly distracted. And meanwhile one was conscious of having spent too long here already: Sam Scott would be — to put it mildly — getting restive. All one needed now, in fact, was agreement on making a rendezvous at or near Debaltsevo; the rest of this was time-wasting.

Schelokov came back to them. 'Fellow can't tolerate the

idea of leaving so much food behind.'

'Oh, was that it?' The matron nodded. 'He does have a point. When half the population's starving.' She turned back to Bob. 'You were asking me — would I have known whom?'

'A nurse by name of Nadia — well, she's *now* Nadia Solovyeva—'

'Of course!' Her face had lit up ... 'In *Letuchka chetiri* — she and her sister-in-law Irina — the very people we've been discussing!' Looking round at the others: 'This *Anglichan* drops on us out of the sky, and he knows our poor darling Nadia!'

'Why d'you say—'

Schelokov cut in: 'You've mentioned her before ... Wasn't she the Princess Egorova, before her marriage?'

'Why, yes—'

'*You* know her too?'

He shook his head. 'My parents knew hers. Years ago. Then Liza Pavlovna here mentioned her and her sister-in-law recently, I wondered then ...'

Bob looked back at the matron. 'Why did you say *poor* darling Nadia, what's—'

'Oh. You didn't hear.' Her eyes had closed as she crossed herself. 'Oh, dear. How *very* sad it is ...' Katya — Katherine — touched Bob's sleeve, told him quietly in English as he turned to her, 'The husband was killed, up on that front.'

Looking back on it afterwards, it seemed to have been a time less of decision than of reaction. Almost like waking suddenly from a long sleep — waking late, so there was this immediate, driving urgency — and no need to decide on what had to be done because that decision had already been taken — somehow, at some earlier stage ... The only problems that needed to be sorted out — at once, and largely by blundering right through them — were questions of detail and how best — quickest — to have everyone else recognize and accept the situation as it was.

Scott in particular, of course. But lack of time was to

one's advantage. And that murky sky — a threatening backdrop to the fact there wasn't much more than an hour of daylight left. Scott wasn't going to stay on the ground a minute longer than he had to.

The girls were easy. And the matron, naturally quick in her grasp of essentials, agreed instantly. Doctor Markov was obviously pleased, though puzzled by the sudden change of plan. While Schelokov seemed to take it for granted, as if it was what he'd have done in any case.

Which left only Scott.

He'd seen them coming, and was climbing out of the observer's cockpit. Bob, Schelokov and the two girls, each of whom had a bundle of personal essentials gathered hurriedly from their tent, Bob telling them as they ran towards the aeroplane — Scott was in his own cockpit by this time, standing, shouting at Bob for God's sake to get a bloody move on — telling the girls, 'The man who sent me to find you is Colonel Temple, Royal Marines, Staff Officer (Intelligence) on our naval staff in Constantinople. When you get to Novorossisk all you need do is identify yourselves to any RN ship's captain and ask him to contact Temple. One exchange of signals and you're home and dry.'

Schelokov added, trotting along beside them, 'And in England all the church bells will start ringing, huh?'

'You've been so kind to us, Boris Vasil'ich.' Mary, smiling at him as she ran. '*So* grateful.'

'*Nye za shto* ... You were more than kind to *me* — remember?'

Katherine panted, 'Perhaps we'll see you at Novorossisk. Or somewhere.'

'Somewhere better than that, I hope, Kate. London, Boris?'

'Yes.' Katherine again. 'Somewhere where people don't keep dying all the time.'

'I'm going with *him*, Katya.'

Bob glanced at the Russian: thinking he might have misheard, or misunderstood. Schelokov adding, 'But still, perhaps one day—'

Scott bawled, 'Cowan, for Christ's *sake*, man—'

'Sorry.' They were at the 'plane: the girls breathless from exertion and excitement, Scott glaring down at Bob. He panted, ' *Very* sorry, Scott. Fact is—'

'You've got to swing this damn thing for me — remember?'

'Yes. Right.' Standing below the cockpit, looking up at him. 'But I'm not going back with you. So these two girls *can* — right?'

'Have you gone raving mad?'

'Scott.' He pointed northward. 'There's another *letuchka* — people I know—'

'I don't *believe* this!'

'These two *must* be got out, Scott. Those were Bolshe- viks just down the road there — huh? And it's a deuce of a long way to Debaltsevo — with the cavalry encirclement in progress. All very well just hoping for the best when there was nothing else we could do — but now there *is* . . . Look, you need to get started *now* — right?'

'So how on earth will *you*—'

'Come on, Mary. Take a hold there. Foot in here. That's it. Then — here . . . Well done — now climb in.' He'd taken her bundle from her, took Katherine's as well now. 'Up you go, Katherine. I'll hand these up. Squeeze in as best you can — and there's a strap . . . That's the way . . .'

'How do we ever thank you, Commander?'

'You don't . . . Listen, this man in front is Major Sam Scott. Doesn't sound very friendly at the moment, but he'll see you through all right. Oh, one of you better wear that helmet, so he can talk to you, and vice versa . . . Scott, be a good fellow, show them?'

'Be a good fellow, he says. Damn four-flushing . . .'

The protest tailed off. He was standing in his cockpit, leaning over to help the girls install themselves. Bob called up, 'It all fits, Scott. If you'd think about it. This *letuchka's* moving out tonight in horse-drawn carts. They'll probably head along the line for Debaltsevo, and if you find your- self in a position to have a train sent up to meet them, they'll bless you for it. And listen — this other *letuchka* —

remember the yarn I spun about the girl who married the count? Well, *she*'s there — way up in what's effectively Bolshevik territory now — and her husband's been killed. So — I don't have any option ... Well, *do* I?'

Scott was sitting, now, staring down at him. He nodded. 'Good luck.'

'Thanks. Same to you. Ready for start-up?'

'Of *course* I'm bloody ready!'

'Right—'

'Wait. She may start just on a swing, but thanks to the time you've had me waiting she's not exactly warm now, may need the full routine. So try it, but if she doesn't fire the first time—'

'All right.'

He ducked round to the front, set his feet carefully as he'd been taught, put his hands on the prop and turned it until he felt the compression.

'Contact!'

'Contact ...'

He flung it round, the engine fired immediately and he stepped back, dodged aside as Scott opened his throttle and the machine lurched forward. Scott pulling his helmet on and then raising one gloved hand, thumb up, and the two girls waving frantically. Schelokov was beside him. The machine's tail swung as Scott straightened for his take-off parallel to the railway tracks. Throttle wide open, then, and a roar of power. Rolling forward slowly at first, but speed building fast. It didn't look too bad from here, but recent experience told him what those girls would be feeling — like twin steam-hammers, more or less — until he'd got her really skimming.

Tail up. And — lifting ...

He hoped to God the weather wouldn't close in before Scott got them back. And that he'd make it before dark. The arrival at Kupyansk would be something worth witnessing. You could just see it. Kinkead and most of the other pilots — including Jim Davies — expecting one outsize RN lieutenant-commander and receiving instead two rather pretty girls.

He'd been waving; he lowered his arm now and asked Schelokov, 'Did you say something about going with me?'

The Russian kept his slitted eyes on the departing 'plane. 'You object?'

'Not at all. I'd be very glad to have your company. But — why, just because your family knew hers?'

'Put it this way.' They were both still watching the bomber as, steadily gaining height, it banked round through north towards the east. Schelokov said, '*You* are concerned for them — or anyway for *her* — and you must know damn well that getting up there won't be any joyride. And you're an Englishman.'

'My father was a Scot, and my mother was Russian.'

'Delighted to hear it. But effectively, you're British. That uniform you're wearing ... Incidentally you'd better get rid of it. There's a ragbag of clothing here. Men come in dressed in rags or soaked in blood, they have to be kitted out.'

'All right. You were saying?'

'You're an outsider — truly, if you'll forgive my saying so — and ready to involve yourself. But I'm Russian, you might say fractionally responsible for the mess we have here. And there is the — parental connection, from way back, one does feel — some slight obligation ... A small factor, but it's there. My people are dead, incidentally.'

'Hers too.'

'Murdered?'

'Yes. I don't know any details, she only mentioned once—'

'The details tend to be abhorrent. Better *not* know ... But on a more positive aspect — well, these *letuchka* nurses and doctors have been risking their lives for ours, after all.'

'Yes ... D'you think these will get through all right?'

'With luck. Please God. In present circumstances, nobody's safety can be guaranteed, Commander. They're much better placed than the people we're going up to find, that's all.'

'Travel in the dark, will they?'

'Yes. We should do the same, I suggest.'

The 'plane had gone out of sight. Bob agreed, 'Whatever you say. If I'm to have the benefit of your advice and military experience, I'd be a fool not to accept it.' They'd started back towards the tents. 'Have you been with this *letuchka* out of the same kind of concern you now feel for the others?'

'Well, when they were at Valki I brought a party of our wounded to them. This was in my sergeant's role. As it happens, I'd been slightly hurt myself. This ...' He put a hand up, opened the collar of his greatcoat. There was a gouge in the flesh, scar-tissue still raw-looking, along the side of his jaw, under that ear and creasing through the grey hair on his neck. He folded the collar back, covering it. 'One bullet in this shoulder too. It was a machine-gun that did it. I wasn't using the arm on this side much, but this up here was the awkward one, I couldn't speak well.' Touching the swell of his jaw ... 'Anyway, I had a platoon of fifteen men, all walking-wounded, with stretchers and a cart we'd commandeered, and we brought these much worse cases to them. We should then have returned — after getting ourselves more or less patched up — to what at that time was still referred to as the front, but—'

'Just a minute — while I think of it — why did you bring them to this *letuchka* when the other — number four — would've been closer? Or wasn't it?'

A sideways glance: 'D'you have a map in your head?'

'Not at all. But I can envisage *that* part.'

'D'you have a map at all?'

'Unfortunately not.'

'Nor have I ... Anyway — the answer to that question is we're talking about a different section of the front. We'd come from midway between Kharkov and Poltava, and this was the nearest, at Valki. There wasn't any real front by then, in that area. We were still holding the bastards but the situation was what they call "fluid" — holding our ground in spots but not in others, you might say. The hope was to hold them up long enough for a major regrouping to take place behind us. Anyway — my platoon with their

minor injuries refused to come back to the fighting.
Having got so far, they preferred to keep going.' He
shrugged. 'We're used to that sort of thing by now, of
course. Or should be. Personally I'm not, never will be. I
was at the Nicholas Cavalry School at St Petersburg, for
some years of my youth — if you've heard of it—'

'Of course. I spent my own childhood in St Petersburg.'

'So. To cavalrymen it's known — was — as "the Glorious School" ... And from it I went to — well, to a particularly famous cavalry regiment. I'm not prepared to
mention its name — ever. It simply — disintegrated, after
the Revolution in '17. Men whom one had trusted with
one's life just — rode away. The work of trained agitators,
of course, preying on simple minds. Perhaps we hadn't
realized quite *how* simple. Or we realized but gave insuffi-
cient thought to it.' He shook his head. 'Now, I believe
more clearly than ever that there are circumstances in
which a man can no longer justify the preservation of his
life, even when it's in his power — and on the face of it
legitimate — to do so. It doesn't have to be an emotional
thing. Simply a matter of balancing values against each
other. You could take this as a little more of my explanation to you, I suppose. Anyway — what I was telling
you—'

'Your men deserted.'

'Yes. And I stayed with the *letuchka* at first because I
did need treatment for these scratches and then because it
was in a very dangerous situation, and both Dr Markov
and Liza Pavlovna — well, in particular, those two young
girls appeared so — so *extremely* vulnerable. You'll understand, if you know our Bolshevik friends and their little
ways. I stayed, anyway.' He stopped, short of the tents.
Annushka was at the bigger of the carts, loading bedding
into it, but the others weren't in sight. 'I hope I've now
accounted for myself well enough, Commander. Would
you in turn care to explain your — well, your solicitude for
Nadia Solovyeva?'

He thought about it for a moment. Then nodded. 'Well,
Boris Vasil'ich — last year I was with our Royal Naval

flotilla on the Caspian, and I became involved with Count Solovyev in a mission to get Nadia Egorova as she was then and Solovyev's sister Irina away from a place called Enotayevsk, where they'd been in hiding. We did manage to get them out, and in the course of it I came to know them quite well. Then later I heard from Nadia that she'd married Nick Solovyev.'

'Was that a surprise to you?'

That hard stare again. Bob told him, 'Not entirely. There'd been talk of an engagement, although when I was with them I think she hadn't made her mind up.'

'Then she — what, wrote to inform you—'

'Yes.'

'I believe I understand.'

'Understand *what*?'

'Oh.' A shrug. 'Don't be offended. But as you implied yourself, it's as well to comprehend each other's motives. And your reaction when they told you — as if you'd swallowed a cat . . .'

'Solicitude' was some word for it, he thought. Nothing like any word he'd have chosen himself, to describe what he'd felt for her since about the day after he first set eyes on her.

Although one *did* of course feel solicitous for her, in this context. Knowing how hard she'd take it. Having committed herself, made the decision and married Nick Solovyev, committal would have been total, grief now as shattering as if she'd been genuinely in love with him.

He didn't believe she could have been. For various reasons, but one memory that had stuck and tended to come to mind whenever he'd pondered this question was of a whispered conversation across a kitchen table in Enotayevsk: Nadia talking about Nikolai and Irina Solovyev, telling him, 'They're a little crazy, you know. I'd never realized before.' He'd then asked her, 'But you're going to marry him?', and she'd shrugged, murmured, '*He* believes so. All I've ever promised is I won't marry anyone else until these horrors are over.'

But she *had* married him. And having taken the decision, she'd have put all that ambivalence out of her mind and probably out of memory too. Especially as his widow, when he'd died fighting for everything that he and she believed in. The fact she'd ever hedged her bet would have no more relevance than some long-forgotten dream might have. And you'd have to adopt that view of things yourself. Give her the protection and whatever else she'd need, let the rest take its course.

Get there, first. Just *get* to her.

10

'I hope you're not as despondent as you look, Commander.'

Markov was holding a match to the wick of an oil-lamp, and the glow of soft, sputtering light was illuminating Bob's face as well as gleaming yellowish on the tent's macintosh side. Daylight had been fading during the past half-hour, while they'd been eating stew out of tin plates with wooden spoons — except for the Tartar, who'd used the blunt, broken-nailed fingers of one hand, guzzling at it like an animal. Markov added, addressing the matron who was sitting bolt upright beside him on one of the canvas-covered, straw-filled pallets, 'Ought to have some vodka to cheer him up. Cheer us *all* up, eh?'

Bob told him, 'Believe it or not, I was counting my blessings. Thinking how lucky I am to have Boris Vasil'ich with me.'

'Lucky for you, certainly.' He had the lamp going now. 'Less so for us. *Much* less so ... But great heavens, if that's how you look when you're feeling *lucky*...'

What he'd actually been thinking at that moment had been that without Schelokov he might well have been biting off more than he could chew. The route, for a start — with no knowledge of the country and no map. And basic military skills — evading cavalry patrols, for instance ...

They were going to travel by night and lie-up by day. Travelling in a *dvukolki* since there was one to spare; Markov's reduced team couldn't have handled a second one as well as the larger *fourgon*. The *dvukolki*'s canvas hood had a red cross on it and nothing anyone could think of would remove that, in the time they had now; there was some discussion as to the dangers and illegality of travelling under false colours. Bob had proposed, 'Why shouldn't I tell the truth? I've come looking for some British girls, came to you — not here, I can be vague about the geography — and you lent me the cart.'

'Good.' Schelokov had nodded. 'Good. British and non-belligerent. Errand of mercy. They'll still shoot you in the back of the head and bury you in the forest, but—'

'What about you?'

'Ukrainian — deserted from Petlyura's rabble. Since then I've been working as a driver — came with the cart, so to speak.'

The doctor had nodded. 'Not bad.'

Bob said, 'So I won't need the Russian Army gear you were offering me, after all — since I'm going to be myself. The only thing I *would* like is to swap my cap for a warm hat.'

Much better …

They'd loaded the *dvukolki* with an assortment of gear selected by Schelokov. Bob thinking wrily while he was helping with it that if he'd been doing this on his own he'd have been setting off with virtually nothing but a pistol and ammunition in one pocket and a pipe and tobacco in the other. Now they had transport and a tent, tinned food, cooking equipment and other items including two Lee-Enfield rifles which had been left behind by Schelokov's own men when they'd deserted. Taking up more space than anything else was fodder for the horse — a shaggy little mare by name of Mishka.

Bob had asked him — supper had been in preparation, they'd been loading the bales of fodder — supposedly hay, but more like straw — 'Do we *need* rifles?'

A shrug … 'Be surprised if we didn't. Other factors apart, that's wolf country — potentially.'

'Ah — well.' He'd nodded. 'I see … But in general terms, Boris Vasil'ich, I'd like to have this clear — I want your company, and I value your help enormously. But I'm not setting out to fight Bolsheviks. As far as I'm concerned the object of the expedition is to find that *letuchka* and get them away — please God without shooting anyone — or being shot at.'

'The latter—' Schelokov agreed — '*I'm* in favour of.'

'Apart from anything else, you see, as a foreigner I've no damn *business*—'

'Half-Russian foreigner?'

'An officer of the Royal Navy — servant of the British Crown—'

'Of course. Of *course.*' Schelokov's hand gripped his shoulder. 'I was teasing you. Don't *worry*, Robert Aleksandr'ich ...'

Now, in the tent, he was reassuring Dr Markov — the doctor having expressed regret that he was going with Bob instead of staying with the *letuchka* — 'You'll be all right, Aleksei Mikhail'ich. Truly. You don't need me, from here on.'

'What about bandits?'

'Well.' He shrugged. 'Get *them* anywhere. Deserters foraging, is all most of them are. As you know, of course ... But we haven't been bothered by them here, have we? I rather doubt they'd interfere with a *letuchka* anywhere.'

'Surely that would depend how hungry ...'

Bob asked Schelokov, when he could get a word in, what the likely shape of things would be in the Valki area, and Markov chipped in, 'A great deal more dangerous than here. Why he's so set on going. *Letuchka chetiri*'s in a far worse situation than we are, so being the fire-eater he is—'

'Much the *same* as here.' Schelokov told him, frowning, 'And "fire-eater" be damned ...' Turning to Bob: 'Valki's only about thirty miles away, you know. All right, thirty miles is thirty miles, but—'

'The Reds won't be there in force yet, anyway.'

'In force — no ... As far as we know, they're still fighting in the Kharkov area — and around Poltava, supposedly. Those are the crucial centres, and for the time being this area's — well, back of the moon, you might say. Except for — infiltration, and as we were saying earlier there's bound to be an encircling movement by cavalry squadrons — which we haven't seen yet, so it'll be a *wide* encirclement. Closing the ring, then mopping up inside it while they regroup for the next push. Well, they might even drive straight on down the line to Rostov *now*. Depends on how much blood our lads have drawn. It hasn't been all one-sided, you know.'

Markov looked troubled. 'If they go straight for Rostov — well, good God, what chance have *we* of—'

'I only said they *might*. It's most unlikely. If I had to bet on it, I'd say you'll have left Rostov behind you a month before they'll have a *hope* of—'

'Please God. Because otherwise—'

'Forget it. Please. I spoke without thinking. Put it out of your mind, Aleksei Mikhail'ich ...' He turned back to Bob. 'The infiltration process — advance units occupying the villages, setting up Red Guard regimes, and so on — one of their priorities will be to round up recruits. Boys, and men who've deserted from one side or the other — mainly from ours, in the present state of affairs.'

'No questions asked?'

'Not many — if they volunteer. Meaning if they come quietly. Oh, some'll be for the chop — senior NCOs, for instance. And any officers or former officers — that goes without saying. But the rest — cannon-fodder is all they want. And they're strong on the indoctrination business, of course. It's also a fact that success such as they're having at the moment is a great persuader. Nine out of ten'll swear blind they've been bright red right from the start, once they're convinced they're going to win. Anyway — getting back to the point — they'll have taken over the villages, there'll be shootings and hangings, torturings and so forth. Red Guards are authorized to kill or torture as they consider appropriate, you know. They've even got a word for it now — *Samosud*. Meaning every man his own executioner. Oh, and the scouting troops will be out in the country looking for stocks of food or fodder — and transport — horses ... And hunting down fugitives like this fellow we have here.'

'What about the railway towns?'

'In this area that means Karlovka and Konstantinograd. I suppose when they've secured Poltava — which for all we know they may have done already —'

'They'll come down the railway.'

A nod. 'When they're ready.'

'The railways are vital.' Markov was adjusting the lamp's wick. 'Literally. When you look at a map, they're like the arteries in a body.'

'Not a bad analogy. Over these plains they're the only way you *can* move an army fast — and supply it, reinforce it and so forth. Also they carry the telegraph lines — when infiltrators or saboteurs haven't cut them. They have been, of course, keep doing it, that's why nobody ever knows what's going on ... But believe me, Aleksei Mikhail'ich, you'll be well away before their armoured trains come blasting down *this* line.'

'I *have* to believe you. Otherwise — well ...' The doctor pulled out a pocket-watch, tilted its face to the lamp — 'might as well die of typhus ... But right now — since minutes make hours and hours make days—'

'Yes. We should start.' The matron reacted quickly, as if she'd been thinking so for some while. 'Annushka, we'd better see to our patients.' She asked Schelokov, 'Are you setting out at the same time as we do?'

'Why not, *Mamasha*.' He leant back, pulled aside a flap of the tent and peered out. 'It'll be dark enough by the time we're on the road. And it's snowing. Good.' He looked round at the Tartar: 'Horses, my friend. Tents ...'

Half an hour later they were on their way, Schelokov driving the *dvukolki* and Bob on the bench beside him, wearing a fur *shapka* instead of his naval cap. The matron had promised she'd look after his cap for him, in the hope they might meet again — 'somewhere, some day ...' His own farewells with her and the others had been brief, but lengthy and emotional between them and Schelokov. Then with the Tartar driving the heavier cart, the *fourgon*, with the two wounded men and the nurse Annushka in it, and the matron handling the two-wheeler with Dr Markov as her passenger, the small cavalcade had trundled away, lurching over the road that linked the river bridge to the railway crossing, and then dwindling south-eastward, parallel to the tracks. Schelokov waited until they'd vanished from sight, into the gathering darkness and the blinding effect of snow driving almost horizontally on the icy north-east wind; then he flipped Mishka's reins, bumped the *dvukolki* down into the road and to the left, towards the crossing.

'All right, Robert Aleksandr'ich?'

'Fine. I'll gladly take over, when you like.'

'Yes. Later. But I'll tell you how we'll go now. After we cross the railway here we'll keep to the road until we have trees close on our left. Then we'll turn off that way, circle this end of the wood and turn up on the west side of it. That way we'll have the whole forest between us and the patrol who fired at you.'

'Should be sheltered on that side, too.'

'Perhaps. But we need it to snow, to cover our wheel-tracks. In fact that's very important, Robert Aleksandr'ich ... Peculiar first name you have, if I may say so.'

'There's no equivalent in Russian. But the short form in English is "Bob".'

'Bob. Easier to remember, at least.' He flipped the reins: 'Come along, Mishka. Pick your feet up, old dear ... Bob — those rifles you didn't think we'd need. Be a good fellow, get them out from behind you there, load them and put them down beside us?'

Dozing. Not having had all that much sleep lately. But with a whole day of sleep ahead — once they got to wherever ...

'You awake, Robert Aleksandr'ich — Bob, I should say?'

'Yes, what's—'

An arm out, across his face: 'Trees. See them? I'm going to turn off here. Whoa-up, Mishka ...'

It was still snowing. The trees were a dark mass on the

left, dark even in pitch darkness. The darkness was under the forest's overhang, of course — no more than fifty or even thirty yards ahead. Schelokov muttered, 'Here we go, then.' Pulling round to the left, Mishka's hooves scrabbling on the low bank and the cart lurching into the dip, then up and over. Schelokov talking to the horse meanwhile, a stream of flattery and encouragement.

'Not quite the sort of horsemanship they taught you at the Nicholas School, I imagine.'

A snort ... 'One learnt to ride a horse as if one was part of it. That was the main thing. Bookwork didn't take much of one's attention, I can tell you. Younkers, they called us. Cavalry language for cadets. When you were commissioned you became a cornet — second lieutenant is the equivalent. Riding a horse, use of swords and lances: and the very peak of it all was the mounted charge. The order was *Out swords, lances for the battle!* Nobody will ever hear *that* bellowed out again.'

'I suppose not.'

'We were outdated before the war even started. But we did some good work, for all that. Won some battles. *I've* led a charge, let me tell you — and there are damn few alive who have ... Latterly they had us fighting mostly on our feet, of course. Except for scouting, from time to time.'

There were trees on both sides now, and it was slower going over this uneven ground. Although the snow would have provided a cushioning effect, and the road hadn't been exactly a billiard-table. Schelokov added, 'You're quite right, though — from *that* to driving a bloody donkey-cart ... In the best of causes, mind you. But still ... Tell me this now, Bob. I understood about one word in five when you were explaining yourself to Katya and Maria — that you were sent from Constantinople to Sevastopol, then—'

'You talk English, then?'

'Understand, a little. Couldn't put more than three words together *into* English ... What I was about to ask, though — d'you have *carte blanche* to wander around rescuing this girl and that?'

'No. My job was to get those two out, that's all. Now I ought to be getting myself out — double-quick.'

'So — you'd say you were inadvertently delayed here for a while, is that it?'

'Haven't given a thought to it, to be honest ... But — yes, I suppose — *if* anyone demanded an explanation.'

'Which isn't likely, do you mean— or are you saying you don't give a damn?'

Meaning — now he came to think about it — well, the second proposition, really. The Everard Philosophy, you might call it. Remembering Everard's professed disregard of regulations and Admiralty approval — or rather *dis*approval.

He explained, 'Truth is, I'm due for release from the Navy almost any time now. Our war's finished, and it's all I joined for.'

'What'll you do, then? D'you have money — land, in England?'

'As it happens, I'll be going into business.'

'What sort of business?'

'Well, my father was an importer and exporter, and in shipping and marine insurance. In Russia — all his life. Made a success of it, and quite a lot of money.'

'Good for him — but he'll never see a rouble of it now!'

'*He* won't — I'm sorry to say — because he's dead. But years ago — after the 1905 revolution, to be exact — he decided to transfer all his assets and income to a company in Scotland. Investment company, based in Glasgow. Some lawyers there are looking after it at the moment.'

'So he saw the writing on the wall.'

'He saw it could happen again, yes.'

'And consequently you're a rich man?'

'There are considerable resources. So — great opportunities ... It'll be exciting.'

'Well. I congratulate you. Your father was a wise man and you're a lucky one. Everything to live for, eh?'

He hadn't discussed any of this with anyone. Not even with Nadia. But here — in a Russian forest in the middle of the night, probably because of the sense of isolation —

like being in some other world, talking about that other, utterly remote one ... And it meant more, now, *was* exciting — because there was the hope — expectation — of having her to share it with.

Schelokov added: 'We must try to ensure you do get back to it.'

When he woke next the cart had stopped. Schelokov had woken him.

'See there?'

The pinpoint of a fire, inside the wood. The mare had seen it too — having let her head droop, she'd now lifted her muzzle from the snow to gaze in that direction.

'Deserters' camp?'

'Or some of our friends in bivouac.'

'Wouldn't they have sentries posted?'

'Should — but there aren't any here. We'd have been challenged — or shot at.'

Silence for a minute. Watching and listening ... Then: 'Deserters, or some such. May as well push on.' Slap of the reins on Mishka's rump again ... Getting the cart started was the hardest work, of course. 'Good girl, good girl.' Glancing to the right again, at the flicker of firelight showing sporadically between the trees. '*Very* good girl. Pick of the bunch, you are, old dear ...'

'Shall I take over?'

'If you like. If you've slept enough.'

'Yes. Sorry — but I *was* tired.'

'Nothing to be sorry for.' Schelokov passed the reins to him. 'Keep the edge of the forest on our right. I don't know that I'll sleep, but if I do and you have any doubt of anything don't hesitate to wake me. Otherwise when you get to the top end of the woods. Then we'll decide whether to camp there or cross a few miles of open ground first.'

'How many nights like this one, would you think?'

'If it goes well — two, after this ... But listen — if it stops snowing, that's it, *we* stop. So wake me for that too.'

'Because of our wheel-tracks — if it stops snowing?'

'Exactly.'

'From that point of view, travelling by cart's not such a good idea, is it?'

'No. But even on foot one leaves tracks. And one has to weigh advantages against disadvantages. The main consideration as I see it is that we may have other people to bring back with us—'

'Oh — of course—'

'— and they may not all be fit. So transportation—'

'Of course ...'

A silence, except for the rumbling of the cart, and Mishka's plodding hooves. Then: 'Driven one of these before, have you?'

'I've driven pony-traps often enough. Much the same.'

It was heavier-feeling, that was all. Especially with all that fodder in it. But once the cart was rolling and when you weren't taking corners the weight made no difference — except maybe to Mishka, who'd no business to complain, when it was her own rations she was hauling.

Schelokov had reached down for the rifle on his side. He was holding it across his knees, clicking the safety-catch on and off, leaning forward to peer out into the curtain of quietly falling snow and the solid-black backdrop of the forest.

Bob lifted the reins, as Mishka stumbled. 'Hold up, girl ...' Now the cart's wheels hit it — left one first and then the other, lurching over. He asked Schelokov, 'What happens if we break a wheel?'

'Well — there's no spare. We *should* have sleds, of course.'

'That's what I mean.'

'So happens we don't. Unfortunate, this time of year, but — there you are ... We do have tools, though — and a sailor's supposed to be able to turn his hand to anything, isn't he?'

'I've heard the theory.'

'But — on the subject of eventualities generally, Bob — there's one thing I'd like to say to you.'

'Go ahead.'

'Speaking of bringing them back with us, as we were ...
Well, when we get near Valki, I can take you to the place
where Aleksei Markov's *letuchka* was, and it's where
Letuchka chetiri would have established themselves when
they arrived to take our place. Not in Valki itself, there
was typhus there — as there is now in most villages ... But
the point is, we can't expect to find them still in that
precise location. They'll have moved out — well, probably
southward, the way they were supposed to have been
withdrawing.'

'And in fact haven't.'

'As you say. But another aspect of it is that if they *are*
still in that vicinity it probably isn't because they *want* to
be.'

'You mean — for one reason or another they haven't
been able to move out.'

'Yes. And — it's none of my business, Bob, but it's
obvious you have some — some degree of — personal
involvement. I'm trying to forewarn you, therefore.'

'Not to count chickens.'

'Exactly. But I'm not just saying it — the plain truth is
they *should* have joined our friends down there quite a
while ago — and they haven't. But they can't have stayed
put either, so—'

'So — God knows ...' The cart listed heavily — the left
side crashing into a hole of some kind ... But it was all
right — wheel still on, still turning ... He muttered — with
his mind on Schelokov's warning, not on any cartwheel —
'Damn soon *will* need those tools out ...'

Schelokov had fallen asleep, after another half-hour or so
of intermittent conversation. Before he'd finally dropped
off they'd heard wolves baying, from some distance inside
the forest, and it had put Bob's mind back to Dr Markov's
somewhat cryptic remarks on the subject of *letuchki*
having to leave badly wounded men behind. The implication had seemed to be that he himself had been forced
to do so, much against his will. Schelokov had confirmed
this. Specifically that Markov had had no option but to

abandon some — having had no room for them in the *letuchka*'s carts, and no hope of saving their lives either — and in general terms that during the years of war wolves hadn't been hunted, so there were more of them than there'd ever been before.

He'd added, 'And they get lucky, sometimes ...'

He was slumped with his head back, now, swaying and jolting to the *dvukolki*'s erratic motion, with the rifle aslant between his knees. It was still snowing, and Mishka was getting sluggish. Hardly surprising: she'd been hauling this load for hours, and the snow wasn't exactly an aid to progress. She'd developed a side-to-side lurch like some old seadog's rolling gait; it could have been a form of protest. Plodding with her head low, harness creaking, the cart's wheels rumbling and a regular squeak on the offside now. Maybe there'd be something in the back there that would serve as lubrication, when they stopped. Might even be some hub grease: wouldn't be surprising, knowing Schelokov.

For whom, thank God. And for Sam Scott before him, for that matter. And Everard before *him*.

End of the wood?

This was rather like keeping a watch alone at sea: staying alert — eyes, ears and brain — to one's immediate surroundings while in the back of one's mind the thoughts ran on. Like background music that switched itself off at crucial moments ... And here, now, having noticed that the trees *were* thinning ... The same density off to the right, but that dark mass of them receding. The *dvukolki* had been continuing dead straight, he was certain, and to stay close to the forest's edge at this point would have meant hauling Mishka's head round.

Top end of the wood, therefore. *Had* to be, although one hadn't expected to come to it this soon.

He nudged Schelokov. 'Boris ...'

Galvanic movement: and the rifle seeming to levitate itself into its former action-ready position. 'Huh?'

'We're at the end of this stretch, I think.'

'Ah.' Upright, staring round ... 'Ah, *well* ...'

Wolf chorus back there again. If one had been alone — and on foot, as one would have been — that sound would have been fairly chilling.

'Mishka's tiring, Boris.'

'Never. Heart of a lion, our Mishka has. Endurance of an elephant. Besides which she's been eating her head off and done no work for weeks.' Schelokov grunted. 'You're right on this, though. North edge of this section. And still snowing, fortunately. Excellent ... So — well, wait just a minute ...' He ducked down, and after a moment's fumbling a match flared. A muttering down there ... 'Hour and a half of dark, yet. So — why not ...' The match had gone out, and he was pulling himself back up. 'Head *that* way, now. North-west, roughly. I've this field compass, d'you see. All we have to do is line Mishka up on north-west — like a boat, eh?'

'Right. Hard a-port.' Joking, in the wilderness. If you could call it joking. Making it a gentle turn anyway, for Mishka's convenience; while reflecting that if Schelokov really believed the chances were so slight, not only would he not have come himself, he'd have tried to dissuade anyone else from starting out.

It was a good thought to hang on to. The kind you needed.

Glancing at the dark profile beside him: 'Compass in your hand and a map in your head. I was thinking while you were asleep — where I'd be without you, God knows.'

'Oh, you'd have managed. But it's memory of the ground itself, not any map. And far from infallible, unfortunately. Might've paid more attention if I'd known I'd be coming back. All right this far, but later ... Well, as it happens there's a small river — tributary of the Vorskla, I think — that I'm counting on as my ace.'

'We'll be all right, then.'

'A few other things too — which I'd have told you about if you'd been doing this on your own.'

'Are we about on course now?'

'Near enough. It's a big enough target to hit, anyway ... Thing is, Bob — so you'll understand what we're doing —

it might not be snowing by the evening. Might *well* not, can't snow for ever ... So if we'd holed up on the wrong side of this open ground — well, we'd have had to sit tight, wait for more. That, or risk laying a trail, you see. There'll be stages when we have to, but here and now we don't, so—'

His voice had tailed off. He was leaning forward, peering into the darkness. 'Damn. Easing off *now*...'

Within minutes, it had stopped completely. But there'd been no question of not pushing on, and after about another hour — which was the time it took before they had the next forest-mass in sight ahead — there were still only occasional flurries of wind-borne snow, in short-lived, whirling squalls.

Dawn wasn't far off, either. They were both very much aware of the wheel-tracks they'd left carved into the snow behind them — with daylight coming now, and cavalry patrols about ...

Into the trees, though, eventually. Mishka perking up a little, at this stage. Schelokov admitted, 'She's earned *her* day of rest.'

'What'll we do — hobble her?'

'Tether her. See to her needs, and give her a drink and a square meal. Breakfast for us, too. Tea and a tin of whatever we've got. All right?'

'One sleep and the other keep watch?'

'Not necessary. I'll show you, in a minute. Here — give me the reins?'

He drove about four hundred yards into the wood, angling this way and that to pass between the trees, and avoiding the more open areas where snow lay. Then they stopped, took Mishka out of the shafts, put a bale of fodder and a blanket on her back, led her some distance northward and tethered her in a place where she'd have room to move around and to lie down and roll if she wanted to. Schelokov then went off to bring the tent from the cart, leaving Bob with instructions to clear the compacted snow from Mishka's hooves and rub her down, then tie the blanket on her. She was already munching, and seemed to take these various attentions for granted.

Schelokov came back with the tent, which they pitched a few yards clear of Mishka's field of movement. Then there was more gear to fetch — rations, rifles, cooking utensils, bedding ... He asked Bob as they trudged back for it, 'D'you see any method in my madness yet?'

'Well. You've parked the *dvukolki* where anyone tracking us would just about fall over it—'

'They'd find it, investigate it, and we'd hear them. Hear them arriving anyway — before that, I'd hope — and the *dvukolki* will delay them while they search it. As long as they're no cleverer than most ... We won't be able to see them at that stage, but more importantly they won't see *us*.'

'But they'd search around, and—'

'I'd pitch the tent much farther from Mishka if I could. Problem is the wolves. On her own — and tethered—'

'God yes.'

'Also she's our warning system. Ten to one anyone coming after us would be on horseback, and she'd let us know. All right, maybe they hear *her* — but even then, before they've located her you and I are in cover, ready for them, we know what we're up against in terms of numbers, we're watching them over the sights of our rifles — and they have *not* see us ... Those *just-in-case* rifles, Bob?'

He smiled. 'All right.'

'But you see — seriously, there's no reason to think they'd have the advantage. Unless there were literally dozens of them.'

He nodded. 'It's good thinking.'

'Some more of the same for you, then. Those tracks we've left — I'd be happier if we hadn't, obviously. But it's quite on the cards that nobody'll pass that way before it snows again. And unless they're *looking* for tracks they're no danger to us anyhow.'

Setting-up camp and settling Mishka down took about an hour. Dawn was well established by the time they'd finished. Schelokov by that time had a small fire going and a pan of snow-water on it for the tea; a bigger pan of packed snow would be left on the embers finally, to provide a later drink for Mishka. Supper meanwhile was a tin of corned beef divided between them and eaten cold, with black bread baked at the *letuchka* — conceivably by Mary Pilkington and Katherine Reid.

Who'd have spent a comfortable night, Bob hoped, in the train at Kupyansk. Might even be on their way south in it today, if the CO — whatever his name was — had managed to get their engine back ... But it was a good feeling, to have got those two out, to have achieved the purpose of the mission. In the RAF people's hands they'd be safe enough. Budyonny's cavalry might be a threat, but those aviators could be counted on to extricate themselves, all right.

Extraordinary, though — staring into the fire, on which the water had begun to boil at last, Schelokov lifting the pan in gloved hands to pour it on to the tea-leaves in another — astounding to realize that only three days ago he'd been on board *Terrapin*, had only just up-anchored and left Sevastopol.

Three days. Incredible ...

'Here you are ... I regret we have no sugar.'

'My God, the hardships ...'

'Black tea — a Russian drink for a half-Russian.' Schelokov poured his own. 'Tell me, Bob — your mother—'

'Died in childbirth. Not mine, a second one. I was — oh, nine, then.'

'In St Petersburg, you said.'

He nodded. 'You know all about me, now. What about your own family? You're not married?'

'It was unusual for any but the most senior officers in a regiment like mine to marry. For one reason and another.'

'In the Navy they call it being married to the White Ensign. But — what about your parents, then?'

Hesitating. Covering it by trying to sip at tea that was too hot to touch. 'I suppose — if you really want to know ...' He put his mug down. 'My father — Vasil Timofeevich Schelokov — was a general. He spent his life in the regiment in which I myself also served, but he retired before the war started. He was quite old, over fifty when I was born. The — er — syndrome I mentioned — late marriage? And — well, my family's estate was at Tsivylsk — between Kazan and Novgorod. I'll confine this to the very recent past, Bob, if you don't mind. He was in a wheelchair — had been for several years. And — they sent him down a long flight of stone steps, in the chair. Broke his neck — I *hope* it did, an eye-witness, former servant, later told me that it did. I say I *hope* because they — did other things to his body afterwards.'

'Some crowds of Bolsheviks — did this ...'

'Peasants inflamed by Bolsheviks. They marched in great hordes from one estate to another — picking others up along the way, so the vast majority of them wouldn't have been local people. They'd have to join in, though, or *they*'d be for it ... He'd been good to all his tenants, left to themselves I'd be astonished if there'd been a hand raised against him. Friends in the neighborhood used to tell him he was too generous and easy-going, made *them* look bad ... An officer in the old style, you see — it was natural to such a man to look after his own people.'

'And your mother?'

A long breath ... 'I don't know, exactly. Nobody seemed to know. Or it could be that they wouldn't tell me.'

'Christ.'

'It's hard to know what to say, isn't it?'

'I'm sorry I made you talk about it.'

'No harm done, my friend. It's in one's mind in any case.'

'Yes — I'm sure.'

A nod: eyes on the fire. 'A lot of the time.'

'Any — er — brothers, sisters?'

'One brother, older than me, killed in '15. No sisters, thanks be to God. But my mother — she was there, some of those creatures were holding her — physically holding her — when they pushed the old man over. It's a very long, steep flight of granite steps, leading down from the front of the house, which is built on a hillside. And they dragged her into the house afterwards. She was — much

younger than my father. And beautiful — *elegant*
describes her well ...'

It took him some time to get to sleep. Mental imagery of
the old general and of his wife — alone and defenceless in
a mob of brutes. The beginnings of a clue perhaps to Boris
Schelokov's motivation? His having stayed with Markov's
letuchka, as he'd said, at least partly because of the two
young English girls and what he'd seen as their extreme
vulnerability: *if you know our Bolshevik friends and their
little ways* ... And his readiness now to come to the
others' help. Nadia's — in one's own mind. One said *they* and
them, but one meant *she* and *her* ... Dozing off, then,
with Nadia talking to him from wherever she was now, her
calm grey eyes smiling into his, and her whisper *Don't
worry, my darling, I'm waiting for you, we'll be together
soon* ...

Then he was wide awake — instantly, having been
asleep by this time for hours — wakened by Schelokov
who'd pushed at him, muttered urgently 'Hear? *Hear?*'
Their two pallets filled the ground-space in the tent and
he'd woken him in the course of moving — crawling out,
shedding a blanket that had covered him. They'd both
slept in their overcoats and gloves. He was on his left side
then, half out of the tent and reaching back right-handed
to pull the rifle up to where he could use it while Bob
groped for his own — listening to hoofbeats, hooves
drumming on snow-covered ground, jingle of harness or
weaponry. Wheeltracks like a scar on the surface of the
brain as Schelokov glanced back, beckoned and then
crawled on out. Following: fur hat on, at the last moment,
and pausing between the tent's flaps, seeing Mishka with
her head up and ears pricked, then Schelokov ten or
twelve yards away looking back and pointing, telling him
silently *that* way ... Into cover, one that side and one this,
and where Mishka would not be in the line of fire if they
approached from where you could hear them now.

Where the *dvukolki*'s wheeltracks entered the forest. Or
near there. They'd find no tracks from the trees' fringes

inwards. They'd push straight on in: or wait long enough to spread out like beaters. Depending on how many of them there might be ...

A voice called — something indistinguishable — from farther away than one might have expected. Outside the forest, he guessed. Not that you could be sure ... But everything else had gone quiet, by this time — so quiet that the sound of the top round of .303 slicking into the breech and the bolt clunking forward and over — which he'd tried to do quietly — was almost explosive in the stillness. Safety-catch off. Nobody had answered that distant shout. High branches moved in the wind and ice-particles rattled down. He was prone, on his belly and elbows in a fuzz of undergrowth, with a tree's roots for cover to the front and forest litter as camouflage around the rifle's barrel.

Waiting ...

Hearing nothing now except forest sounds. Wind in the tops of the firs, and branches rubbing against each other. He decided that when there were targets in sight he'd wait for Schelokov to start it. Unless circumstances decreed otherwise. But two rifles, each with ten shots before you had to change the magazine — if this was only a small patrol, and you had them in clear sight before they knew it ...

You'd have to kill them all, he realized. For the simple reason that one could neither take prisoners, nor let any go.

Still no sound, and nothing moving.

Might have been just two or three of them, and they'd decided they needed a stronger force to make a job of it. Could be scouts for a larger troop: they'd have ridden back to bring the others up. *Or* — there could be half a dozen of them creeping into this forest — with eyes and ears no less sharp than your own — worming from tree to tree ...

But Mishka had relaxed. Her head was down, and she'd shifted round so that the tethering rope was now quite slack. She wouldn't surely have lost interest so completely, he guessed, if there'd still been other horses in the offing.

A lump of snow or ice fell heavily, hitting a branch and dislodging a shower of ice crystals. Schelokov's voice then: 'Coming your way, Bob.' Visible, then: half up, brushing dirt off himself and his rifle as he approached, stooping slightly, through the trees. 'No battle this afternoon. Thought we were in for one.'

Bob pushed his safety-catch on as he got up. 'What d'you think—'

'God knows.' A shrug. 'Except they were on the edge there, then took off.'

'You're sure?'

'I don't think they came into the trees at all. But I'll tell you when I've had a look. We aren't the only ones who leave tracks. And look at Mishka. *She* knows they've gone . . . I'll be five minutes.'

Bob was with Mishka when he came back. Keeping her company, and watching the forest. When he saw Schelokov coming — after nearer fifteen minutes than five — he went to meet him.

There'd been four or five horsemen, apparently, they'd come up around the outside of this wood from the south and must then have seen the *dvukolki*'s tracks; they'd milled around, cutting the snow up over a wide area and generally confusing the picture so that it had taken Schelokov some time to sort it out.

'That was when we were hearing them. But then instead of following the tracks into the forest, they went the other way, as if they thought we'd come *out* of it. Maybe assuming the *dvukolki* would've been going the way they'd been heading themselves, but inside the trees. The tracks did seem to slant out, rather. But they're still idiots!'

'Mishka's hoof-prints?'

'Exactly. They have to be real clowns!'

'But the odds are they'll catch on, sooner or later, and come back?'

'Possibly. Depending on — well, one, the depth of their stupidity, and two, what their orders are, what latitude they have. If they were *en route* from say Karlovka to

Zmuyev, for instance, as distinct from patrolling this area
… But — who knows. They *might* come to their senses.
For one thing, before they get very far those wheel-tracks
are going to vanish. From where it was snowing? At that
end the tracks will have been covered. If their corporal or
whatever he is has any vestige of a brain, wouldn't that tell
him something?'

'So do we wait for them, or move?'

'I'd say move. Northward, as far as we can through this
forest, then stop for a meal and to rest Mishka, then set
out again when it's dark.'

'Will we be crossing open ground then?'

'Unfortunately — yes.'

'Leaving more tracks.'

'Unless we have more snow. But — short of flying —
which in a *dvukolki* nobody's yet managed, that I know
of—'

'Hang on … I'm only thinking — we can't help leaving
tracks — if it doesn't snow — but we don't have to do it
with four men on our heels. If it *is* only four or five, why
don't we wait for them and get it over with?'

'It's a tempting alternative.' Schelokov nodded. 'I
thought of it too. Location and timing according to our
choice, not theirs … But do we *want* a battle? I thought
you especially did not.'

'I want to get there — that's all. Quickest way possible.
When we talked about it then we weren't thinking of this
kind of complication, were we? But you're the expert,
so—'

'Well, I say we move on. If we wait, it could be for
nothing — wasting time … But moving on now we still
have the option — if we find they're still after us?'

11

Dusk seemed to be starting at ground level and growing upward through the trees — whose tops were hardly moving, when you looked up into that greyish light overhead, looking yet *again* for signs of snow. All afternoon — during the slow transit through the forest and then here in camp — praying for it . . .

It was time to start now, tracks or no tracks. Mishka had eaten all she wanted, and sucked up most of a pail of snow-water. She was between the shafts of the *dvukolki* and Bob was buckling the straps, telling her — in Russian, of course — what a beauty she was. She wasn't: not by a long chalk. Short-legged, wide-beamed, rat-faced, shaggy . . . The only pretty thing about her was her name, the Russian equivalent of Teddy Bear.

'No snow tonight, Mishka. Trust to luck, that's all . . .'

He'd stopped, listening.

'Hear it?'

Schelokov — he'd been loading pots and pans into the back . . .

Hoofbeats.

'Bob—'

'Yes.' He'd already thrown the rope of Mishka's halter back around the tree where it had been before, and was flipping two half-hitches into it. She'd heard, meanwhile — had her head up, came up against the rope as she tried to turn — Bob leaving her, grabbing his rifle as Schelokov thrust it at him and pointed at thicker cover on the far side of the small clearing. '*There*—'

They weren't more than forty yards from the forest's edge. You could see the last of the daylight there, fragmented by the dark verticals of the trees. There were no wheel-tracks to lead the horsemen in at this point — in several miles of thick forest, there was absolutely no reason they *should* ride in here.

He was ready for them, anyway. As ready as one ever could be. Skull pounding with the drumming hooves — rhythm of several horses cantering — and taking long, slow breaths to slow his heartbeat. In less tense circumstances — targets either cardboard or, at sea, floating tins and bottles instead of flesh and blood — he'd excelled at this ... Safety-catch off, crouching behind a wide-boled fir ten yards from where Mishka was doing a little dance between the shafts, craning her neck round against the tension of the rope. Schelokov was somewhere beyond her, and in the centre of the clearing a low mound of earth and snow covered the place where their fire had been.

This would be the same bunch, he supposed. They'd have been back over those tracks, but probably farther than that too. Following the wheel-tracks to where they'd have been erased by last night's snowfall and then returning to the starting-point — having realized their mistake — wouldn't have taken much more than an hour, or two at the most, and the interval had been — six, seven hours ... Might have been back to their base, wherever that might be. Not the farmstead, which would be too far, but wherever it might be, to change horses — or stand-down, in which case this could be another troop that had taken over the duty.

Though why the interception of some cart seemingly on its way north should be thought worth such effort ...

They were pulling up. The tempo of the hoofbeats slowing, then disintegrating. And a shout ... He squirmed down, full length, with the rifle-butt tight into his shoulder, cold smooth wood and metal against his bearded cheek. Recalling Schelokov's *We still have the option*: even if the 'option' had been forced on one ...

Sounds were confused now. Horses jostling around, and men's voices — none of it distinguishable. Then one clear shout of 'Turn back here, do we?'

Guessing — because they'd reached this corner of the forest?

He wasn't sure whether to feel relieved or disappointed. It couldn't be a big group out there — Schelokov's 'four or five', probably — and if they'd come into the forest the action might have been effectively on one's own terms. Shooting from cover, when although they'd be looking for you they wouldn't know *where* to look: and would be dead — some would, anyway, before they did know.

On the other hand — if one *didn't* have to ...

Neither the killing nor the chance of being killed was all that attractive. And at stake beyond one's own survival was — please God — hers.

Toss-up. Either way.

That voice again — or one like it — and others were answering.

Turning back?

Sounds drawing *left*, though.

Continuing the way they'd come. Hoofbeats settling into that same rhythm — cantering, northward ... Obviously had paused here not because they'd had any reason to think the *dvukolki* might be in this top end of the woods, but because this did happen to be the top end — north-east corner — of them. And as likely as not guessing that the cart over which they'd made fools of themselves earlier might have taken advantage of their absence to push on northward.

Schelokov grumbled as they met at the *dvukolki*, 'That's our route they've taken — damn them ...'

Bob slid his rifle on to the seat of the *dvukolki*, and reached in for Mishka's bridle. 'If we can't move out—'

'Can't just sit here, either.' Schelokov pulled the magazine out of his rifle, ejected the round from the breech and caught it, slid it back into the magazine ... 'Might detour. Out *that* way —' a gesture north-westward — 'and then work round. But — long way round, and time we can't afford to waste. Open ground too — I think ... All right, if we knew they'd *keep* going ...'

Bob cut him short: 'Coming *back*?'

They weren't only coming back, they were already close — *too* close. He'd dropped the bridle, was reaching into the cart for his rifle — uselessly, *much* too late, but even Mishka hadn't heard them — until now, she certainly had *now* — fighting the head-rope, trying to rear against its pull — the rush of hoofbeats thunderous — out of nowhere, right on top of them.

But — *passing.* Even though Mishka's whinny might have been heard in Taganrog — they'd gone by. *Gone* ... While having been completely off-balance through those few seconds you were still seeing it as it might have been — horsemen crashing through the trees, sabres drawn and aimed ...

'Christ.' He was ashamed of his own fright, found some slight compensation in the gleam of sweat on Schelokov's broad forehead. He slid an arm round Mishka's neck. She was still trembling too — for her own equine reasons. He found his voice: 'Solves the immediate problem, anyway.'

'Yes.' Schelokov picked up the bridle. Sorting it out as he moved to Mishka's head: and getting his mental breath back, no doubt ... Glancing at Bob, over her withers, almost a challenge to anyone to imagine he'd been rattled in those few seconds ... 'I'd say this is the same patrol commander, probably in a dither about the light. Hoping to pick up our tracks before dark. Possibility of snow during the night, too — he'd be anxious about that. But he'll camp now, start looking again first thing in the morning.'

'And he'll find them, won't he?'

'Unless it does snow. Always a chance, you know.'

'So tell me this. If it's a silly question, I apologize — but why should they have this burning interest in us?'

'Wheeled transport going *north* — the way things are up there? Entire populace migrating south, or trying to?' He was checking over Mishka's harness. 'Clandestinely, what's more, not as if we were travelling by day...'

'Yes.' Bob slung the reins back to the driving position. 'It *was* a silly question.'

'Anyway, let's get going. We can start out on that

fellow's tracks. Fox him for a while, in the morning — if he's *really* stupid.'

Neither of them talked much in the first hour or so. Schelokov was driving, Bob beside him with both rifles, thinking most of the time about the tracks they were leaving and which would still be there in the morning for the cavalry scouts to find and follow. There was no doubt about it, no point in wishful thinking about new snowfalls. The fact it wasn't only their own survival that was at stake but ultimately the *letuchka*'s was about the worst aspect of it.

What one needed, to supplement present efforts — as well as for anything like peace of mind — was blind faith. It wasn't easy to acquire — or to hang on to. The fears lingered, and Schelokov's account of what had happened to his parents coloured them. In particular, the curtain he'd drawn over precisely what they'd done to his mother: thoughts travelling from there via Nadia — the connection being only in the imagination but no less frightening for that — to this present situation, the wheel-tracks which couldn't have been any clearer if you'd been laying a trail deliberately.

He swallowed — tasting the pipe he'd been smoking when they'd started out. Only half a pipeful at a time now, and limiting smokes to two a day. He had only what was in his pouch, the rest of it being in a tin in the canvas holdall which he'd left in the train: and he'd been sharing what he had with Schelokov, who'd had none at all.

Wolves howled mournfully, somewhere behind•them. Impossible to guess how far behind. Close enough to have upset Mishka, *that* was for sure ... Schelokov was calming her, or trying to: then calling over his shoulder into the darkness, '*Damn* you, go feast on Bolsheviks!' To Mishka again: 'Steady, old girl, *steady*! They're not after *you*, you scrawny beast ... But *wouldn't* they love it if you turned us over ... Eh, Bob?'

'I dare say ... Boris, listen—'

'*That's* my girl ...' Turning back to him: 'Huh?'

'I've been thinking. Seems to me that as things are now we can't win. Either they catch up with us, or if they don't we could be leading them to the *letuchka*. So I'd say we've got to try something of the kind we were talking about before.'

'Well ... In principle, I agree with you. But — you do realize, I suppose, there'd be no guarantees attached?'

'We mightn't get away with it, you mean.'

'What I mean is we might end up dead. Especially if — you may not have considered this — we may well have a larger force after us now. If those were only a scouting party — with the main force wherever they've camped?'

'D'you think that's likely?'

'It's certainly not *un*likely.'

'But still a perfectly good chance—'

'We'd have *no* chance. Imagine it — half a platoon, say — eighteen men against two?'

'But it *might* still be that small party. I think we've got to take a chance on it. Because otherwise — unless there's some alternative — if you've any better ideas?'

'No. Only miracles. An immediate heavy snowfall, or if they gave up, turned back at the boundary of the area they're expected to police.'

'*No* alternative, then.'

'There isn't, that I can see.' His breath plumed in the black, frosted night. 'So let's look at the practical aspects. Where, when and how ... *Where* is easy — wherever we find ourselves in the morning. I don't have any detailed memory of the topography, but we can pick our ground when we come to it. *When* — the answer to that is any time after dawn. Their initiative, of course — all we can do is be ready for them. In the morning sometime is a safe enough bet — they won't be hanging back and waiting for it to snow, you see ... Then, *how* — well, would you feel happy with some such arrangement as we prepared this morning — parking the *dvukolki* as a lure, setting an ambush?'

'You're the soldier, Boris.'

'I dare say we can improve on details, here or there.

One for instance is that I think Mishka should be tethered much farther away from where we camp. Don't want her warning them.' He added, 'Taking her chances, of course, as far as *those* creatures are concerned.'

Pausing again; listening to a renewal of the wolves' chorus. Further away, though, this time. He'd shortened rein, ready to cope with Mishka's playing up again, but she'd decided to let it go ... 'Bob, here's a fresh line of thinking for you. Looking beyond the fight itself — if we're going to do this, and on the whole I agree, we *have* to — I think it might be a good idea to continue from there on without the *dvukolki*.'

'Leave it there?'

'Hide it somewhere — not there, exactly, but in the area — and go on on foot. Because even if — *especially* if all we're up against is our little troop of scouts — and we make a real job of it — well, others coming after them will be looking for a horse and cart, won't they?'

'Others coming after them? Then what have we achieved?'

'We'd have stopped the close pursuit, Bob. Stopped it literally *dead*. Isn't this how *you* envisage it? Then if we shed this cart — well, we disappear ...'

'What about Mishka, when we dump the cart?'

Bob had driven for about three hours, then half an hour ago Schelokov, who'd had a good sleep during that time, had taken over again. There were scatterings of trees here, not forest but its outskirts, and they were steering the *dvukolki* through them whenever possible. Less in any hope of hiding the tracks than to look as if that was what they'd been trying to do. Schelokov yawned loudly — looking up at the sky and the first signs of dawn, then murmuring as if he hadn't heard that question, 'Better get into forest soon. *Very* soon.' His head turned. 'What? Something about Mishka, you said?'

'What'll we do with her, when we dump the *dvukolki*?'

'Oh. Well.' Another yawn ... 'What do you think?'

'We can't just leave her, so the obvious thing is take her

with us. Although I suppose tracks are an issue, even without the cart ... But if any of the *letuchka* people needs to ride, we might be glad we'd brought her.'

'That is — a point ...'

'Also if we decide to pick up the *dvukolki* again—'

'Not unless it's snowing day and night by then. As it's turned out, you were damn right when you said maybe it wasn't so clever.' He was angling left, to pass through a copse of leafless birch. 'Although mind you, if the snow had kept up ...'

'Made better progress than we'd have done on foot, surely?'

'We've also achieved the honour—' Schelokov jerked a thumb back over his shoulder — 'of an escort of cavalry.'

Bob had glanced back involuntarily ...

'Not *that* close ... Having their breakfast now, I'd guess. Or just had it, saddling up ... Tell you one thing, we're not leaving any tracks here, to speak of.'

'Well — let's not lose them—'

'Don't worry ... Are you any good with a rifle, Bob?'

'Oh, I — manage.'

'You'll need to do more than *that*.'

'As it happens I'm quite competent. What about you — with your shoulder?'

'It's mended now. No problem.'

'I've noticed you don't use that left arm much.'

'I'm right-handed.' He glanced round. It was light enough now to distinguish features, at point-blank range. He shrugged. 'All right, so I rest it when I can.'

'Does your jaw hurt still?'

'Would, if I had to hold a rifle on that side. Lucky I don't ... Bob — *there*. See? Not bad timing after all, eh?' He was pointing ahead and slightly to the left, to forest-edge standing solid, jet-black in the familiar beginnings of the pre-dawn glow, with a hazy, mist-like foreground leading up to it and a grey sheen overhead. Five minutes ago that grey had been funereal black, allowing no differentiation between sky and forest.

Schelokov shifted on his seat: an adjustment less to the

beginnings of a new day than to the tenth hour on a hard
plank bench ... 'Half a mile, roughly. Then the hard work
starts.' Flipping the reins: 'Come on you old she-goat ...
Bob, the whip's behind you there ...'

In the grey early-morning light and the forest's gloom the
camp-fire's orange glow was the only splash of colour.
Setting this scene *had* been hard work: fast work too, with
daylight growing rapidly and no time to waste. Schelokov
had set the fire and got it going while Bob had taken
Mishka with a bale of fodder to a tree a hundred yards
away, then hurried back to pitch the tent. They were about
five hundred yards inside the forest, in a clearing of sorts,
an area of sparser growth with a diameter of about sixty- or
seventy-five yards. They'd parked the *dvukolki* in the
centre, and he'd put the tent up ten yards north-east of it. The
fire was about the same distance north-west — due west of
the tent. So the three points formed an equilateral triangle
with its apex downward, marked by the *dvukolki*.

They'd also prepared hides for themselves, one west of
the *dvukolki* and the other — Schelokov's — east, each
fifty paces from it. Bob's paces, in his seaboots. From
either hide only a few trees impeded the view across the
clearing, and all the surroundings of the *dvukolki* —
behind which a man might conceivably take shelter —
were open to crossfire from one hide or the other.

The rifles were in the hides, with their sights set to fifty
yards. This happened to be the lowest setting, and was
also the optimum range at which they expected to be
shooting, the way the scene had been set. Schelokov swore
the sights had been zero'd recently and could be trusted.

Bob joined him at the fire.

'They'll be on their way, by now.'

'Should be.' The Russian's eyes gleamed in the fire's
glow as he looked up. 'What d'you want for breakfast?'

'Whatever we've got. But water for Mishka's a priority.'

'Well. This is about ready.' His fire, he meant. He'd
been patiently feeding it with bits of fallen timber and
then fir-cones, building its centre to a solid red nucleus of

heat. The cones glowed almost like coal. He reached for the big pot now with its contents of packed snow, and set it down on the stones, which were in the fire itself. 'That'll be for her Highness, then. What about corned beef?'

'Again?'

'It'll be different today. The bread's rock-hard.'

'Why not cut up the beef and let the fat soak into the bread, heat it all up together?'

'Well — why not. Take a little while, of course.'

'Personally, I could wait. Especially if I had some tea. If there's time—'

'*If* there's time.' He shrugged. 'All right. Tea now, *Boeuf Cowan* later.'

Bob had laughed: remembering Sam Scott saying something about tomfoolery easing the strain. Tomfoolery wasn't exactly Schelokov's stock-in-trade.

Mishka had had her drink and Schelokov had made tea, Bob taking his mug of it back to where he was doing his listening out.

They'd be coming at their own pace, he guessed. Knowing they'd be covering the ground a lot faster than any cart would. And no doubt confident that they'd have it all their own way.

They would, too — if there was a crowd of them. Visualizing them as they might appear at this moment — a double file, trotting in the *dvukolki*'s easy-to-see, north-leading tracks. Eighteen or twenty riders, say, rested by a sound night's sleep and with a good hot breakfast in their bellies: forward units of a currently victorious army, full of the *esprit* that comes from battles fought and won.

Or — the small scouting team. *Please*, let it be just those five?

He drained his mug of black tea, and went back to Schelokov at the fire.

'They're a long time coming.'

'They must have realized by now that we hole-up for the daylight hours. Might even be giving us time to get to sleep.'

He smiled, squatting down on the other side of the fire. 'Starting as stupid, they're becoming craftier every minute.'

'Made one mistake, that's all.'

'I sincerely hope *this* isn't one.'

'So do I.' Reaching over for the mug. 'But it's the right thing we're doing, Bob, the only thing we *can* do. If it goes wrong, don't blame yourself.'

'*If it goes wrong*, for God's sake—'

'All right — all right . . .'

A longish pause, then. Listening, hearing nothing.

'What you said just now, Boris Vasil'ich, about them reckoning to find us asleep — they *will* assume we're in the tent, obviously. So it wouldn't do to have any cooking in progress, would it?'

'If you're telling me you're hungry—'

'No, I'm not. Not telling you, I mean — it's a fact, but I can wait. If you can.'

'I was going to suggest we might have a slice of the corned beef cold, to be going on with.'

'Well—'

'Could be quite a *long* wait, otherwise.' He tossed a few cones into the fire. He'd collected a mound of them. 'Another thing, Bob, is we'll be busy afterwards, won't we.'

Busy clearing up, he meant. Something of a euphemism, when one thought of what it might involve. He got up. 'A *zakuska*'s a good idea, anyway. Give me a shout?'

It wouldn't take long to open a tin and cut out two rations of beef, but the fire itself and Schelokov's occasional movements made a certain amount of noise, and anyway he didn't want to spend too long away from his listening-out position, which was in the direction from which one expected them to come, and no further than this from his own hide. He glanced around before going back there. The tent looked natural enough. He'd put some gear in it — not much, but a corner of the ground-sheet showed at anything like close range, and if a flap blew aside — or was moved with the toe of a boot, for instance — you'd see bedding. The fire looked about right too; from the circle of ash and unburnt ends of branches you wouldn't doubt that it had been left to burn down.

Mishka wasn't in view from here. The closer-standing trees outside the clearing made a barrier that was impenetrable to sight from any distance.

But none of these preparations, he thought as he passed the *dvukolki*, its shafts tilted skyward by the weight of gear and fodder in the back, would make any difference to the outcome if there were eighteen or twenty men on their way here instead of five.

You could have spun a coin. Heads they didn't stand much of a chance, tails *you* didn't stand any at all. The stakes being one's own life and Schelokov's and — ultimately — hers.

Please God. Because if her life did *not* depend on what happened here, the whole effort was futile, it would mean you'd come too late.

He sat down, with his back against a tree. Same one he'd leant against before. He'd been moving rather frequently between here and the fire, he realized, because moving around was easier than sitting still.

It was mid-forenoon when he heard them. By that time they'd both begun to think there might be something in that speculation about miracles — the acme of wishful thinking, that the pursuit might have reached the limits of its own territory, given up ... The single slice of corned beef had meanwhile only sharpened their hunger, so they'd gone on to preparing and eating the *Boeuf Cowan*, which hadn't been at all bad.

He was offering Schelokov his tobacco-pouch when they heard the patrol approaching. Freezing for about one second, with the pouch held out across the fire's embers and Schelokov reaching a hand out to take it. Then they were running to their hides.

Flat, cuddling the Lee-Enfield. His borrowed brown *shapka* would be good camouflage, he hoped, blending well into the drab colouring of the forest floor. Navy

greatcoat less so — except that it was mud-stained and
he'd cut the epaulettes off the day before. In any case he
was half-buried in the pine-needles and the other debris:
like some kind of nest.

Not a sound, now. All he'd heard had been hoofbeats,
and now he couldn't even hear that.

Gone by — *again*?

Not after following the tracks this far, surely ... Unfortunately the cessation of those sounds hadn't been noticeable because one had been on the move oneself: now, if
Schelokov hadn't heard them too, one might have
doubted—

Nonsense. They *had to* be there. With the edge of the
forest five hundred yards away, if they were making efforts
to be quiet you *wouldn't* hear them ...

Keeping his breathing quiet as well as slow. With the
thought — after another minute, maybe two — that these
people might be a lot cleverer than he and Schelokov had
allowed for, might be surrounding this place now, might —
given long enough — come from any or all directions ...
In fact, you *would*—

Then — a hoof struck a fallen branch. Loud, unmistakable — and a lot nearer than the forest's edge. If that hoof
had cracked into one's own skull the brain would hardly
have been jolted any harder.

So — they weren't *there*, they were almost *here*. Heart
banging: banging hard ...

Unlikely that twenty men could be approaching through
thick forest quite so silently? More likely to be only three
or four?

But whether it was three, four or six, the rest could be
outside, waiting while the scouts drew this cover. The rest
of them sitting their horses quietly out there, waiting.

Long, even breaths. Head right down, watching over
the rifle's sights and the heaped litter. Watching under his
brows, showing as little face as possible, and absolutely
still.

He saw the first one then, at a range of about eighty
yards, and moved — *very* slightly — to settle the rifle's

foresight, its tip level with the shoulders of the backsight's 'V', on the man's breastbone just about where the highest button below the turned-up collar would be. Sombre greenish-brown Russian army uniform ... He'd halted: reins taut in his left hand, holding the horse as still as a rock while he first glanced around the clearing, pausing at the fire then concentrating on the *dvukolki* and the tent. His horse — it was black — meanwhile swinging its head to the left, tetchily jerking at the reins, and staring directly at this hide. If Bob had fired now the bullet would have passed between those pricked ears to the new point of aim he'd been forced to settle on for the moment, the smudge of white face and forehead, and aiming at where the bridge of the nose would be. Range say seventy yards. Sights set for fifty: so an inch higher, the forehead, where the whiteness showed right under that tall *shapka*, which had a red badge of some kind on it. Red star, probably. Trotsky's new army getting itself organized even to the extent of a common uniform, or elements of one. Now he'd raised one arm, seemed to be signalling to others — or *an*other — to come forward. The same hand and arm then unslinging the rifle that had been slung diagonally across his back — bringing it round and resting it across the pommel of his saddle.

Probably an NCO. This would be Schelokov's area of expertise but one did know that mounted officers didn't carry rifles, only revolvers and sabres. Unless Bolsheviks were different ... There was another rider behind him now — on his right, the far side. And one *this* side — further back. The three of them advancing slowly — tight-reined, rifles cocked upward with their butts resting on thighs or saddles.

Sixty yards ...

A fourth was in sight then. On this side of the leader, pushing up between him and the man on his left, nearest to oneself. Schelokov had said he'd take the leader, if one of them made himself obvious as such ... *If not I'll begin with the man nearest to me and you take whichever's your own nearest. And so on. But let me shoot first, Robert*

*Aleksandr'ich. I won't start it until there's a good chance
we'll bag them all. Wait for my first shot — then fast and
straight, eh*? Bob had asked him what if there were a
dozen or more, and he'd shrugged, told him *Then all our
worries will be over very quickly.*

Only four, so far. And they'd stopped again, the leader
putting one hand up, and the others reining in immediately. *Softly, softly, sleeping men in that tent, let's not rush
it* ... The nearest horse, whose rider would be one's own
first target, was a grey. There was a dun-coloured animal
between that one and the leader, and a chestnut on
Schelokov's side. It was a shame — a tragedy — about the
horses. They'd discussed it at length, neither of them
readily accepting the necessity of killing them, but having
to face the fact that you couldn't let them go, galloping
advertisements of what had happened here — or somewhere near. Saddled and bridled, at that — if you did *not*
shoot them they'd be gone in seconds, telling the story as
clearly as if they could speak ... Just as obviously, you
couldn't take them with you; and it would hardly be doing
them a kindness to leave them tethered for the wolves.

They were coming on again. The leader diverging to his
right — away — to pass on the far side of the *dvukolki*, on
course for the tent. Exactly as had been anticipated by
Schelokov. The one on his right was staying with him —
had fanned out farther to their right, no doubt so as to
cover the far end of the tent. Envisaging the rabbits
bolting ...

They'd be behind the *dvukolki* in a moment. But not
from Schelokov's angle of sight. Schelokov would have his
sights on that leader: would have had all this time, but
now he'd have his safety-catch off and a finger curled
around the trigger ... One's own sights meanwhile rock-
steady on the rider of the grey: ready for it to start at any
moment although not expecting it *quite* yet. Schelokov
would wait until his man had passed the *dvukolki*,
probably — so as to have all the others well inside the
arena, none out on the fringes from where if they weren't
brought down in the first few seconds they might stand

some chance ... The grey's rider was tall in the saddle and narrow-shouldered — long-legged too, and so long-stir-ruped that his legs were almost straight. Brown greatcoat and breeches, black boots, the same red badge on his fur hat. The leader was passing out of sight behind the *dvukolki*. Range on the grey as near fifty yards as it would ever be. Bob's view of him was in half-left profile, point of aim now the heart. He wanted his own first shot to go off so close to Schelokov's that there'd be virtually no interval between them. Then switch like greased lightning to the dun. Fine big horse, that. Big man on it too. It was on the far side of the grey and half a length behind. That one's most natural reaction, he thought, would be to pull his horse's head round and spur for the thicker cover—

Schelokov's rifle cracked, Bob squeezed his trigger and the grey's tall, thin rider was flung backwards: the other *was* tugging his big mount around and Bob's sights were moving to him, he'd flipped the bolt back and snapped it forward again in one swift movement, but at that moment he saw what he should have seen before and hadn't — a fifth man, visible as all hell now as his horse reared, half-round too and well back, a damn sight *too* far back, too near cover and a hasty exit: Bob's second shot sent him over his nag's head as its forefeet crashed down, and two more in very quick succession — needing two because the man's body had been in the way — killed the horse. Then back to the big dun, whose rider was *not* running as anti-cipated, was standing in his stirrups with his rifle up and aimed at Bob — who must have shown himself when he'd needed to be lightning-fast in nailing that other one. The Russian had fired again — and missed again — not sur-prisingly, from that cavorting horse, into which the rider-less grey had just cannoned — and Bob's fifth shot killed the big man as the dun pranced round, turning its rump this way — which was *not* so good — but he had the grey's head in his sights then, and killed it, and in the next second a bullet from Schelokov brought the dun crashing down in mid-stride halfway back across the clearing.

*

Schelokov said, 'Clean sweep. My God — when you said you could "manage"—'

'Well.' He shook his head. Gazing round. 'Poor bloody animals ...'

'I know.' Schelokov had taken his revolver out of its holster. Opening it, he span the cylinder, snapped it shut again. 'I know ... Have to make sure of them now, though. Men *and* horses.'

The thought was sickening. Despite this having been his idea and at least half his doing. He had a fleeting memory of his father telling him — in some previous age — *You're a bit of an old softy, you know* ... He glanced back at Schelokov. 'I'll fetch Mishka. Sooner we're out of here the better — don't you think?'

The grey eyes held his for a moment. Bob thinking that the earlier talk of clearing up was nonsense. For one thing, two men couldn't move five dead horses — even if there'd been anywhere to put them.

'Yes.' Schelokov must have come to the same conclusions. '*Soglasno*.' He added as he turned away, 'The wolves won't mind.'

12

Dark night, and snowing, blowing too, Mishka trudging through it like a laden mule. She was wearing a saddle and bridle for which one of those five cavalry horses had had no further use, as well as saddle-bags with as much tinned food in them as they'd hold. Two sacks of fodder balanced each other, with camping gear between them; Schelokov's rifle was in there too. Mishka was an unhappy-looking creature, with the hump on her back and the sacks bulging out on either side, a ground-sheet covering it all. Bob plodded on her right, Schelokov on her left with the reins looped round his arm. It had been snowing since midnight and the road was defined only by a low bank on Schelokov's side and an occasional snow-crowned fence-post on the other.

They'd left the north-western edge of the forest soon after sunset and followed a compass course over open country, downhill all the time, until Schelokov had found the river which was at the bottom of the valley, below the road. He'd left Bob with Mishka and gone on alone to find it, to make sure this was the Valki road, and since then they'd been trekking northward with the river somewhere below them on the left and a hillside that was gradually steepening on their right.

They could have brought the *dvukolki*, if they'd known it was going to snow like this. No tracks of any kind were being left tonight. But the *dvukolki* was in that forest — somewhere in the middle, nowhere near either the scene of the ambush or their eventual point of departure — in a hollow, and camouflaged with all the fallen branches they'd been able to find within about a half-mile radius. It might be found — but surely not for a while. There was nothing to lead any searcher to it, for one thing, and for another the scouting troop's tracks to the killing-ground would have been obliterated hours ago by this snow. So the disappearing trick — that troop's and the *dvukolki*'s — would seem to have been accomplished.

Barring really evil luck: or circumstances unknown, unknowable.

The wind was from the north, the snow coming in it at an angle of about thirty degrees to the horizontal, into their faces most of the time as the road wound this way and that between the high ground on one side and the river on the other. Eventually — before dawn, Schelokov had promised — they'd come to a river-bridge with the road that crossed it branching off this one. They'd keep straight on, staying on this side of the river, and find abandoned farm buildings on the right about two versts — a mile and a half, roughly — from that fork. *Letuchka syem* had established itself there, he'd explained, because Valki, the village itself, had been full of typhus, and at this farm they'd had the conveniences of the road for transport and the river for water — the river hadn't been iced up at that time — and a few farm buildings still with roofs on.

Bob broke a long silence. 'Still going to be there before daylight, are we?'

'Please God.' He added, about six paces later, 'Damn well *have* to be.'

Meaning; *we'll be in trouble if we aren't* ...

But in these conditions he couldn't know how far it was, or how fast — or slowly — they were moving. The snow was more than welcome from the point of view of covering tracks, but it wasn't contributing much to progress. Mishka obviously hated it. That, and being used as a pack-horse. He sympathized with her: for a third reason too, the effect that scene in the forest had had on her. She'd been terrified — trembling, fighting the routine processes of being harnessed into the *dvukolki*, her eyes rolling white in fear.

Her head and eyes were plastered in snow now. He

reached left-handed to brush some of it off, but she tossed her head, rejecting his advances.

Can't blame her, he thought. A man who murders horses ...

He asked Schelokov, 'When we do get there, d'you have any kind of plan?'

'There are woods along that strip. Beyond the farm — maybe this side of it too, I don't remember. But we can get into cover somewhere along there. Camp, feed this animal and ourselves, then reconnoitre. Then — depends what we find, eh?'

What — or *whom* ...

It didn't bear thinking about — the possibility that in just a couple of hours — hour and a half, maybe ... In fact, it was *not* a possibility — or at least it was highly improbable — that they'd still be there, in the same place or anywhere near it.

Schelokov had been right when he'd warned against counting chickens. Wiser and safer not to count on *anything*. Also to bear in mind that when or if you did find them — find *her* — you wouldn't be exactly home and dry. From here to — say Taganrog, for instance — was something over two hundred miles.

He'd dreamed of her, last evening, in the two hours or so which was all the rest-time they'd had before starting out. There'd been horses in the dream, and a river in the background — not this one, must have been the Volga, the Enotayevsk connection — and an overwhelming feeling of happiness, Nadia's long, lithe body in his arms, her own arms tight around his neck and her voice in his ear — *Bob, oh Bob, my darling* ... The moment had been as real as life, the timbre of her voice more clearly recognizable than it had been in actual memory at any time in the past year. He could hear it again *now*: until the recollection was wiped out by Schelokov's voice, raised to beat the wind's buffeting along this hillside ... 'Robert Aleksandr'ich — asleep on the march, are you?'

'Not quite.' Mishka let him wipe the crust from her eyes this time. 'Only — thinking ...'

'Well, listen. When we go back south — with or without your *letuchka* friends, Bob — I think we should take a different route. Not through country where a scouting troop has disappeared into thin air.'

He thought about it. The words 'with or without' raising a mental block, a conflict between the reflex response *We certainly will have them — her — with us*, and the feeling that such a concept was too good — too *glorious* — to be real, actually come true ...

He grunted. 'You mean they might be looking out for us. I dare say you're right. But—'

'Might make for Kupyansk. Or Debaltsevo. Although by that time — well, depends how soon we can start, of course ...'

Bob remembered that Schelokov hadn't been entirely confident even that Dr Markov and his party had had all that good a chance of getting to Debaltsevo. And that had been two days ago. Such uncertainties were exacerbated, of course, by the complete lack of communications, one's having no idea of what was happening here, there or anywhere.

Schelokov had muttered something else.

'What's that?'

'I said, I wish you'd kept the other rifle.'

He thought, Oh, God, *again* ...

'I did explain, Boris Vasil'ich—'

'Point is, if we go south by some other route we can't recover it. And in the present state of things — especially when you're as useful a sharpshooter as you are — well, God almighty ...'

They'd been through this before. He'd cached his Lee-Enfield in the forest, along with surplus canned food and other gear they couldn't carry. The prime reason — which he'd explained at the time, in what had been quite a heated argument — was that the farther north they travelled the greater the chances were of being stopped and interrogated, that in such an event he was going to admit to his true identity and that he'd come to find some British nurses, and in this non-combatant role the possession of a rifle would be difficult to justify. Especially when it was the twin of Schelokov's and he and Schelokov — who was now carrying identity papers he'd taken from one of the cavalrymen they'd killed — would be representing themselves as chance travelling companions.

Schelokov was now — according to his new papers — Ivan Leonidovich Krotov, born in the Ukraine in 1890. The date of birth might be a problem — if it was noticed — since with his grizzled beard and generally mature appearance he couldn't possibly be twenty-nine. With luck, nobody *would* notice: with even better luck nobody would be looking at his papers anyway. But if he did have to account for himself, his story would be that he'd been recruited into a hussar regiment in 1914, deserted to the Red Army in 1918, had been taken prisoner near Kiev earlier this year by Petlyura's Ukrainian nationalists, who'd forced him to join them, and got away from them a few weeks ago during a skirmish with White cavalry near Elisavetgrad. He'd been on his way to rejoin the Red Army on the Kharkov front, and had fallen in with this Englishman who was looking for some English nurses. As the Red Army wasn't at war with England — so far as he, Krotov, knew — he'd seen no reason why they shouldn't join forces for the journey.

It was a good story from Bob's point of view, since it fitted in with his own intention of being himself.

Schelokov was grumbling on about the rifle. Reminding Bob that he hadn't wanted to bring rifles in the first place ... 'And if we hadn't, where'd we have been now?'

Bob agreed, 'You have a point, there.'

'I have, *haven't* I!'

'On the other hand, here's another. When we have the *letuchka* people with us, the last things we'll want are battles. We can't fight our way out, Boris Vasil'ich — only way we'll manage it is to *sneak* out ...'

*

Beginning to worry, now, about how much further ... The high ground on their right blocked out the eastern sky but there was a hint of dawn's beginnings in the darkness overhead. Maybe one felt it more than saw it, but it was there all right.

So there might be — what, another hour of darkness?

There'd been a lull in their exchanges, since the renewed argument about the rifle. But Schelokov now cleared his throat, turned to spit down-wind, and reopened communications.

'Incidentally, Bob, where did you learn to shoot like that?'

'Oh — I suppose at sea, mostly. What we'd call a dog-watch exercise. The dog-watches are in the early evening — after working hours. If you can imagine a ship steaming along quite fast, you have a man up for'ard chucking sack-fuls of bottles and tins over the side, and you pot at them from the quarterdeck — that's at the stern end — as they wash by. In any kind of sea they're dancing around quite a bit, and you have to be damn quick.'

'Personally, I should be damn sick.'

'No, you'd get used to it. But what about you, anyway? You were shooting at least as straight as I was.'

'I'm a soldier — I'm *supposed* to shoot straight. Well, it's true, for sport we used to shoot quite a lot. Pig, wolf, bear ... From horseback, often enough ... Bob — d'you hear something?'

The howl of the wind, and it's booming on the steep hillside. Mishka's bellows-like breathing, and the regular thudding of her hooves ...

'Whoa. Whoa ...' Her head was dragged round to Schelokov as he pulled her up. Bob heard it too then, and his first thought — duration about one second — was of an avalanche, rock-slide. But it was coming from ahead: and it was hoofbeats, he realized — on this road ... Not just a few horses, either, it was like a — well, muffled, but less so every moment — like a rolling of massed drums. The volume of it was mounting steadily — rapidly — drowning the wind, filling the dark valley. Cavalry — approaching, head-on ...

Schelokov had Mishka half-round, hauling her to the roadside. He shouted, 'Over the bank here — take her head on that side!'

With so much weight on her back, she did need help — took some controlling, too, beginning to go mad ... Her hooves scrabbling and sliding while they hauled at her, pulling her up, exerting brute strength — having to, with not even seconds to spare — both assuring her insistently it was all right, old girl, all *right*, come *on* now, *there*'s the girl ... Over — and down, in deep, soft snow, all three of them floundering thigh-deep in it — Mishka frightened and by this time *very* excited, plunging around and off-balance anyway under her load — visibility nil, no way of knowing what was even a yard ahead — a sheer drop to the icebound river, for instance — while what might have been a whole regiment of cavalry was thundering past on the road above them. It wasn't only sound, the ground was shaking — sound and reverberation lessening two or three times for the space of a few seconds and then rising again — *another* lot — separate platoons or squadrons or whatever ...

Schelokov shouted, 'This'll do, Bob! *Whoa*, girl ...' He'd clamped his hand over Mishka's nose, pinching the nostrils shut so she couldn't whinny. And you could *see* them now: against the sky, a slab of movement composed of men and horses not so much in silhouette as in contrast to the static darkness around and over it: a moving, jogging entity. Another gap — then more ... God only knew how many: and the power, the sheer weight and mass: an earth-tremor that went on and on. Mishka fighting to get her head free, Schelokov cursing, having to watch out for her front hooves. It wasn't easy to keep your footing even without *that* hazard. He wondered — semi-stunned by the continuing roar — a *thousand* of them? But — drawing away to the right again ...

Either this was a bigger gap, or—

No follow-up. The tail-end of it — at last. No sight now, only sound, lessening and drawing right. And none at all coming from the left. After — what, five or six minutes ...

Sound diminishing fast, southward. You could hear the wind again.

'Bob — check the road's clear? Then come back — if you would ... It'll take both of us to get this damned animal up there — eh?'

'All right ... What was it — a whole regiment?'

'Probably. A number of squadrons, anyway ... But look it's going to be bloody *daylight* soon, so—'

It wasn't daylight, even when they were back on the road and trudging north again, but dawn was a clear threat now. And the snow was falling less thickly. Or that could have been an illusion, an effect of the changing light. They were looking for the bridge by this time as a matter of real urgency: not only daylight's approach but an obvious possibility of more cavalry following that first lot.

Meanwhile — one destination, one route to it. *This* one.

They were both — all three — still winded, and Schelokov was limping.

'Boris — how many squadrons in a regiment?'

'Six. And a hundred and fifty swords, not counting officers, in each squadron. That was *our* system.'

'Might have been a whole regiment, d'you think?'

'Yes. Might well.' He was peering ahead and to the left, probing the thinning, snow-flecked darkness. Adding after a few moments' pause, 'We knew we wouldn't have long, didn't we?' Another pause. For a moment he thought he'd seen the bridge: but he hadn't ... 'But — as they say, one swallow doesn't make a summer.' Muttering, then: 'Can't have already passed it. *Can't ...*'

'Might be part of the great encircling movement everyone's been expecting — Budyonny's masterstroke, forty-eight hours late?'

'Might. And if it is—'

'There'll be more coming.'

He'd flung an arm up: 'There it is! *There!*'

The bridge was a hump in the semi-darkness off to the left. The road junction was closer — about fifty feet ahead where the bank curved away, following the branch-road towards the bridge. Once you had it in focus it became quite clear to see: but in rapidly improving light, of course ... Not that from their point of view 'improving' was quite the word ... Schelokov telling Mishka, 'Come *on* — not so far now, you — you *thing*, you!'

Because she'd trodden on his foot ...

'Two versts, you said.'

'Something like that.'

'Then it *will* be light, before—'

'If we come to woods before we get there, we can stop there and then.'

That cavalry force had come from or through Valki. You didn't have to be any kind of tracker to see they hadn't come over the bridge. Or any kind of genius to deduce that if there were more coming this was the road they'd be on.

On the other hand, just because one regiment had passed through ... He looked past Mishka's nodding, plodding head at Schelokov's dark, limping profile. 'Boris, if it's at all possible I'd like at least a quick sight of the farm, before we hole up.'

'But the priority must be to get off this road and into cover. Can't have it both ways, unfortunately. At least—' Pausing, evidently thinking about it ... 'It's just possible we *can*. If my memory's not playing tricks ...'

He was gazing up at the hillside ... It was farther back from the road than it had been. River bending left, Bob guessed, and the line of the road following its course. There *was* a bit of a curve to the left ... But Schelokov was right, anyway: irrespective of more cavalry regiments on the move there'd be civilian traffic on this road soon. With daylight coming, and a village just up ahead: and civilians who'd remained in their villages or farms when the rest of the populace had fled south wouldn't be *anti*-Bolshevik.

In other words, if they saw suspicious-looking strangers on the road they'd run and tell someone. The military, or local Red Guards, for instance.

'Boris — I was going to ask you, back there — where

does that other road lead, over the bridge?'

'Bogodukhov. Where *Letuchka chetiri* was before they moved down here. *If* they moved, that is.'

'Ah. Right ...' He did a double-take, then: 'Are you saying they might not have left Bogodukhov?'

'If they hadn't started the move in time, it's — conceivable. Reds were on the point of breaking through — *were* breaking through, here and there. If they'd been slow off the mark they *could* have been trapped up there.'

'But — if that *is* the case—'

'There'd be nothing you or I could do for them. But it's only just one of several possibilities, Robert Aleksandr'ich, there's no reason—'

'No. I — realize ... Here's another question, though. Assuming they did come down, how would they have found this farm — the place we're looking for now — when Markov's *letuchka* wasn't here to meet them?'

'Either they'd have had a guide, or the location would have been detailed in their orders. Kharkov — Army headquarters — were administering and supplying both *letuchki* by that stage. Probably others too. Base hospitals were out of it. Markov was getting whatever orders he did get by despatch rider, same would have applied at Bogodhukov. What's more, we left supplies here for them — whatever Markov didn't have room for in his transport.'

'Left some wounded, too?'

A grunt ... 'By no means willingly, I assure you.'

'But no danger to them from wolves *this time*, he said.'

'Because they were in the farm buildings.'

'Ah. I see ...'

'See *there*?'

Woods — a thinnish growth of pines close to the road, about a hundred yards ahead, thickening into a dark mass as it climbed the hillside. Schelokov was jubilant ... '*Chudno*! Perfect!'

Bob looked from the hillside to the sky, the growing light. He nodded. 'Just when we need it.'

'And *where* we need it. I couldn't trust my memory, precisely. I was hoping, but—'

'Close to the farm here, are we?'

'I think *very* close. And from up there—' a gesture towards the wooded hillside — 'I won't speak too soon, but I *think* it's a godsend.'

Proof of it had to wait a while. First there was the traverse from the road to the trees — during which time if anything had come along this stretch of road they'd have been in full view — and then a climb through woodland which at some stages was so steep that they had to zigzag — to a comparatively level patch that seemed good enough for a camp site. Then the unloading of Mishka, and anchoring her to start with on a long tether in a more open area where she could move around and lick up snow if she was too thirsty to wait for her water, which was going to be a long time coming. Material had to be gathered for a fire first, and the fire then built up, and even then it was a lengthy process. Having had to leave non-essential gear behind they hadn't burdened her with the largest cooking pot; snow had to be melted in the small one and poured into her canvas bucket until there was enough for her to get her snout into it. Meanwhile one pot-full was used for making tea.

Schelokov had made only a small fire, and selected the driest of the fallen timber, so as to keep smoke to a minimum. The north wind helped with this. It was a bitterly cold wind, but it carried the smoke away southward to lose itself amongst the trees.

Schelokov murmured, opening a tin. 'You won't believe me when I tell you what this is.'

'There's only one thing they put in cans that shape. And we've no bread to go with it, have we?'

'Some crusts.' A movement of the head: 'Almost gave 'em to *her*. Thought better of it, luckily. We'll have *Boeuf Cowan* again.'

'Let's have more tea meanwhile. I'll do it ... What other food have we got with us?'

'Fish. Type unspecified, but it's always sturgeon. And

farsh.' Farsh was a kind of sausage-meat. He added, 'And more corned beef, of course.'

'Of course.'

He'd moved Mishka in closer to them by this time, rubbed her down and given her half a sack of fodder. Leaving three days' supply, if she could subsist on that kind of ration. Probably could not, he guessed. Certainly not if one was going to give her any work; in fact after the exertions of the past few nights she probably needed feeding up, not dieting ... A lot would depend on how long it might be before they started south: and it could become even more of a problem if as Schelokov had suggested they went by some different route, not by way of the forest where they'd left the *dvukolki* with a few bales of fodder in it.

Might be safe enough to let her graze on the edge of the wood. Somewhere out of sight from the road. Alternatively, perhaps find some local supply of fodder.

At the farm, for instance.

Where Nadia might be — *now*? Within a mile or so of where one was sitting at this moment?

All right — first things first — But he'd been moving and working like an automaton, with his mind full of her. Images of how it would be, when they met. Whether she'd even recognize him. The prospect was almost frightening, as well as thrilling.

When they finished their meal, Schelokov produced a canvas pouch bulging with tobacco.

'*Makhorka*, God help us. Better than nothing, though.'

Markhorka was a very strong and evil-smelling, shag-type tobacco.

'From — one of those five?'

'From the late Ivan Krotov, no less. Tell you what, though — you smoke your own, and I'll use this. As long as yours lasts, that is.'

'Well — if you don't mind—'

'I have a confession to make, Robert Aleksandr'ich ... No, nothing to do with pinching this fellow's tobacco. Much more — basic, than that ... The fact is — I've only gradually allowed myself to recognize it — I really enjoyed that business yesterday. It was a pleasure — an actual pleasure ... You disapprove: obviously it wouldn't have been like that for you, eh?'

'Not pleasure — no ... But satisfaction, definitely. Killing them as the only alternative to having them eventually kill *us*?'

Schelokov shrugged. Stuffing his pipe ... 'Beyond that plain necessity — although you're perfectly correct, of course — the point I'm making is that I found it truly — as I say, *pleasurable*.'

'But you must have killed Bolsheviks before this?'

'Certainly. But this was — personal, wasn't it? Just the two of us. And they were hunting us, so we destroyed *them*. Nothing to do with soldiering, the field of battle and so forth. That's like being part of a machine, there's nothing — personal, about it ... I'll tell you — even if it shocks you, Robert Aleksandr'ich — the only fault I'd find with our action yesterday was that you got three and I only got two.'

'Well — luck of the draw. And that third one's horse would have got away if you hadn't nailed it.'

'Minimal satisfaction in that.' He put the pipe in his mouth, leant to the fire for a burning stick. '*Technical* satisfaction, some personal regret. Whereas Bolsheviks—' sucking, holding the glowing end of the stick on the bowl — 'I truly hate.' Puffing ... 'Never realized it before. The extent—' puff, puff ... '— the utter *loathing* ...'

His pipe was going. He tossed the stick into the fire. 'Sorry. I'm boring you. Shocking you first, then boring you.'

'Not in the least, Boris Vasil'ich. Neither. Not at all surprising, either.'

'That I should ramble on about my — feelings?'

'That you'd have such feelings.'

The grey eyes met his, through smoke. 'Perhaps it's not. But not to have realized it until now ... Grows in one, I suppose, without one's knowing it. And telling you my story ... Never talked about it before, you see. Then an affair like yesterday's — the personal involvement as distinct from straightforward military duty...'

Five minutes later, both with pipes going, they started northward across the hillside. Having left their bedrolls near the fire, with the groundsheet under them. One blanket each; the third was Mishka's, and she was wearing it, Bob had put it on her after she'd finished rolling. As they set off she swung her head round, watched them as if she was wondering where the hell they were off to without her.

It was three of four hundred yards to the edge of the wood. Fully daylight now; you could see the gleam of it, light reflected from a surface of glistening snow outside this partial gloom. It wasn't easy going; there were a lot of fallen trees and thick undergrowth, including brambles, and the hillside was pitted as well as steep. Schelokov led, carrying his rifle, Bob following in the *makhorka*'s stink.

They *might* still be here, he thought. If for instance they'd had a lot of wounded, more than they could have moved with them, and hadn't been prepared to abandon them ... And they might well have not been interfered with — yet — in this backwater, largely depopulated as it was.

Back of the moon, Schelokov had called it ...

He'd stopped at the edge of the trees. Motionless, cradling the Lee-Enfield, gazing down across the open hillside. Then glancing round, beckoning ...

'Bird's-eye view, Robert Aleksandr'ich.' He turned back to it, pointing diagonally down-slope as Bob came up beside him. 'Every bit as good as I'd hoped for.'

The whitened slopes ran in folds and curves clear down into the valley, steeply at first but then in easier gradients, became finally more or less level pasture surrounding a cluster of derelict farm buildings. Grey stone and broken timber, roofs mostly fallen in, half-burnt timbers showing up starkly black where they were in shelter from snow. No smoke, no signs of life or movement. A track led to the farmyard from the road, through a copse of what was probably birch, and ran on beyond into more pinewoods that had bare hillside above them. Perhaps a quarter of a mile beyond the ruins of the farm a single chimney was visible among the trees.

It wasn't snowing now. He'd thought it was, but the snow blowing in the wind was being lifted off trees and hedgerows.

'That's — *it*, is it?'

'Where we were.' Schelokov nodded. 'Doesn't look like anyone's there now.'

'Well, we didn't expect—' He let that tail off: asking himself *Didn't we*? Pointing, then: 'What's the chimney?'

'It *was* a small manor house. The owners of this land — all this valley — lived there. People of no great consequence, small landowners, but apparently the usual rabble came for them. Much the same as I described to you. As it happens this was Markov's story — I suppose he'd have heard it from some local person. Someone from the village, perhaps. The only difference from the usual pattern is that *there*—' he gestured towards the farm — 'these people's tenants tried to protect their master and his family, so the mob killed them too and destroyed the farm as well as the house. Not as effectively — there's nothing left of the manor, except a wall with that chimney on it. The rest of it was made of timber, burnt to the ground.' He took the pipe out of his mouth, spat, shook nicotine juice out of the stem ... 'As for the farm — the well in the yard down there was stuffed with corpses. Including children's. This was before I got here. Markov cried when he told me about it. He'd had them pulled out and buried, but they still couldn't use the well. His Tartar drivers used to haul water from the river.'

'What happened to the murderers when the Volunteer army got here?'

'Murderers?' Schelokov squatted on a fallen tree-trunk. He shook his head. 'Phantoms, more like.'

Smouldering socks would have smelt better than those pipe-fumes. Even the ones Bob was wearing inside his seaboot stockings. He said — thinking of Nadia — 'You mean nobody'd know, or—'

'Or admit to having been within a hundred miles.'

He sat too. It had been a long night's walk, and he'd had less than two hours' sleep in the past two nights and a day. Leaning forward, elbows on his knees, staring down at the cluster of wrecked buildings. It had the broken and deserted look, he thought, of a nest that crows have ravaged.

Ravaged *twice*?

It was a form of cowardice, of course — to imagine the worst, in order to protect oneself from any shocks that might be coming. The coward and his thousand deaths . . .

'Bob?'

Glancing round: 'Sorry. I was—'

'We should go back and sleep now. Then when we've rested take it in turns to keep a watch here. If you agree . . . Never know — might learn something. Then go down there when it's dark.' He glanced up, at higher and lighter-looking cloud than they'd seen recently. 'May not be as dark as we've been used to, eh?'

13

The bare trunks and limbs of birches were black and silver against some last vestiges of pink-flushed cloud. The land was dark, the humped shapes of the farm's ruins hard to see as darkness filled in the space around them. The nearest was twenty or thirty yards ahead; it had been some kind of barn but was now skeletal, possibly only still standing because its sparse frame offered so little resistance to the wind.

Schelokov pointed. 'Track turns into the yard there — between the shed and the stables I was telling you about.'

He'd mentioned them as being still intact. Stone-built, apparently, better built than the rest of the farm because it was where the landowner had kept his own horses.

They'd started down from the hillside camp as soon as the light had begun to fade. If they'd waited, getting down through the wood might have been fairly hazardous. Then at the bottom they'd been amongst the straggle of trees that stood along the high side of the road — cover enough, in the growing dusk, would have been good enough even if there'd been yet more cavalry on the road. Several detachments had clattered southward during the course of the afternoon — one big formation, regimental strength Schelokov had said, others smaller. Schelokov's estimate was that about fifteen hundred horsemen had passed during the daylight hours — plus however many might have gone by while he and Bob had had their heads down during the forenoon and early afternoon. So with last night's formation, you could say two and a half thousand in the past twenty-four hours.

Bob had commented, over their meal of tinned fish an

hour ago, 'Your "back of the moon"'s getting crowded, Boris Vasil'ich. Just as we arrive, they start flooding south.'

'There was a trickle before, wasn't there? Scouts, of course — the ones who chased us, for instance, and the detachment you saw from the air. So now — it makes sense.' He'd nodded. 'Be useful to know their objectives, wouldn't it? Ekaterinoslav, perhaps. Or to secure the railway towns. One thing's sure, they won't be hanging around in that wilderness we've come though. All right, the railway towns — Karlovka and Konstantinograd, on that line — but otherwise—'

'Kupyansk, Debaltsevo—'

'Not *these* units. There'll be other forces, on other routes. And on the railway, before long.'

'Won't make our withdrawal any easier, anyway.'

'Did you expect it to be easy?'

'I'd *hoped* to have been in and out again before it got to this stage.'

'At the time you and I set out, you hoped that?'

'Oh.' Trying to remember. Only four days back: it seemed much longer. 'No, I suppose—'

'You weren't giving yourself time to think about *anything*, Robert Aleksandr'ich. For reasons which we both understand. *I* was, though, I knew very well it could turn out like this. But if the clock were put back, you'd make the same decision again now, wouldn't you?'

'Well, I suppose—'

'No "suppose" about it. So the hell with worrying about it. The objective's unchanged, we're here where we aimed to be — despite a few hurdles along the way — and as for the journey back — it's wide-open country down there, plenty of forest, even with women to look after we can hide in it — eh?'

Pep-talk, he'd realized. Nodding ... 'When we *do* start south, Boris Vasil'ich — with this invasion in progress, it might be better to make directly for Taganrog, say, rather than nearer places we can't be sure of.'

'Yes. I agree.'

If one could be sure of Taganrog, even . . .

The track that led off from the road was on their left, with a branch curving right into the farmyard and the main line of it continuing into the pinewoods that surrounded the former manor house. Schelokov had stopped. Wondering — Bob guessed, by the way he was looking this way and that — whether to use the track or slant to the right behind this barn's remains and the rear of other sheds. There was an enclosure on this side — yard, paddock, whatever, the tops of fence-posts had been visible from the hill — and one could have approached that way.

He'd grunted. 'Wait here a minute?'

Vanishing trick, then — down into the drive and towards the wrecked barn. Moving inaudibly, under the sound the wind made in the trees and damaged buildings. And knowing his way around, of course. Just as well he did: prospecting these ruins in the dark wouldn't have been a very practical endeavour otherwise.

Mightn't be all that productive anyway. Just happened to be the only starting-point one had.

Darkness was still thickening as the minutes passed. Continuing meanwhile on that line of thought: what small chances one did have, realistically . . . But also that Schelokov had been absolutely right: given the decision to make again *now* . . .

'Bob?'

Stocky figure materializing out of nowhere . . .

'Here.'

'There've been cavalry here. I'd guess a scouting patrol, and probably this morning. Their tracks aren't even dusted. And it was coming down hard when we got here, remember?'

'Might they still be here?'

'No. Came and went. The later hoofmarks — superimposed on others — were made by the same number of horses leaving.'

'Can you *see* that much?'

'Feel, mostly.' A hand spread itself in front of his eyes.

'With *this*. See too, with your snout right on it. Like you can see my hand now. But do you get the implication?'

'You mean, the place must be — uninhabited.'

'Exactly.' He touched Bob's arm. 'Come on. Let's look around.'

Down a bank and to the right. At the corner, where the frame of the barn loomed over them, Schelokov pointed at where the track ran on, narrowing into darkness and enclosing trees. 'Two horses went up there, then came back and rejoined their comrades in the farmyard here. It's pretty clear they were just scouting the place out.'

It was about as dark as it was going to be, now. And — contrary to earlier indications — as it had ever been. The scent of fresh horse-manure could have been what had alerted Schelokov to the fact that horsemen might have been here.

'Didn't know you were a skilled tracker.'

'Not much skill in it. Practice, mainly — two years leading scouting patrols into East Prussia. You learn *something* as you go along.'

The stable building was on their left, with its roof still intact. Inside, Schelokov struck a match. Four stables — boxes — with shoulder-height partitions and half-doors to the inner passage, and at the far end a tack-room. Nothing that told one anything.

Second barn on the right, next, on this south side. It had most of its roof still in place, and Schelokov said it had been the typhus isolation ward. Good reason not to linger … A line of posts and wire linked it to a larger building — cow-shed, milking parlour, apparently. There were stalls in it, and in its south side sagging timber doors held shut by a wooden bar opened to the fenced area which they'd seen from the hillside earlier. *Strong* aroma of fresh manure, and the reek of urine: he was glad to be out of that one too — preceding his guide back into the central yard.

'Over here now is the well. In which — you know, I told you—'

'Yes.'

He wondered as they crossed the yard whether the

farmer and his family had been dead before the mob threw them in. And how Markov's people — his drivers, probably — would have set about clearing it. Someone would have had to go down inside, obviously. On a rope, and attach another rope, then be hauled back up — as many times as there were bodies.

'Here. This is it.'

There was a horse-trough, a low stone wall encircling the well itself, and a gallows of heavy timber supporting a joist with an iron sheave for the bucket rope. The rope was in place, around the sheave, and the bucket was in the horse-trough. The sheave turned, squeaking, when he pushed it round.

Schelokov's hand on Bob's arm turned him to the right.

'That — what you see there — was the dwelling-house. No roof, but the stove was in good order, so Markov had the tents pitched inside the walls. They rigged a tarpaulin above the stove.'

Single-storied: a typical *izba* — peasant's house — in which in winter the whole family would have lived around the huge stove and slept on top of it. There was nothing else in there now, except a carpeting of snow, but Schelokov was nosing around while he continued his muttered commentary. 'So this was the living quarters, and all the *letuchka*'s cooking was done on the stove here. The wards were in the stables where we came in, and in the large cowshed on the other side. Also this side — joined to this house — there's a cartshed, and we fixed up its roof while I was here. Needed more room for the patients I'd brought in, you see.'

Most of the damage had been done by fire. The mob must have set light to all the timber buildings, although some seemed to have burned less well than others.

Outside again, Bob waited while Shelokov went into the cartshed. Its roof-line was a continuation of the *izba*'s, then further to the right the hay-shed with its loft — only a clutter of beams up there — rose half a storey higher.

Schelokov emerged.

'Bob — tell you how I see this ... First, I'd say the patrol

that came here must have been looking for a place to
stable horses — remounts, perhaps — or a base for themselves or others. Even a hospital — cavalry need veterinary hospitals, you know, tends to be a problem. But
something of that sort. They made a thorough inspection,
anyway — took time over it, their horses must have been
in the barn there at least an hour or two. But what's more
interesting is *this*. When the *letuchka* was in operation
there were beds, tents and other equipment, all over the
place. Markov had small stoves set up in the makeshift
wards, for instance. And his operating theatre was in this
shed here — under the false ceiling, the floor of the loft.
Well, most of this furniture was scavenged locally, and he
certainly didn't take it with him. And obviously the doctor
or doctors with *Letuchka chetiri* — assuming they *were*
here, for some period of time — would have made use of
it. It was left *for* them ... But there's no table in there now.
Nothing — nothing *anywhere*. And a mounted patrol of
say a dozen men can't ride off with tables, stoves, beds ...'

'Right.'

'But nor could the *letuchka* people themselves — not in
a rush, or at short notice.'

'So your conclusion is they had ample time to pack up.
Didn't have to run for it suddenly. And — probably gone
for some while?'

'As we'd thought was probable, if you remember.'

'But they could have been gone, say, a week or two, and
— look, perhaps I'm being slow, but what would they have
done with all that stuff? I mean—' He'd stopped, looking
round. 'What—'

There'd been a clatter, from the hay-shed behind them.

Silence, now. He *thought* the sound had come from that
shed, but — hard to be certain ...

'I'll take a look.' Schlokov started towards it. 'You stay
here, Bob, and—'

'*Wait!*'

Engine-sound — some vehicle on the track leading up
here from the road. A lorry, truck, by the sound of it ...
He saw it then — weak headlamps, moving left to right,

visible briefly through a gap between two sheds, then it had gone out of sight behind the cowshed — but throwing all those semi-derelict shacks into silhouette as it rumbled on towards the farm entrance.

'Coming here ...'

'Quick — inside!'

Schelokov pulled him towards the hay-shed. The truck noisily changing gear at the corner ... One of the shed's doors was jammed open and the other was missing except for a broken plank hanging from one hinge. Inside, the smell was of rotting fodder — damp, musty. 'Here. Here, Bob ... See — there are rungs fixed to this wall here. Here — where my hand is — got it? Follow me up, eh?' He began climbing — the truck's engine was loud outside there, by this time — Schelokov climbing towards a square aperture in what was effectively a timber ceiling but actually the floor of the loft. The rungs were screwed or nailed to the timber wall, their upper surfaces sloped towards the wall to provide finger-holds as well as footholds. Less decrepit than most of the structures around here: and not a long climb: the loft's floor was only about eight feet from the ground.

It had its own floor-covering, too — several inches' depth of rotted hay, waterlogged and malodorous. He was off the ladder and lying flat on it. Schelokov too. There was a glow of yellowish light down in the yard — stationary now, and the engine was switched off, coughing to itself a few times, wheezing into silence as a man's voice called, 'Keep the lights on, Mikhail ... Hey, there's the well. If the water's good—'

'It is. The lieutenant said so.'

Second visit of inspection?

Cavalry starting their move south, needing conveniently-placed halts *en route*: or — whatever, purposes such as Schelokov had been guessing at, just minutes ago. Conceivably the patrol who'd come earlier in the day had reported on this place as being suitable for whatever they were looking for, and now these — out from the village, perhaps, officials of some sort—

'*Chyort vozmi!*'

An upheaval, close to him in the darkness: Schelokov had moved suddenly and violently. A whimper — not in *his* tones — and more scuffling: a growl of 'What the *bloody hell* . . .' and a thud of impact . . .

'Bob?'

'Yes — what's—'

'We have — company. Hold *still*, you — or by God I'll—'

'Christ — my *nose* . . .'

'Never mind your bloody nose — who *are* you?'

Some creature on its back, Schelokov on top . . . Then at a range of about twelve inches Bob saw he had one hand on this man's throat, and his Nagant now unholstered in the other. Loud metallic click as he thumbed the hammer back. At the front edge of the loft floor: he'd have been inching forward to get a better view down into the yard, and — come up against *this* character.

That noise they'd heard — and forgotten, in the truck's arrival . . .

But if he used his pistol, for God's sake — with those people only yards away down there — even the brief scuffle and the sound of the revolver being cocked had seemed loud enough. Especially when you were virtually on a stage — could have stood up, taken a bow: 'Gentlemen, for our *next* act . . .'

'Excellency — *proshu vas*—' hoarse, anguished whisper — '*beg* you, sir, you're *throttling*—'

Ukrainian accent. It had taken a moment to identify it. Being slightly preoccupied with what was happening in the yard: and how long it would be before they heard or saw . . . Schelokov's mutter: 'Tell me very, *very* quietly who you are and what you're doing here. Or believe me, I *will* throttle you.'

'Maltsev. Ivan Ivan'ich Maltsev. I was — hiding. Saw the motor's lights coming. I'd been watching you — hiding from you, thought *you* must be—'

'Must be what?'

'Don't know, but—'

'What are you doing here anyway?'

'I — live here. Well — around here ...'

'Deserter?'

'Yes. But I had the typhus, and—'

'Deserter from which army?'

Below, two of them were moving from shed to shed. One had a torch, its beam appearing and disappearing as he moved around. Three others waited by the truck. Schelokov was keeping an eye on the scene down there as well as listening to his captive ... 'I was with the artillery — Ninth Infantry Division, Excellency—'

'Went over to the Reds, eh?'

'My comrades did, sir. But I—'

'Deserted from them too?'

'Only wanted — *want* — to get home! I have a young wife, two children—'

'Where's "home"?'

'Kiev. I'd thought it was in White hands still, but they say it's changed again. Petlyura's forces—'

'Changed hands several times. Reds are there now.'

'Yes — and you see, *Prevoskhoditeltsvo*—'

'Quiet!'

The one with the torch was crossing the yard towards the dwelling-house. Torch-beam flickering this way and that, and another man close behind him. Two of the three who were waiting beside the lorry were lighting cigarettes; the flare of a match briefly illuminated one unshaven face and a badgeless cap, military tunic, red armband. The back of the lorry was stacked with bales of hay: the torch-beam licked over it as the other two passed, one of the smokers asking, 'How's it look to you, comrade?'

'*Nye plocho*.' Passing them, on the way to the house. 'It'll do. And that—' his torch-beam lit the front of the cartshed, no more than twelve feet down to the right from here — 'looks as good as anywhere to dump our load.'

'Any signs of *letuchka* habitation?'

'No.' He'd stopped in the open doorway of the little house, shining the torch into it and up at its non-existent roof. 'None.' The man with him growled, 'If they were *ever* here, the old she-goat may've been right and they're in the Crimea by now.'

The one with the torch went into the cart-house, came out again almost at once. 'Dry as a bone in there. But I'll just take a peek in this one ...'

Schelokov muttered, 'If he comes up the ladder, Bob—'

'Don't worry.'

'Good man. And if it comes to it, I'll keep those three busy. Should be able to plug a couple of 'em. The other one — with your fellow — you'll be nearest to him if he's inside, so—'

'Yes, all right.'

'Excellency—'

'Shut up. Move or speak before I give permission, I'll kill you. And if I don't, *they* will.' He'd paused. Then: 'Here he comes.' Bob was worming round to the far side of the access hole. He and Schelokov had both climbed out of it to their left, towards the front of the loft, so that seemed to be the natural way to go and on this other side he'd be behind this fellow, if he did come up.

If he saw the rungs — and then felt it was worth his while ...

Crouching, waiting. In the back of his mind, what they'd been saying about the *letuchka*. Not that one could think too lucidly at this moment. Knowing that at any rate one of them was inside the shed by this time. But no sound, or movement ...

Just standing there, looking round? Guesswork, and visualizing ... The mental picture was of one man standing inside and the other in the doorway. Right under Schelokov, that would put him. But it wasn't *all* just visualized: for instance, light showed with shifting effect in the square aperture as the man down there shone his torch around. Then — drag of boots on the earth floor, and — blinding suddenly, blinding bright, the beam shining straight up through the hole, lighting rough-edged planks and the mulch of rotten hay ...

Lighting *everything*. Up here — all immediately visible, if he'd poked his head up. Not a breath, hardly a blink.

'Weather'd come straight in, see.' Loud-voiced — all the louder for the silence he was breaking. 'You'd get leaks through these planks, anyway. No, we'll settle for next-door.'

The light dipped, vanished. The other voice mumbling that it wouldn't take more than twenty minutes to shift the bales inside. Adding then: 'Due here *tonight*, did you say?' Or it could have been 'Did *they* say' ... The answer was even less audible: and they were outside by this time, the first one calling across the yard, 'All right, comrades — put it in that shed there ...'

'Now let's get down to it, Maltsev. You deserted His Imperial Majesty's service, then ratted on your Bolshevik friends. And now you live *here*, you say.'

They were down below, in the hay-shed on its ground floor, under the loft's planking. The men who'd brought the fodder had left, finally — having taken nearer an hour than twenty minutes over it — and after they'd seen the lorry's lights turning right on to the road, towards Valki, they'd come down from the loft bringing Maltsev with them. Bob had stopped at the bottom of the ladder to receive him from Schelokov, who'd hung on to a fistful of the man's hair until Bob had hold of him. Then Schelokov had come down, pushed him against the timber wall and struck a match: revealing a round, soft-bearded face, round brown eyes like a monkey's.

'Well — should've found this before, shouldn't I ...?' A knife, in a sheath on his belt. It would have been under him, of course, unreachable under the greatcoat. Schelokov said, 'The sheath too. Take it off. And now turn out your pockets.'

'Comrades — please—'

'*Gospoda* will do, or *Prevoskhoditeltsvoli*. We're not your damn *tovarischi.*'

'No — I beg your Honour's pardon—'

'Bob, you need a knife. I've already got one ... What's this, now—'

Feeling it — he'd dropped the match — holding some

small object close to his eyes: then sniffing it.

'Candle-stub. May come in handy. Matches. A spoon, for God's sake ... Where would you have used a candle, Maltsev?'

'Here. Anywhere.'

'I'll let you in on a secret. Yesterday I and my friend here killed five Bolsheviks in the space of less than one minute. D'you think we'd hesitate to snuff out one more — a small, miserable-looking turd of a Bolshevik like you?'

'But — *Vashe Prevoskhoditeltsvoli*, I'm *not* a—'

'You deserted from their army — huh? Have to join something before you can desert it, don't you?' He shook him, his hands like clamps on the little man's upper arms. 'Here's the point, Maltsev. My only interest in your past career is it tells me the sort of man you are. In other words, I know you're going to lie to me, or try to. So here's a warning before we start: straight answers, or we kill you. I'll soon know if you're lying, and you're only useful to us if you tell the truth. *Understand?*'

'I won't lie — I swear—'

'You say you live here. How long now?'

'Oh.' Jerky breath ... 'Perhaps a month, or—'

'Why?'

'Excellency?'

'*Why* live in this place?'

'Excellency — my home's in Kiev, but — as I told you—'

Bob cut in: 'He said earlier he had typhus. Could be—'

'I know.' Schelokov's head turned. 'I know, Bob. It's what made me guess we might have a little treasure here. Leave it to me, eh?' He'd turned back: still holding Maltsev, shaking him again, the round head bouncing on the wooden wall. '*Real* little treasure, aren't you ... Well, all right, let's get to this typhus business. You told me you had it — *pravilno?*' So you're one of the very, *very* few who've lived through it. But you don't look to me like a man with a particularly strong constitution. How do you account for this?'

'I — don't know, Excellency. I suppose — God's mercy—'

'Oh, I wouldn't put the blame on *Him* ... What about doctors and nurses — you wouldn't have been nursed through it in a *letuchka*, by any chance?'

'In a *letuchka* ...'

'Well?'

'You must have known ... Of course, *they* were saying—'

'Is it something to be ashamed of?'

'For a Bolshevik, your Honour—'

'We're *not* Bolsheviks. So you can tell us the truth. In fact, as I explained to you, Maltsev—'

'I was — nursed — in a *letuchka*, Excellency.'

'*Letuchka chetiri*?'

'Here. The *letuchka* took me in. *Here*. And I — lived. And — I can't go to Kiev, I've nowhere else—'

'What were the names of the nurses in this *letuchka*?'

'Their names ...' He was panting like a dog. 'I don't—'

'Maltsev—'

'We called them *sestritsi*. *Proshu, Sestritsa — spasibo, Sestritsa* ... But names ... I'm sorry, Excellency, if I *could* tell you—'

'Where is the *letuchka* now?'

Silence. The hard, jerky breathing: it wouldn't take much to change to sobs ... 'I — don't know ...'

'They left here, did they?'

'Yes. Yes ...'

'When?'

'I — don't remember, exactly—'

'When I asked you where they are now, you hesitated before you gave me a lie for an answer. You're stupid, as well as dishonest, Maltsev. Try it again now. *Where are they, where did they go?*'

'Excellency — I don't know, I can't—'

'*Can't?*'

'Don't know. I swear ... If I ever knew, I don't remember.'

'Like the nurses' names. You don't remember them, either.'

'No. No, I—'

'You've a rotten memory. Two minutes ago you told me you never knew their names. Now you say you've forgotten them! How long since they left?'

'How long ...'

'Yes, *how long*?'

'Weeks. Three, four ... I — since the typhus, Excellency, I don't think straight, don't *remember*—'

'You're lying. Again. I'm losing patience now, Maltsev. I want two things from you, or I'm going to kill you. The first thing is the nurses' names, and the second is where did they go from here ... Bob, this place is as good as any, and I'll do it with his own knife. If you'd be so kind—'

'Yes. Here ...'

'*Prevoskhoditeltsvoli* — in the name of God—'

Bob transferred the knife into Schelokov's hand. 'Here it is.'

'This is your own doing, Maltsev ... No, stand *up*, damn you ...' To Bob — 'Swine's trying to kneel!'

'Mind if I try a question or two on him first? After all, once you've cut his throat — I mean—'

'All right. Go ahead.'

'Maltsev. You say they've been gone several weeks. And you're still living here. So you're also eating here. Eating well, aren't you? You're certainly not starving. Where d'you get it?'

'In the village. People are kind, they—'

Schelokov cut in again: 'People are *not* kind, Maltsev. People are — *horrible*. Look to the wolves, Maltsev, for kindness. Not to your fellow humans. Take me, for instance — I'm going to kill you in a minute, and the prospect doesn't worry me at all ... Bob — I'm sorry, I'd like to get it over with, that's all.'

'How come you're so well fed, Maltsev?'

'They left food here. In the house, where the stove is. It's gone now, all used up, I'll have to—'

'So why tell lies about getting food in the village?'

'It's what I'll have to do *now*—'

Schelokov murmured, 'Oh no, we'll save you that trouble!'

'Tell me this, Maltsev. And don't lie again. My friend here wants to get it done with, you heard him ... Here's the question, now. You don't recall the nurses' names, but what about the doctor? Make a great effort, tell me *his* name?'

Mouth open: trembling. Sweat glistening ...

'Just — *doktor*, we called him.'

'For me, that's enough.' Schelokov pushed him back hard against the wall. 'Wasting our bloody time. All right, Bob — finished?'

'Doctor — Karavayev!'

'Karavayev ...' Bob nodded. 'Good. That's a start — if it's the *right* name.' He asked Schelokov, 'Just another minute? If his memory's started to work, at last ... *Sure* that's his name, are you?'

Aware — although there was no time to think about it in any depth — of new hope. The men who were here and had talked of a *letuchka* could have been referring — in ignorance, not knowing any second *letuchka* existed — even if one did at all — they could have meant Markov's. But now there was Karavayev's: which *had* been here, *had* got away from Bogodukhov.

Maltsev mumbling, 'Karaveyev. Yes — Dr Karavayev.' As if he'd just heard the name for the first time himself, and liked the sound of it. 'But — Excellency—'

'Listen to me. It's possible you have a chance, now. If your memory's stirring, finally. The nurses — give me the *nurses'* names?'

'I can't. *Can't* ...'

'Well — where the *letuchka* was going?'

'Bob, we're wasting time. Those people said something about coming back tonight — remember? I say let's call it a day, get out of here. Kill this creature — and drop him in the well so they won't find him for a while—'

'All right—'

'*Prevoskhoditeltsvoli* — in the name of God—'

'— but one last try. There's a way I might jog his memory. If it doesn't work — all right, *soglasno* ... Think we might risk lighting his candle? I'd like to *see* how he reacts.'

A grunt ... 'Here. You light it.'

One-handed: the other still holding Maltsev, whose panting wasn't far short of sobbing. Bob cleared a piece of the dirt floor with his boot, set the candle-stub down carefully and struck a match. It took two more before it lit. Rising then, holding it between the finger and thumb of his left hand, shielding the small flame with the other.

Maltsev wasn't a *pretty* sight. Sweat, tears, slobber ...

'Now, then. I'm going to give you a name. I want you to tell me if you've heard it before. And remember this is your last chance. Are you ready for it?'

Nodding — so fast, small repetitive nods, that it was like some kind of affliction. His pumping breath endangered the candle-flame.

'Nurses by name Solovyeva?'

He'd gasped. Facial muscles convulsing ... Schelokov swung at him, his fist smashing into the open mouth, slamming his head back against the wall. Bob said urgently — nursing the flame — 'Hold on, Boris, hold on ... Maltsev — you know them, we *know* you know them — and they're our friends, we've come to help them. So — last question now, the last chance you'll get to save your skin — *where*, where *are* they?'

14

Those two cavalrymen had ridden up here as recently as this morning and found nothing to arouse their interest. Other people must have been along this track too, surely, in recent weeks. The area couldn't have been completely denuded of its inhabitants ... Schelokov hadn't believed Maltsev at first, and he still doubted him. The manor house — he'd told Bob again — had been burnt to the ground, leaving one solid wall standing — the only stone wall there'd been in its construction — and nothing else. He'd been up here often enough, he'd explained, in his own convalescent days, had come up into the woods for a quiet smoke, or sometimes with the English nurses when they'd had an hour or two off duty. He'd brought them hunting for mushrooms — like all Russians, he knew about mushrooms, which varieties were edible and which weren't.

'If this is a trick, Maltsev—'

'Your Honour, I swear — on my mother's grave—'

'Be the last swearing you do, if it is ...'

He wasn't giving him a chance. Keeping a grasp on his collar or arm most of the time. Bob following a few paces behind, with his hand in his pocket on the loaded Webley. Mainly with thoughts of wolves. Not that a pistol would be much use in this darkness — except scare them off, perhaps. You'd have got along faster using the track, but progress wasn't too bad now through the wood itself. It gave you the best of both worlds — the open roadway on the left visible enough as a guide, and only patches of crusted snow on the carpet of pine-needles underfoot, so you weren't leaving any noticeable tracks. In the open you would have — for anyone to find in the morning, and no doubt wonder what the sudden rush of visitors to nowhere-in-particular might have been in aid of. And there *would* be people here in the morning, according to what one of those visiting Bolsheviks had said — something about people being 'due back tonight'. Which had been good enough reason not to hang around the farmstead any longer.

Bob didn't think Maltsev had it in him to be tricking them. He'd recovered a little now, but half an hour ago he'd been utterly demoralized. He'd probably have given them the information they'd wanted even if Schelokov hadn't slugged him: as it was, they'd had to quieten him down before they could begin to make sense of his babbling.

One bit had stuck in Bob's mind: Maltsev still down somewhere near their feet, crumpled against the wooden wall, panting, 'If I'd known you were her friends — I'd have *told* you where — told you *anything* — been no need of this ...'

Her friends. Not *their* friends.

Trudging behind the others, left hand up to ward himself off trees and an occasional low-hanging branch. Ought to be at least halfway by now, he guessed. It was supposed to be about a quarter of a mile from the farmstead to the ruins of the old manor. Four or five hundred yards, say. They'd surely covered two or three hundred by this time.

'*Here*, you ...'

Schelokov — jerking Maltsev with him, to pass that side of a pine-trunk. Taking *no* chances: maybe also keeping him in line ... Brutal, but brutality with a purpose. Like that surprise assault — which had made absolutely certain he'd crack ... One thing was for sure: even if one was, oneself, *still* — quoting the Old Man — 'a bit of an old softy', Boris Schelokov as a partner might be counted on to make up for it.

The line kept repeating itself in his thoughts: *If I'd known you were* her *friends ...*

He hadn't questioned Maltsev on it. Through — all right

— lack of courage. Because one of the answers he might have given was — unacceptable.

He'd cannoned off a tree. Rebounding — like a drunk — and Schelokov glancing round: 'All right?'

'*Da, nichevo* ...'

Picturing her in his mind. As if by doing so one might physically *summon* her to be there.

'There it is, Bob.'

The surviving wall was a slab of blackness darker than the emptiness around it; you could just make out the chimney, like the stump of a tooth up there. Flat, open ground; in daylight one might guess there'd be foundations detectable under the blanket of snow. But no *letuchka* here: nothing ... He heard Schelokov ask Maltsev roughly, 'What next? Climb up, come down the chimney?'

'That way.' Pointing with his free arm: 'Over the ridge there, Excellency. About — half a verst from here.'

Bob had closed up to them. He saw Schelokov swing Maltsev round — hands clamping on his shoulders, stooping to peer into his face. 'In tents — or what?'

'The old ruins there. The old house — I *said* ... Tents also, but—'

'Not *this* ruin.'

'The *old* house. Much older. The people who were killed here — the man — they say he was born in it ... No — that his father was. His *father* built this one, see — when he got rich somehow, or—'

'I never heard of any other house. Or ruin. Damn sure Markov didn't know of it either.' Back to Maltsev: 'All right — show us.'

'Excellency — I said half a verst — it *would* be, from here straight to it, but it's better we should go up through the forest and down on the other side of the ridge. So as not to leave tracks from here. She's very — insistent, she—'

'*She*?'

'Solovyeva. She's the *mamasha* now, since—'

'Isn't the doctor in charge? Karavayev, you said?'

'Dr Karavayev died, Excellency. He had the typhus, too.'

'*No* doctor now?'

Again, the implication that there was only one of them. With the repetition, you had to accept it. Either Nadia or Irina, therefore. Spin a coin: heads you owned the world, tails—

Unless Maltsev didn't know they shared the name Solovyeva? If Nadia was using her maiden name, for instance?

It wasn't likely. In fact it was extremely *un*likely. Clutching at straws...

She might be alone here, Irina *not* here. Irina dead, for instance. After all, if a doctor could get typhus and die — and Dr Markov had contracted it, although he'd survived — extraordinarily, like *this* fellow ... A nurse would be as vulnerable as a doctor—

Schelokov was suggesting, '— go the shorter way. No time to waste — and nobody's on our tracks tonight ... Agree, Bob?'

Sweating, inside his heavy clothes. Needing — needing desperately — that straw to clutch at. And — driving the brain hard, forcing himself to deal with this state of panic coolly, logically ... For a start, it was conceivable that Maltsev might have had dealings with Irina, not with Nadia. If Irina was the matron now, her surname would be the one patients would be familiar with. They'd call her *Mamasha*, but any time her name was used it would be the surname. This truly *could* be the answer — because Nadia would be known to the patients as *Sestritsa* Nadia. Just as the two British girls had been known as *Sestritsi* Katya and Maria. And when you thought about it — facing it objectively instead of funking it as he had been — well, if one of them had been in line to become the matron, it *would* have been Irina, who'd been a qualified nurse when Nadia had only been in training. Nadia having been diverted into secretarial work, in the military hospital where they'd both worked in Moscow, hadn't even completed her training at that time.

'Bob?'

'Oh — yes. Yes, I do agree ...'

About which route to take ... Maltsev had been

protesting, imploring Schelokov to go the longer way round. Schelokov had overruled him, told him to shut up ... Adding now to Bob, 'We're not leaving much in the way of tracks, in any case.'

At that stage they hadn't been, but shortly afterwards there'd been several hundred yards of open snowfield to cross before they were back under trees again. He realized that the longer, safer route would have taken them higher, in woodland all the way, in effect covering two long sides of a narrow triangle instead of this short base-line.

Might have been better if they had, he thought. If one had known about that open stretch — and as a navigator, being trained to err on the side of caution ... On the other hand, time *was* a vital factor. With — as likely as not — some cavalry force arriving at the farmstead tonight, and others — hordes of them — pouring south to invest the whole countryside ... She — *they* — would have to be persuaded — somehow — to leave at once, and this wasn't going to be easy. To persuade them to walk out, as it were, at the drop of a hat, leaving the *letuchka* and whatever patients were in it now. It might in fact be more difficult in Nadia's case than in Irina's — in Nadia's circumstances now, having had her husband killed up on this front. Phrases from her last — final — letter came back to mind: such phrases as *Russian to the last drop of my blood*, and *Face death in defence of everything that I love and value* ... And she'd written that even before Nikolai Solovyev had been killed.

In contrast, Dr Markov's observation: *Letuchki have been obliged to abandon their wounded before this* ...

There'd be ancillary problems too, though. Such as walking wounded. She'd want to bring them: but with about two hundred and fifty miles of countryside to cross — territory in which by now there'd be a great deal more Bolshevik activity than there had been a couple of days ago — well, to have any reasonable hope of getting through you'd need all your physical powers, mobility, endurance.

'Excellency — we're close now ... Should I call to them, tell them who we are?'

'All right.'

They'd stopped. Maltsev called softly, 'Hello, there! It's Maltsev here — Ivan Ivan'ich Maltsev, bringing friends! *Mamasha* Solovyeva — two gentlemen here say they're your friends!'

Mamasha Solovyeva ...

Tall, slim, grey-eyed. That cloud of very soft, dark hair. The wide, full mouth and calm, unassertive manner ... However much she may have changed: and bearing in mind that she may not know *me* from Long John Silver — in any case may not give a damn ...

Be here, my darling? Please — *please*, be here?

They'd started forward again, down the snow-covered slope. There was a scent of woodsmoke. Stunted or half-grown trees here and there, but more or less open ground — which was probably how Maltsev had known where he was. Now, you could make out the shape of a tent: and other — tents, or ruins ... A spark of light, then: it flared for a moment then faded into a steady, softer glow.

'Maltsev? Ivan Maltsev?'

Male voice: heavily accented Russian: or intonation, more than accent ... Visible now: an odd-looking figure, down-slope from here, in line with the tent and against that radiance ... Maltsev answered him — calling him 'Ibraim' — while some other person emerged from the tent, light spilling from the open flaps across patchy, half-melted now. A woman's voice then, as she straightened — shapeless, wrapped in a blanket probably — asking '*Kto jhe oni?*'

'*Druzhya, Mamasha!*'

'*What* friends, for God's sake?'

He didn't recognize her voice, at this stage. If it had been Nadia's he thought he *would* have. She wasn't tall enough either. Didn't mean Nadia wasn't here — of *course* it didn't ... He called, 'Irina? Remember Bob Cowan, Robert Aleksandr'ich Cowan, brought you out of Enotay-evsk?'

Two seconds silence: then, 'It's not — *possible* ...'

'It's me, though — believe me ... Is Nadia here?'

Getting close to them, now, to the tent with the light in it — oil-lamp, or a candle. He had an impression of low walls and sloping tent-like roofs — groundsheets or tarpaulins as roofing to makeshift shelters. The man — stooped, long-armed, with a physically crooked look about him somehow — was confronting Maltsev and Schelokov. Bob had stumbled past them and him, to Irina.

'Irina—'

'Robert Aleksandr'ich? Really *you*? I can't *believe*—'

'It's amazing, I know. And for me, astonishing to have found you ... Nadia *is* here, is she?'

He had the impression of someone — *old*. Despite knowing she was in her mid-twenties ... The darkness and the time of night, and the way she was dressed, of course ... She'd given him her hand, rather tentatively. As he released it he was looking past her, searching the vaguely lit area near the tent's opening ...

He heard her say — *thought* he heard her say — 'No, you're out of luck there, Robert Aleksandr'ich ...' Then before he'd had time to assimilate it — defences no doubt resisting, declining to accept it — she'd raised her voice, called sharply, 'Ivan Maltsev! Come here, Maltsev!'

Shrill, commanding ...

Now she'd noticed Schelokov. 'Who's this?'

'Schelokov.' He'd bowed. Bob told her, 'Major Boris Vasilevich Schelokov. A good friend. He was with *Letuchka syem* when they were here, and he offered to bring me to find you. I couldn't have got here without him, either ... Irina — tell me, please — where's—'

'Maltsev.' Hunched — in profile like this more of an old crone than young woman as she faced Maltsev — whose attitude was cringing ... 'Came across the hillside, did you?'

'They made me, *Mamasha*. I'm sorry, *very* sorry — I tried to explain to them — your orders—'

She'd slapped him. Shrilling into his face: 'D'you want us *dead*? You *fool*, damn *fool*—'

'*Mamasha* — I was obeying you, I wouldn't tell them *anything* although they—'

'He's telling the truth, Madame.' Schelokov tried to intervene. 'We forced him to bring us — Commander Cowan having first convinced him of our — *bona fides*—'

'Get *out*, Maltsev. Go away — and don't come back! I told you — didn't I — if ever you came that way again — didn't I *tell* you?'

'*Mamasha*, I tried not to, I tried *hard*—'

'Ibraim.'

'*Mamasha* . . .'

'Get rid of him. I don't mind how, but see he goes . . . Hear that, Maltsev? You'll have no more meals here — that's final, I won't change my mind. Go away, *stay* away — d'you hear?'

Bob tried — 'We did make him bring us, Irina. We told him we'd kill him if he didn't.'

'Ibraim!'

A grunt, as Ibraim shambled towards Maltsev. Tartar driver, Bob guessed. Irina muttered, 'He's been a constant danger. Hanging around just so we'll feed him. I've told him to go a hundred times. Others go, only this one clings . . . *And* he was a Bolshevik — which we didn't know when we took him in . . .' Raising her voice again — Maltsev was backing away — 'I mean it, Maltsev — clear out, I don't *want* you here!'

'Excellencies—'

'Irina—'

Schelokov's hand on Bob's arm: 'Leave it, Robert Aleksandr'ich. If I were you. It's not *our* business.'

'*That's* true enough. What you've come here for, God knows . . . Come in the tent here, anyway — you can sleep here tonight if you want — we'll give you a meal, then—'

'Irina — where's Nadia?'

'Nadia.' Facing him — her face a whitish blur in the darkness . . . 'Yes. Nadia, you've come for. Of course, you *would* . . .' She'd shrugged, turning back to the tent. 'She's with my brother, that's where she is, she's *dead*.'

*

He'd whispered to Schelokov — to the deep commiseration in his eyes — 'May not be true. She's—' he'd touched his temple. Having to reach for *something*, and her imbalance being — to him anyway, at that moment — so obvious, in her brutal tone, some kind of personal triumph in it ... He wished he'd warned Schelokov earlier. He hadn't because he'd counted on Nadia being here. Despite the anxieties, it had been effectively beyond the scope of one's imagination that she would *not* be.

Schelokov's hand on his shoulder for a moment, gripping hard. Bob shook his head, muttered, 'I'm all right ...'

Needing time to think. Establish a perspective, a frame of mind to cope with this — beyond the immediate, instinctive reaction which was to tell himself that Irina was lying, that it simply *could not be true*.

She'd taken the candle from inside the tent and led them to a sort of lean-to shelter. Pine-branches served as roof-beams, slanting from the ground to the top of a five-foot wall of earth and stones and supporting a tarpaulin. There was a portable stove emitting some warmth from a residue of hot ash, and bits of old groundsheet to sit on. She told Schelokov — stirring the ashes and adding some pieces of wood — 'This was a ward. We cook and eat here now. Only seven patients left. When they're gone, it's finished.'

'When they're gone where?'

'Back to their duty. Where else?'

'Their duty. Quite.' Frowning ... 'But — the Volunteer Army — on this front, anyway—'

'You're not suggesting the reverse is permanent?' She looked and sounded contemptuous. 'You — a senior officer, to suggest—'

'I'm thinking of here and now, Madame. The problem of finding duties to return to.' He looked away from her — at Bob, who seemed as remote from them as if he might actually have been alone — or have thought he was. Or — praying ... Schelokov turned back. 'What about *you*, then? When in your view you've finished here?'

'The same, of course.' She dropped the poker beside the

stove. '*My* duty. Another *letuchka* — or base hospital. Whatever's wanted.'

The candle was in a tin, the tin's flapped-back top acting as a reflector, to throw its small pool of light whichever way one wanted it. She'd set it down on a wooden crate serving as a table, and now sat between it and the stove, pulling a bit of the groundsheet under her. Looking up at them then, from one to the other, her eyes glittery in that pale-yellow glow. Her eyes were green, Bob remembered, but no colour was noticeable at this moment. Like chips of glass, colourless in her dead-white face — sharp-chinned, triangular in its cowl of blanket. He remembered having thought of her as having a face like a cat's: and Nadia's quiet statement, *They're a little crazy, you know*...

He wondered if she might be lying, about Nadia. Whether he dared hope she was. She'd been intensely possessive of her brother, jealous of Nadia and — towards the end of the Enotayevsk expedition — suspicious of his own relationship with her.

She might well lie, he thought, to keep them apart. And it would account for that tone of voice: the brazen and brutal lie, wielding it like a club.

Schelokov was saying, '— point is, dear lady, we came to find you and escort you out to safety. I mean your *letuchka*, all of you. The Commander here came to us at Dr Markov's *letuchka* — we were near Karlovka, and as you'll remember — from the time you and Markov's people were together at Bogodukhov — he had some British nurses in his team?'

Bob cut in: 'Was it typhus?'

The cat's eyes burned at him. 'I presume you're asking me about Nadia?'

'How did she die?'

'A *chemodan*. She and our matron and the driver of the *dvukolki* — on the day we were leaving Bogodukhov. There was a hamlet close to us and they were on their way to say goodbye to some old people who'd obstinately refused to leave, and taking them some rations we could spare. Bolshevik guns happened to range on the cross-roads just at that time.'

A *chemodan*, literally meaning a suitcase, was the colloquial term for a particularly heavy-calibre shell or mortar.

'Was she killed outright?'

'Blown to pieces. All three. The horse and cart as well.'

Her eyes were fixed on him, doubtless watching for reaction. But she'd told the truth, he thought. You could tell, sometimes, it was just obvious.

Except—

Nadia — *dead*?

'You'd heard of my brother's death, I suppose. Saw your chance, eh?'

He frowned. 'As it happens, Irina — and as I think I heard Major Schelokov telling you a minute ago — we came in the hope of getting you out ahead of the Bolshevik advance. Dr Markov and the others were extremely worried for you. They'd waited as long as they could — in fact they'd hung on much too long, one can only pray they'll get through … I'd been sent up to get the British nurses out, and they told me you'd disappeared up here—'

'And you knew my brother was dead, so—'

Schelokov intervened: 'Why did this *letuchka* not pull out of here when you were told to?'

'What d'you mean, *told to*? Who's supposed to have told us?'

'Army headquarters in Kharkov. They'd taken over your administration, hadn't they. Orders certainly *were* issued — Markov knew of it, and he'd had his. That's why he was expecting you.'

She shook her head. 'Never had such orders. To move down here from Bogodukhov — yes. We came down with a cart-load of our own patients and found *Letuchka syem* had left others here. Including some who'd died in the interval between their departure and our arrival. But perhaps we'd moved *here* by then.'

'So the despatch rider would have found that place

deserted — no indication where you'd moved to?'

'Wouldn't have left a change-of-address notice for Bolsheviks to find, would we!'

'So it might have been assumed you'd anticipated orders to withdraw ...'

Bob asked him, 'Did I hear you ask whether she's coming with us?'

'Hadn't got quite that far.' Glancing round at him, Schelokov winked. 'Still a few patients here — we'd established this much, and—' he turned back to her ... 'How long before you'll be ready to leave, would you say?'

'Leave — with *you*?'

'It's what we're here for. And frankly, the sooner the better, because—'

'Did you know she had it in mind at one stage *not* to marry my brother?'

Irina was, undoubtedly, mad ... But — how much she knew, or guessed, or what Nadia might have told her — under extreme provocation, for instance, *this* sort of provocation — which after some period of time might wear through even Nadia's cool self-possession ... Schelokov put in — coming to his rescue again — 'Excuse me, but if we might stick to more immediate business for the moment — so I can have some appreciation of the background to your situation here — your doctor in this *letuchka* — name of Karavayev? Died of typhus, that fellow Maltsev was telling us?'

'And that Bolshevik creature survived it.'

'Did the doctor die here, or—'

'Here. Yes. And before that we'd lost Anya Prokofyeva, also to typhus. She was a nurse, very experienced, she had become matron when the others were killed, and when she fell sick I took *her* place. Then Ivan Karpovich — Dr Karavayev — was struck down just after we'd moved to this place. He was dead in three, four days.'

'And are you alone here now, you and — Ibraim?'

'There's a young girl — student nurse — from the village here. Avdotya. Anya Prokofyeva recruited her. Nice child — ignorant, can't read or write, but—'

She'd checked herself — staring at Bob . . .

'Would you be interested in hearing how she came to change her mind back again, and marry my brother?'

'She' meaning Nadia, of course.

Not Avdotya. Nadia — who was dead.

It still wasn't real. One might hope to wake up in a minute, hear Schelokov growl, 'Time we started, Bob' . . . Then — God, the *joy*, to find that it had been no more than a particularly foul dream!

His own voice, though — as if from some other self who was so far detached as to be able to discuss her impartially . . . 'I suppose she — loved him.'

'Rubbish! If she had, why would she have made eyes at *you*?' A snort - derision, anger . . . 'No — I'll tell you. It was *my* doing. That's to say, she was taking no notice of me — of *my* entreaties — so I enlisted the help of Maria Feodorovna.' Schelokov had grunted in surprise: Irina glanced at him, nodded. 'Yes — the Dowager Empress.' Back to Bob: 'Our mother had been very close to her, as you know — as Lady in Waiting, but in any case as friends of long standing. It's why she'd invited us to join her entourage down there at Kharaks, of course. You may remember, it was where we'd been making for — *with* my mother — when we ended up at Enotayevsk. Anyway — Maria Feodorovna was of like mind, I'm pleased to say — for the sake of my darling mother, what *she*'d have wanted — and she was able to persuade Nadia as to where her duty lay.' Irina's look was triumphant, as she finished. 'See?'

'Yes, I do see.'

And it was — something, to have it explained, after all this time. It was the truth, too, made unmistakable sense because Nadia had put a lot of it into that letter. For instance, where she'd written: *Just as Nikki would be broken in his heart and spirit if I had held myself back from his long-held expectation that I would marry him, I would be in torture if I had to wait in safety* . . .

He could see it, now, understand it — as he had *not* understood it until now. Nadia *would* have been impervious

to Irina's attempts at persuasion: she'd had Irina's measure,
all right. But Maria Feodorovna, no doubt with the finest of
motives but she herself on the point of embarking in HMS
Marlborough for passage out of Russia, had persuaded her
where her duty lay.

And she'd listened, and was dead.

'The point we have to decide—' Schelokov broke in
again — 'is what to do *now*. For instance — if we waited
here a few days, would you come with us? A few days to
make arrangements for your patients, or get them on their
way?'

'You'd wait *here*?'

'Not necessarily—'

'No.' Bob reminded him, 'Mishka — she'll need feeding,
and—'

Schelokov told Irina, 'Mishka is a horse. We've made
camp in the woods back there, left her tethered ... Look
— if we said we'd wait one week would you commit yourself to coming with us then?'

'A week.' She was frowning. 'I don't know. If the last of
them is strong enough by then—'

'Again — *no*.' Bob didn't look at her. 'You'd have to
make the decision now, and stick to it. Personally, Boris, I
think a week's far too long. Another thing is we can't take
any walking wounded with us. We'd take Irina — and
Ibraim, I suppose—'

'Even a week—' Irina reached to poke the stove — 'I
couldn't *promise*—'

'In that case—' looking at Schelokov — 'there's no point
in our waiting even a day.'

'You see—' Schelokov began explaining to Irina — 'the
Bolsheviks are moving south in strength now. Cavalry, as
we've been seeing for ourselves, but also by this time no
doubt on the railways.'

'Yes. Avdotya gets news from the village. Her aunt's
there still. It seems they're going to use the farm we were
at, too. Some — as you say — cavalry use or other. We'd
anticipated it, anyway, it was the main reason Dr Karavayev decided we should move to *this* place. Formations of

cavalry had been passing southward on the valley road, and a place like that — with stables — naturally they'd make use of it.'

'Your Dr Karavayev would have been much wiser to have pulled out altogether.' Schelokov added, 'I imagine the move itself wouldn't have been too easy, anyway — short-handed, and with no road?'

'There was the doctor, and Ibraim, and another driver. He's also died, since ... We had one *telega* and one *fourgon* — the other *fourgon* we'd sent directly to Kharkov with wounded — from Bogodukhov, before we left. So we lost that cart *and* its driver. And our other *dvukolki* smashed itself up — the axle and one wheel, on the way down here. That was the second one; the other — I told you ... But with those two carts we were able to move the patients and all our material as far as the ruin — you know where I mean, the wall with the chimney on it, like some kind of monument — and then from there — on foot, and with stretchers.'

'Where are the carts and horses now?'

'I sent them into Valki, in exchange for food. One of the horses they may have butchered — what they sent us first was certainly horsemeat. Now we get flour, and whatever they can spare — very little, I may say. In fact if it wasn't for Avdotya's aunt—'

'You must have realized you wouldn't be able to move again, without your transport.'

'Moved where?' The wild stare ... 'Look — right after the move, we'd sent the horses and carts back to the farm. I don't know what Dr Karavayev would have done later, but he fell ill then and died, and it was all up to *me* — with one young girl to help me — oh, and Ibraim of course ...'

She'd glanced round — as Ibraim crept into the shelter and squatted just inside the tent-like entrance, with his eyes fixed on her. Bearded, long hair tied in a knot at the back of his head, savage-looking, but the dark, slanted eyes never leaving her. A phrase for it might have been 'dog-like devotion' ... If that *was* devotion? She went on — addressing Schelokov — 'I had no feed for the horses,

and it wouldn't have been safe to let them graze freely.
Then we had snow ... But in any case I've no use for
transport, now. When the last of our patients leaves, that'll
be the end of this *letuchka*. If we can only be left alone
that long ...

Schelokov nodded. 'Brings us back to the question of
whether you're coming with us. If we did wait a week?'

He looked at Bob, who held his gaze for a moment and
then turned away. He'd already said he thought a week
was too long. The thought of spending a week here —
even a day — was sickening.

If Nadia had been here, he'd have waited a month — a
year ...

And if he'd been here alone — without Schelokov, who
was suggesting to Irina that she might think about it, give
them a firm decision by this evening — he'd have left now,
this minute.

A *chemodan*. The shrieking plunge of it, out of
nowhere. Nadia, and the matron and a Tartar driver, a
dvukolki and a horse. On an errand of mercy, incidentally.
Flash and thunderclap, a cloud of smoke quickly dissi-
pating, the hot reek of explosive. Debris: blood staining
the surrounding snow. At that time, that moment, he'd
have been in Constantinople: at work — or play ...

She'd been married. It hadn't been a monastic life, in
Constantinople, not by any means.

'Robert Aleksandr'ich—'

Back to earth ...

'Most of the night's gone. We wouldn't want to be
caught blundering around on that hillside, would we? If
there's a platoon at the farmstead now? Suppose we spend
the day here — sleep, enjoy a meal if we're offered it.
Mishka's a tough old bird, she'll last one day without
us ...'

The stove had been hot enough by then for a pot of *kasha*
— gruel, containing scraps of bacon — to be heated on it.
Irina had left the candle with them, and retired to her tent.
They'd sleep in this shelter when they'd eaten. She'd

warned them against letting the stove overheat; it was at the back of the shelter where the roof was highest, but that was still timber and tarpaulin right above it.

Schelokov had murmured when she'd gone, 'Plenty of bees in *that* bonnet.'

'She's mad ...'

'Robert Aleksandr'ich, I'm *extremely* sorry.'

'You warned me, didn't you?'

'Oh ... One didn't actually *believe*—'

'I don't believe it now. At least — I do, I know it's a fact — but it's unreal, I keep feeling I'll wake up and—'

'Another warning — with apologies. When you do wake up, it'll be worse.'

He could see the truth in that. *Dreading* it. Thinking, *Better stay awake* ...

'Grit your teeth, Robert Aleksandr'ich. Remember it's happened to other men — *many* others. Different circumstances, but—' a shake of the greying head — 'all you can ever do is grit your teeth.' Stirring ... 'This may be hot enough, I think.'

'Boris Vasil'ich — if when the evening comes she's still not certain about coming with us in a week — don't press her?'

'No. We do have some — obligation, though. And—' glancing round at him, from the stove — 'we both have to think how we might feel in — say, a year's time, if we hadn't done all we could?'

'If *we're* alive in a year ... But — such a *bitch* ...'

'*Volchitsa*. Wolf-bitch ... Here, it's plenty hot enough ... Jealousy, is it?'

'Of Nadia. Yes. And a sort of crazed devotion to her brother. She'd have preferred to have him all to herself. Resented Nadia for that reason. That was how it *was* ... Since then, I'd guess the possibility of Nadia preferring someone else — me — and rejecting her brother — that would have appalled her, too. Nadia told me once that they were both crazy. And *he* began to crack up a little, at one stage ... I think she'd still have hated Nadia, but even more the idea of Nadia turning her beloved brother down.

In a sense turning them *both* down, as she might see it ...'

'Pity you couldn't have kept Nadia with you, after the other business.'

'I know. But—'

'Wouldn't have been possible, I suppose.'

'Hardly ... But incidentally — in case you had any other impression from Irina — Nadia and I did have an understanding, but we'd done nothing, absolutely *nothing*—'

'You don't have to tell me, Robert Aleksandr'ich. Here. It's ready, help yourself ... Changing the subject — I think the *volchitsa* made a grave error in throwing Maltsev out.'

He needed a moment, to readjust, shift wavelengths ... Then he nodded. 'I was trying to tell her so — if you remember.'

'And I said leave it, it's their business. I was wrong there, if the worst came to the worst it could be very much *our* business. But I doubt if you'd have changed her mind, in any case.'

'In a rage, wasn't she? Absolute fury. Here you are ...' Offering him the ladle. 'Wolf bitch is right.'

'Except wolves aren't stupid. To have Maltsev out there now on the loose — the farmstead as his alternative abode, presumably, and Bolsheviks moving in — if they are — lots of them around anyway — and he knows all about *this* place, must hate her now — if he didn't before, but she was his meal-ticket then — and no reason to love *us*, poor fellow.' He was helping himself to the porridge ... 'Come to think of it, *I'd* sooner not wait here a week.' Glancing at Bob. '*Another* mistake I've made, eh?'

Even half-sleep was bad. Half-dreams, in half-sleep. In one of them Nadia asked him, '*Why* could you *not* have kept me with you?', and in his subconscious or semi-conscious thinking the answer seemed to be that he could have, could have brought her with him to Krasnovodsk — which was where he'd ended up himself and been greeted as some kind of hero. He could have married her there, just as Nick Everard had married *his* girl, a week ago. It would have been easier, in fact — in those circumstances, with temporary hero status, there'd have been no problem about getting permission. All above-board, proudly fluttering White Ensigns and an arch of his brother-officers' swords.

Awake, he'd asked himself *Could I have?*

Only if he'd more or less kidnapped her, at sea. The Solovyevs wouldn't willingly have transferred to the other ship without her. And although there'd been something going between himself and Nadia by that time, they hadn't arrived at any clear understanding, they'd barely had a minute alone together. She might well not have been ready to defy them.

The three of them had been as sick as cats, too. And he'd had his own technical preoccupations . . .

But Nick Everard would have managed it — grabbed his chance while he had it — *wouldn't* he?

Spilt milk. More literally, split blood. One life thrown away, and the other—

Time would tell. At this stage its value seemed — questionable.

As daylight came he was awake and sitting in the shelter's entrance, with the stove's warmth behind him and a frozen section of the camp-site taking shape outside in steel-grey, cloud-filtered early light. In his close-up view was the end of the tent in which Irina slept, and to his right an earth-wall on the other side of which there had to be a shelter like this one. Ends of cut branches protruded over it, with a tarpaulin lashed to them. Beyond — visible through the gap between the tent and the end of the wall — uneven snow-covered ground with patches of undergrowth and saplings and the stumps of other saplings — a lot of those, it would be where these roof-beams had come from — and behind, hardening out of the darkness as it faded, the encircling backdrop of forest.

There'd been no snowfall in the last twelve hours. Their own tracks would be leading clearly in this direction not only across the area now in his view but also across that much larger stretch of hillside which they shouldn't have crossed. Maltsev's would be there too, he guessed, leading back the other way. Unless on his return journey to the farmstead he'd obeyed orders, taken the long way round. It seemed unlikely that he would have. And surely he *would* have gone back to the farm: seeing that there was no other shelter except for the forest itself.

A male voice called, '*Zdrastye, Sestritsa! Sestritsa — pojal'sta!*'

He'd heard — he realized now — some kind of domestic activity a moment or two earlier — a clatter of pots or perhaps it had been a stove's iron lid — when he'd been preoccupied with those other thoughts. But a girl's voice now ... '*Da — momyent, momyent...*'

'We're hungry in here, *Sestritsa*, little darling!'

'You'll *stay* hungry too, if you're cheeky!' Then she was in his field of view, and had seen him too. 'Oh. Oh ...'

'*Dobroe utro.*' He lifted one hand in greeting. She was crossing the open ground towards Irina's tent, carrying a tin mug that had steam rising from it. A short, sturdy-looking child with a round, pink face encircled by a scarf that covered her head and was tucked inside the raised collar of a military greatcoat. Locks of yellow hair showed under the scarf, and the coat had frayed lower edges where a foot or two of material had been lopped off. She'd stopped, was staring at him, her mouth slightly open. He'd look to her like some kind of bearded ogre, he realized. Although she ought to be used to such apparitions — the country being so full of them ... He smiled. 'You must be Avdotya.'

'Yes. I am!' *Big* smile — ingenuous and infectious. 'Like some tea?'

'That would be *very* kind. But you'd better see to your hungry patients first?'

He went inside. His undervest and the socks which he wore inside his seaboot stockings had been hanging above the stove, and they were now warm and dry. He pulled off his sweater and shirt, put on the vest and hung the shirt where it had been. Socks on, then: the oiled-wool stockings could have an airing now. First time they'd been off his feet in a week ... But this was luxury, one had to make the most of it.

Schelokov was half awake. He told him, 'Tea coming in a minute.'

'Uh? Tea, you say? Did you say—'

'Yes, I did. Hang on.' He'd heard the girl passing back the other way, humming to herself. 'Avdotya!'

'Hello ...'

'There are two of us in here, Avdotya. Thought I should mention it — in case you really meant it, about tea?'

'I know.' She nodded towards the tent. '*Mamasha* told me. Ibraim will bring it to you, though.'

Back inside, he told Schelokov — he was sitting up now, stretching — '*Mamasha*'s orders. Did you hear? No young girl's safe with us. With *me* anyway.'

'She'd have nursing duties that keep her busy, I imagine ... Are you all right, Bob? Did you sleep?'

He nodded. 'Thanks.'

'Gritting the teeth?'

'You're a good fellow, Boris Vasil'ich. Extremely kind. But — let's forget my problems now?'

'Excellent! Life goes on — uh?'

On the surface, it had to.

Ibraim brought them black tea and chunks of black bread. His family home had been on the Nogai Steppe, he told Schelokov in his broken Russian, but he hadn't seen either it or them since 1916, had no idea whether any of them were still alive. He called both of them 'Your Excellency' — *Vashe Prevoskhoditeltsvoli* — but never cracked even a hint of a smile. Bob commented when he'd left them, 'Face like a mask.' Thinking, *Hallow'een mask, at that* ... Schelokov had muttered with his mouth full of bread that Tartars invariably called you 'Excellency' right up to the moment they cut your throat.

Irina came by, then, on her way to attend to the patients.

'Did Ibraim bring you your breakfast?'

'Yes, thank you very much.' Schelokov was studying her with interest. In this light you could see that her eyes were green — and her hair light-brown, tied back behind her head. Her eyes were set deeper in her skull than Bob remembered. Or perhaps it was more that her cheek-bones were more prominent. Short rations, he guessed: and tight nerves. You could almost *see* the quivering nerves. She could have been Schelokov's own age — not young enough to be his daughter ... He'd added, 'Slept like logs, too. First night under cover for quite a while.'

'You'll keep the stove going, will you?'

'Of course.' Bob offered, 'If you want any wood chopped—'

'That's Ibraim's work.' *Cold* green eyes: definitely feline ... 'Thank you, all the same.'

'Nice little thing, your Avdotya.'

'Meet with your approval, does she?'

'I was wondering — you said she's a local girl — what'll happen to her when you leave?'

'I've told her I'll take her with me.'

He exchanged a glance with Schelokov. Irina added, 'In point of fact my predecessor, Anya Prokofyeva, made that promise. But in any case I haven't decided yet whether I'll go with *you*. So — in due course—'

'Quite. But if her family's in the village here—'

'Only an aunt. Her father and brother were both killed fighting on our side, and her mother died of typhus. The aunt's a widow and her two sons are away somewhere in the Red Army.'

'My God ...'

'We Russians do have our problems, you see.'

'I know it. Remember, I'm half Russian.'

'Half British, too. When you've had enough of it, you'll leave. Sail away, leave us with—' a sweep of one hand — '*this* ...'

She did have a point — which had been put to him often enough before, in one form or another. But if he'd given her the standard answer — that he was a serving officer, had to do as he was told, she'd almost certainly have been ready with something like 'Such as chasing after other men's women'. He shrugged, therefore, kept his

mouth shut — he hoped disappointing her — and she
turned to Schelokov. 'Avdotya will be going into the
village now, Major, and I have my own work to do. We
don't usually have a midday meal, but if you're going back
to your camp when it's dark this evening — *is* that your
intention?'

'Yes.'

'We'll give you a meal of some sort before you leave.'
On her way out, she paused, pointed out past the other
shelter. 'Beyond that stand of birches, there's a stream.
Ibraim keeps an axe there, to open a hole in the ice — it
closes up again, of course. And anything else, ask him. He
speaks very little Russian, but he understands.'

They'd both slept, off and on. There'd been a few flurries
of snow outside, but the shelter's low ceiling contained the
stove's warmth with soporific effect. Conversations came
in spasms when they both happened to be awake. Hopes
that Mishka would be all right, and that Maltsev, as a
deserter from the Red Army, might keep himself to
himself. And that Irina, come sundown, would refuse to
make any commitment to leave with them.

'She'll manage on her own, in any case. Better than we
could, probably. She's not a wolf bitch for nothing.'

'And we'll start south tonight, eh — if she says no?'

'I'm for it. Definitely.'

'Risk using the road, d'you think?'

'The alternative's to go over the top — up through the
wood and then head south along the crest. I've no idea
what the terrain's like up there.'

'Might be less risk on the road going south — if all the
traffic's going that way...'

'Sleep on it, shall we?'

If *she*'d been here, the prospect of the return southward
would have been — beyond description, unimaginably
thrilling ... But now, it was merely what he had to do — or
attempt — for some reason that wasn't entirely clear ...
You might say — Schelokov would have, if he'd asked him
now — that it was natural, *of course* any sane and healthy

person did his best to stay alive and free — etcetera. But this assumption — if you believed in any kind of after-life and had it as much in mind as he did now that the only people he cared for to any really profound degree were already dead — wasn't exactly blinding in its logic.

He'd heard women's voices, at one stage, so Avdotya must have returned from the village. And another time when he'd been only dozing he'd heard men singing, a baritone solo with a deep-voiced chorus in support, a very old Russian song — *Stenka Razin*, a ballad about a river pirate of that name.

Schelokov had woken too, had been smiling as he listened to it. He'd suggested, 'We should join them.'

'Later, perhaps.'

'All right. Supper time. When we're ready to move ... I just woke from a dream, Bob — Mishka was being attacked by wolves.'

'Christ. You don't think—'

'Don't *think* — but it's on the cards. Depending on the wolf population in this region. And their food supplies. We've left her longer than we meant to, haven't we?' He fingered the scarred side of his face. 'Dreams are crazy things.'

He nodded. 'I've been having some.'

'Ah.' The soldier's head turned. 'Just remember — it's happened to others, *they*'ve stood it ... Also, Bob, however terrible it is *now*—'

'I know.'

That was the answer to the other question, too.

He'd fallen into a much deeper sleep, then, and Schelokov must have done the same. They had no warning, heard nothing of the troop's approach — which had had to be across open ground, and it was still late afternoon or early evening — didn't know a thing about it until Irina was outside the shelter screaming 'Get up, *up*! Robert Aleksandr'ich, Major, *vstavayete* — they're *here* — Oh God, *God*!'

Like regaining consciousness from coma. There was shouting — but who — where ... Horses then — arriving at the gallop, slithering and crashing to a halt, and immediately — rather as if her screams had precipitated everything — a bedlam of noise all around, and Irina's final screech silenced by a solid *thwack* — the flat of a sword, he learnt afterwards. Horses neighing, orders being shouted: he was on his knees with the Webley in his hand — he'd slept in his greatcoat, as always — jerking the action back to get a round into the breech, seeing Schelokov on his stocking'd feet — crouching, the roof was too low to stand — with his revolver aimed at the entrance but unable to fire because Irina was there in it, filling it as she fell inwards and backwards. He had a vision then of a rearing horse and its rider sliding down to land right in the entrance astride her now prone body. Schelokov had fired twice by then but the same sword sent his Nagant flying; Bob hadn't got even one shot off because his gun hadn't cocked as it should have, and by this time there were four of them inside the shelter, there'd have been no point. He'd surrendered, two rifles were covering him, Schelokov had his arms up too and a sword-point at his throat. One of them pulled the Webley out of Bob's hand, and another — no rank insignia but he seemed to be in charge — yelled '*Out — outside — von, poshli!*' One of them had been hit by one of Schelokov's two shots, had his right hand clasping his left arm and was cursing. They were dragging Irina out by her feet, long heavy skirts riding up above her knees, and the one pulling her stopped where he'd got to, knelt down and began wrenching the skirt higher, having to lift her legs and bottom with each jerk as her thighs and long woollen knickers became exposed. Bob moved without thought, having the weight and power to thrust his guards aside: they'd grabbed him again but he'd aimed a kick at the kneeling man's face. Futile — didn't even have his boots on — but all of this had taken about twenty seconds, straight from deep sleep into shock and now blind reflex fury. His kick didn't connect, that man had rocked back out of its range, and the two whom Bob had almost but not quite thrown off had got new purchases on his arms. At the same time, adding to the quality of nightmare, he saw Avdotya struggling in a cavalryman's arms, heard her scream in her small childish voice 'Mamasha! Oh, Mamasha! Oh please, Jesus—' The man had forced both her arms behind her, his bearded face was nuzzling at her throat — might have been trying to tear her clothes open with his teeth — and a colleague was running to share the fun. Bob roaring, fighting like a madman to get free from the two clinging to his arms; while another horseman cut his way out through the side of the other shelter — slashing the tarpaulin open with his sword.

Exploding out: 'Seven of the bastards! Kill 'em, shall we?'

'Yeah!' It was the sergeant — or officer, whatever he was — behind Bob, now. He'd left Schelokov, whom he'd been questioning inside, and he had Maltsev with him. 'Swords — don't waste bullets!' He flipped the Nagant around in his fist, brought it clubbing down on Bob's skull.

15

The screaming could have been a sound-effect out of hell — as one imagined hell or dreamed of it. There *had* been a dream-like element to start with, but the screaming hadn't stopped now that he was awake or half-awake — in *some* degree of consciousness. Conscious of the cold and pitch darkness, and the scream swelling into an even wilder abandonment to agony — with the over-spill here of horror, the hair standing up on the back of his neck and down his spine and an image forming, its outline shaping and then detail hardening, as if it were created *by* that sound: a triangular, sharp-boned face suffused with blood — *black* with it. Green pinpoints for eyes, and her throat and the veins in it swollen to what might be bursting-point.

Then — liquid ... The distorted features, and the scream — glottal, bubbling through liquid as it drowned.

'*Christ ...*'

His own voice, speaking into silence. Cold, hard-beaten clay under his face. Music then, starting up out of that same silence? Not close, nowhere close at all, but—

Curtain down, orchestra striking up?

A hand found his shoulder, closed on it, just as a fact stood out clearly in his stirring memory. *Nadia, dead ...*

'Back with us, are you ...?'

He'd whispered — thinking of Nadia, who'd gone virtually in a puff of smoke — 'Thank God. Oh, thank God ...'

'For small mercies?' A chuckle. 'I wonder which ones *they'd* be.' The voice was familiar but only just audible. Boris Schelokov's, of course. 'Welcome back anyway, Robert Aleksandr'ich.'

'What in God's name *was* that?'

But he knew damn well what — or rather who — it had been. Not the little girl. Impossible to imagine any such sound issuing from — being forced out of — that small, childish throat ...

And it was no dream. Might have started in one but certainly wasn't now. He'd have made it a dream if he could have. Right back to — oh, Sevastopol ... No — to the other *letuchka*. At least he'd got those two out.

His fingertips told him that the back of his head was a sticky mess.

'Boris Vasil'ich — where are we?'

'Stables.' Schelokov's hand squeezed his shoulder, then left it. 'The tack-room at the end — remember? Only place they could shut us up. Door's wedged — wedge in the latch — and there's a guard on the other door.'

The music was real, not some aberration as he'd suspected it might be. Incongruous, but there right from the moment the screaming had stopped, and louder now than it had been to start with. He was on his face with his fingers clawed into some sort of hard earth flooring. Clay, probably. A stink of piss but not — strangely — of horses, of horses themselves or of their excrement. Yesterday — last evening, if that was yesterday — the place had reeked of it. Well — not this place, especially. Only generally, and that other barn.

That was an accordion, and there were men singing to whatever tune was being squeezed out of it.

There'd been singing earlier, he remembered ... Then remembered better: no connection — those had been Irina's patients.

'*Seven of the bastards. Shall we kill 'em?*'

'*Yeah! Swords — don't waste bullets ...*'

A revolutionary song, this one. Shoulder to shoulder, the people's triumph. *Svoboda, Raventsvo* ... The squeeze-box panted a suitably discordant background to it.

'Are you there, Boris Vasil'ich?'

'Well — unfortunately ...'

'How did we get here?'

' *You* came on a horse — across its withers, like a corpse. Head dripping blood — for all I knew you *were* a corpse. Rather envied you — and not just because you were getting a ride ... The two girls travelled the same way, except Avdotya had her hands tied. She wasn't unconscious, as you and Irina were. She sobbed all the way. Screamed now and then. Well — hysterics. Made them laugh — would you believe it?'

'Believe *anything*, of them ... Did you come on foot, then?'

'Ibraim and I came between the stirrups, as the saying goes.'

'Meaning what?'

'Cavalry expression. When you put a prisoner between two riders, two horses, and he has to run between them. In my case, with no boots on. They used their whips too, the sods ... You've no boots on either, in case you didn't notice. How's the head?'

'Hurts. Where's Ibraim now?'

'Here — by the door. Mutters to himself now and then — gets too loud, I've had to quieten him a couple of times.'

'What does it matter, if—'

'As I said, there's a sentry on the outer door. Changes every half-hour. So none of them has to miss the fun for too long, I suppose. I imagine they've got some vodka, helping things along. Sounds like it. They have a fire, too, earlier on it blazed, you could see its light — up there ... But — answering your question — I'd sooner not invite attention. Especially not have them know you've come round — might want to question you?'

'Ah ...'

'Speaking of the damage to your head — they haven't even left me a match that I could strike, to look at it. I've only made sure you were on your belly. It was a hell of a whack he gave you.'

'From behind, I suppose.' He remembered the young girl struggling in that creature's arms, and that he'd been fighting to get to her. Then nothing more.

'Rifle-butt, was it?'

'Revolver. The shit of an NCO who's in charge. As you say, from behind. He'd been shouting questions at *me* — a lot more since then, I can tell you, I'm black and blue — and another of 'em had an arm-lock on me, also that little turd Maltsev was between me and you. There were two of 'em holding you, but I think you were on the point of breaking free when he laid you out.'

'So it was Maltsev brought them. As we guessed he might, I remember.'

He was attempting movement, while digesting all this information. He knew enough about the damage to his head not to want to think about it. Nothing one could do about it — except hope for the best, leave it to mend itself — if it was going to — and meanwhile ignore it, try to — manage ... Hands flat in the clay floor now, and drawing his knees up. Then levering himself up — slowly, cautiously. Thinking about Maltsev — that they *had* anticipated something of the sort, and done nothing — just, as it were, crossed their fingers, heads in the sand ... For food, warmth, rest.

'We should have cleared out, when we realized he'd be a danger to us.'

Mother of God ...

Must have groaned, then. Schelokov asked, 'Want help?'

'No. *Christ* ... No — thanks ...'

Resting ... Noticing suddenly that up near the apex of the end wall was some kind of ventilation hole, with silvery light showing through it. Blinking: not trusting his eyes ... But — a narrow slot, about half the width of the wall where it narrowed there.

'Am I seeing things, or is there a moon?'

'There's a moon. Off and on. Cloud did seem to be thinning, didn't it, during the day. Must be breaking up. Well — to some extent, it's covered some of the time, or has been.'

'As well we aren't on our travels, then.'

'Because we might be caught?'

'Well — you have a point ... Not as sharp as I should be — yet.' Catching up — or trying to ... Realizing that the hole in the wall would be how he'd seen they had a fire. Then — from the thought of moonlight — wolves — 'Oh, God, just remembered — Mishka, tied to a bloody tree up there!'

'Yes, I know. I was thinking that if the worst comes to the worst we might tell them where she is.'

He thought about that — and about what 'the worst' might amount to. But Schelokov was right, there was no reason she should suffer. And they might welcome the gift of a horse — even a short-legged, barrel-bodied, shaggy animal like that one.

If she was still *on* her short legs, by this time.

He asked Schelokov, 'What d'you think's in their minds for us? Why take us alive like this when they slaughtered the others?'

'Remember that, do you?'

'Only the order to kill them.'

'Well, you've missed a great deal. But you're right, of course, I remember — it did all happen very quickly at that stage. Then as far as you were concerned — *wham* ... But the killing — slaughter, you're right again, that's a better word for it — it was a rare spectacle, you might say. Not just an earful, like it's been here — and you've missed 99 per cent of *that*, even ... Some of the patients were quite mobile — two of them hobbling on crutches which I'd say Ibraim must have made for them — how the hell *she* thought they could have gone back to active duty in a week, or anything like it, is a mystery ... But — well, naturally the poor devils tried to get away, and —' he drew a deep, loud breath — 'these fellows caught them, and — I've seen action, Bob, really savage close-quarters fighting with sabres and no quarter asked or given, but I tell you, never anything like that kind of — the word's murder, but to them it was *sport*. Cat-and-mouse — you know?'

'Why haven't they killed us too?'

'Maltsev told them about us. And he'd got you down as a foreigner. Your uniform, for one thing, and a tendency to talk to yourself in English, for another. Yes, you do. You have that in common with Ibraim here, he natters to himself in *his* own barbarous tongue ... So — I admitted it. You were going to tell them the truth about yourself, you told me, didn't you? I told the NCO you're British, Royal Navy, and that you were here to find some British nurses. Who in fact aren't here, we don't know where they are, probably in some other *letuchka*.'

'What about yourself?'

'I came along as your guide and companion. I'm Krotov — Ivan Leonidovich. The papers I — acquired?'

'Yes ... So did he accept—'

'Unfortunately he decided the Cheka might want to question you — *us*, I should say. He's sent a man off with a despatch — to Kharkov, I think.'

'Thirty miles?'

'Say a hundred versts there and back. Unless he gets to some telegraph that's working, in which case he'll save himself a long ride. The message is do they want us, and if so will they come here or should we be sent to them — which would take up some of his manpower that's allocated to patrolling down here, see — that's what they're here for, apparently, to police the road — so he'd need orders. He told his man to be back here before dark tomorrow.'

'Gives us the rest of tonight, and tomorrow.'

'There's more, if you want the whole picture.'

'Affecting us?'

'Not — directly—'

'Later, then.' He was up on his knees now. It was all right as long as he didn't move his head, or jar it by any other abrupt movement. Also to move without thinking too much about it — without *expecting* it. If it was going to hurt, it would hurt — and you'd know it, didn't need to anticipate it. To move as smoothly as possible, was the secret. And to concentrate the mind on other matters. Like this about the bloody Cheka. CHEKA standing for *Extraordinary Commission to Fight the Counter-Revolution*. They were the professional inquisitors, torturers and executioners. One could understand they'd be interested in a foreigner who'd been netted here in the backwoods of nowhere, and that they'd want to question the foreigner's accomplice as well. It was very unlikely they'd believe the first cover-story they were offered.

Strange, that thinking on these lines should alleviate pain.

Well — it didn't. It stopped you thinking about it, that was all. What you were thinking about instead was *future* — discomfort, say...

Might be better to keep off that, too.

'Why Ibraim, though?'

'Uh?'

'What would they hope to get out of Ibraim?'

'I don't know. But they might think he'd spill whatever he did have for them. I heard Maltsev tell the NCO that Ibraim was Irina's hatchet-man. So if they thought the *letuchka* had been involved in some kind of conspiracy with us—'

'Then surely they'd save the girls for the Cheka too.'

The concertina — or accordion, whatever it was — was ending its current rendition in a long, off-key wail.

'They can still question them I imagine.'

'D'you really think so?'

'I don't know...'

'That scream — just as I came round—'

'Yes. And no sound since.... Frankly, for her sake I'd *hope*...' He paused ... 'Anyway, they're only *letuchka* staff. I doubt they'd expect to get anything of interest out of them. They'll shrug *this* off — "boys will be boys", don't you know ... You and I are the mystery men, the ones they'll want to suck the brains out of ... Oh, incidentally, Maltsev told the NCO that I'd told him we killed five Bolsheviks in sixty seconds. I'm sorry, Bob. They'll haul us over the coals for details of *that*, you can bet your life. I've made a lot of mistakes, I'm afraid.'

'What did you say about it to this NCO?'

'Denied it. Said I was only trying to frighten Maltsev.'

'Well, that's believable.'

'To the Cheka?' A snort ... 'The Cheka believe *nothing* they don't sweat out of you with red-hot irons!'

He was on his feet now. A bit wobbly, but — not too bad. Getting better, in fact, every minute. Physically, anyway. He thought part of the improvement might be due to not having the blood pumping into his head as it had been when he'd been lying flat. Like he'd seen it pulsing in that swollen throat ... Might be the answer to the metaphysics of it, the vision he'd had and which he could still recall in graphic detail: that he'd part *felt* it, thus making the image so appallingly real. He was leaning on the wooden wall for support — wooden partition, rather, between this tack-room and the stable next to it. Thoughts still on the subject of the Cheka and prospects of survival — or rather non-survival, which was a comparatively nice word for a number of other, extremely unattractive spurts of imagination. Over the last year or so one had heard a lot about Cheka methods. Including a report that they were using some of the former Chinese Labour Corps — ditch-diggers, menials formerly employed in the Imperial Army's rear echelons — for the more important torture-sessions. The Chinese were specialists, apparently, perfectionists who took great pride and pleasure in such work. He told Schelokov, 'Wouldn't make much difference, I'd guess. If this is any comfort to you, Boris Vasil'ich. I mean they'll kill us anyway — when they've finished with us. You might imagine *I*'d have preferential treatment — as a foreigner — but in the first place I'm half Russian, so they could ignore the other half if it suited them, and second — well, look at all I've seen and heard. In their shoes, would *you* let me go, to tell the tale abroad?'

'I might think twice about it.'

'Damn sure you might. And I'm sure you'll agree *you* don't stand a chance.'

Ibraim spoke then, out of the darkness — his nasal tones coming as a surprise, when he'd been so quiet and presumably immobile that one had forgotten he was here. He blurted, 'No chance me, also, I think.'

'Did they knock you about at all, Ibraim?'

'Beat — beat hard. But no hurt.'

Perhaps hurting Tartars wasn't all that easy ...

They were singing again. An old Cossack ballad, this time. Intrepid Cossack — *Udaloi Kazak* — riding alone, above the river slowly-slowly, through fog and lashing rain ...

'Boris Vasil'ich — this partition's seen better days.'

'What d'you mean?'

'I mean the boards are loose. Can be moved — prised back.' He put a little pressure on one of them: the nails in it groaned as it shifted, and he stopped immediately. 'Hear it?'

'Yes.' Schelokov was beside him. 'Not that it could help us much. Except ... No. No, it couldn't. There's an armed sentry on the other door — *and* a dozen more of 'em, when we haven't even got a toothpick ... Maltsev took his knife back from you, by the way.'

'Did I have his knife?'

'Yes. I gave it to you, when I took it from him. Anyway — you're right, this *does* give — quite easily ... There aren't any horses in there, incidentally — just their saddles and bridles, so they're under guard same as we are. Two birds with one stone. Horses are in the barn across the yard ... Look — tell you *what*—'

'Excellency.' Ibraim was on Bob's other side. He could smell him as well as hear him. 'I beg Your Excellency ... I, Ibraim — getting out this way, kill the soldier?'

'Wait, Ibraim. Great minds think alike, they say, but — wait, just a minute ... Bob, I'll tell you what we have here. My guess — more than a guess, the door's been built up as well, it was a half-door like the others, now has a top on it ... I'd say this was another stall, and at some stage they converted it to a tack-room. Fellow who lived up at that ruin and kept his nags here — until then this partition would have been only five feet high, like all the others.'

'And unlike the door, the new bit's flimsy.' Bob said, 'I'm going to sit down for a moment. Sorry, but—'

'We will, too. Ibraim — sit. Sit here, talk ... Bob, listen, I think there *is* a way—'

Avdotya screamed. High, thin, piercing, a child's scream of pain ...

'Christ almighty...'

Ibraim began, '*Gospodin Major*—'

'Wait a moment, Ibraim. No good just rushing out there. There are three of us, thirteen of them, we have to plan it carefully or we get nowhere. Except dead. Understand? Shut your mind to that, now — what's going on out there ... Bob — how fit are you? Or conversely—'

'I'm fit.'

'For action? Think you could handle a rifle like you did the other day?'

'Fit for anything except having to listen to much more of *that*.'

'Even with you on top form — and myself ditto — it's a devil of a slim chance. And with you in the state you're in — whatever you say, however *willing*...'

His voice tailed off. They were singing, and the squeeze-box was being played again. She'd only screamed once since that first time. Schelokov resumed, whispering, 'All right. Listen. The sentry out there changes every half-hour — has been doing so, anyway — and the last change was about five minutes before you came back to life, Bob. So — quarter of an hour from now, say. The point is, we need two rifles. Am I making sense?'

'Perfect sense. Thirteen men, you said—'

'Eleven. We'll already have killed the two whose rifles we'll be using.'

'*Right*.' He managed not to shake his head, but he damn near had. 'I'm being slow. Sorry — go on.'

'Ibraim — d'you understand all I'm saying? *Ponimayesh*?'

'*Ponimayu.* But I, with my bare hands — *s'rukami*—'

'Yes. Indeed. The first one, certainly, probably the second too. First, the one who's on duty now. Bob, you wait here — please. You may not like it, but we need you to be at your best, or as near as you can get to that, and the longer you have between now and then the better. Quarter of an hour ago you were still flat out — *remember* that.'

'All right.'

'Ibraim — you, with me, we climb through, go to the other door — *very* quietly. When we're ready — when *I* say, not before — I throw the door open, you grab the sentry — cover his mouth, don't let him shout — pull him inside—'

'Kill him.'

'Yes. Quietly. No sound.'

'*Ponimayu.*'

'If the door's locked — I don't think it can be — we'll have to force it open. Shoulder to it. Wouldn't take much doing, nothing here's all that robust, but in fact I doubt there can be a key or that the lock would work. I can't remember there being any latch on it, even. Could be a bolt ... Anyway — we kill this first one, then leave the door ajar. When the other one comes, he'll think his friend's inside. We'll let him come in — farther in the better — I'll shut the door and you kill *him*, Ibraim.'

'*Khorosho.*'

'Or if he hangs back — no reason he should, but *if* he does — we nip out and grab him. Tell you what — I'll have the first man's coat and cap on, just in case—'

'And I just bloody sit here ...'

'Yes, Bob. Leave this part to us ... Ibraim — when we're prising the planks out here, then getting through, we'll time it with the noise from outside there. Including any screams. And you do exactly what I say, and nothing else — uh?'

'*Konyeshno, Gospodin—*'

'Boris — soon as you're out, pull the wedge out of this door before you start all that?'

'Of course. But you stay put, mind. Three of us'd be falling over each other anyway ... Christ, it's a madcap scheme, isn't it?'

'I wouldn't say so. In the circumstances. No — I've no ideas how you'd better it.'

'Instant bloody planning ... Bound to be some snag, something I haven't allowed for — *can't* allow for—'

'So why worry?'

'Well — you're right ...'

'It's got to be *now*, hasn't it — or as likely as not, never.'

The music was as loud as it had ever been. Schelokov's hand rested on Bob's shoulder as he pushed himself up. 'Ibraim — when the noise stops, *we* stop. Understand?'

The wedge must have come out without a sound: he was close to the door and heard nothing until it opened and Schelokov whispered, 'There. Sit tight now.' He could see him: there was a ventilation slot halfway along the front wall, high up, and although the moon must have been cloud-covered there was enough light for him to be in darker silhouette against it. Then he'd gone — *through* it, ghost-like, Ibraim a crouching shadow that vanished with him. Bob squatted, then sat — in the open doorway, and avoiding the natural inclination to lean back. His head still throbbed, but much less painfully than it had.

If it was only superficial damage — stunning, with lacerations and bruising — he'd be damn lucky.

Hugging his knees: forehead resting on forearms. Listening ...

Here, close-to, nothing. Outside, forty or fifty yards away, the concertina wheezed out some dirge-like tune. Nobody singing now. Sleeping maybe. He had no idea what time it was. It had been early evening and still daylight when they'd knocked him out. Could be midnight — or before, or after ...

Then — more howl than scream — '*No — o — o!*'

Avdotya: her protest drowned out then in a roar of cheering.

Cheering ...

Close on his right, though, a thud, the sound of splintering timber and the start of an explosive '*Nu — shto takoi—*' that was cut off by a different kind of impact, followed by a clatter — something falling, weapon perhaps, his rifle — and then regular, short gasps — muscular effort, Ibraim's — crushing, strangling ...

Half a minute passed — roughly ...

'*There.*' A muffled thud.

'Well done.' Schelokov's voice, low-pitched, in rather the tone he'd used when being nice to Mishka. 'Let's have him in here. Here, I'll take—'

Another clatter like that first one. 'Damn it . . .'

They'd cheered again, outside there. It was best not to allow one's imagination any scope in that direction. Better to confine the reaction to *Be dead soon, every one of them* . . . The total obliteration of the patrol — troop, whatever it was — was in fact a prime necessity. Same as on that recent occasion in the forest, you couldn't afford to let even one of them get away. It was obvious and unarguable, but happened also to suit one's inclinations. Except that the chances were they'd die quickly — a mercy none of them deserved. Mightn't be all that easy, either: with the varying light, and good cover all around. Anyway — cross one bridge at a time . . . He was outside now, in the passage, straining his eyes towards movement down at the end to his right. The moonglow didn't reach that far, he couldn't make out individual figures or what they were doing. But hinges creaked, and he heard Schelokov mutter to Ibraim, 'I'll be back in two seconds.'

Coming this way now . . .

'All right, Boris?'

'So far. One down, one to go . . . My God, I'm glad Ibraim's on *our* side . . . Here, now — present for you, Robert Aleksandr'ich. It's a cavalry rifle, shorter and lighter than you're used to. There's a clip in it and four spares in this pouch. Five rounds in each clip.'

'Bloody marvellous.'

'All right, are you?'

'Yes — fine—'

'Fine, he says . . . Anyway — this has a peep-sight, Bob. God knows how it's set — hundred metres, as a guess. Try it against the light there, get the feel, so—'

'Learn to suck eggs too, shall I?'

He eased the bolt back — there'd been no round up the spout — extracted the magazine, checked the rounds in it by feel and the spring-pressure under his thumb, and reloaded. Sliding the bolt forward, carefully, with his ear

down to it to hear the top round come off the top and
snick into the chamber. Schelokov murmured, 'You realize
we're going to have to kill all of them?'

'I was just thinking about that very thing. And this time,
Boris Vasil'ich, *I'll* take pleasure in it.'

'Yes. Yes — by God ...'

He'd gone. Bob hefted the rifle, trying it for weight and
balance and for the length of its stock against his shoulder.
Then the peep-sight: peeping at moonlight which had
been brighter in the last minute or two but faded at the
precise moment he put the gun up to it. Didn't matter —
as long as it came back again — when they both had rifles,
and eleven men to kill.

Eleven men who were now singing. Unaccompanied,
now. Squeeze-box artist taking a breather, perhaps.

He sat down again. Knowing it could be a long wait.
The fact sentries had changed round at half-hour intervals
didn't mean they'd maintain the same routine all through
the night. They might have been on short shifts only while
— well, while the *entertainment* was in progress.

Assuming it was finished, now?

Much quieter, certainly. That last — *final* scream?'

But in the name of God or the devil or any other Power
that might have anything to do with it, what justification
could there be for the existence of such creatures?

Ibraim had either strangled that one or broken his neck,
or both. But *slow* strangulation would be best. One would
have liked them to have time to comprehend *why*, understand how unfit they were to live, or to masquerade as
human beings. And there had to be *thousands* of them.
Foul and unspeakably cruel as tonight's performance was,
it wasn't any isolated incident. One had heard of dozens.
Even just recently — Schelokov's story of his parents, for
instance. And right here, the family who'd lived at this
farm. And for that matter Nadia's own people. He
remembered her saying once that it wasn't *her* fault she
was a princess ... *My father was a prince, that's all. For
which crime incidentally he and my mother were literally
torn to pieces ...*

Music, again. Improvising, by the sound of it.

If Nadia had been here, could one have found the self-control to sit and listen while they played their games with her? Irrespective of the circumstances — the fact that making any move too soon would have been suicidal, therefore have done her no good either — would it have been physically possible to wait, while the games went on?

Thank God, again — *and again* — for her death.

Resting his head forward again. It felt better that way, throbbed less.

'Relieving Tikhonov, are you?'

'Tha's it, comrade, tha's it!'

'Well — in that case—'

The music — and two or three voices raised in song again — made the rest of the exchange inaudible. But you'd heard what mattered — relief sentry on his way ... He called, 'Hear that?'

'Yes.' Schelokov observed in a whisper, 'Comrade Tikhonov will soon have company.'

Tikhonov being the former owner of this rifle. Bob pulled the tack-room door shut. The outer door was being left ajar to entice the new man in, and it wouldn't do for him to see this one standing open.

A cheer. Then a single voice making some sort of speech. Words indistinguishable ... Laughter, when he finished. It was quite a long time now since Avdotya had screamed that protest, and considerably longer since Irina's.

Assuming that *had* been Irina.

You'd know. Before long, you'd know. Better not to make guesses. You'd know soon enough.

Stomach shots, he thought suddenly. Wherever the angle made it possible. The thought of it made him feel a little better. Although there'd be some risk. A man with a bullet in his gut, even in agony — which one would hope for — might still be a danger.

'Hey, Tikhonov! Second helping, comrade — if you've rested it long enough?'

A chuckle ...

But — *wrong*. Not from the same man. From another — with the same delicate sense of humour, of course — but a second man, following. And the first one now too damn close to risk him hearing—

But — *the hell* . . .

'Boris — *two* coming! Another close behind the first!'

'*Chyort* . . .'

'Let the first one come on in. I'll shoot him. You get the other.'

He reached for the rifle, pushed the door open about two inches, squirmed around to lie full-length with the tip of the rifle's barrel in that gap. Settling to it, wriggling into a comfortable position . . . Schelokov had neither acknowledged nor argued.

'Tikhonov, what are you doing in there? Sleeping it off?'

The outer door creaked open.

'Comrade Tikhonov?'

The other one called sharply, 'See if the prisoners' door's secure!'

'Right, comrade . . .'

There could have been only yards between those two: and the words one hadn't heard must have been something like 'I'll go along with you, see if the *Anglichan*'s come round yet.' The *Anglichan* meanwhile had the rifle tucked into his shoulder and a small circular area of thickly-filtered moonspill like a disc of fog in the peep-sight.

Safety-catch — *off*.

This one was going to be lucky. One couldn't go for a stomach shot at this stage, he had to be shot dead. The shot itself would make enough noise, God knew. But — no option . . .

The second voice growled, 'Where the fornicating hell *is* that blithering idiot?'

He'd stumbled in the doorway. But that was number two. Number one was a shadow darker than its background, outlines firming as it grew into the circle in the rifle's raised backsight.

The others' voice again — he was inside now — 'Where the hell—'

Bob squeezed the trigger. The rifle's crack was louder than he'd been expecting — confined space magnifying it, of course — but his target jolted backward, flinging its arms outward, the rifle which had been slung on one shoulder clattering down against the wall as the body crumpled. Simultaneously the beginnings of the other man's yell of '*Christ, what—*' were cut short. There was some grunting like pigs rooting and a heavy impact against one of the wooden partitions, boots crashing against it too. Then only Ibraim's straining gasps of effort. He began articulating them: 'There. *There*. Ah, *there* . . .' He was in a crouched position with the man bent backwards across one knee, hands clamped on his throat, forcing the head back and downward.

He'd let him drop. Schelokov muttered, '*He'll* want no second helpings.'

Bob's man was dead and messy. The bullet had smashed through the bridge of his nose on its way into the brain. The range had been near-enough point-blank, of course.

The music had stopped. A voice called from the farmyard, 'What's going on there, comrades?' and Schelokov answered from the doorway — muffling his voice, somehow or other — 'S'all right! S'all right, *tovarischi*!'

'Who loosed off, then?'

'Tikhonov! Thought he saw a wolf!'

Laughter, and jeers, and the name Tikhonov repeated in derisive tones. The squeeze-box started up again. Schelokov shut the door: then changed his mind, pushed it open again to let in some moonlight. 'Robert Aleksandr'ich, you saved our bacon.'

'So now let's get on with it.'

'Yes — indeed . . . Well — we have our two rifles, and one revolver. This was the NCO, this last one — handgun, you see . . . Ibraim, can you use a Nagant, shoot *straight* with it?'

'How many hours to daylight, Boris?'

Ibraim had grunted affirmatively, and Schelokov had given him the NCO's revolver. Answering Bob's question: 'Don't know, they took my watch. Well — unless one of these beauties has one ... But I don't think it matters, anyway. Tell you why later. As you say — first things first. First thing being — Bob, see what your man had in his pockets, will you? I'll check this one. But—'

'First thing being—' Bob said it for him, crouching beside the man he'd shot. His head was hurting badly, pulses of pain that had started with the shot itself. 'First thing is get out there and kill those—'

'Exactly. But also—' a hard expulsion of breath — 'I wish to God we had a doctor with us. Hey — box of matches. *That's* something, we can check the rifles' sight-settings, now ... Ibraim, this knife any use to you?'

16

The moon was hidden behind cloud. They'd made sure they could count on it at least for a few minutes, then he'd started with Ibraim close behind him, loping doubled across the entrance from the roadway and into the cover of the ruined barn on that far corner. Out behind it, now. Feet like blocks of ice, and head pulsing rather like a drumstick hitting it at about every second step. Disconcertingly, there'd been a break in the music just as they'd been crossing the open ground: in imagination he'd seen the squeeze-box artist stopping, peering across the yard: 'Hey — what's *that* ...'

Slowing now, he glanced back to see Ibraim was still with him. As he was — close behind, close enough not to lose touch in the dark, and content to follow although he obviously knew this place intimately, having lived and worked here with the *letuchka*.

With the first barn's gaunt remains between them and the farmstead — invisibly so at this moment, but a reassurance against the moon happening to break through — Bob was looking for the fence that enclosed the cattle-yard behind these buildings, behind the cowshed in particular. The cowshed — in which all the horses were stabled — was Ibraim's destination. He himself would be stopping before that, at the barn that had about half a roof still on it. And Schelokov was going the other way, round behind the stable building and from there, if he found he was in good enough cover, across to the well. Otherwise he'd settle himself for the time being anyway at that north-east corner of the stables. The well would be a much better

position for him: closer to the targets, and with its low
surrounding wall and timber superstructure as his blind. If
when the time came they were still around their fire, he'd
be shooting at a range of only about twenty-five or thirty
yards.

The fire was between the well and the roofless *izba*. It
was only a dim glow, now. Festive-looking and keeping
them warm, no doubt; you could guess the men were
sprawling on the ground around it. They'd have had the
stove inside the ruined cottage for cooking their evening
meal, and this fire outside it for warmth.

For conviviality, you might say.

He was squeezing the box again, now. It sounded like a
hymn, and they weren't singing to it. There'd been no
singing for the past quarter-hour or so.

Fence-posts. Wire sagging loose … That was the top
strand, the lower one was taut. He stepped over it, saw
Ibraim doing the same. Ibraim was fortunate enough to
have his boots on — short ones that laced around the
ankles and presumably hadn't been considered worth
taking — but none of the three dead men in the stables
had had boots that Bob could get his feet into. Schelokov
had been luckier, was wearing the NCO's.

There'd be a wider choice before long. Schelokov had
observed drily, 'If there isn't, Robert Aleksandr'ich, boots
will be one of many things you won't ever have to think
about again.'

He stopped — behind the second barn — and caught
Ibraim by an arm. Pointing to where he was going … 'All
right?'

A whisper: '*Khorosho*.'

'Nothing until I shoot — eh?'

Ibraim had said he understood, but it was as well to
make certain. Misunderstanding could cost lives — the
wrong ones. Which weren't exactly gilt-edged, in any case.
He'd nodded again and slid away. He wouldn't be going
into that shed — causing a disturbance among the horses
— but to its corner where a fence ran between it and this
nearer barn. Part of the enclosure to the cattle-yard, the

farmstead end of it. The idea of placing him there was based on the theory that if any of the cavalrymen made a run for it they might well try to do so on horseback — bareback and without any bridles, but that wouldn't deter them — and once mounted they'd be difficult to stop — in the dark, anyway. Posting Ibraim within a few feet of the door they'd have to go in by seemed like good insurance.

He was invisible now against the cowshed's dark end wall. Bob picked his way carefully into the partly-roofed barn — which had served as the *letuchka*'s typhus ward, he remembered Schelokov had said — and to his right, then, into the part that had some roofing on it and was also the end nearest to the fire. The concertina was being played rather quietly, lazily, now, as if the musician might be falling asleep over it. Might well be … You didn't want them *all* asleep, though. At least one man had better be awake and moving. Shambling off for a pee, for instance. You'd kill him, and as he dropped there'd be others jumping up.

As long as one had some light to shoot by, for God's sake. That was the most important factor — the moon. As important as it was uncertain. Half an hour ago when he'd first seen moonlight through that tack-room wall, the pattern had seemed to be longish periods of light with comparatively brief eclipses — in other words, less than 50 per cent cloud-cover — but now it seemed to be the other way about, more cloud than clear sky. Could even be total cloud-cover — change in the weather terminated, in fact, reverting to normal. Certainly no stars were visible. But there again, until the moon broke through and lit the sky as well as the land, you couldn't be sure. Thin cloud hid stars, did not always obscure the moon. And the clouds were fairly racing over, from the north-west; changes could come suddenly.

If there was total cloud-cover up there now — or anything like total, because one needed a clear spell lasting at least several minutes — there'd be nothing for it but to wait for the first light of dawn. Minimally five hours — going by the dead NCO's German-made pocket watch.

Hell of a long time: the only advantage being that at least
after that long wait you'd be sure of it, you'd know darkness wasn't going to clamp down with some of them still
alive and scattering into the surrounding countryside. That
was a danger — was the reason one needed a long clear
period. And to see it coming, see clear sky up there to
windward. But in every other way the thought of waiting
any such length of time wasn't at all a happy one. For one
thing because if there was any chance of saving the girls'
lives, the sooner you could get to them the better that
chance might be. *If* there could be any such hope ...
Although there again — supposing they *were* still alive —
how would you cope — with no medical knowledge whatsoever? And how to move them — in whatever state they
might be? Because one away or another you *were* going to
have to get out of here — as fast and as far as possible. For
one thing, the despatch rider who'd been sent with a
message to the Cheka in Kharkov might bet back sooner
than expected. If he'd found a working telegraph line, for
instance, got his message through that way. He'd be back
sooner or later anyway, and he wouldn't be alone here for
long, but there might well be other visitors even sooner —
other cavalry units, possibly, or the ones who'd come in
the lorry might come back.

Sooner the better, therefore. *Now* wouldn't be too soon.

The end wall of the barn had partly disintegrated, and
the remains of the roof had slumped here and there where
its support was gone. Any incautious move — especially
when you were groping around like this by feel — might
bring more of it crashing down. But one of the gaps —
planks either fallen out or removed for repair work elsewhere — seemed better placed than others. Although
you'd be shooting from a semi-crouched position: knees
bent, anyway ... Well — this would be among the least of
one's potential inconveniences. In fact if the upright at the
corner — heavy timber, part of the barn's supporting
frame — was strong enough to lean on ...

He tried it out. Left shoulder against it, then his weight
on it gradually. Not being too keen on the notion of the

whole structure collapsing: or even of small bits of it landing on his head.

It was taking his weight, all right.

The music sounded close, from here. And the fire *looked* close. Still only its glow, though, not a damn thing else. Well — *visually* nothing else, but — straining his ears, thinking he might have imagined it — and he hadn't — a low growl of men's voices.

Sleepless. They'd had an exciting afternoon and evening, those boys. Lots to talk about. And that was fine. Talk, lads, stay awake ... And meanwhile — moon. Moon, *please*?

Rifle up, and its barrel out through the gap. Ready, waiting. It was in his own hands, now — for him literally to call the shots. Schelokov would have been in position several minutes ago, either at the end of the stables or at the well, and their arrangement was that Bob would start the action as soon as he was in place and ready and the light was right for it, with targets visible and attainable.

They didn't seem to have missed Tikhonov or the NCO yet.

One hadn't anticipated any long wait for the moon, of course. With the enormous good fortune of having a moon at all, one hadn't envisaged a reversal of that stroke of luck — and just at the wrong moment. The wait should have been only a few minutes. Although — all right, one *had* discussed the possibility of having to wait until daylight. So that excuse — blaming the moon — mightn't be entirely valid.

It was spilt milk, anyway. The plain fact now was that at any minute they were going to start wondering where in hell were those two comrades: and then they'd remember the shot they'd heard ...

Christ.

Instant planning, Schelokov had called it.

Watching the glowing rosette of their fire's embers, meanwhile. Nothing else to look at, no movement. Wondering what alternative plan — if one *had* foreseen this — might have been better. If one had maintained the ambush in the stables, for instance, waited for them to catch on and come investigating — whittled them away a few at a time? But hindsight didn't help *now*. What one needed now was an instant alternative, a plan of action for when they did finally catch on. For instance — when they did, wouldn't some of them rush down to the stables?

Move back to the stables, wait for them?

Second alternative might be to stalk them where they were now. Creep up, start the business at close range. Drawbacks being that you'd be out of cover, levelling the odds — stacking them the wrong way, in fact, since numerically it was more than three to one against: you'd also be throwing away one major advantage, the fact that you were both pretty good as snipers.

There'd been a sudden movement at the fire, then …

A shower of sparks: and he'd heard a thump. One of them had tossed something — a piece of timber, plank or something — into the embers. And now voices — angry-crowd sounds, shouted complaints, and another voice shouting them down — laughing uproariously … That would be the man who'd thrown stuff on the fire, disturbed their slumbers. You could see him — just — the fire was beginning to burn up, enough to light up his boots to start with, and glitter on a belt-buckle — something bright, anyway … Then his face, a pale blob — as he stooped and half-turned away, reaching for more timber and throwing it on — all dry wood, probably rotten, the flames fairly leaping as he piled it on. You could see others too now: they were sitting up, you saw the lightness of faces and hands although the rest of them in their sombre-coloured uniform coats was hardly visible at all. Becoming more so, though, as the fire blazed up.

Another of them on his feet: stretching …

Then — loudly — 'Where the devil's Sergei Ivan'ich?'

'Yeah.' More of them stirring. 'Yeah — Tikhonov too. Didn't they come back yet?'

'Hey, there!' Yelling towards the stables. 'Hoy, *tovarischi*!'

Three — four — on their feet now, and the fire filling

the whole yard with its light — lighting the front of the *izba* and the cartshed and the end shed too, the hay-shed with the loft. Even over here — the cowshed. And the well-head could have had floodlights on it. Schelokov would be keeping his head down — that close to them he'd *better* be ... Another strident yell — from one of them at the fire who had his hands up to his mouth, bawling towards the stables: 'Sergei Ivan'ich, what you doing, comrade?'

Another of them growled, 'Grilling those bastards, maybe.'

'Oh — yeah ...'

And the time had come. The moment: there might be a worse one but also there might never be a better. Bob fired, and he'd shifted his aim to the next man before the first had hit the ground, killed this second one and had a third in his sights, but that one went down sprawling right into the fire — Schelokov's shot, and a leap of flame and sparks as his man collapsed into the blaze. So that was a round saved, and he used it instead on one who was half up to his feet but must have been thinking better of it — hesitating in that half-risen stance and probably about to get down again *quick* when Bob's third shot put him down for good.

None of those had been gut-shots, as he'd promised himself earlier. The timing, sense of urgency, making maximum use of the God-sent illumination didn't allow for any such indulgence.

Silence, now. No targets, nothing moving. His head was throbbing and his ears ringing from those shots. Smell of singeing — the one who'd fallen into the fire, of course. Fire still blazing high — flames and shadows dancing, nothing else. No moon — forget the bloody moon ...

He knew he'd killed three, and he'd seen two others go down to Schelokov's marksmanship. Five, therefore: and five from ten left five. Five still on their feet.

Except — not quite. One crawling: a hump moving from left to right against the flickering background of firelight, and looking from here like the back of a giant tortoise. The ground sloped mostly upward in that direction, towards the fire and the line of buildings, so that this crawler was — in naval terms — hull-down. Demanded one's full height, therefore — and a gap in the planking higher than that other. Point of aim behind the shoulder — a certain amount of guesswork in it, but aiming for the ribs close to the armpit — as near as it seemed possible to judge ... He fired, the hump convulsed and then dropped flat, out of his range of vision, and in almost the same moment a spurt of flame from above the well — then the hard *crack* of Schelokov's rifle — brought a scream and the sight of a man somewhere back beyond the fire — halfway between it and the *izba* maybe — twisting away — apparently on his knees, but he was as it were hull-down there too — with his arms out and a rifle falling. A second shot — Schelokov driving his point home — finished him.

Seven? He thought so. Seven down, three to go ... And another rifle-crack: but it hadn't been Schelokov's, the flash had been somewhere to the right and Bob had only been aware of it in the corner of his eye. Someone shooting *at* Schelokov, he guessed — rather than at oneself — because Schelokov had fired only seconds before, marking his position at the well; this character would, so to speak, have taken him up on it. Bob was watching that way now, waiting for him to fire again. He had an idea that the shot had been made from a certain height above the ground, and a distinct possibility therefore was the loft — where they'd been hiding when Schelokov had found himself cuddling up to Maltsev.

Maltsev — for God's sake. Not thirteen to start with — *fourteen*. So there'd be four left, not three. That rifle's flame stabbed into the darkness, and as the sound of it reached him he was squeezing a shot off at the flash. Definitely from that end shed and at the loft-floor level, and there'd been another shot on the heels of his own — from Schelokov, obviously, although he hadn't seen it. Schelokov must still have a whole skin, anyway — which was comforting to know. And there'd been no reaction this time from their target. So — *possibly* ... Safer to reckon on there still being four, but it might well be only three now. Including Maltsev, of course, who wouldn't count for much. Meanwhile that was five rounds he'd fired: he'd jettisoned the empty magazine and was snapping in a full one. Five shots — four kills, one result unknown. Not bad: but he was thinking it might be a good idea to move from here now — having made one's position pretty evident by this time, and with at least three of them still on the loose. And nothing happening — time maybe that something was *made* to happen ... He thought Schelokov would probably *not* shift his position; he could move from side to side of the well's surrounding wall, or shoot over the top of it, and this gave him a certain flexibility even thought they'd obviously know in general terms where he was. Also, to move from that well in any direction at all would involve crossing open ground — which was now lit up and doubtless under keen surveillance. Schelokov would stay put, for sure.

There'd been no sight or sound of Ibraim, meanwhile. But he'd be there: and they didn't know he was. So they might for instance try getting to their horses from the rear — out of the top-right corner of the yard into the cattle paddock, and down behind the buildings — but if they did it wouldn't help them much, as he'd hear the horses reacting to their arrival and be in there himself like a dose of salts.

So *he* was well placed and had to stay there. If anyone was going to move, break what seemed to be a stalemate, it would have to be oneself. And the move should be towards the hay-shed or the cartshed, which was surely where they'd have holed up. They'd have backed away from the fire and into those sheds right when the shooting started, he guessed. Not into the *izba*, which would have been closer to them but was also closer to Schelokov — as well as particularly well illuminated, with the fire right in front of it.

A problem was that in the course of transferring oneself from A to B — which could only be done by moving round on the blind side of the cowshed — the way *they* might come to their horses — you'd be leaving a lot of this central area uncovered. Schelokov couldn't cover all of it from his position — certainly not as far as a man crawling or belly-creeping was concerned — because of the down-slope and general unevenness of the ground. Second problem was that there was no way of letting the others know you were moving or had moved — that you were not something to be shot at.

Shift from this corner, anyway — for the time being. It would be idiotic to stay put, where they must by now have one positively located. Move to wherever there was a hole to shoot through and a reasonably good field of fire, but somewhere nearer the other corner, the one nearest to the cowshed. That stench on the wind, he realized, was the odour of burning human flesh. The target Schelokov had poached, in the first few seconds of the action, and the fire having burnt away the clothing. It was a sickly, sweetish smell which one had encountered before, at sea. Moving now: the width of the shed being about twenty feet, the limit of one's range of transfer. Enough, anyway: just so you weren't where they thought you were ... He passed several apertures on his way along the end wall that would have been usable and might have allowed for a better field of fire than he'd get further along, but to maximize the distance from that corner seemed desirable — common sense suggesting that the survivors, whether there were three of them or four — had only two targets that they knew of, were aware of their locations and would be keen to tilt the odds in their own favour.

Right. *Here* ...

Long-range firelight flickered on the front wall of the cowshed — its near corner being only a few yards to his right. Ibraim was not visible: but shadows were deep there, this side of the corner. There was dead ground over the slight rise between here and the fire, but only enough of it to hide a man crawling. It wouldn't be dead ground to Schelokov anyway. The well — its upper part — was still in his sight from here, but to the left of it his view was cut off by the corner he'd just left. While almost directly in front of him — slightly right, in fact, immediately to the left of the cowshed's obliquely slanting frontage — he had the roofless hay-shed and its loft at about forty or forty-five yards' range. The fire — still burning well — was from this angle exactly in line with Schelokov's end of the *izba*.

Beginning to find the continuing stillness uncanny. Watching narrow-eyed across the illuminated farmyard area: well aware that the passage of time was one's own enemy, very much to *their* advantage: in fact if they could hold out, maintain the status quo, that was all they'd need to do, just hang on and wait for developments from outside ... Then a rifle cracked from the vicinity of the well — of which from here he could only see the timber superstructure — and he was on his toes for any answering shot or shots, ready to shoot at such flashes. But — nothing ... Except — he caught his breath: to the right of the carthouse — closer but on that line of sight — glory be, yet another of those humps — moving left — another crawler. Then he'd lost it — before he'd had a chance to get a shot off ... About halfway between here and those buildings, he guessed it *had* been. Confusing, though, in that tricky light and the spread of darkness over low ground where it was blanked off altogether. But crawling left, he'd have been making towards the well? Or at an incline, diagonally across the yard towards the stables — or even — well, *here*, this—

On him. Back *on* him again ...

For an easy shot, too. That guess a split second ago had been dead right — it was the very recently vacated corner of this shed the man was making for. And bad luck, *tova-risch* ... He had the dark hump of him in the peep-sight now, was conscious of being about to take a very easy shot indeed, therefore taking it perhaps a bit easier and more slowly than he should have done, when the crawler put him off his stroke by — bafflingly, in that instant — seeming to change shape. Rearing up ... Then a long arm going back over the right shoulder — a smooth, oddly familiar movement, despite its having taken one completely by surprise — the message to the startled brain being *Mills-*

bomb — grenade: he squeezed his trigger as the bomb went lobbing high towards the corner of the shed where he'd been half a minute earlier, and his shot missed: he'd fired just as the thrower launched himself forward in a natural follow-up dive for cover against the blast of his own missile. He was only too well aware of having missed, but for the moment postponing any second shot, ducking low in the corner with his forearms protecting his head and with his backside to the blast, by the time the bomb either bounced on or broke through the planking near the other corner. Thunder-clap explosion, splash of flame: that noise like ripping calico was of grenade fragments whirring through the barn's dark emptiness and rotten timber.

Back up then — jack-in-a-box reaction — for the delayed second shot. Bits still falling from as much as remained of a roof ... And something — at first impression, could have been a huge dog — bounding from the right, the cowshed's corner, while another form rose — the bomber — came up from the ground to meet it. Rifle still slung — having needed his hands for crawling and bomb-throwing — and a glint of firelight on the knife in Ibraim's fist, then the two silhouettes had crashed together, fused into one image, Bob watching over his rifle's sight — not through it, no chance of getting in a shot at this stage — and seeing the merged bodies separate after three or four seconds' grappling, one part sliding down and the other stooping over it. Making sure of a job already done, he guessed. Ibraim half-straightened then, came in his loping run with the dead man's rifle trailing from one hand to this shed's bomb-blasted corner. Bob was watching for flashes by this time, rifle-shots from any colleague who might have been covering the bomber's approach. Nothing, though. Nothing except the flickering light and the stink of roasting flesh.

'*Gospodin* Bob!'

'Here, Ibraim.' Rather struck by that novel form of address — 'Lord Bob', near enough — as well as startled by the style of his arrival. He'd actually smashed his way in through that corner: unstoppable: as though in a frenzy of rage — or triumph. Rage, more like ... But muttering to himself now in his own language: mostly expressions of astonishment, it sounded like, and some intermittent praise of Allah. Bob, still watching the sheds across the yard, gave the Tartar's dark shape a glance and a nod as he arrived beside him. The man had, after all, tried to save his life. 'Good work, Ibraim ... Only two alive now, I think. One for sure, could be two.'

He'd arrived at certain other conclusions meanwhile — continuing the thought-process about where the survivors might be, and about shifting his own ground, and the need to ferret them out — them, or him — and get this over ...

Point one: he, or they, would be in the loft of the hay-shed. It was the obvious place because they'd been more or less trapped in that line of buildings to start with, the hay-shed was the most distant from the fire's light, and from its loft you had a more commanding view than from anywhere else.

Two: he/they might be on the point of trying to break out. If so, they'd try it by way of the cowshed. The grenade attack a preliminary to it? But running for help, knowing you couldn't get anywhere on foot — in the dark, and wading through snow — with the nearest help or communications at Valki, three or four miles away. And being a horseman ...

So — you had to (a) maintain a guard on the horses, and (b) move towards dislodging the survivor/s from the hay-shed. If they *weren't* going to run for it that was where they'd be aiming to sit tight. And the fire, for God's sake — he'd just noticed this, although it must have been happening progressively for some time — was dying back again.

Distantly, wolves howled.

'Ibraim. Listen to me now ...'

Minutes later he was at the corner of the cowshed — top-right corner, the cattle-yard side of it. When in less than another minute he moved to give himself elbow-room and

poked his rifle around the corner, he'd be shooting diagonally across this end of the shed, upward into the cartshed
loft. Range — allowing for the slant — approximately
thirty yards.

As he'd outlined the scheme to Ibraim — who'd just left
him, slinking away soundlessly into the darkness — *he*
would have had this job. Ibraim would have used the rifle
he'd picked up from the man he'd killed a few minutes
earlier, and he'd have been shooting from inside the
cowshed, through some aperture or other in this end wall.
But the Tartar had pointed out in his distorted, monosyl-
labic Russian first that he'd never learnt to use a rifle and
second that the cowshed wall was solid, built of logs and
with no apertures in it. He'd also indicated that in his view
he'd be better at the other part of it than Bob would be —
lighter, quieter, faster on his feet and handier with a knife.

So he was the ferret and Bob would provide the
covering fire: giving him one minute — less than that now
— to get himself to the side of the hay-shed — the blind
side, from the farmyard — from which point when Bob
started shooting into the loft he'd creep round to the front,
and inside, and then — well, act like a ferret.

Forty seconds to go.

Schelokov, Bob hoped, would see which way the shots
were going and catch on to what was happening. He'd also
realize that the best thing he could do was stay where he
was, to prevent any breakout across the yard.

Bob had five rounds in the rifle in his hands, five in the
second rifle — which he'd propped against the wall beside
him — and two spare magazines in his pocket. Twenty
rounds: one shot every three seconds, say, for the first
half-minute, and then — well, depending ... The half-
minute might be all it took.

Twenty seconds, now.

The fire had died down surprisingly fast. Dry tinder
very quickly consumed, of course. What had been a blaze
as little as five minutes ago had reduced itself to not much
more than embers again. The corpse slowly cooking in its
glowing core couldn't be doing much for it, either. But the

rapid loss of light was a very good reason for making this move now.

Ten seconds. Reminding himself to watch out for grenades. Might or might not have some up there, but from that elevation he'd be in lobbing range if they did have.

He raised his gun, pushed off the safety, murmured under his breath as he stepped out and back a little *Good luck, Ibraim*...

Ibraim set off as if the rifle had been a starting-pistol, was round the corner — hugging close to it — with the second shot a spark of flame in the corner of his left eye; and then he was inside — a crouching shadow soft-footed on the carpeting of rotted hay — by the third. This time he heard not only the *crack* of the discharge but also the bullet's impact somewhere overhead. Knife in his right hand, left hand out as an antenna, his slanted eyes boring into the dark: fourth shot, an audible but comparatively soft impact and a gasp that became a groan. Ibraim was by this time flattened against the wall near the ladder — that set of wooden rungs — as still as a post and staring up, getting the rectangular hatchway into focus, the faint vestige of light from outside making it *just* discernible. Two more shots meanwhile, one burying itself in the front edge of the loft floor and sending splinters flying, the next passing through and out into the night sky; and another now — a steady rhythm of firing, you could have matched the beat of it by counting: two, three, *crack* — two, three, *crack* ... Ibraim's eyes riveted on more than just the empty hatchway now, he was watching a bulge of darker shadow curving one side of it, a shape that was manoeuvring itself into the gap, on to the rungs. *Crack* — two, three — smacking impact — in timber, somewhere up there — and gasps of effort, a hand clawing for the top rung, the body half-filling the splintery-edged hole and the wall creaking as weight came on the rungs: *crack*, two, three — tenth round, not that Ibraim had been counting, he was watching this man climb slowly, laboriously down the rungs, with a jerky movement due to the fact he was using only one arm.

Another shot: but there'd been a longer interval, this time. As if he'd *known*. Which he didn't, of course, didn't have the least idea. Half a minute gone and two magazines emptied, that was all, he was spacing the shots out now to make them last, keeping them high, watching for results ... Ibraim inched forward slowly into range, then sprang — left arm clamping around the man's neck, wrenching his head back. The Bolshevik had had his rifle slung on the right shoulder, and it fell, that arm striking back powerfully but ineffectually with the elbow, and then groping — uselessly, Ibraim had him pinned, body arched back against his own, was reaching around now with his knife arm — *crack*, and a rattle of debris falling — so as to stab upward from the front, locating the exposed throat between the turned-up points of the greatcoat collar, below his own horizontal left forearm. The first prick of the knife's point galvanized his victim into a frenzy of resistance — a convulsion of terror, shock — straining to turn away from the blade, right arm flailing ... Ibraim held him as in a vice, pressed the knife halfway to its hilt in the bulging windpipe and then twisted slowly, letting him feel it while he died.

Outside, the rifle cracked again. Seconds passing: two, three, four, five ...

Count to ten. Having worked the bolt, pushed a new round in.

Something had to be happening in there. Ibraim wouldn't be just standing around. There was — or had been — at least one of them in there: after his own second shot there'd been one in reply, and he'd aimed his third round at the flash. Nothing since.

Nine — ten—

Hold it ...

Ibraim, emerging. At least, a dark shape: and any of those others would have been running, not just coming out as if for a breath of air. But a thick, peculiar shape ...

Then he'd dumped the burden he'd brought out with him, spilling it off his shoulder to crash down in a dark heap on the trodden, muddy snow. Standing back with his arms spread, facing this way, identifying himself. Bob lowered his rifle, scooped up the spare and went to meet him. There wasn't much light at all, by this time. Ibraim saw him coming and turned away, calling, 'Other one—' gesturing up towards the loft— '—also dead. I bring ...'

The other one was Maltsev. He had three bullets in him and had had no rifle, seemed to have been used as a sandbag, this other one probably firing over his prone body. Ibraim brought him out and dropped him beside the other. Bob had meanwhile called to Schelokov, who'd started over in this direction but stopped to bank up the fire with more dry timber. It was already picking up.

'Well done. Well *done*.' Sombre tone, though, no elation in it. Both of them — all three — grimly aware of what they might face now. Flames crackling behind him as he came on towards them, and the light spreading — lighting a number of bodies behind the fire, between it and the *izba*, and Bob's crawler out in the middle, and beyond that the grenade-thrower.

Schelokov gestured towards the cartshed. 'In here, I think.' A jerk of his head towards the *izba*. 'I looked in there.'

Bob nodded slightly, leaving it to him. Ibraim was motionless too, with his knife still in his hand. A moment ago he'd stooped and wiped its blade clean on Maltsev. Schelokov's right hand moved across his chest to sling the rifle over his left shoulder; then he'd stopped in that shed's wide entrance — his back rigid, shoulders square — staring in where the dancing firelight would be throwing his own shadow.

'Oh, Christ. Oh, *Jesus* ...' It was a moan. 'Jesus, *no* ...'

17

Irina had been on her back, naked, and her throat had been slashed from ear to ear, her head lolling back so that the wound gaped open. Green eyes open too, glistening — upside-down, as it were — through a mask of blood. Before they'd killed her she'd been virtually ripped apart. Blood covered her from head to toe, and the details of her injuries had been such that having seen them one might have wished to have been born blind. But you *had* seen them, and however quickly you looked away or shut your eyes your brain had taken a photograph that would stay in it for life. They'd have cut her throat presumably when they'd decided she'd had nothing more to offer them. That scream would have marked the moment, which for all her terror might in its hideous way have come as a mercy. Not that that word was anything but incongruous here. There'd been none for Avdotya either. Her body, a dozen feet away from Irina's had been scarlet in its own blood and like a rag doll, all broken. Nothing left unbroken, some joints actually reversed. They hadn't cut her throat but her neck had been twisted like a chicken's.

Riding south, several hours later, having turned one's back on nightmare in the physical sense but in every other way bringing it along — in the certain knowledge that it would be yours for life — however long or short that might be … While in contrast Nadia, in his thoughts of her now, was a survivor, the one who *had* been shown mercy.

Except that perhaps this horror needn't have come about at all. Then there'd have been nothing for her to have been spared. If one hadn't come here? Uninvited and unwanted, blundering in?

But she'd have been dead anyway. *Was* dead. Which changed the world around one. So — what difference ... In this aftermath of nightmare not all one's thoughts could have been spoken aloud or were truly acceptable even to oneself. Riding — trotting, now — with Schelokov ahead of him and Ibraim behind with the spare horses, thoughts and memories churning to the drumming rhythm of thirteen horses' hooves on the road's hard-packed snow, he could just about persuade himself that it would have happened anyway. Or that something like it would have. That Irina had been mad, should have got away weeks ago, irrespective of the condition of her patients. Dr Markov's bitter comment came to mind: *Letuchki have been obliged to abandon their wounded before this* ... It was all — in that area, *extremely* confused. Actions, incidents, conversations, details of the past hours' sickening as well as backbreaking work ... In no special or noticeably logical sequence, but probably starting with an exchange between himself and Schelokov, at some point in the early stages — when they'd both been figuratively speaking knocked flat by the initial, visual shock. He'd asked him — but really more asking himself — 'What kind of *men* — *if that's what they were*—'

'*God knows. God knows...*'

'*We shouldn't have let them die so easily.*'

A shrug ... They'd been in front of the *izba*, in the fire's light but upwind of its stink, that shapeless black thing in it. Those were the recalled visual images. And Schelokov's hands shaking so violently that he'd had difficulty stuffing *makhorka* into his pipe. Which with all the other things that had been taken from them had been in that same shed, at the back where fodder and stores were stacked. Put there ready for examination by the Cheka, no doubt. Schelokov had muttered, 'Tell you the truth, Robert Aleksandr'ich, before we started I did have some thoughts of not giving them a quick and easy death.'

'Yes.' He'd nodded. 'Difficult, thought — in the circumstances.'

'And one simply wanted them *dead*.'

As indeed they had been. Fourteen of them. Three in the stables, six in the vicinity of the fire, one beyond the corner of the *izba* — a man who'd been trying to outflank Schelokov by working his way round behind the well — and the two crawlers out in the open yard, and Maltsev and his companion in front of the hay-loft.

'So now — what?'

There'd been decisions to make and then a great deal to be done, and no time to waste. The most difficult — and frightful — decision had been how to dispose of the women's bodies. It had been accomplished, in fact, half an hour ago. The final sequence in the nightmare: although in point of fact 'disposal' might still be in progress. But — to all intents and purposes — it was done.

Burial would have been the obvious thing, but the ground was iron-hard, deep-frozen, it would have taken all day to excavate a grave even if you'd had tools for it. In fact you had rock-hard ground, no tools and very little time. And — this had been implicit between himself and Schelokov — there'd been no question of leaving them for others to see or even know about. For the representatives of the Cheka, for instance, when they arrived, or for other cavalrymen to gawp at.

One solution which they'd discussed had been cremation. In that cartshed with its content of dry fodder — lie them on a bed of it and toss some burning timber in. But the blaze would have been visible from miles around, and Schelokov had pointed out that this could be fatal to their own chances of getting away now. 'I've thought it out, Robert Aleksandr'ich. We'll get a good start, if we do it right. A day or more, could even be several days — and then we're clear. Depending on what we run into down there, of course. Here and now the vital thing is to leave no traces of what's happened.'

'No — traces . . .'

Puzzled: gazing around at the sprawled bodies. All of which had bled. Although the freezing temperature did reduce the period of bleeding. But as well as the butchery in the cartshed there'd been blood and other mess in the loft, the stables, on the snow out there in the open, and pooled in the muddy, trampled ground around the fire.

He'd look back at Schelokov. 'If we had about a week — and shovels, mops ...'

'No. Think again.' Puffing at his pipe, getting it going ... 'If we get down to it *now*, Robert Aleksandr'ich — three of us hard at it. All right, we won't eliminate every trace, but we can make sure what's left doesn't tell them anything. Believe me, I've worked it out. For instance, the bodies — not those, but those *things* — we'll put in the well.' A nod towards the fire. 'Including what's left of that one.' Glancing at him, then. 'But I'm sure you'll agree — not *theirs*. Not with that *filth*.'

'Of course not.'

'With luck it'll be a while before they're found. As long as it'll hold them all — I've no idea how deep ... But — best way to set about it might be to stack them all beside the well first, so until we dump them we'll have access to water for the clean-up. Fill that trough, too. And where there's mess in the open we can wash it away as well as we can, then spread snow over what's left. Come to think of it, same thing inside — using hay, and the litter that's in there.'

'Well. We can try, anyway.' Bob had tossed more broken planking on the fire. There was a heap of it, piled against the *izba*'s front wall. The flames engulfed it at once, lighting the whole place up, and he turned back to Schelokov. 'What about Irina and Avdotya?'

This was when they'd discussed the impossibility of digging a grave, and the idea of cremation, a funeral pyre: which in fact was not only impractical in the context of Schelokov's wider plan, but unsatisfactory because total destruction couldn't be guaranteed.

Schelokov had taken the pipe out of his mouth.

'Bob, look here. It isn't easy, this — problem. But there's no time for lengthy contemplation. So let's say we'll take them with us, to start with. Wrap them — in greatcoats, say — bundle them up. Then — well, we've got horses, we'll be taking all the horses—'

'*All?*'

'Look — these uniforms — Red Army ... Be a bit stained and some'll have holes in 'em, we'll just pick the best that fit. And as I say, we have good horses here. You can be sure they'll have been fed and watered, incidentally — but Ibraim can see to that, he's a horse-handler, it's his job. And you see — we've got uniforms, and horses, rifles to sling on our backs, swords at our sides. I'll show you how a cavalryman wears his sword. We'll be leading this bunch of remounts — thirteen of 'em, three under us and ten running with us. All cavalry formations need remounts — replacements for animals killed or lamed — and we'll be bringing these to some unit that's supposedly down there ahead of us. This way we can move in daylight — use the roads, or follow railway lines — d'you see? I doubt anyone we meet will think of asking to see our papers ... Get the idea?'

'Well — yes ...'

It seemed — so easy. A natural ... Not that it came anywhere near answering the question about the women. He'd nodded, though, postponing that. 'We should get along pretty fast — with spare horses too.'

'Exactly.'

'Take Mishka along with us?'

'No.' He'd frowned. 'I hate to say it, but if she's alive it'll be a miracle. I heard wolves up there — didn't you?' Glancing at him, catching the uncertain nod, then looking down at the former NCO's watch. Conscious of the passage of time ... 'Anyway, we must see to her. If she's got away with it, we could bring her down to the road and turn her loose for someone to find. But—' a shrug — 'we couldn't take her. She'd never keep up, for one thing.' Pushing the watch back into his pocket. 'Have to get up there, anyway, I don't want to leave that Lee-Enfield. And we can take *them* up with us.' He'd thrown a glance back towards the cartshed, and now his grey eyes held Bob's. 'If you follow my line of thinking?'

He thought he did. Staggered, initially, by the enormity of the proposal: but facing also the lack of alternative.

And the certainty that the girls themselves would have chosen anything rather than to have their remains left either with their murderers' or where they'd later become objects of interest to others of that same kind.

'As I said, this isn't easy, Robert Aleksandr'ich. Don't imagine *I* think of it without — extreme reluctance ...'

They'd wrapped them in their own coats — Schelokov's well-worn Imperial Army greatcoat and his own naval one. Having already selected the best of the dead cavalrymen's outer gear for themselves. Most of the hard labour had been over by this time: fourteen bodies piled beside the well, and the mess cleared up everywhere else. They wrapped the girls' bodies and carried them out of the shed, leaving them out there while they applied themselves to the worst job of all, cleaning up inside. Bob at any rate working with his eyes open — and the firelight from outside for illumination — but with his brain, as it were, shut off. Meanwhile Ibraim had been seeing to the horses, putting saddles and bridles on all of them. There'd been minor tasks as well, such as packing rations, ammunition and a minimal amount of cooking and camping gear into the saddle-packs. Then when the cartshed was as clean as they could make it and they'd also cleaned themselves up, had no further use therefore for the well, they'd dumped the fourteen bodies. Including the half-burnt one, which was tipped in from a plank. Fourteen thudding splashes. Also ten swords and nine rifles, and various other unwanted gear. Ten saddles would have gone in too, but with the corpses already in there a quantity of saddlery would surely have been visible above the water-level. The basis of Schelokov's plan was that whoever came to occupy the farmstead now would find it deserted, the patrol out on some military duty — with their horses, obviously, the only way a cavalry patrol *would* be out. The messenger who'd been sent to contact the Cheka knew there'd been three prisoners here, but it was hardly likely they'd guess those prisoners could have taken over — causing the entire patrol to vanish, along with its horses. The assumption would be either that they'd taken the prisoners with them or that the prisoners had escaped and they'd gone after them. But at least there'd be some passage of time before they began to suspect the truth; and meanwhile the Cheka visitors could drop that bucket in on its rope and draw water to make their tea, if they were so inclined.

The saddles would be dumped somewhere along the way, wherever there was a ditch deep enough to hide them. Remount horses came bare-backed and in halters — headstalls and leading-ropes — Schelokov had said. There were no halters here, so these nags would be bridled but only saddled temporarily. And setting out from the farmstead, down the track and on to the road and turning south there, one horse had the two wrapped bodies tied on its back. There'd been no moon, not even a hint of it behind the clouds; and the fire would die down quickly enough, untended, although it had still been throwing its light across the empty yard behind them as they'd ridden out — with about two hours of darkness left at that stage. Schelokov had been leading the burdened horse from his own saddle, Bob following on a very large black gelding — over sixteen hands, Schelokov had estimated — and Ibraim behind them with the other nine in tow. Then after a few hundred yards they'd turned off the road into the straggle of trees at the foot of the hill, and Bob and Schelokov had dismounted, leaving Ibraim with a dozen animals to look after while they climbed into the wood with the thirteenth and its load.

On the way up there'd been no sound of wolves. Only their own and the horse's panting breaths and stumbling progress as they zigzagged up between the trees and through undergrowth, having to go carefully and make detours around steeper parts and obstacles here and there. When they'd arrived here they'd made the climb in growing daylight, and coming down — thirty-three hours ago, roughly — had been in the dusk. One had been aware enough of the hazards, therefore, to have been looking out for them as well as for wolves. For whom Schelokov had prepared what he called wolf-scarers — balls of hay on short lengths of twine cut from the hay bales. It was an old-established peasant device, he'd explained, in common use for centuries by those travelling by sleigh or horse-and-cart between villages in wolf country. Except that they'd tend to use straw more often, and longer lengths of rope. When the wolves chased after them they'd light the bundle and throw it out to tow astern, and the packs would keep their distance.

Approaching the level where they'd left Mishka, the horse had objected to further progress. Schelokov had had his work cut out to keep it moving. He had his own persuasive and coercive tricks, but even these failed after another thirty or forty yards.

'This is a waste of time, Bob. We'll tether him here and I'll go on up. Stay with him, will you? Here — I'll leave you one of these.' One of the hay-balls. 'Got matches?'

'Yes. Somewhere . . .'

'Have 'em ready. Look, better have two of these things. Leaves me four, that's plenty. If you hear 'em getting close, light one and sling it at them. They don't like being shot at, either. Don't shoot when you can't see, though.'

'Can't see a bloody thing.'

'You will when you've lit one of those. See their eyes, the light reflected in them. Now I'm going up to get that rifle.'

'And Mishka, if—'

'Can't you *hear*?'

He did, then. Had probably had the sound in his ears for some minutes without realizing what it was. But it was in the sound of the wind, and he'd been breathing hard and the horse hadn't been exactly quiet. He could hear it — *them* — clearly enough now, though. From some distance — fifty, a hundred yards, whatever — snarling and whining and the tearing and crunching of hide, flesh, bone . . . Imagination might have played some part on his interpretation of the amalgam of sounds, but it couldn't have derived from much else.

Schelokov muttering, 'Stand *still*, you damn creature . . . Here, Bob, this tree here, I'm—'

'All right.' He'd groped for and found the taut reins, which Schelokov had succeeded in clove-hitching around a birch-trunk. The horse now jerking at it hard enough you'd think to break the leather, Schelokov growling, 'Easy, easy ... They aren't after *you*, old fellow...' To Bob then: 'Weren't so busy, they'd have heard us long ago. May have anyway. Wind's in our favour, far as scent's concerned ... Got your pistol ready? Handier than—'

'Yes — all right ...'

Should have wished him luck. Too late: he'd gone. Bob wanting rather badly to have this over with. Better still, not to be here at all. To wake up, confirm you'd been dreaming, that the only reality had been this sense of *un*-reality. How could it be real, actually happening — to be stuck on a frozen hillside with two corpses and, close by, a pack of wolves tearing a horse apart? But start further back than that: wake up in Sevastopol, in the Kist Hotel, still waiting for news that didn't come: Nadia still alive, *all* of them alive ... 'Steady, old fellow! *Easy*, now ... We're in the same boat, you and I ...' Probing the darkness. By the sound of it, some of them were fighting, up there. Nothing to see except the horse's bulk — it was trying to rear, against the pull of the tether — and the black pillar of the tree itself, the darkness similarly but less distinctly streaked within a radius of a dozen feet or less. Watching mostly uphill, where Schelokov had vanished and where the sounds of wolves competing for meat — Mishka's — were coming from ... And a flare of light, up there — with an instant, complete cessation of all sound, then after a few seconds the start of low growling, and the volume of it rising while the flare became a nucleus of bright fire which soared then from left to right. And the *crack* of Schelokov's rifle. No — his revolver, that had been. Second shot on the echo of the first, and the horse surprisingly still, after all that panic. You could imagine it was straining its ears and keeping still so as to hear better: he ran his hand up its sweat-damp neck and found the ears *were* pricked forward. The glow up there had begun to fade, but Schelokov was putting a match to another ball and again one saw its flight, the flickering effect of tree-trunks between here and there: a wolf's high yelp, then a shout of 'On my way down, Bob!'

'Right ...'

With enough light from that thing to see by — but still concerned not to be mistaken for a wolf, and shot at. But whether they'd follow him down, or go back to their meal ... Still a glow up there, that second hay-ball smouldering. Bob had the Webley in his right hand, the other with the ends of twine wound round it and patting the horse's neck — muscles quivering under that sticky coat. 'Bob?' Schelokov came slithering down, stopped himself against the tree. 'Couldn't get the rifle. One of those sods damn near got *me*. Bob — old friend — cut them loose, those two ... No — I'll do it, you light a scarer, will you?'

'Now?'

'Yes, *now*, Christ's sake—'

Hadn't thought there was any need. Fumbling with matches ... Hearing the snarling then — a whole orchestra of it — and appreciating there *was* need. Not all that easy, though, to strike a match, shield it while it lit and keep it alight while getting it to the ball which was dangling on three feet of twine.

Try it the other way about. Hay-ball up close to the left hand, and strike the lucifer close against it. Thumb through the trigger-guard of the Webley to leave the rest of that hand free. Crouching, for better shelter from the flame ...

It flared, the hay caught, he let the twine run out through his fingers as he straightened, his gut tightening at the sight of a score of pairs of yellow eyes blazing at him, a half-circle of them ... Schelokov called 'Throw it!' — while the horse danced, whinnying, throwing its head up, jerking repeatedly at the tether, its eyes showing white with terror, and Schelokov just about off the ground, hanging on to its head to hold it down. Bob had lobbed his hay-ball at the vicious, glittering eyes, caught his first-ever sight of wolves as the burning missile flew sparking towards them and they retreated, scattering. He had his pistol up, fired at one particularly large animal which had only pirouetted then stood its ground — snarling, fangs bared, eyes like a devil's ... He'd missed, fired again, and Schelokov shouted, 'Give me a hand here!' A hand at getting the first of the two bodies down. This was his own greatcoat, which had Irina's remains in it, bound like a parcel with more of that twine. 'Here will do.' Near the foot of the tree but clear of the lashing hooves. 'Get the other down? It's loose ...' Loose and slipping, slipping into his arms as the horse half-reared again. Schelokov must have realized he had no knife. And if he'd tried inexpertly to use his sword — in the dark, at that ... He lowered Avdotya's body in its wrapping of Schelokov's greatcoat to the ground beside Irina. Schelokov had cut the twine on that first one, and now he did the same for Avdotya. 'Better light another scarer.' Because that one was fading, the snarling yellow-eyed shapes were all around them and edging in again. All it would take would be for that big one to give the others a lead. You wouldn't last a minute — *half* a minute ... 'Light it and throw it down close to us here. Got two more, don't worry.' He'd been crouching but was on his feet now, half-erect, stooping to throw both coats open and expose their contents. The wolves wouldn't gawp: one thing they were not was *voyeurs*. Bob struck a match, lit his second hayball, held it swinging by its tail of twine. But you could only do that for a few seconds without the twine burning through, or burning your arm off. He tossed it to land a few feet away, and Schelokov thrust another at him: 'One more. I'll untie this animal. When it's alight, throw it at the nearest of 'em. I'll need a hand with this bugger then. One hand each, spare ones for pistols — huh?'

Retreating, finally ... Controlling the horse between them: it was primarily a matter of not letting it bolt. That was hard work on its own. There was no need to shoot, since after they'd started down the wolves didn't close in on them or follow. They had other scent, other interest, didn't so much close in on *that* as rush in, as the light died and the forest up there darkened.

*

Riding south, with the high ground on their left still holding back the dawn, although it was leaking up into the clouds overhead and beginning to reveal the shape of the snow-covered land around them. This long, straight road, with the bank on their right and the ground beyond it sloping down into lingering darkness; there was a river down there, and it was over this bank they'd scrambled with poor old Mishka, taking cover of sorts while a squadron of Red cavalry had thundered by.

At that time, he'd thought of Nadia as being alive. Had known she might not be, but had believed she *would* be, had still counted on finding her, bringing her south with them to safety, and eventually — although he was aware that as Nick Solovyev's widow she wouldn't be the same Nadia Egorova whom he'd known a year ago, and that she might still harbour such notions as she'd expressed in her letter, about not leaving Russia — *eventually*, to Britain. That was how he'd envisaged his own future as little as three days ago. But now, if there was any future at all — anything beyond this present preoccupation with trying to stay alive — presumably for *some* purpose . . .

What purpose, though? In the light of recent events wasn't it, to say the least, egotistic — after all that, and above all with Nadia dead — to have any concern at all for one's own skin?

Except you could argue that — egotistic or not — it was natural. The urge to survive being a matter of instinct, not reason. For instance his father — to whose memory he still tended to turn for guidance, when he felt the need of it — the old man would certainly have shrugged off any such doubts or self-questioning. As likely as not he'd have dismissed it all with a brief expletive and a favourite aphorism of his: *It's pluck that gets home*.

It derived, Bob remembered, from the turf, horse-racing. And pluck, he might have added, didn't ask where *was* home. It just bloody well got on with it. The old man being thoroughly entitled to his views on the subject, too, having been through a great deal of adversity himself, emerging from it with flying colours largely because he'd been just about stuffed with pluck — from birth onwards.

He was thinking about his father and the gruff exterior under which he'd concealed a softer heart even than he'd credited his son with, when Schelokov reined back to ride beside him.

'Been thinking, Bob. What we were saying earlier about where we left our *dvukolki*, Mishka's fodder. If we were caught there, how could we have known about it unless we'd dumped it there ourselves?'

'Right after having killed those scouts. So they might have a watch on it.'

'Exactly. Also, it's too close. We should get twice that distance before dark. And two other considerations — one, this first day's important, we want the maximum distance behind us, and two, it'd mean a dog-leg, off our straight course towards Taganrog. Better to head south-east right from scratch, pass well to the north of Petrovka, I'd say. D'you agree?'

'Yes. Anyway you've got the map.'

'*That* doesn't take us far.'

'No. Of course ...'

The map had been in the inside pocket of the NCO's greatcoat, and it only covered this immediate area, not even as far south as Petrovka. Its main interest was that it had the name, or rather number, of the detachment's regiment stamped on it. They were planning to make use of this, for want of anything better, in their own cover story if they needed one.

Bob added, 'Horses may get hungry, though.'

'Not if I can help it. We'll be working 'em hard, they'll need their rations. Have to find food for them wherever we are. Commandeer it, if we have to. We're Red Army, after all.'

'Christ ...'

'Well — in for a penny ... How's the head?'

'This cap doesn't suit it. But otherwise — a lot better than it might have been.'

'You were very lucky. How about your boots?'

'They're all right.' He'd pulled them off one of the dead cavalrymen — one with large feet. His own seaboots, which had been in the cartshed with their other things, wouldn't have got even their toes into the stirrup irons. He added. 'For riding, anyway.'

'Good. Talking of riding, d'you think you could handle say three of the loose horses? Three each for you and me, leaving Ibraim with four. It'd look more natural — to a cavalryman's eye, that is.'

'Don't see why not.'

'Good. *Chudno*. You'd have made a good soldier, Robert Aleksandr'ich.'

'Better sailor, though.'

'Wishing you'd stayed where you belong — eh?'

'The thought's occurred — once or twice.'

'Well — you'll be back there, in due course. Spewing your heart out, wishing you were back *here* ... Any *papirosi* left?'

Russian cigarettes — a couple of inches of rank tobacco in a cardboard tube. There'd been several packets of them with the stores in the cartshed, and Bob had stuffed a few into his pocket. He gave Schelokov a pack now; cigarettes were easier than filling pipes, on horseback. Bending to light his own: with his beard down close behind the blanket-roll across his horse's withers, cupping the flame in his palms ... Then: 'Our Tartar friend's a trump, isn't he?'

'Thank God for him!'

'When I was in the Caspian, they were hand-in-glove with the Turks. Only ambition to slit Armenian throats. And loot ... But this fellow — he's remarkable.'

'I'd say he was devoted to Irina Solovyeva — she'd have been good to him, I suppose — and he's transferred the loyalty to us. There's also the fact he wants to get to his homeland.'

'The Nogai Steppe, you said.'

'Exactly. I told him if he stayed with you he'd get damn close to it. Tikhoretsk, I had in mind — from there he'd be in spitting distance of home, and it's on your route to Novorossisk — eh?'

'*My* route. Not yours?'

'My dear fellow ... I'll see you on your way — please God — but what would draw *me* to Novorossisk?'

'You're saying you intend to stay in Russia.'

'What else? *Where* else?'

'You're entitled to a passage out, and I'd make sure you got one. Seems to me, Boris Vasil'ich, the way things are going—'

'The way they *will* go, if we all run away. I flatter myself I can still be of some service here.'

'But — realistically, don't you think—'

'No. I don't.' He lifted his hands. 'Get your snout up, you donkey!' It was a chestnut he was riding, almost as big as Bob's black giant. You could see shades of colour and other detail now, as the light grew. 'Even if I did — agree with you that we're beaten, that's what you mean, isn't it? — well, you're not necessarily wrong, it's certainly how it looks at this moment. But—' he shrugged — 'such things can change, you know, very quickly. It's quite on the cards we might turn the tables — again, eh, as we've done before?'

'D'you think Denikin will put the pieces together again?'

'Yes. Or Kolchak will. Wrangel, perhaps. It's important, of course, that your people continue to supply us.'

'To be frank, I wouldn't say it's likely.'

'Giving us up as a bad job, are they?'

'There's a lot of political argument in England. A War party that wants full involvement — to restore the Romanovs—'

'Out of the question.'

'Fellow called Winston Churchill wouldn't agree with you. But others say it's none of our business and we shouldn't be involved at all. The result's been a botch-up — which gives strength to the elbow of the mind-our-own-business brigade. It's a hopeless mess, they say, so pull out before it gets worse.'

'Your Royal Navy too?'

'I'm afraid so. Except in the Baltic, where it seems we've been doing a good job.'

'Doesn't help *us*.' He rose in his stirrups, looking down into the valley, where you could see a loop of the iced-up river now. 'Anyway — this is a depressing conversation, Robert Aleksandr'ich. Personally, I prefer to believe there may be a miracle around the corner.'

'Let's pray for it.'

'Do so. Please. But for now, listen. Any time from now on we're likely to run into some of our beloved comrades. It'd be very surprising if we didn't. So let's have our stories straight and matching. We're from the Twenty-third Regiment — hussars — of General Budyonny's Fourth Cavalry Division. I'm comrade Sergeant Krotov, you're comrade hussar — what is it—'

'Galanshin.'

'Galanshin. Right. Better sharpen *my* memory ... But our Tartar friend gives no name except Ibraim, speaks better horse than Russian. No papers — deserted from the other side, they'd conscripted him against his will. I'm his sergeant, I vouch for him. And our story is we had to wait at the veterinary depot at Kursk to collect these nags and bring them on. We were told — three weeks ago, so we're in the dark now — that our lot would be deployed towards Taganrog. That's all we have to go on, we're just doing our best to comply with orders.'

'It's good.' Bob nodded. 'Better make sure Ibraim's got it in his head too?'

'Yes. I'll drop back now and have a talk with him.'

'In horse?'

'Oh, I'm fluent ...'

All you'd need was confidence. If you didn't doubt yourself, *they* wouldn't. He remembered Nikolai Solovyev's brilliant acting, on a railway platform policed by Red Guards, and his explanation that the secret was to *be* the character you were playing, *think* like him.

On the surface, that mightn't be too difficult. And if

one slurred the words a bit, distorted the vowel sounds —
and confined one's conversation as far as possible to
grunts and monosyllables ... Wearing a full beard had its
advantages too, facially one wouldn't give much away.

In about mid-morning there was a branch off to the
right — to Karlovka, the map suggested. They'd held
straight on, on what was then more of a track than a road
but had been used very recently, cut up by horses' hooves
and with fresh droppings here and there. Cavalry for sure
— probably from Karlovka or that direction, would have
turned east on to this track at the fork. The dung was soon
not only fresh but steaming, and rounding a bend into a
long, straight stretch with a farmstead on the left and open
fields both sides, sure enough there was the tail-end of a
body of horsemen climbing a rise and then diminishing as
they passed over it and into the dip beyond.

'Better slow down.' Schelokov glanced back over his
shoulder, signalling to Ibraim with one hand while he
pulled his horse back into a walk with the other. They still
had saddles on all the horses — not having come across
any suitable dumping-ground yet — and there was no
point in arousing other cavalrymen's curiosity when you
didn't have to. Although you wouldn't want to be slowed
down like this for long, either. Every mile counted, every
hour. It was going to take the best part of a week, this trip,
and the longer it took the less likely it was that Taganrog
would still be in White hands when you got there.

Then beyond Taganrog, Rostov. Rostov-on-Don being
the gateway to the Caucasus and to Novorossisk, as far as
anyone coming from this direction was concerned. If
Rostov *did* fall—

Well. You'd be really up against it, then. Discover for
sure whether or not you *did* give a damn about personal
survival.

Denikin would surely hold on there, though. If he
didn't, *he'd* be finished. He'd probably hold Taganrog as
well. If he had any troops left to hold it with.

That cavalry squadron was swinging off to the left,
northward. Making for Zmuyev, perhaps. There was

nothing much else up that way, between here and Kharkov — not that the map showed, anyway. It was a rotten map, gave hardly any detail. But they *had* turned off. Schelokov grunted, pushed his horse into a trot again.

The track beyond the point where that outfit had left it hadn't been used in recent days by anything except carts. Farmers' *fourgons* from and between the farms they'd been passing, no doubt. And there'd be a village ahead there somewhere, Bob guessed. There'd been none since Valki, which was now a long way behind them. Virgin snowfields, meanwhile, on both sides of the track, and woodland a few miles distant backing the undulating whiteness on the left. Clouds pressing lower than they had been, and a darker grey now, passing over swiftly on a wind that had veered from north-west to north. Snow would be coming before long, for sure. And whereas on the way up they'd prayed for it, to cover the *dvukolki*'s tracks, now it would not be welcome at all — could only make the going harder, slow one down.

It was early afternoon when they found a place to dump the saddles. Pine-woods close to the road flanked a valley with a stream in it which the road crossed by a timber bridge. Up among the trees, undergrowth crowded down on both steep banks, ravine-like, and the saddles went in there — out of sight from the road and into a mass of briars. The three of them changed to fresh horses, at this point, saving time by ditching the saddles they'd been using, having only to tighten three other girths and transfer the saddle-packs and blanket-rolls. They also divided the riderless animals between them, as Schelokov had proposed earlier. The whole business took only about fifteen minutes. They'd made tracks between the road and the wood, of course, but you could reckon on their being snowed-over soon enough.

On again. Conscious of being well into the second half of the daylight hours now, and that before dark they'd need to find some place to stop where there'd be fodder for the horses. Ideally a farm with a barn or stables they could sleep in. It was a matter of some concern, with no certainty about it — for instance, no way of knowing how many scavenging units of Budyonny's cavalry might have passed this way before them. On the other hand you didn't want to start prospecting for a place too early, wasting time. Schelokov said finally, 'Have to chance it, Bob. When the light's beginning to fade, time enough ...'

They were lucky, that first night. Hardly realizing at the time *how* lucky. For one thing that the snow had held off until about the last half-hour that they were on the road — and even then was only light stuff flying on the wind — and more importantly that the first farm they stopped at was exactly what they'd been looking for. The farmer was a man in his sixties with a crutch and a wooden stump in place of his left leg, his wife an enormous creature who groaned as she heaved herself along, seemingly had something wrong with her vast hips. There was a big shed, and hay in it. The man told them, 'They took my cows, to feed the Army. I've one horse, that's all, pulls the cart, and *he* won't outlive me, poor old devil. Leave us enough hay to keep him until the spring, that's all.'

He had pigs, in another outhouse. Bob had found them when he'd been nosing around, before they'd started out again at first light. The snow had been coming down more heavily by then. The farmer had asked him not to mention the existence of the pigs to anyone else ... 'Or they'll come and take *them*. Give us paper money that's not worth — well ...' A gesture, wiping his behind. 'That's what it's good for, eh? Folk here say they'll be taking our land too, once it's over ...' Small, sharp eyes suddenly worried, then, and a hand on Bob's arm: 'Mind you — there's plenty that cries out to be put right, *I*'m not one to stand in the way of progress ...'

The second night was adequate — fodder plentiful, but shelter for men and horses worse than at that last place — but nearing the end of the third long day's march — snowing hard, horses and men plastered with it and visibility down to a hundred yards or less even before the light had begun to fade — after drawing blank at the first two places they'd tried there was a sense of real desperation. At the first one an old woman had told them there was no fodder in the place at all; soldiers of one kind or another had stripped the place bare, and if they chose not to believe her they could search ... At the second — where there seemed to be no barn anyway — nobody answered the door although the cottage was certainly inhabited — tracks in the snow, and a strong scent of woodsmoke.

They rode on to the next. Schelokov muttering, 'If we'd been real Bolsheviks we'd have smashed the door in. Stabled the nags there in the house.'

It was getting dark by this time, and they mightn't have seen the next farm if it hadn't been for a glow of light in a window, an oil-lamp flickering through failing light and driving snow.

'Third time lucky — please God.'

'Amen.'

Wheeling in. The horses were very noticeably flagging; they'd been driven hard all day, and the going had been rough. Bob added, 'Even just shelter. Then we could find food for them in the morning.' He and Ibraim reined in, Ibraim having already taken over Schelokov's spare horses to free him for knocking on doors. They'd come up fifty yards of track between lines of fence-posts whose tops were only a foot or so clear of the snow, and into the yard where there was some shelter, partly from trees planted to form a windbreak. The light still burned: it looked as if a curtain had partly collapsed inside that window, or they'd covered it inadequately with a blanket. Yellowish light seeped out across trampled snow. There was a well to the left of the house — roofed, on timber piles — and the dark loom of a barn behind it. Schelokov rode into the pool of light — in the lee of the house, where only a few snow-flakes blew around — then slid down and approached the door.

'Hello!' He tried knocking, then stooped for a piece of firewood from a pile there, used it as a hammer. 'Hello, there — if you please!'

A shadow crossed swiftly between the light and the window.

Silence.

'Hello, inside there! D'you want me to freeze out here?'

Sounds of bolts being pulled back: then the door inched open. Light was visible in the slit which expanded into a pale rectangle. Widening: then a dark figure filling it, blocking most of the light. Schelokov began in his quiet, persuasive tone, 'We're in search of shelter, and fodder for our horses. Only three of us, *batushka*, but we've a dozen horses—'

'Fodder—' an old man's voice, raised in protest — 'for *twelve*?'

'Thirteen, to be exact. But if you have *any*—'

'No. No — truly, captain—'

'Sergeant, *batuskha*. Or just "comrade" would do. Was that your son, by the way?'

'Son? Where? No — no, I'm on my own here, I swear—'

'I'll believe you. Even it if means I have to disbelieve my own eyes. But our horses need something in their bellies, d'you see — and shelter for the night.'

'Shelter, you can have. In the barn here. Only don't touch my fowls or the goats. I beg you. Fodder — well, there's a little, it's not good and it's all I have for the goats. They took all my good hay — and the cow, they—'

'I'm sorry to hear it. But this is extremely kind—'

'No food in the house, mark you!'

'No, no ... We have food for ourselves. Only the horses—'

'Nothing like enough for that many. It's rubbish anyway — mildewed, and—'

'Anything's better than nothing, *batushka*. We won't lay a finger on your livestock, don't worry. And whether or not that lad's your son — nephew, grandson — your business, I never saw him. Oh — we can draw water from the well here, can we? But one thing — if you'd be so kind as to put a pot on your stove — if I knock on the door in an hour's time, say, a jug of hot water for our tea?'

There was a yoke lying near the well, with two large buckets, and a trough in the barn which Ibraim filled. Schelokov told Bob when they were inside, out of the wind and snow, 'There was a lad in the room with him, where the light is. Nineteen, twenty — military age, anyway. Ten to one he's a deserter. Ran into the other room where it's dark, when I knocked. The old boy knew I'd seen him. Hence this—' he glanced round — 'abundance ...'

The barn was in good repair but it wasn't very large and it was now crowded. The chickens had taken to the rafters, there were five goats and now thirteen horses and three men. The fodder, which as the old man had said was rubbish, was in a boarded-off corner where the goats couldn't get at it. Bob and Schelokov distributed it as fairly as possible among the horses while Ibraim took their bridles off and unsaddled the three they'd been riding.

'Bloody stiff ...'

Hobbling, in fact. Schelokov nodded. 'Two long days — when you're not used to it.' He shrugged. 'Quite a few more to come, mind you.' He was opening tins — Red Army rations. These contained salami, and they'd be sharing a loaf of black bread between the three of them. He added, 'Without fail, we must give these animals a proper feed tomorrow. I'll tell you — give you some idea of what they need — horse rations in my own regiment were nine pounds of oats and nine of hay per horse per day. On top of that they had all the black bread our soldiers couldn't eat. Our hussars had enormous rations, there was always a lot left over.'

'Those were the days, eh?'

'You could say so.' A shrug. 'Just seemed normal at the time. One of a lot of things that would go on for ever.'

It was like sleeping — or trying to — in Noah's Ark ...

Dead tired, certainly, but also stiff and sore, which the barn's hard earth floor didn't exactly help. One good thing was that although the back of his head was still sensitive — he couldn't even think of lying on his back, for instance —

the throbbing had stopped, if he didn't touch it it didn't hurt. Another was that the body-heat of thirteen horses and five goats kept the place fairly warm.

The horses were restive, probably from hunger. And this was only the third night of the long journey. From here to Taganrog would still be the best part of two hundred miles. Thirty miles a day, Schelokov had said, would be very good going for horses that were well fed and rested — and in good conditions, not deep snow and a blizzard such as was blowing out there now.

18

It had been snowing all night and still was, swirling thick and heavy in a gusting wind from the north as they walked the horses south-eastward, two hours after daybreak. Horses' heads hanging, the men peering forward under whitened brows, seeing sometimes as far as thirty yards ahead, often less. Caps, coats and horses plastered white, horses' rumps and left sides more so than the rest. Ice-crystals formed quickly — especially in beards, tails and manes.

He'd dreamed that Nadia was with them, dressed like them as a cavalryman except that her dark hair had been flying free. He'd remonstrated with her about this, and she'd told him that it was how Nikki liked it. Evidently they hadn't told her that he'd been killed, and she'd believed she was on her way to join him in some base area, Bob acting only as her escort. It had been intensely worrying to him that he hadn't been able to break through to her with the truth, which was that Nick Solovyev had been half-eaten by wolves; this was the condition in which they were going to find him, but Bob couldn't tell her, warn her. He'd woken in a sweat and with a scrawny chicken pecking at his sleeve, which had horse-dung on it. Full consciousness had come with recognition of the farmyard stink, Ibraim's snores and the stark reality of the situation like a kick in the head: *Two hundred miles to go, and no feed for the horses . . .*

Schelokov dropped back to ride beside him. Bob and Ibraim each had five unsaddled horses behind their own, leaving Schelokov free to prospect farms as they came to them. They'd been on the march about an hour now and haᵈ passed only one, which had been no use. Their host of last night had told them they hadn't a hope of finding any supply of fodder within a day's ride, at least.

'Thinking, Bob — we mustn't be put off too easily. Farmers are living on *something*, they have carts, must have horses to pull them, horses don't live on air. So, they've got it hidden. And if it's a case of them or us — well, just their bad luck, eh?'

Alone again — thinking about that, with the phrase in mind *When the devil drives* ... Schelokov had dropped back to talk to Ibraim. Morale-building exercise: last night and this morning the Tartar had barely said a word, seemed totally self-contained behind that mask-like, slant-eyed face of his. He talked to his horse occasionally, but that was about all. He rode slumped, long-legged, boots dangling, his feet rarely in the stirrups, and he was answering Schelokov's chat now with no more than grunts.

Bob watched the sides of the track for farm entrances. It wouldn't be difficult to pass one without seeing it, under all this snow, and with Schelokov preoccupied back there he probably wasn't keeping much of a look-out himself. Bob consequently wasn't looking ahead much, as he had been before, and with the depth of snow underfoot and its blanketing effect on sound generally as well as vision, he'd had no inkling that there might be even a single horseman on the road ahead of them, until suddenly — as it were, out of nowhere — there were shouts, dark forms looming, horses back on their haunches and whinnying, others swerving aside ...

The impression was of fifty or a hundred of them, in those first seconds of surprise. In fact it was a platoon of thirty-six.

'*Hey* there, comrades!'

Another yelling back over his shoulder, 'Lieutenant! Comrade *Leitnant!*'

'*Zdrastye, tovarischi!*'

'*Zdrastvuite!*'

A few had unslung their rifles, or begun to, had then

recognized fellow-cavalrymen and were re-slinging them on their backs. Well-fed, fit-looking horses quietening too, after the brief flurry of excitement ... Schelokov spurring forward: 'Hello there, comrades!' Their horses filled the narrow road, jostling each other now as a small man on a big grey pushed up through the middle of them: 'What's *this* bloody circus?'

'Comrade, you the leader here?'

'Shikhin — lieutenant. You?'

'Sergeant Krotov, comrade. With remounts I'm supposed to be taking to Taganrog or thereabouts. But *tovarisch Leitnant*, perhaps you could advise me. In a bit of a fix, you see — reckoned on getting fodder for these nags along the way, but no such fornicating luck — and they're bloody starving — farmers *say* they don't have any hay, oats, any damn thing at all, so—'

'Where're you from, comrade? Damn it, Taganrog — that's a hell of a long ride, my friend! Not ours yet, either — far as *I* know ...'

Schelokov gave him the story. Horses from the veterinary establishment at Kursk: had to wait weeks instead of days, out of touch, consequently, but orders were orders and nobody'd changed them, consequently he was proceeding with these remounts towards Taganrog, come hell or high water. He'd little doubt he'd locate the regiment somewhere down in that area, anyway. But dead or lamed horses wouldn't be worth delivering, and if the comrade lieutenant could tell him where he might get the poor brutes a decent feed and a day's rest, in this benighted wilderness ...

'My advice is to ride to where we've just come from, comrade. Provisional headquarters of this region. If you're taking 'em along slow — well, you'll make it in six hours, I'd say. Six or eight.' He was running his eye over the horses. 'They've enough left in 'em for that, I'd say?'

'*Have* to. But where—'

'You'll cross a railway line in — well, walking pace, say two hours. Then take a fork due east. That's turning off your route for Taganrog, but — on *that* road there's nothing ... Left fork, soon after the railway. The land's all fenced there, you'll see it all right. Heading east then, see. And you've got the Donets river ahead then — I don't mean close, but you're getting into the Donets basin, coal country, that's what's important to us, why we're going to hold on to it now no matter *what*, d'you see.'

'Is there reason to believe the bastards might be in a condition to counter-attack?'

'Could be. Who knows. But we're organized now, we've got their measure ... You were in it, up there, I suppose?'

'They moved us east from Kiev. We took *that*, a while ago. But the Kharkov front was broken before we got there. Then I was detached — well, as I've explained ... You were in that show, were you, comrade?'

'The thick of it ... Got a map there?'

'No—'

'Christ! No *map*?'

'I told you — damn-all. Because we'd've been up with 'em by this time, if—'

'Here. Take a look at this one. Memorize it, comrade ...'

'Helpful fellow, that Shikhin.'

Pyotr Shikhin: he'd told Sergeant Krotov to mention his name to Captain Fedorenko at the cavalry headquarters, explaining that Shikhin had directed him there in the certainty that Fedorenko would allow him to rest and feed his horses before setting off again on the long ride south.

They were riding stirrup to stirrup, with a string of horses behind, then Ibraim with *his* string. Bob said, 'On the road like that is one thing, Boris Vasil'ich. But actually to bed-down in a Bolshevik headquarters ...'

'No reason we shouldn't get away with it. We fooled *him*—'

'But as I say — just a brief meeting, on the march. *And* with this damn stuff to hide all the blemishes.' The snow, he meant. It did have a camouflaging effect. 'Quite another thing to stop in some kind of headquarters establishment — spend a day or two — my God, *fraternizing*?'

'Robert Aleksandr'ich — please, listen. We fooled him completely. And why not — he'd no reason to be suspicious of us. Now we go to this Fedorenko with an introduction from his brother-officer Pyotr Shikhin — he'll have even *less* reason to look askance at us!'

Plodding on ... Thinking about it. The conclusions being that one had very little option, really. Certainly no good alternative to suggest. He shrugged. 'All right ... But — supposing it *is* as easy as you say, and we get away with it — what then?'

'Then we're a lot better off than we are at this moment.'

'In the short term — yes. And I agree, we have to — risk it. In the spot we're in now — all right. But we'll still have — what, a hundred and eighty miles to go — two hundred, even?'

Schelokov was brushing accumulated snow off his now heavily-bearded face. Turning down-wind then to blow it out of his moustache ... 'What I'm hoping is they may have another depot further south that we can aim for. With Comrade Fedorenko's blessing, d'you see.'

'A tour of Red Army establishments—'

'Once we're in, we're *in*. Now, we have Comrade Shikhin's endorsement of us. After that, as long as we play our cards right we'll have Fedorenko's. Eh?'

Silence — except for the softly thudding hooves, creak of saddle-leather, and the wind ... Bob thinking that there had to be *some* limit to one's luck ...

'Listen, Robert Aleksandr'ich.' Schelokov reached over, patted his shoulder. 'There's no reason to expect problems. All right, we'll have to be *very* careful. And if it turns out it's tricky — well, we'll go back to scrounging from farms, thereafter.'

'What if word's sent out from Valki — three escaped prisoners, thirteen horses—'

'Ah — well — *then*, I grant you—'

'Like walking into a cage.'

'But we don't know they have the telegraphs repaired yet. Even if they caught on that quickly, it mightn't be easy to get word out very fast. In any case it's unlikely they'd be

so quick: and even if they were, they *can't* know which
way we've gone. Then again — would anyone believe
escaped enemies of the revolution would ride into their
cavalry headquarters and ask for a night's lodging?'

'No. Not unless they were bloody lunatics.'

Late in the afternoon they turned into the ornate gateway
of what must have been some nobleman's country seat.
There'd been about a mile of high wall and a smaller gate
— barred, with a 'No Entry' board on it — before they'd
come to this one.

A soldier with a red band on his arm emerged from the
gatehouse. A hand up to keep the snow out of his eyes as
he stared at them ... 'Where you from, comrades?'

'Kursk. If it's any of your business.'

They'd agreed on certain rules and principles, one of
which was that Valki should not be mentioned. Schelokov
told the guard gruffly, 'Looking for Comrade Captain
Fedorenko. He commands here, am I right?'

'Delivering remounts, are you?'

'I'll tell the comrade captain what we're here for, lad.
Where'll I find him?'

'At the house.' A wave of the hand. A driveway led
through snow-covered parkland towards a distant view of
roofs and chimneys. Another man had appeared in the
gatehouse doorway, was leaning there, not in any hurry to
leave its shelter ... The first one said, 'Miserable-looking
bunch you've got there, comrade.'

'*You*'d look a damn sight more miserable — if you'd
come as far as they have.'

He'd glanced at Bob, and laughed. Bob grunted, staring
contemptuously at the soldier.

'Your name, comrade?'

'Krotov. Sergeant.'

'Unit?'

'Twenty-third Regiment of Hussars. *Was*, anyway.'

The man blinked at him. Then: 'All right, comrade
sergeant. Follow the driveway, report to the guard up
there.'

Schelokov glanced back at the others, and flipped his reins. Another guiding principle was not to say or explain more than was necessary. Ibraim would speak virtually no Russian, Hussar Galanshin would be more surly and taciturn than most, and all three would be obviously played out — wanting only to see to their horses, have some sort of meal themselves, then sleep. Sergeant Krotov, moreover, would ask the comrade captain's permission for the three of them to sleep with their horses — being determined, as an experienced and cynical as well as conscientious NCO, that none of them should disappear while in his charge.

The house was fairly large, of classical design with a pillared central portico, a two-floored middle section behind it, and extensive single-storey wings. There'd been a four-man guard on the front steps, clustered in that shelter from the driving snow, and one of them had led Schelokov inside while Bob and Ibraim waited out here with the horses.

These guards were beardless boys, recruits by the look of them. Edging rather diffidently out into the forecourt now, probably embarrassed at having been caught skulking in the dry, and by the sharp contrast between their own indoor look and these new arrivals' heavy plastering of snow. Not to mention the way they sat their horses out there, ignoring it.

'Have you — come far, comrades?'

Bob stared at the boy who'd asked it. He asked *him*, after a short silence, '*Novobranyets*?'

A nod, and an embarrassed glance round at his friends. He *was* a recruit. He'd blushed slightly. Bob looked away, shifting his hold on the reins of Schelokov's horse, yawning.

Easy, really. Until they rumbled you . . .

He wondered what had happened to the owners of this house. In general terms, it wasn't difficult to guess. Details were better left obscure. One had heard — and *seen*, now — more of that kind of detail than you'd want in any lifetime.

Ibraim seemed to have fallen asleep. Perhaps he had. Schelokov had told him of times in his experience when troopers had slept in their saddles when actually on the march: in tight formations, stirrup to stirrup, riders nodding off while the horses kept on, mile after mile. Ibraim's chin was on his breastbone, and his slumped body might have had no bones in it, have been dumped there in the saddle like a sack of flour.

Five or even maybe ten minutes, Schelokov had been in the house. Fedorenko might be keeping him waiting before he saw him, of course. Or he might be tearing holes in his story. *So who commands the Twenty-third now, sergeant?* Might even have a Cheka man there grilling him. All major military units and establishments had Cheka representatives, to keep an eye on security, political attitudes and so forth. At Enotayevsk, in fact, Nadia had worked as secretary to a Cheka boss whose job had been to collate reports from the various military outposts in that command.

If she'd been here now — here, this minute, dressed as a cavalryman — her hair shorn, of course, not as it had been in the dream — and her lovely features hidden in a great-coat's upturned collar . . .

You wouldn't have come here. Couldn't have chanced her being seen at close quarters. The very thought of it: you'd have been in panic — even if she'd remained as cool as he guessed she might have — you wouldn't have been able to breathe, or think straight . . .

A voice from the steps woke him out of daydream: 'Very well, then, comrade. I may see you again before you leave.'

'Most grateful, comrade Captain!'

He'd got the voice and intonation exactly right, Bob thought — watching him come quickly down the wide steps, stride across to take his horse — a wink as he took the reins from him — then swing himself up. Glancing round at them then: 'We're in luck, comrades—'

'Show them to the stone stables, Losev.' Fedorenko, calling down to one of the young guards. 'Then find

Corporal Fomin, tell him these horses are to have all they need.'

Schelokov saluted, wheeling his horse to follow the boy, who was setting off at a run along the west frontage of the house. Then with some distance behind them he told the others quietly, 'Everything we wanted. Including a hot supper in about an hour. Glad we came now, Robert Aleksandr'ich?'

You *had* to be glad of it — of shelter, food, new life in the horses. Only two things were wrong: one, it seemed so easy that you could hardly believe in it lasting, you had this feeling it could explode in your face at any moment. For instance — suppose the Twenty-third Regiment was billeted somewhere in this region and Fedorenko knew it, might have suspected something and sent a message to them? It was possible: all you actually knew of the Twenty-third was that you'd annihilated a small detachment of them up at Valki. They could have been *here*, even. Calculated risk ... Or not even that — just a *frightful* risk.

Except that it was only your own neck on the block. All right, your own three necks: but it did help to remember how much worse it might have been. It even allowed you to hope you might get away with it — simply because objectively the issue wasn't of such vast importance.

The other snag was that this was only a stop-gap answer to the main problem — the distance to be covered, and the time factor. Fedorenko had told Schelokov that in his own estimation Taganrog was likely to be in Red hands within a few days. Rostov and Novorossisk would be the targets then, with the primary aim of stopping the flow of seaborne supplies to Denikin. He'd spoken of the port of Novorossisk solely in that context, with no reference to its being also the Whites' only remaining escape route. But what one was facing now, in brutal fact, was what Colonel Temple must have foreseen when he'd wound up that signal with the words *Your return here by first available sailing is therefore authorized*.

Perhaps one should have taken the hint. But at least those two nurses would be out by now — and might not have been.

Now, in the old manor's stone-built and stone-paved stables, supper was about finished although the horses were still munching happily. There was as much hay for them as they wanted, and a few handfuls of oats as well. The platoon which had been on the road this morning — Shikhin's — had been quartered here and another should have arrived to take their place by now, but — Fedorenko had guessed — might have delayed their move, waiting for weather conditions to improve. If they arrived before Sergeant Krotov left with his remounts, there was other accommodation for them anyway.

'Less palatial, apparently. Sheds or some such. Anyway, we won't overstay our welcome — eh?'

'Start out at first light?'

'Well.' Schelokov frowned. 'Might let 'em give us breakfast, don't you think?'

They'd fetched their supper from the kitchens at the back of the house, being accompanied there and back by Corporal Fomin, who was a cripple with a twisted leg. A horse might have fallen on him at some stage in his career. They took mess tins and mugs from the saddle-packs with them, and were issued with buckwheat gruel, goat-cheese, tea, and three loaves of black bread. Better rations than usual, Fomin said, on account of one whole platoon being away.

'So we're in luck, comrade.'

'You are that. Timed it just right.' Glancing around at the weather, as he hobbled back to the stables with them. Bob aware that *he* was more or less hobbling too — stiff as hell, and sore. The stiffness might have been slightly less acute than it had been the night before, but the saddle-sores were worse. Fomin was saying, 'Snow's letting up, I'd say. Might have a better day of it tomorrow.'

'You've done us proud anyway.'

'It's a pleasure, comrade sergeant. And great days we're living through, eh? Victory just around the corner?'

When he'd left them, Schelokov commented, 'Simple fellow. Means well enough. My regiment was stiff with men very much like that one.' He'd added as they'd settled down to eat, with bales of straw to sit on, 'Speaking of which, there's one thing really frightens me, Robert Aleksandr'ich. Here — and anywhere like it that we may find ourselves next — fellow like that, face to face round some damn corner, and it'll be an hussar from my old regiment. Couldn't *help* but know me.' He touched his beard. 'Even under this disguise. Walking into that kitchen just now, for instance — one of the cooks, it might be. Imagine it — *Hey, your name's not Krotov...*'

Dropping off to sleep — preparing to — on a blanket spread on straw — he concentrated his thoughts on Nadia. For pleasure — of a bitter-sweet kind, but still pleasure — and to escape present anxieties which otherwise tended to nag on, in and out of sleep, and even more in the hope that any dreams might be of her and not of events at the Valki farmstead.

That was a dread. So — Nadia ...

As he'd last seen her — which was how he tended to remember, visualize her — that last snapshot in his mind again. Not that she'd been exactly at her best. Pale, tired, bedraggled, on the pitching deck of a little German-built torpedo-boat — in the middle of the Caspian and in the aftermath of what had been a very rough sea. It had still had plenty of movement on it. There'd been another ship's boat tossing alongside, and he'd been saying goodbye to her — under the eyes of Nick Solovyev and Irina. Irina positively hawk-eyed, and Nadia very much aware of it so that her manner to him — Bob — had been so reserved that it had been actually hurtful, had seemed to be a cruel denial of the relationship that had been developing between them. But he'd had a message — a contact address — scrawled on a screw of paper in his hand, and in the act of kissing her goodbye — or rather, touching her cheek with his lips, which on its own had been enough to sharpen Irina's green eyes — he'd opened his right hand

against her left one, palm to palm, she'd felt the small wad
of signal-pad and her fingers had curled, enclosing it.
Turning away then she'd had it hidden, and there'd been
no change or sign of anything in her face or manner. He'd
realized afterwards, when he'd had time to think, that she'd
needed the Solovyevs at that stage, for her own security —
to be taken with them to the Crimea. Hence the formality,
having to mind her p's and q's with Irina. But if one had
only been quicker off the mark, *not* always needed so
damn long to think ... In fact he'd pondered this only a
day or two ago, but it seemed much less fanciful now —
that he really could have, *should* have — instead of saying
goodbye, should have begged her, 'Stay with me — please?
Don't go with them. I love you — let *me* look after you?
Marry me? Nadia, my darling—'

There'd have been a most frightful shindy with the
Solovyevs, but you'd have weathered it. And she'd have
been alive today.

Nadia, darling ... So sorry ...

He pulled an arm free from the blanket, used a corner
of it to dry his eyes.

He woke out of a heavy, dreamless sleep, at what later
turned out to have been two o'clock in the morning, with
light flickering, a blast of freezing wind — snow in it, even
— and a lot of angry shouting. The light was from an oil-
lamp held aloft by a stranger — cavalryman, the one who
was doing most of the shouting — and the stables' main
doors were open with snow swirling in and a crowd of
men and horses out there. The dismounted man with the
lamp was bawling at Schelokov — who was on his feet but
still had his blanket round him — '—no damn business
here, you and your bloody nags! Get 'em out, I tell you,
take the bloody lot of 'em and—'

'Comrade lieutenant.' Fomin, the corporal: he'd
squirmed in, with that dipping and twisting limp of his,
squeezing in through the pack of horses blocking the
doorway. '*Tovarisch Leitnant* — excuse me, but these
comrades are here by order of the commanding officer. It's

the truth, comrade, he'll tell you himself—'

'At the gate they assured me these stables — they're *my* stables, damn it—'

'But you were overdue, comrade.' Schelokov spoke in his sergeant's voice, a bit of a Moscow accent. 'Captain Fedorenko assumed the weather'd delayed you. But he told me if you did turn up there were other stables you'd use.' He nodded towards the boxes. 'My horses here — remounts, we're in transit southward — needed a good feed and a night's shelter. And *we* needed a night's sleep — begging your pardon, comrade.' He shrugged. 'We'll be out of it in the morning, see.'

The lieutenant stared at him. A tall, slim man with a trimmed black beard and wide moustache, small hooked nose. Glancing at Bob: then at Ibraim who was still flat out in his corner. Back to Corporal Fomin then, resignedly: 'Which other stables, comrade?'

A minute later, Bob pushed the doors shut behind them. The oil-lamp was still burning; Fomin had taken it from the lieutenant and hung it back on its hook. Schelokov, still blanketed, was walking down the line of boxes, peering in at each horse in turn. Coming back now. 'Doesn't seem to have disturbed them much. But two o'clock, for God's sake ...'

Bob was pushing his straw together, prior to re-laying his blanket over it. 'Thought we had trouble, for a moment.'

'You took a while to wake up, I must say.'

'Not as long as our tame Tartar.' Ibraim had slept through all of it, hadn't moved. 'Did Fedorenko tell you what that lieutenant's name was?'

'Volodarski, I think. Yes — Yuri Volodarski. Why?'

'Doesn't have the manner of a Bolshevik, does he.'

'Well — quite a few joined them who should know better.'

'Anyone *you* knew?'

'No — thank God ...' He'd remade his own straw bed. 'You going to douse that lamp?'

*

Surprisingly, Volodarski paid a second visit to them at first light. They were stirring anyway by that time, had the lamp lit and were getting their gear together, on the point of going over to the kitchen to fetch their breakfast ration of tea and bread, when he pushed the doors open and came in, shutting them quickly against a blast of wind and snow. Bob had already ascertained that the weather wasn't very much different from yesterday's.

'Comrade Sergeant Krotov?'

Schelokov shut and latched one of the boxes, and came down the flagged passageway.

'Yes, comrade *Leitnant* Volodarski.'

'You know my name.'

'Captain Fedorenko mentioned it, in the conversation I had with him.'

The tall man nodded, put out his hand. In fact he wasn't any taller than Bob, but his slimness made him look it. 'Wanted to catch you before you left — to apologize for disturbing you last night. May have been a bit rude, I'm afraid.'

'No bones broken, comrade *leitnant*.'

'Well, good.' A glance at Bob. 'Good morning, comrade.' He nodded to the Tartar, then turned back to Schelokov. 'You're heading towards Taganrog, I'm told.'

'Yes. Did you come up on that route?'

'No. Across country, from Debaltsevo. That's more easterly from here, you want to go more directly south. But that's the other thing. Corporal Fomin tells me you have no map and you're worried about where to stop and get feed for your horses after this. I just want to suggest you ask for guidance from any patrols or formations you meet along your line of march. Bound to meet *some* — and they've all come from somewhere and have to be going somewhere — to state the obvious, but—'

'Exactly how we heard of this place.'

'There you are, then. Should be the answer to your problem all the way along. And as to the map — I've no spare, but if you want to make a copy of mine I'm sure Captain Fedorenko 'd supply pen and paper — huh?'

'Take me a week, comrade. But if I could just have a good look at it—'

'Of course. Here.' He moved closer to the oil-lamp. 'Now — you see where we are now — here, this cross.'

'Yes. Yes ...' Schelokov peered at the map. Narrowing his eyes in the poor light. Volodarski said, 'Of course, if the railway was open through Debaltsevo — which it isn't, I hasten to add — that'd be your easy way of getting down there. Two days' ride to Debaltsevo, then sit back and enjoy it, eh?'

'If our people had secured the line *and* Taganrog — or Korsun, even.' Schelokov shrugged. 'Not yet, eh?'

'Unfortunately not. Good enough going to have taken Debaltsevo this soon, *I*'d say.'

'Certainly. What well-handled cavalry can do, eh?' He'd seen enough of the map. 'Thank you, comrade.'

'*Nye za shto.*' Folding it carefully. 'In point of fact there's a very rum situation on the railway line at Debaltsevo. Well — to the north of it.' He checked the time, on a wrist-watch. 'Look, I must be off. Haven't been to bed yet, d'you know that? And you want to be on your way.' He stopped with his hand on the door. 'This train, though — extraordinary. Stuck there — we've got it trapped, you see — full of foreigners. English pilots, no less — Royal Air Force, would you believe it? With their machines, what's more, flying machines, on flat cars — just damn well *sitting* there!'

19

The horses were moving at an easy, steady canter, having no problems with the foot or so of soft snow overlying a hardbeaten base. Churning it up, though — more than fifty wide, powerful hooves throwing up a great wake of it to cloud away across virgin snowfield on their right. Snow was still falling too, but it was a thinner fall than yesterday's and riding east they had it behind their left shoulders, with a visibility range ahead of several hundred yards.

Bob asking himself — the question in his mind fairly constantly — whether this could be true, was possible ... The same train — carrying the squadron's 'B' Flight? Or whether it might be the other 'A' Flight, which was Scott's. Sam Scott's voice echoed in his memory, explaining in his patient way, *The one we expect to find here at Kupyansk is "B" Flight, Kinkead's. "A" Flight — to follow, if it does, seems unlikely now — is mine ...*

It seemed even more unlikely *now* — that they'd have sent a second flight up when they hadn't even deployed the first. Or at least hadn't decided to at that stage. They'd been waiting for General Holman, and for their own CO — and of course for an engine to move the train ... How long ago — a week? More — eight, nine days. And still only less than a day's slow travel south from Kupyansk ... *Could* have been that much delay, obviously: one hadn't envisaged anything like it, that was all. And to have sent the other flight up that way would have been lunacy: the object at that time had been to get the train out before it was too damn late.

Before, in fact, they got trapped. As it seemed they had.

Two days' ride to Debaltsevo, Volodarski had reckoned when he'd first mentioned the railway — as a potential means of transporting the horses south, once the lines were open, etcetera. But they were aiming to make it in one day, not two. You wouldn't cover that distance in the daylight hours, obviously but it might be better anyway to get there after dark. Undoubtedly the horses were going to suffer: although in theory each rider could change mounts twice. So that if the journey took fifteen hours, say, no single horse would actually carry a man's weight for more than five hours.

Any that went lame along the way you'd turn loose. The fewer the better because the pretext would be that you'd come to entrain them for Korsun — or Pokrovsk even. Having been given to understand — Schelokov would say — that the railway was functioning and that whole area was in 'our' hands by this time.

Volodarski had walked over to the house with them, when they'd gone for their bread and tea. He'd been on his way there in any case, for a cock-crow call on Captain Fedorenko, and Bob — sore and stiff, trying not to hobble — had asked him why the train with the airmen and their flying machines was being allowed to 'sit there', as he'd said it was. Why not storm it, pull the bastards off and shoot them?

The lieutenant had grinned at Schelokov. 'Fire-eater you've got here!'

'Same question's been in my own mind, though, comrade *leitnant*. Been flying in support of the counter-revolutionaries, haven't they, those foreigners?'

'Well, they have, you're right. But it's in our own interests to act with caution. As it was explained to me, certain negotiations are in progress. You see, there's good reason to believe that all the English forces — "military missions", they call them — are in process of being withdrawn. Including those aviators, of course. Well, obviously we don't want to provoke any change of heart. Clearly an option would be to storm the train, shoot them or take them prisoner. But it'd raise a storm in England — might even result in larger forces being sent, in reprisal. There'd be no legality in that but — could happen ... So the position is — or was, when I was there — we'd told them that if they off-loaded their flying machines, secondly handed over any Russians who are with them, and thirdly gave their word to clear out of our country and not come back, then we'd allow the train to proceed. It'd be to our advantage, you see — we'd get them off our hands, and we'd have those machines.'

'But if they're still there — or were, as you say — seems they can't be accepting the terms. So — excuse me, comrade *leitnant*, I still don't see—'

'Why we don't storm the train and take the machines for ourselves anyway.' Volodarski's tone had been that of a man exercising patience. 'As I explained — we'd sooner avoid an incident that could be used as an excuse for — further interference. As I also mentioned, negotiations *are* in progress. At the time I left — midday of the day before yesterday — one of our leaders was said to be on his way from Moscow to take charge on the spot.' The lieutenant had stopped, and pointed at the back of the house. 'Small door there. Oh, you know, of course ... So — I wish you a good journey south, comrades, and may you be among the first into Taganrog.'

Bob had murmured as they went on towards the kitchen, 'This is a bombshell. To put it mildly. If we could get to that train—'

'Yes ...'

'Think he was telling the truth?'

'Hardly invent it, would he?'

'It's just so — incredible ... And why's he so damn friendly?'

'*Smarmy* is the word I'd use. I'd guess because he's a fish out of water — as you noticed yourself. Also hedging his bets. Sergeants have been known to become colonels overnight, in this rabble.'

'So we believe it about the train. And if we *could* get to it, Boris Vasil'ich—'

'Let's get to the rations first.'

They'd collected Ibraim's as well as their own. Bob acting like an automaton, his thoughts centred on that train. Visualizing it standing there — as if it was waiting for them ...

Outside, on their own again, he'd looked at Schelokov.

'Debaltsevo?'

A wag of the grizzled head. 'Better give it a little thought, Robert Aleksandr'ich ...'

They'd discussed the various angles, for and against. The big attraction in it, obviously, was that in opting for it you'd shed that rather frightening problem of the distance to Taganrog, the time it would take to get there and the fact it might fall to the Bolsheviks within days. When the train did move south, according to Volodarski's account it would be doing so as an outcome of current negotiations, would in fact have a *laissez passer* from the Bolshevik hierarchy. So it would get through — whoever held Taganrog or, for that matter, any other place. The train would get through, and you could bet that three men on horses probably would not.

It didn't seem likely that the RAF on the train would agree to hand over any Russian personnel they had with them. This had worried Schelokov, to some extent — on his own account and Ibraim's. Bob pointed out that if some commissar was on his way down there to conduct negotiations, it followed that the terms *were* negotiable; and he thought that Kinkead — or Collishaw, whom he hadn't met but would be the same sort of man — would be much more likely to agree to off-load aeroplanes — perhaps with vital components missing — than to hand over Russian friends, knowing they'd have either a bullet or a rope waiting for them.

An argument *against* trying for the train was that conceivably it mightn't get away at all — if the negotiations foundered, and eventually the Reds did storm it. But this seemed very unlikely too. The Bolshevik leadership would *not* want to provoke warlike reactions in Britain. Especially at this stage, with complete withdrawal very much on the cards. Why foul *that* up? Political attitudes at home were ambivalent, and Trotsky, Lenin and company surely must know it.

'Another point, Boris Vasil'ich, is we've no idea what may be happening behind us by this time. Whether the Cheka may have worked out what transpired up there. I'd guess it won't be many days before they set the dogs on our trail.'

Schelokov had nodded. 'I agree. It's been worrying me too. So happens there's been nothing we could do except keep going.'

'But now there *is*.'

'Yes. Yes, I suppose ...'

They'd crossed one railway line yesterday and had another to cross today. In early afternoon, probably. Yesterday's had been a line directly south from Kharkov leading to Ekaterinoslav or thereabouts, and today's was also from Kharkov but running south-east — it joined the line which came down through Kupyansk at a point well south of Debaltsevo. One had to approach any railway line with caution, not knowing for sure whether the Reds might have brought it back into use and be sending troop trains or armoured trains down it. It wouldn't have been operational even as recently as yesterday — or Volodarski would have mentioned it — but things were changing fast and they'd be exerting every effort to get their 'iron roads' into commission as soon as they could. Particularly when the land was snowbound as it was now, so that without the railways the only possible large-scale movements were by cavalry. This line might have been out of action for quite a while — blown up, probably, somewhere or other. But it could be in use again now, and in any case railway lines were as often as not patrolled. That was the point: one could probably bluff one's way through all right, but one wasn't looking for delays of any kind, or confrontations that could be avoided. As Schelokov had put it, any long run of good luck had to come to an end eventually.

He'd made this somewhat obvious statement a few hours ago, in the course of a discussion as to what they'd do if they found the train had left before they could get to it. It was a frightening contingency, which one might have to face with a bunch of knocked-up horses in tow and no known refuge anywhere. But he'd also been speaking in general terms, and Bob's answer had been that he didn't think they'd had more than a reasonable share of luck this far anyway. It wasn't luck to be handier with a rifle than the opposition was, or to set a scene for an ambush so the odds would be heavily in your own favour. Not to have been caught napping by the team with the lorry — *that* had been luck, and so had stumbling on to the wretched Maltsev. But being caught at Irina's camp — nothing lucky *there*. Getting out of the stable — it had been luck that there'd been a physical way out, the loose planking, and that their captors had been as slack as they had been, but it hadn't been *luck* to have taken immediate advantage of those factors.

He'd called — shouting over the drumming of the horses' hooves — 'Mistake to confuse good luck with initiative, Boris Vasil'ich!'

A sideways grin ... Schelokov had started the day on the chestnut that was his favourite, and looked relaxed, comfortable in the rhythm of the canter. Shouting back, 'Also a mistake to pay ourselves compliments too soon, Robert Aleksandr'ich!'

They changed horses when they reached the railway line, having been in the saddle then for five hours. Schelokov and Ibraim had carried out a quick examination of the horses, and pronounced them sound.

'Luck's holding — this far. But they're tiring — and that compounds itself, you know?'

One-third of the way, roughly, at that stage.

There'd been no trains on the line; the rails themselves were snow-covered. No signs of patrolling either. They'd walked the horses for a spell, while choosing a point of departure where a track from a crossing pointed more or less in the right direction. Schelokov was navigating with the help of his pocket compass. And starting off again —

in a mood of affability, pleased at the way the horses had been holding up this far — he demonstrated how to put a horse directly from a walk into a canter, without its having to progress through a trot. It was a matter of watching (or feeling, when you'd learnt how to do it) the fall of the animal's feet. When the offside rear leg was coming forward, you put your weight down on that side just as the hoof was about to touch the ground; the horse went down on to that leg and, willy-nilly, straight into the cantering action.

'Simple, eh?'

He'd done it at the first attempt. 'Any other little tricks?'

'Dozens. These swords we're wearing, for instance—'

'That's something I've meant to ask. I thought cavalrymen had sabres — curved things, not—'

'Some do. More usually officers and NCOs — in most regiments, invariably officers in full fig, parade kit. But it depends. There are uhlan and dragoon regiments as well as hussars, for instance. And Cossacks, with different traditions again. As for *us* — my God, but we looked smart, Bob! You should've seen us . . .'

Reminiscences flowed, then — in a shout, the only way one could communicate — as the white miles rolled under them. About his cavalry school, for instance, where bookwork was minimal, the achievement of very low marks in any written or technical tests virtually *de rigueur*; and in his own famous, unnamed regiment, duty officers smuggling the ladies of the town in for night-time entertainment.

'You'd have to do something, I suppose. Seeing as you weren't allowed to marry under the age of sixty?'

'Usually a *little* earlier than that. But one achieved it, of course, by ensuring that one did not become involved with women of the kind one *might* have married.'

'Reserved yourselves exclusively for the tarts, eh?'

A frown: 'I'd say, for the courtesans. The *demi-monde*.'

'Ah. I beg their pardon.'

'As I believe I mentioned—' the brief smile was ironic — 'we were an *extremely* exclusive regiment.'

Straight-faced, then. Erect, staring directly ahead, barely moving to the motion of the canter: a cavalry officer on parade, with his squadron in line behind him, other squadrons behind that one and the Tsar himself up on the saluting-base. He'd glanced sideways finally, found Bob watching him, and shrugged. 'We pay for our follies — eh?'

The black gelding on which Bob had started the day but from which he'd changed at the first stop went lame in mid-afternoon. Ibraim saw it and howled at Schelokov, who called a halt. He and Ibraim dismounted and inspected the limping animal, then they went on again at a walk — but only a few hundred yards, to a farm entrance where Schelokov dismounted again, knotted the slack of the reins so they weren't dangling, and turned him in towards the house.

'You're excused old fellow. Good luck to you.'

One foreleg was swollen, apparently, by damage to a tendon. Schelokov commented as they started off again, 'We'll be damn lucky if he's the only one we lose.'

They lost two more before dark. Progress became slower then, and they'd been riding for sixteen hours when in a crossroads hamlet two shawled women told them after a lot of deliberation that Debaltsevo was '*That* way, Captain. But — bless you, it's a long ride — and be dark soon enough—'

'The railway line, mother. The one that goes from Debaltsevo towards Kupyansk — if we keep straight as we're going now, will we come to it?'

The women conferred again, and concluded that they would indeed, in ten or twelve versts. 'But there's no train would stop for you!'

'No. I'm sure not ... Is there a horse-trough here?'

There was, so at least the horses had a drink, then. They were in a fairly bad way by this stage. Neither Bob nor Schelokov felt like discussing it, but they were both well aware that if the train wasn't where it was supposed to be, or if they couldn't get to it — well, you couldn't go on all night, would have to halt *somewhere* — rest, eat …

Ibraim muttered while the horses were drinking, two at a time, '*Loshadyi* tired. Not run more, Excellency.'

'I know.' Schelokov had an arm round his own mount's neck. 'We all know it, don't we, old dear.' Then in a low growl, 'Do *not* call me "excellency". The word is comrade.' Raising his voice: 'Not much further now.' Although the least distance it could be was what the women had said — ten or twelve versts. He murmured to Bob, 'Might have to beg another night's lodging from the military.'

'If we could find any.' Mounting again: not without difficulty. In fact it was a fairly superhuman effort. One felt not far from the limits of one's own endurance — as well as physically handicapped in certain specific areas. Additional strain sprang from awareness of what was being inflicted on the horses: and the question arising from that — where you'd be without them, if the worse came to the worst. Three men on foot, hundreds of miles from anywhere. Possibly three *hunted* men. It made one realize how good the remount story had been — while it lasted … He called to Schelokov — settling himself in the saddle very carefully — 'If we run into a patrol, ask for directions to some cavalry depot?'

'And look for the train in the morning. If it's still there. Yes.'

He reminded himself — by way of keeping his own spirits off rock-bottom — *The darkest hour* …

But it was a long way, to the dawn. Quite a few dark hours to come, before that one.

Riding on, meanwhile. And *on* … The snow might have been falling rather more thinly than it had been.

Another hour. Forcing the horses along. By this time it seemed incredible that earlier in the day there'd been spells of gaiety and optimism, the feeling that one had been coming to the end of an ordeal, seeing light at the end of the long, dark tunnel. All promoted by one's thoughts of the train, of course, the heaven-sent solution to all other problems.

Schelokov called back — at some point — 'Has to be some military presence near the rail track. If we can get that far. They'll have a camp, of sorts. As far as we're concerned, two birds with one stone, eh?'

Not bad thinking — once a seized-up brain had solved the cryptogram. If there were soldiers besieging the train, and they had some place to go home to: and — touch wood — if they happened to be cavalry with feed for horses ... You'd beg a night's shelter and sustenance and then push on ostensibly for Debaltsevo but actually for the train after daybreak. What was more — the brain though sluggish was beginning to chug around again, after a fashion — what was more, in consorting with the military you might find out what sort of guard was being maintained on the train.

If these nags could stay on their feet and in motion that long, poor devils. And if, when you did know where the train was and all about the troops who'd surely be surrounding it, there was any way at all of getting to it.

Among less depressing thoughts buzzing in his head was what Schelokov had told him about hussars falling asleep in the saddle on long marches. Realizing that it would indeed be quite easy to drop off. But — jerking upright in sudden alarm — that unlike those cavalrymen you *would* drop off — literally—

'Bob, look there!'

'Lights ...

He *had* been dozing. At least, felt as if he had. Muzzy-headed, detached from his immediate surroundings, foul taste in his mouth. All he'd eaten throughout the day had been black bread and goat-cheese, from a pocket, crumbled in the fingers of the left hand ... He was still shaken by having damn nearly fallen off. If Schelokov hadn't shouted then ... They'd come over a rise and were on a downhill slope; he was gazing ahead through the slanting snow, over the black undulations of horses' rumps, past Schelokov's broad shoulders ... A light like — moonrise?

And closer lights as well. Couldn't be moonrise: with full
cloud-cover, and snow still falling, as it had all day ...
Schelokov was a black cut-out against it all: cap moulded
to the shape of his head, shoulders pulling round as he
half-turned to call back, 'Road-block. Soldiery ...'

The lights were oil-lamps in the hands of two peasant
women, and there was this glow — suffused but wide-
spread — behind them. A much larger and quite different
source — not moonlight but of that order — a sheen of it
here on the knee-deep snow. There was a cart — a four-
wheeled farm wagon — in the ditch, facing this way more
or less, one wheel up on the road at an angle to the cart's
side which suggested it might not be all that well attached,
and a mule in the shafts with an elderly man tugging at its
head. At least he had been doing so, was giving up now,
looking round at the sounds of their approach. While
further on, forty or fifty yards down the slope, there was a
barrier across the road and a group of soldiers some of
whom were coming this way. Black figures with that haze
of light behind them, capped heads down, rifles slung,
shoulders hunched against the driving snow.

Schelokov called as his horse came to a halt, 'What's
going on?'

'Ask *them*!' One of the women had screeched that
answer. The approaching soldiers were shielding their eyes
against the snow as they stared at this pack of horses and
the men on them. The older of the two women — they
were both stout, looked as if they were wearing tents
— told Schelokov in her high, penetrating tone, 'The road
we've always used, and they won't let us, made us turn
back — see, that's how *this* happened! Our youngest
daughter in labour — only reason we're out this time o'
night — now we must go back and t'other way round,
damn soldiers say—'

'Quiet, woman.' Her husband said, 'We'll *go* t'other way
round, that's all. Only doing what they're told, these lads.'
The soldiers were close now. 'Isn't that the truth, comrades
— and you'll give us a hand, now — eh?'

'What we've come to do.' Stopping, peering through

patchy darkness at the three of them and the bunch of horses all with their heads hanging ... 'What's this, then?'

'Making for Debaltsevo, comrade. To entrain these remounts southward. If they'll last that far. You could tell me — please—'

'I'll tell you you won't be entraining anything tonight, comrade. Or tomorrow. Entraining to go where, anyway?'

'Korsun. Comrade, I have orders—'

'And you can shit on 'em. No trains are moving — that's one thing — and you can't pass this way, that's another. If you want to get to Debaltsevo, you'll need to go the same way these folk here will — the track off to your left back there — that's going south, parallel to the rail line, see — then turn left, and down the hill to *that* crossing. Over the line, up the hill and turn right. Got it?'

'Thanks. But — anywhere around here that I can get shelter and food for my horses?'

'You can't *here*. Town's full of bloody cavalry, though.'

'Are you *going* to give a hand here, comrade?'

The plea had come from one of the other soldiers, waiting at one of the cart's rear wheels. The peasant at the mule's head was also waiting — with nervous impatience, glancing anxiously at his wife, who was still muttering complaints. The scene was dreamlike: after the interminable hours of riding, locked in one's capsule of anxiety and exhaustion, this was some other world — an irrelevance, with so much still undecided, in the balance ... He heard Schelokov ask that other one, 'How far from here into the town?'

'Five versts, near enough. No different from what it'd be this way. Listen — you'll see a train on the line to your left as you cross over: don't leave the road or you may get shot at.'

'*Shot* at?'

'That's what I said. Stick to the road — eh?'

'Hey, wait a minute! When I get shot at, I like to know who's shooting, and what for ... What if I bloody well *want* to leave the road?'

'Christ.' He'd been turning away, towards the cart.

'Number of times I've had to tell it ... All right: there's a trainload of foreigners we've trapped here. This side of the train I mentioned.' An arm flapped, pointing down the road past the barrier. 'Here. They want to go south, we're holding 'em, see. That's why this road's closed. Got it, now?'

'The foreigners' train's close to *this* crossing, is it?'

'Ah, you've a head on those shoulders, all right. Congratulations, comrade!'

'Comrade sergeant, as it happens.'

'Makes two of us. So how about harnessing some of those nags to the *fourgon* here?'

'No harness. No ropes even. And the horses are about knocked up. Tell me, though — who'd shoot at us?'

'*Please* — comrade—'

'Yeah, all *right*!' He'd snarled it at the old man: turned back to Schelokov, then. 'Now let's get this over — and you on your way. I'm not saying they *would* — just *might*. Well — if they thought you'd come from the train, they would for sure. See — we've a block on the line down here. One post this side and one the other — these lights, see, lorries' headlights? And snipers there watching — both sides. Other end, where you'll cross, snipers in *our* train — same procedure, watching that end of it. Killed one last night, as it happens. Making a run for it — he *thought* he was ... Understand why we don't want the place cluttered with spectators?'

'Killed one of the foreigners, d'you mean?'

'No, a Russian. Traitor. There's some of *them* on board too ... Now you know it all — eh?'

'Why not attack the train, finish it?'

'That question's being asked every five minutes, comrade. And the answer is we're doing what we're bloody told — all right?'

'Well — I suppose—'

'It's still a good question. Specially with an armoured train sitting there in Debaltsevo. On the up-line, see. Steam up here, blow that lot to smithereens any time they want — eh?'

'Well — perhaps when they're good and ready—'

'Yeah. Tell me *when*, that's all ... Getting along now, are you?'

'Yes. Right. And thanks.' Schelokov told Bob and Ibraim, 'Turn 'em around, comrades.'

The soldiers were stationing themselves at the cart's wheels, the sergeant at this near-side front one that was up on the road. Ibraim had his horses turned, and Bob was pulling his round. Schelokov called back as he brought his own up past them, 'How far to this turning, comrade?'

'Oh, Christ almighty—'

'No distance.' The old man bawled it. 'Stone's throw.' Then in a lower tone, 'Now, you devil —ready — *pull*!'

'What d'you think, Robert Aleksandr'ich?'

'Whether to try for it now ...'

'That, or push on into the town. Saving these nags' lives perhaps — and get on with it tomorrow. Not exactly on top form, are we.'

But after this, the horses would need more than a single day's rest. Assuming there was stable-room available anyway. No guarantee of it — or that any unit would have feed to spare. And arriving with horses in this condition ...

One thing reassuring was that the train's departure was obviously not imminent. But then again — you were *here*, in spitting distance of it, and it might not be so easy to get as close to it again.

'Shall we decide when we've seen how it looks down at that crossing?'

'Yes. Yes, good. *Very* good ...'

As the old man had said, it wasn't far to the turn-off — into a narrow lane, wooded on both sides and running along the crest of this ridge. The next turn, the one down to the railway crossing beyond the trains, couldn't be far either — the length of two trains with some unspecified gap between them. A few hundred yards, he guessed. Thoughts came as it were in weak flashes, faded away into oblivion when you found they didn't lead to practical

conclusions. For instance, if one did get to the RAF train
— God knew how, without being shot — what about the
horses? He held on to that one for long enough to realize
that (a) you'd have no option but to turn them loose, and
(b) ten wandering cavalry mounts wouldn't escape notice.
And the sergeant at the roadblock had seen them, would
report there'd been three Russians with them.

In his mentally fuzzy condition, what difference this
would make wasn't entirely clear to him.

Well. He'd guess that three Russians had boarded or
tried to board the train: three more to be handed over
before the train might be allowed to leave.

Except there might well be three bodies stiffened in the
snow by then.

'Think we could've passed the turning?'

'Could. God knows.'

'That cart may not be far behind us.'

At this crawling pace, it wouldn't be far behind. Unless
that wheel had fallen off. None of the light from the lorries
down at the crossing was visible above the trees which
enclosed this lane.

'All right, Ibraim?'

'Ibraim *khorosho*. Horses — not.'

'But not far now, either. Truly not far.'

'*Loshadyi* finish.'

'I know. But not far. *Nyedaleko* . . . Bob, here it is.'

It was no wider than this connecting lane, but had been
used quite a lot in recent hours. Not surprisingly — since it
led to a railway crossing, and the other one was shut.
From here now it would be roughly the same distance
down to the railway line as it had been from the ditched
cart to that first turning. That long stone's throw . . . There
were woods on both sides here as well, and a fairly steep
down-gradient. The trees gave shelter from the falling
snow but they also interrupted one's view down towards
the trains.

Schelokov suggested, 'They'd have their lorries at *that*
crossing — the road that's in more regular use — because
it's wider. Room to turn around, and so forth.'

'The *fourgon* didn't manage it too well.'

'I mean down near the tracks. They'd be off the road, I imagine, but they'd need good access for other vehicles — bringing recharged batteries for all that floodlighting, for instance.'

'Or petrol. Keeping the engines running.'

'Didn't hear any, did you?'

'Not sure one would. But — hey ...'

Light — filtered through trees at first, then as the wood came to an abrupt end — on this left side, the side that mattered — you could see a searchlight beam shining along the tracks and spotlighting the engine of a train that was standing there.

The train. Sam Scott's train, one might call it — while still finding it hard to believe in. The idea that that crowd — and the two girls whom one had thought of complacently as being out and free by this time — had been sitting in it, stuck either at Kupyansk or here, all the time one had been up at Valki ... But they *had* — because there they *were* ...

Up here, meanwhile, they were still in some degree of cover — the dark background of the trees — the three of them sitting on their tired horses silently, studying the scene below them. The railway tracks were about sixty yards down the hill, and the train with the searchlight on its roof stood black and square in an aura of its own snow-reflected light ten or fifteen yards to the left of the crossing. There wasn't much of it. Engine — at this end, facing towards Debaltsevo — a tender, and one box-car. Like some child's toy that had been left out at bedtime. The searchlight was on the box-car's roof, the end of it nearest to the RAF train.

'Snipers'll be in that car. Either a door open in the end of it to shoot through, or it's one of the loopholed, armoured kind. I'd guess at that.'

'They'd be keeping a look-out towards this road as well, though, surely?'

'I don't know. Their job's to watch the other train. And they aren't expecting to be attacked. Cat watching a mousehole doesn't look out of its backside, does it. They're only seeing the end of that train, the engine, at that. Whatever happens along its sides must be covered mostly from the other posts.'

'You'd think they'd have put trucks here too.'

'Road's too narrow. In any case they've got your friends pinned down well enough.'

Bob glanced around. 'If we went off this road — back up a little, then along through the trees—'

'I don't think so, Robert Aleksandr'ich. Anywhere near the trees' edge we'd be in view from both ends. Not a hope we'd get down to the train — sniper fire from both directions—'

'Enfilading fire . . .'

'Bravo. *Said* you'd make a soldier.'

'Make corpses, if you're right — however we try to—'

'Well — it may not be quite *that* hopeless . . .'

He was silent for a few moments: Bob waiting, seeing no way that wouldn't be suicidal. Then, from Schelokov: 'What we need is a close look at it down there.' He'd pointed down towards the crossing. 'I'll go down. If you and Ibraim'll stay here with the horses—'

'You're proposing to ride down there and — what, see if you do get shot at?'

'Well.' Leaning forward in his saddle, peering down. Second thoughts, perhaps . . . The lane's down-gradient levelled about twenty yards short of the embankment, then the rutted, snow-covered track ramped up over it. It wasn't much of an embankment, by the look of it from here. Probably enough for melted snows to run off, and for drifts to form at the sides, not on the tracks. Schelokov muttered, 'You see, I really doubt they'd be taking notice of what goes on along the road. As that fellow said — roughly . . . If I'm guessing right, snipers in that box-car will be all they've got here. And there's no reason they'd be looking out any other way. In fact the front of the train there — and the crossing itself — that's effectively dead ground.'

'To those other posts, you mean.'

'Oh, certainly, to them. *They're* blinded beyond the end of that train — by the searchlight, surely!'

'Could be — I suppose ... Boris Vasil'ich — suppose we *all* ride down, and loiter on the crossing while you see what you want to see?'

'Perhaps ... And then — yes, either they'll challenge us or they won't. If they do—' he shrugged — 'answers as now well-established. I'm Krotov, etcetera. Curious about this train. No reason anyone wouldn't be. Huh? But if there's no challenge — well, that's something else. We'll *know* they're blinkered, then.' He nodded. 'Yes, that's good, Bob, excellent.' He glanced round at Ibraim: 'Come ...'

Into the open — darkness of the trees behind them, faces to the light, and the horses more or less allowing the slope to carry them down towards the railway. It wasn't all *that* steep. Steeper than the other road — which would be another reason why that one was more suitable for the lorries. With chains on their wheels, no doubt. Bob was following Schelokov's example, leaning well back in the saddle to take weight off his horse's forelegs. Below them the stubby train's silhouette was black against the pale, partially illuminated background, falling snow slanting continuously into a radiance very much like moonglow. A strip of flat, open snowfield extended in both directions on this side and on the other too — though less visibly, over there — with the low ridge of the railway embankment dividing them and the searchlight's narrow beam glinting on the steel, lighting the RAF train's engine but then losing itself in the spread of light from the other crossing.

The RAF train — in about one-quarter profile — profile gradually narrowing as they rode down towards the line — was showing no lights of its own. A glimmer here and there would be reflections of the headlamps' beams. They wouldn't have steam up, on that engine, so there'd be no power on the generator for lighting. They'd have oil-lamps, probably. And stoves in the passenger coaches, for warmth and cooking. In those respects they'd be comfortable enough.

But you could imagine a carriage door swinging open, that sudden interruption of the flood of light: and snipers' eyes instantly at their rifles' sights, fingers tensing on triggers ... The poor devil who'd made a break for it last night wouldn't have stood a chance.

Down into the dip of the lane, now. The ramp up to the line ahead of them was darkly shadowed. And that blackness halfway up the lane on the other side was woodland crowding its edges. They couldn't have stationed lorries here. But Schelokov was right, they hadn't needed to. This toy train with the light on it was, so to speak, the stopper in the bottle: and it wasn't only blocking the line, any would-be escaper from the RAF train who might think of crawling out this way — out of the lorries' floodlighting — would find himself speared on the searchlight beam.

And then riddled.

Not that it was really a searchlight, as such, with that very narrow beam. More like a ten-inch Aldis. Spotlight, more than searchlight.

'Robert Aleksandr'ich.' Schelokov leant towards him, spoke quietly over the backs of the horses between them. 'I've developed this plan of yours a little. When we're on the tracks there, you and I stop. Pass your nags over to Ibraim — now. He can go on up the road with them, up to those trees, and wait either until we join him or until I call him down to us. All right?'

'Right.'

He was giving Ibraim his instructions now. Bob pulled aside to let the Tartar ride up past him, closer to Schelokov, and as he passed handed over to him the reins of the two horses he'd been leading. Ibraim took Schelokov's from him too, even before he'd got it all clear. Schelokov finished: 'If I whistle—' he demonstrated a whistle, very softly — 'come back here on foot — no horses. Leave horses in the trees—' pointing — 'there ... *Ponimayesh*?'

'*Ponimayu.* But, *vashe prevoskhoditeltsvoli,* if *no* whistle—'

'Stay there, and we come to you.'

They let him and the riderless horses take the lead up

the ramp. Then they were picking their own way up it and on to the railway track.

'Go on, Ibraim.'

Schelokov turned his horse between the rails, facing the dark loom of the engine ten or twelve yards away, with the diffusion of light beyond it — but no light here at all, you were right in its shadow — and dismounted. No challenge — yet ... Bob slid down too. Enduring twinges of agony in the process. At this stage he'd no idea what Schelokov's intentions might be. Watching him moving like a wounded crab — which was probably a lot better than *he*'d do, when he let go of this animal. He was hanging on to it still, with an arm up over the saddle. Fall flat, as like as not — have to crawl, hands and knees ... The thought jolted his imagination, gave him — in conjunction with that thought of an escaper crawling out under the RAF train — a hint of what might be in Schelokov's mind. Looking away to his right then, seeing Ibraim and the seven horses bunched around him rising out of the dip on that side, beginning the climb towards the trees. It struck him that in this instance what Schelokov had at some earlier stage referred to disparagingly as 'instant bloody planning' might not be at all bad. To any observer's eye, that party moving so painfully slowly up the hill might be the same one that had come down from this other side a few minutes ago.

Schelokov meanwhile had taken a quick look up each side of the train, and was now squatting close to its snow-plough snout, getting his head right down to peer under-neath, along the rails.

'Bob — here.'

He grunted, let go of the saddle. Agony in his hips and spine. 'Jesus ...'

'Stiff, eh.' Schelokov was getting to his feet. He whis-pered, 'No look-out this way — right?'

'Seems not.'

'That's point one. Point two — assuming it's an armoured wagon with loopholes, sniper or snipers watching out of that end. How many of them in there, would you guess?'

'Watching both sides of the train — say two. Keeping watches — and hour on, an hour off, say — makes four. Plus an NCO?'

'Five. There might be only one sniper on the job and one sleeping, but — say five. Next point — they have sliding doors both sides, these wagons. And since they aren't expecting to be attacked, chances are the doors won't be fastened. May be on one side, mind you ... But equally — same reasoning — if they *were* bolted, and I banged on the side, gave them some load of eyewash—'

'They'd open up.'

'Exactly. And there you have it. Five of them, three of us, and we'll have the advantage of surprise. We'll crawl under — you'll have realized, I dare say. See any snags I've overlooked?'

'After we've done this — what, we crawl along the track?'

A nod ... 'Down the middle.'

'But in that beam – are you so certain—'

'That they can't see anything beyond the engine of the train — yes. They've got *their* lights on its sides, but the front of that engine's as much dead ground to them as this is — and all the searchlight does for them is blind them.'

'You don't think we'd show up against it?'

'No. We'll keep low — right down on the sleepers, between the rails ... All right, Bob?'

'I suppose so.' He slid his right hand into his coat pocket, to the Webley. All it had shot at so far had been wolves. Schelokov had turned to face up the hill; cupping his hands round his mouth, he let out a high, thin whistle to bring Ibraim down. Bob asked him as he turned back, 'What about these horses here?'

'Let 'em wander. Nothing else we can do.'

'And the farmcart — could be here any minute?'

'If it's coming, it'll come. Last thing they'd want is trouble ... I'm sorry about the horses, they're sure to attract attention. Sorry *for* them too, but—' He'd checked himself. 'Listen — one very important thing. We're not so far from the posts at the other crossing there, and we can't risk alerting them. So — no shooting, eh?'

Staring at him, through about three feet of semi-darkness. Thinking — what, bare hands? *Swords*, for God's sake? Schelokov's hand closed on his arm, then: 'It's them or us, Bob. Remember that. *Always* remember that.'

20

Ibraim — a stooping, ape-like figure in the dark lee of the engine — unslung his rifle and laid it down beside the other two, between the rails. He'd led the horses off the road into the trees and removed their bridles, he'd told Schelokov. He was a good man with horses, did what was best for them without having to be told: Schelokov had commented on this and expressed approval, before embarking on a rapid, pidgin-Russian exposition of what had to be done now.

Rifles would have been an encumbrance, from here on. Unfortunately — from Bob's viewpoint. Other considerations apart, the rifle was his weapon, not this fancy-dress item — which was all the sword in its scabbard on his left hip had been until now. He'd never thought of actually using it — except once, on that hillside with the wolves, when he'd thought of it retrospectively for cutting twine, and been glad not to have had the idea sooner, feeling that out of sheer ineptitude he might have cut an arm off. On ceremonial occasions in the Navy one had worn a sword, of course, but only as a decorative object — symbol of authority, naval tradition and so forth. No resemblance whatsoever to *this* weapon, which had an edge like a razor's, a point like a needle's and a weight of steel to carve through a man *and* the saddle under him — or so Schelokov had claimed, in that period of reminiscence earlier in the day.

Schelokov had finished his briefing of the Tartar.

'Bob. When we're under there, I'll check whether I can see which side they've been using, which side the door's likely to be open. But also, I think it's preferable not to

burst in with weapons in our hands. Trojan horse routine
— get in there first. Then when we're inside—'

'I'll take my lead from you.'

'Yes. Good man.' He grasped Ibraim's arm, pointed at
Bob. 'You follow *him*, eh?'

'*Khorosho.*'

'Come on, then.' He turned away, got down on his
hands and knees and crawled around the side of the snow-
plough, into the low, dark void behind it. Bob pushed his
own scabbard back out of the way — as he'd seen Schelokov do, rather like a man flipping back the tails of a
morning coat — and followed him.

It was more a matter of wriggling than crawling, once
you were underneath. In places you couldn't raise your
head more than inches: particularly not wanting to renew
damage to the back of it. Not being exactly a shrimp,
either, didn't make it any easier, nor did the stiffness from
something like eighteen hours in the saddle. Although
one's arms and shoulders took the brunt of the effort; in
fact after some experimentation it devolved mostly on the
right arm alone, since the left one was needed for keeping
the sword-scabbard out of the way. If you let it drag, it
clattered. Right forearm flat, therefore, dragging oneself
forward in steps of about six inches over snow-covered
cinders, stones, intervening sleepers. Keeping the head
right down out of harm's way, but also having to watch out
for Schelokov's boots — and telling himself meanwhile
that this was something that simply had to be got through.
The only way forward — *out*. And, as Schelokov had
reminded him, *Them or us . . .*

But even accepting the necessity — which is what it
was, no question about that — he was appreciating for the
first time that aiming a gun and squeezing a trigger was
really child's play, in contrast to what he imagined the next
few minutes were going to be like. Pull a trigger — finish.
Or at sea — the best of all worlds — fire a shell or a
torpedo, and whatever the result it would as often as not
occur literally miles away. He'd had a conversation with
Sam Scott on this subject, he remembered. Scott had

asked him whether he'd ever killed a man face to face, and
he'd told him yes, he had. In that business at Enotayevsk.
Scott had been surprised: and then, later, critical: *Got to
hand it to this guy. Knifes one, breaks the other's neck.
Both times from behind* ...

If Scott was on that train, he'd have some new stories
for him now. Or — *by then* ... Except — on very brief
reflection — that one wouldn't much want to tell any of it.
To Scott or to anyone else. Never, probably, to anyone at
all. But in any case, as far as Sam Scott and that train were
concerned — well, you weren't *there*, yet, and it wasn't by
any means a certainty that you ever would be. For
instance, this business of being limited to the use of
swords: if they had pistols in there, and their wits about
them?

They *would* have pistols. And certainly did have rifles.

Schelokov pushed his head and shoulder back under the
wagon. Lying parallel to the rail, sort of rolling over it,
swivelling in. He'd been out there checking by sight and
feel for tracks, indentations by men's boots under the
surfacing of new snow. 'Out this side, Bob. Ibraim ...'

Very cautiously. You were right under them here. And
there were steel rails for scabbards to clink against.

Emerging — beside Schelokov, on the west side of the
wagon, the side they'd had in view when they'd come
down the hill. You were in some shelter here from the
falling snow, which swirled overhead in a fall-out of brilliance from the spotlight. Ibraim also out from under now,
on his right. The three of them close together, flattened
against the planking, with the light up to their left and
about half the wagon's length away, throwing its thin beam
down the track at the other train.

The thought of crawling out there — eventually, after
this — crawling out along the track, effectively *in* that
beam ...

Forget it. For the moment ... Schelokov, on Bob's left,
had waited to see Ibraim emerge, was now reaching up,
groping for the iron handle on the door. He'd found it:

was checking below the door now for the step. One only, quite high off the ground: pointing it out now, wordlessly, to the others. Then glancing down at his left side, easing his sword an inch or so out of its scabbard then pushing it back. Glancing along at the others again — seeing they were ready, watching *him* ...

He reached up again, grasped the handle, thumped on the door with his free hand.

'Comrades, visitors here! Permission to enter?'

He was up on the step by that time, putting his weight on the door and sliding it back with its runners squealing. 'Sorry to disturb you, comrades ...' There was a glow of soft light from inside: and he was in it, in silhouette on the threshold for a moment and then *in*. Bob following, Ibraim scrambling up behind, and a man's voice telling Schelokov, 'Welcome, comrade but who — if I may ask ...' The hot smell of a coal stove, and its warmth in the dim lighting from an oil-lamp, that voice demanding, 'Christ, how many more of you? Look, shut that bloody door, whatever—'

'Bob, watch the door?' Schelokov turned back to the lit interior. 'Comrade, it's like this. When the time comes to storm that train—' Ibraim was inside, Bob slid the door across to bang shut, turned with his hand on his sword-hilt — slamming his mind shut too — just as Schelokov grunted, '*Sorry*, comrade,' and the one who'd been on his feet — with a revolver in his fist, but the fist opened and it dropped now — bearded, bald, capless and coatless in this warmth — the bald head lolling sideways, Schelokov's sword — in one sweep, rasping out of the scabbard and the steel's swift glittering arc terminating in the angle between neck and shoulder on the man's right side, virtually separating head and neck from the torso, the stubby body as it were draped in a scarlet fountain as it folded. Initial shock had exploded into a bedlam of screams and shouts by then, the wagon was a seething crush of men straight out of sleep into — *this* ... One rushing at Bob — or at the door — screaming for help — God's, anyone's ... Bob's sword still only half up took him on its point, thrust

on in — through — the boyish face in close-up in the
lamplight, eyes rolling white and the mouth wide open in a
scream of agony that was lost in the surrounding noise and
a gush of blood. The sword had gone in at an upward
angle, probably into his heart; he had difficulty extracting
it as the body collapsed close against him. His impression
at that moment was of about a dozen men fighting to
escape and most of them screaming: a sword swinging up,
reflecting light, swinging down, the thud and a crunch of
bone, and from the end — where Ibraim was — a howl of
'I surrender! I *surrender*!' He'd have died, on that word.
All of this happening in what felt like a lengthy but also
compressed period of time: in fact, something like half a
minute at the most. He'd wrenched his sword out of the
boy he'd killed and seen a man crawling towards him out
of the thick of it, other bodies — crawling over one and
dragging himself this way — towards the door — then as
Bob lifted his sword he saw *him*, twisted half over on to
his side, had a revolver in the hand he'd been using to pull
himself along with and was slowly lifting it — struggling
to, having barely the strength to tilt its barrel upward. His
other arm was clamped across his belly — ineffectually,
blood gushing out around it. All of this in one picture —
sepia and scarlet, and as it might have been in the flash of
a single magnesium flare — as Bob moved towards him
but also out of the line of fire. The man must have been
blind by then, had had a sight of him a second or two
earlier but was aiming only vaguely at where he *had* been
when the sword smashed down to finish it.

Whimpering . . .

It was the only sound, other than men's hard breathing.
One's own included — gasps almost like sobs. The
screaming must have finished very suddenly: he hadn't
noticed the actual cessation. Well — two or three seconds
could have passed since it *had* ceased, and now there was
only this whimpering — which could have been a child's.
A soft impact, then, and *it* stopped. Ibraim straightening
— at the far end of the wagon, where the snipers would
have been — wiping the blade of his knife on the other

sleeve. His sword was in that hand, and the knife in his right. Beyond him one rifle was still propped with its barrel out through one of the loopholes, and the other was clutched in the arms of a boy who'd been decapitated. Ibraim sliding his sword into its scabbard — left-handed with the knife still in the other hand. He had blood all over him: slitted eyes shifting around — looking for movements, obviously — but his face as mask-like as ever, utterly without expression. Schelokov said, panting, 'There were seven of them. *Seven*, for God's sake.' He'd been well blooded too. Staring at Bob now: 'Well. Earned *your* butcher's apron, by the look of it.'

The essential was to move fast. Move *now*.

Nothing on the outside looked any different. Peering out through the loopholes the snipers had used, one saw the floodlighting around the train down there exactly as it had been — no change, and no movement anywhere.

Seemed — uncanny. As if there *should* have been some sort of reaction to so much noise. Even though it had lasted hardly any time at all.

Schelokov had just suggested — having *his* problems, Bob guessed, in getting his thoughts together — 'Might even get the train moving out tonight — possibly? Need to shift this one, obviously, but — look, your friends' train might push it, shunt it off somehow?'

'They won't have steam up on that engine, Boris Vasil'ich. Any more than this one has. Take an hour or two to raise steam, I imagine. *Might*, I suppose — but there again—'

'Let's get over to it, anyway. Before we get other visitors here.'

He was right — others *might* come. Change of watch, or a commander checking — whatever ... But this business of the transit from here to the other train was a major problem now. Schelokov was convinced that the spotlight would blind those snipers to movements between here and the RAF train's engine, while Bob felt equally certain that to appear even for a moment out there would be suicidal.

Against the spotlight's dazzle, he thought, you'd show up like a cut-out target on a shooting range.

'So what's your alternative?'

'Don't have one. At least, nothing that wouldn't tell them they've got trouble — like as not provoke an attack on the train. Incidentally, the armoured train your friend said they've got standing by at the station — that's the *real* menace, isn't it? What you just said about moving the RAF train doesn't take account of it either.'

'So what's this idea you have that might provoke attack?'

'If we shot those trucks' lights out before we started. We've got snipers' rifles here—'

'My God, yes ...'

Staring at each other. Both about half alive, still, among the litter of those who weren't, and the sickening blood smell. The simple truth being that you'd be dead if you did *not* keep going, and thinking sanely. Sanely enough at least to know you did *want* to remain alive — which only a few days ago had seemed at least questionable ...

Schelokov, he thought again, might not have been as clear-headed as usual, at this stage: he was certainly grasping at *this* straw ... 'You're right, Bob! Shoot out the headlamps, and switch *this* one off ...' Glancing up to where cables looped around a corner stanchion led from a stack of motor batteries to a trapdoor in the roof at that end. Access to the spotlight, obviously. Schelokov frowned — the sight of those wires giving him another thought — 'You'd think they'd have rigged a field tele-phone between here and the other posts, wouldn't you?'

'Probably don't have any. But — Boris Vasil'ich — wait a minute ...'

There was a stepladder propped against the wall near the batteries. He'd looked for one, after seeing that hatchway and the cables, realizing there did have to be some means of access. Stepping over the young sniper's headless body, he pulled the ladder out to set it under the hatch: Schelokov murmuring 'Hold on', stooping to take hold of a booted leg and pull that one aside. The deck was slippery, you had to be careful. 'There you are. But what's this for?'

'The light should be adjustable. Solve our problem, if it is.' He stopped on the ladder to push the hatch up, then went up another step, and another, until he could get his head into the hatchway and his arms out through it. Head and shoulders out — right out in cold, clean air — a blessing in itself after the charnel-house stink inside. He was looking down the beam, with the falling snow drifting through it from right to left, at an end-on view of the RAF train's engine. A wisp that could have been smoke — but wasn't, must have been either imagination or — refraction, the light playing tricks. But the whole front of that engine was illuminated, from its snowplough upward: and with any luck, a very small adjustment would make all the difference. At least, *enough* difference.

It *had* to be adjustable ...

It was. Even without loosening the hexagonal knob which he found on the side of the casing. A slight squeak came from its bearings as he applied firm but cautious pressure upward. The beam lifted: it was still centred on the engine, but higher than it had been. The lowest two or three feet of the engine, and its snowplough, were now in darkness. You could crawl out now *under* that silver beam.

The watch on duty in the engine's cab from midnight to 0400 consisted of Flight Sergeant Hodges with Airmen Price and Peabody, and one of the Russian civilian railwaymen whom they all called Ivan. Watches had been maintained on the footplate day and night since they'd been trapped here, as a precaution against any attempts to remove the engine and also in order to keep the boiler fire alight. This was the Russian's job. Economy with fuel was obviously essential, but by keeping a low fire going you'd be able to raise steam quickly when, or if, the need or opportunity arose. When there was some breakthrough in the present stalemate, for instance. If the bastards decided suddenly they'd had enough, the thing would be to move out quick before they changed their minds.

'Wouldn't lean out too far, lad, if I was you.'

Peabody pulled his head and shoulders back in over the edge. He was well muffled against the cold, with a wool scarf filling all the gaps between his greatcoat collar and the RAF cap, and gloves on the hands that grasped his Lee-Enfield. He was taking his turn as lookout, Hodges and Price inside the cab taking advantage of the warmth from the furnace.

He told them, 'Shifted the light, those buggers have. Shinin' right up, now. Wasn't before, was it?'

Hodges took his pipe out of his mouth, and growled, 'Somethin' to do with all the hollerin' and yellin' we heard, p'haps.'

Peabody glanced at him, shrugged, looked upward again. 'Over the top now, see?' The beam caught the falling snow in it: snow-crystals glittering in the brilliance … None of it settled in or on the cab, because of the warmth from the furnace. Hodges said, 'Be annoying the customers on the 'illside, I dare say.'

'Wouldn't show that far, I reckon …' Peabody looked to his left: 'Hah. Workers of the world on the bleeding march again, lads.' He watched Ivan coming from the tender, bringing one large shovelful of coal to throw into the furnace and keep it going. Hodges and Price had to move out of the way for this.

Peabody, gazing back towards the lights on the parked lorries, began to sing *Why are we waiting*. Ivan hooked open the left-hand furnace door and slung the coal in, landing it exactly where he wanted it. Straightening, he pushed the iron door shut with the shovel and told Peabody in English, 'Russian peoples also sing. But now, sad songs only.'

'Wouldn't say *that* was a jolly one, exactly.'

'Sing us one o' yours then, Ivan old cock!'

Price joined in: 'Yeah! What about Ochie What'sit?'

A voice called — out of nowhere — 'You — in the train — d'you hear me up there?'

'Gawd, what the '*ell*—'

'Shurrup, Pea-brain! *Listen!*'

Silence. A long way off, wolves were howling. Ivan's hand moved as if to cross himself, stopped as Hodges asked, looking round at their startled faces, 'Who's the ventriloquist, then?'

'I suppose I am.' A man's head and shoulders were materializing in the space between the engine and the tender, expanding upwards beside the steel plate that bridged the coupling. Lifting his hands as a rifle-barrel swung towards him ... 'Don't shoot — d'you mind? I'm British — my name's Cowan. Lieutenant-Commander — Navy ... Look — is Major Scott still with you? He knows me, d'you see ...'

'Really is *you* inside there?'

Scott's brown eyes quizzed him from the seat opposite the one he'd flopped down on. He added, 'Thought I was dreaming when he told me. You *real*, Cowan?' Scott had only minutes ago been woken out of sleep, and showed it, but was in other respects immaculate. Moustache neatly clipped: Sam Browne and buttons gleaming in the oil-lamp's glow. Vaguely shaming — if one had cared — given a damn for *anything* at that moment except for having got here, achieved the miracle. Although even now — well, only as far as *that* miracle went. It had been like this all the way along: you scraped through one crisis, and more or less immediately faced the next ... Scott glancing at Schelokov — grey beard, bloodshot eyes — then at the Tartar who'd hunkered down in the corridor, from where he could watch them both with that dog-like, wooden-faced persistence, through the open doorway. On their way through into this passenger coach Bob had stopped to remove his swordbelt and sword, then the filthy, blood-splashed greatcoat — after extracting the Webley pistol and spare magazine from its pocket; he'd dropped them in a heap and told the young pilot whom Scott had sent to fetch them — lieutenant, name of Beasley — 'Might tell them to burn that.' Throwing his Red Army cap on top of it: 'And that. Go in the furnace, couldn't it?' The others had followed his lead, shedding their coats and caps, but retained their swords. Ibraim had been additionally burdened with half a dozen rifles which they'd brought from the other train, thinking they might have been needed here. Bob had added as he'd shambled on, 'Burn every damn stitch, when I've stripped.' He'd known by then about the furnace being alight, having seen its glow through a small glass peephole in the iron door while they'd been waiting, and asked the airmen about it — before Beasley had arrived, stammering 'Commander Cowan — sir? Major Scott's compliments — oh—'

He was duty officer, had been sent by Sam Scott while he, Scott, was in the process of turning out, and he'd noticed Schelokov, then, not having been aware that there were any others besides Bob. Bob had introduced them — Major Boris Schelokov, late of the Imperial Russian Cavalry, and Ibraim as his batman.

They stank: and were as much aware of it as these people whom they could see reacting to it. But at least having dumped their coats they weren't so noticeably blood-spattered.

In the compartment, Bob stripped off the tunic which he'd taken from one of the cavalrymen at the Valki farmstead, threw it out into the corridor. Tea was being prepared for them, and some kind of food — supper being reheated probably. Scott murmured — he seemed uncharacteristically stumped for words, poor fellow — 'Been through it a bit, haven't you?'

'A bit.' He nodded. 'But listen — isn't time for chat, now. I know we're filthy, we stink — fix all this later, tell you about it — later ...' Words weren't coming easily to him, either. 'Here and now — look, who's in command — Colonel Collishaw, is it?'

'Ray Collishaw flew General Holman from Kupyansk to Novo Cherkassk. That's Denikin's HQ now. Holman's concerned with the withdrawal of missions, and Ray was to set up arrangements for handing our crates over to the Volunteers. Including these — which the Bolshies want to get their dirty paws on.'

'So who's—'

'Marcus Kinkead. You met him, didn't you.'

'Any chance he'd join us?'

'On his way. Turning out. I sent Beasley.'

'Right. Good. Thing is, you see, this train ought to be moved — I mean *now*—'

Davies looked in, then. Jim Davies — Captain, MC — as spick and span and surprised-looking as Scott was. He had Bob's sword with him: Beasley hadn't known what to do with it, apparently. 'He said you'd told him to burn it, but—'

'Anything you like. Keep it — souvenir — or throw it away.' He nodded, thinking that with Bolshevik blood caked on it it would make an excellent souvenir. He personally didn't want it in his sight, that was all. The throbbing in his head came and went: at this moment it wasn't as noticeable as it had been. He raised a hand, as in greeting — or farewell — 'Good to see you again, Davies. But — if you'd excuse us now — awfully sorry, but—' turning back to Scott — 'Tell 'em to get steam up, could you? I'll explain when Kinkead comes, but—'

'Speak of the devil.' Scott glanced up as the Flight's CO stepped past Ibraim and stopped in the narrow doorway. 'You remember Commander Cowan, Marcus—'

'Of course I do. But how in hell did you get here?'

Bob shook hands with him, shook his head at that question, introduced Schelokov — apologizing again for the state they were in — and then, with Kinkead still standing and Scott leaning forward with his forearms on his knees — mouth slightly open in continuing surprise — put the situation and his proposals to them as succinctly as he could manage. Listing points in what seemed a logical sequence, starting with the fact that the blockading train now had only dead men in it.

'How the devil—'

'We killed them.' Second point: it was likely there'd be an attack on this train. From what the sergeant on the roadblock had said, there was undoubtedly a general feeling amongst the troops that action should be taken, and Bob's instinct was that the Bolshevik leadership would lose too much face with their own people if they continued to allow a trainload of pro-White foreigners to resist their demands.

Three: there was an armoured train in the station at Debaltsevo. Armoured trains carried heavy guns as well as troops. If they decided to make use of it — and you could assume it was there for some purpose — that would be that.

Schelokov had fallen asleep. If Bob had been able to make this dissertation in Russian he might have managed to stay awake, but the flow of English had proved too much for him. He had his head back against the board partition; Bob could see the scar of his wound through the grey hair on this side of his jaw and neck. He'd heard the heavy, regular breathing, and seeing now that he was asleep he told the two pilots quietly, 'This man's a bloody marvel. Without him I wouldn't be here now, that's certain ... Listen — d'you have an engine-driver or some such who could join us? Thing is, that train we've come from — if you moved this one up, then took that one's brakes off—'

'Push it along in front of us?'

He'd nodded, indicating Schelokov again: 'His idea, originally. But there's more. One needs — you know, the technicalities ...'

Kinkead shouted down the corridor to Beasley to send for someone called Baibakov, then came in and sat down beside Scott. 'Baibakov's a good egg. Hates the Reds like poison, bless him. He has two civvy assistants — firemen — and a bunch of Volunteer Army recruits they drafted into the job at Kupyansk. Rules 'em with a rod of iron.'

Bob nodded. Barely hearing him, letting that information — which seemed somehow off the point — wash over his head while he got back on track ... Thinking: *Debaltsevo — the armoured train. Plus troops in the station, presumably* ... 'Major — how many officers and men in this Flight?'

'Ninety. With Scott here and Davies, ninety-two.'

'How many rifles?'

'Oh — enough to go round. Officers have revolvers, of course.'

'We brought a few rifles with us, too.'

'I saw them out there. With that — er — Tartar, is he?'

'Yes. Don't underestimate him, either. He's — extraordinary. In action — you wouldn't believe it ... But listen — machine-guns, could you take some off your aircraft?'

Scott nodded. 'Already have.'

'Made holes in some of the box-cars to fire through.' Kinkead explained, 'In case of the attack which you say we should now expect. It was always a possibility, obviously — although I personally doubt it could be quite as imminent as you believe.'

'Could we have the furnace stoked up, anyway? If you decide *not* to move you could always let it die down again, but—'

'All right.' This time he shouted without moving from his seat: 'Beasley! In here, a minute!' Looking back at Bob: 'Go on, Cowan.'

'Could you mine the track behind you here with aircraft bombs?'

'Could, surely. Armourers'd be happy to display their skills.'

'But one problem's those headlights, isn't it. We could shoot 'em out, of course, but then you'd be giving them notice—'

'Sir?' Beasley was in the doorway. Narrow, boyish face, enormous moustache. Kinkead threw him a glance: 'Tom, tell 'em to raise steam on the engine, would you?'

His eyes sparked: 'Raise *steam*?'

'Yes. Full blast. *Now*.' Turning back to Bob. 'We could do it if we sacrificed the two Camels on the flat-car at the end. Break that coupling and set the mine there under it. Be working under cover, then, they wouldn't know it was happening.'

'*Damn* good, Marcus!' Scott added, 'You'd sabotage the Camels first, wouldn't you ...? Did we take the guns off those two crates?'

'Probably. Why don't you check, Sam. But — yes, Cowan, we can mine this track. What about the armoured train — any ideas?'

He nodded. 'Depending on what your engine-driver may have to tell us. Does he talk English?'

'Oddly enough, yes. Even the firemen do, a little.'

'Right.' He woke up to the fact that the Webley, which he'd been toying with in his lap, still had a round in its breech. He took the magazine out, ejected that round and fed it back into the magazine, put the empty gun down beside him. All these pilots were wearing revolvers on their belts, he'd noticed. Concentrating again now: or trying to ... He asked Kinkead, 'Do we know how far south the Reds are in control now?'

'Well, *we* don't. We've been isolated here for — what, five days now. And at Kupyansk a bloody age before that — before we got an engine!'

'Those two girls all right, Scott?'

The Canadian nodded. 'They're great kids. We all love 'em. Gone bye-byes now, of course.'

Kinkead said, 'They're one reason there's been no question of doing any kind of deal with these bloody people.'

'Yes. Of course.'

Scott asked him, 'Did you find that other *letuckha*, Cowan?'

'Sam — time's short, on this—'

'Yeah. Sorry.'

'The point is—' Bob got back to it — 'how far south from Debaltsevo we'll have to steam before we're in friendly territory. I do know they haven't taken Korsun yet, for instance. That's — from Debaltsevo, say sixty miles?'

Kinkead's eyebrows rose. 'Not so damn far!'

'Mind you, they'll have cavalry operating much further south — moving in on Taganrog even, by now. But as far as this line's concerned, or the towns along it — couple of hours' steaming, say?'

'Are you *sure* they aren't in Korsun yet?'

'Well — yesterday, we were told they weren't. By a

lieutenant in a Red cavalry depot. He'd been down this way quite recently — told us about this train, in fact.'

'Red cavalry . . .' Scott whistled. 'You really *have* been in it.'

'Yes.' He met the Canadian's widened eyes. 'Have, rather.'

'Major.' A tall, brown-faced man in railway uniform — Navy-like blue serge shiny with age and service. Exposing a dome of bald head as he removed a battered cap. 'You wished to speak with me, Major. And you have ordered the raising of steam.'

'Have indeed, Baibakov. Come in, sit down.' Kinkead nodded towards Bob. 'This is Commander Cowan. He reckons he can get us out of here. Raising steam so as not to waste time if it still looks like a sound proposition after he's picked your brains.'

'My brains — such as they are — are at your service, Commander.'

'Thank you . . . But I didn't say *I* can get us out.' He shook hands with the railwayman. 'Only have some ideas how you might get *yourselves* out.' Glancing at Schel-okov's inert, deep-breathing form: 'He and I — and that Tartar out there — well, we just had a battle, of sorts, and before that we were in the saddle for eighteen hours. Several days of much the same kind before that too. Fact is we're played out. It's up to you, Major. I'm giving you the idea, that's all. Dare say you'll improve on it. Hope you will . . .' The mind drifted, had to be hauled back, held on a shorter tether. Glancing at Scott: 'Did you say there's tea coming?'

'Damn, I'm sorry!' He shouted, 'Pickerell — where's that tea?' To Bob: '*Very* sorry, Cowan—'

'Help keep one *compos mentis*, that's all.' In fact, the thought of a mug of strong, sweet tea was like something out of a dream of paradise. He turned to the railwayman: 'Questions, now?'

'Please.'

'First — when you have steam up on this train, could you move up to that one that's blocking the line, have someone board it and take its brakes off, then push it ahead of this one?'

'As long as the person who alights can do so without being shot.'

'There's no one alive in that train now.'

'No one — alive?'

'Seven in the box-car, all dead. Look, whoever fixes the brakes could also disconnect the batteries from that spotlight. But — there's more to this ... D'you know the rail system in Debaltsevo — where the points are, for shifting from one line to the other?'

Baibakov touched his left palm with a finger of the other hand. 'As well as I know *these* lines.'

'There's an armoured train there now, on the up-line. They're holding it there in readiness for an attack on this one.'

'Ah.' Looking at Kinkead. '*Well*, Major ...'

'Question is, is there a set of points on the far side of the station, connecting the two lines?'

'Yes. This side also.'

'So you could stop, have some of your people jump down and switch the points, then give that blocking train a good shove to send it over?'

'That could be done. But—'

'Then your team would switch the points back, get back on board and you steam on.'

Kinkead objected, 'They'll have troops on the ground, surely? Won't just stand and watch all this.'

'Where your riflemen and machine-gunners come into it, Major.'

'Ah. Well — I suppose ... But what's to stop the armoured train pushing the damn thing along with it, same as we'd have been doing?'

Baibakov nodded. 'My own thought, also.'

'So think about *this*. You've a big load of cans of petrol on this train, haven't you. Didn't you bring up a whole wagon-load to Kupyansk, Scott?'

'Sure we did. Didn't leave it there, either.'

'So while we're raising steam, amongst other jobs — like

issuing rifles and ammunition — what about shifting some of it up to the front end here. Then when you move up to fix the other train's brakes and so forth, pile it into that box-car. Better warn whoever you detail for it they won't find it very congenial in there. Bodies and so forth. In fact a good blaze wouldn't come amiss.' Looking at Kinkead. 'Easy enough. You'd have some Bickford's cord, I imagine? Make a damn great fire-bomb out of it. Over those points, light the fuse, leave it to explode behind you. *Then* they won't clear that line in a hurry — and all you need's a good head start — eh?'

'But—' Scott pointed downwards — 'We'd need a second mine on *this* line. Otherwise they'd merely switch—'

'Yes. Struck me just this minute. And — why not? Have it ready — have the armourers make two mines instead of one. Second one just beyond the points?'

Kinkead began, 'Mightn't need the first one, in fact. Unless there's a train we don't know about behind us here. But perhaps we *should* play safe on that ... What is it, Sam?'

'The wagon with the gas in it is only about one car from the end — right? So why shouldn't we move as much as we need up front here, and use the rest of it to fix *that* wagon as a fire-bomb too. Then all we'd need do is uncouple it — wherever we want, uh?'

'Capital.' Kinkead nodded. 'Even if it's, say, three or four from the end — who cares, we can lose some ... Sam, your idea, your task. You look after everything at that end, will you?'

'Sure.'

Kinkead asked Baibakov, 'Would you sketch the layout of lines and points for us?'

'Certainly, Major. If you have a pencil, piece of paper—'

'Tea, sir? Sorry for the 'old-up. thought you'd be wanting it with the meal, like, and that's not—' Pickerell checked, grinned at Bob. 'Welcome back, sir!'

'Thanks.' He moved his head, indicating Ibraim. 'Have

you got a mug for him?' Pickerell had to dodge out of the
way then as Kinkead went to the doorway and bellowed,
'Beasley! In here!' Schelokov groaned and shifted slightly,
but didn't wake. Kinkead said, glancing at him as he came
back inside. 'See what you mean about being played out.
Going to wake him for his tea, are you?' Turning to Scott:
'Sam, might be an idea to mount a Vickers each side of the
engine. On the cab, d'you think? Or on the tender, if that's
easier ... Well, I'll have Halliday see to it.' Beasley
arrived, then: 'Ah, Tom. All hands on deck, as the
Commander here might say. Rouse 'em out — everyone,
no exceptions ... Baibakov, how long before we have
steam?'

In his dream he heard a machine-gun firing. He was in the
Kist Hotel, that was Kotter's gang up to their tricks again,
and he remembered with a pang of fright that Nadia
should have been arriving at just about this time. He had
to get down there — should have *been* down there, for
God's sake — but as he struggled to get out of bed it
lurched — the entire Kist Hotel had lurched. He thought,
Earthquake. Get her out, quick ...
    'I don't *believe* this!'
    Her voice?
    Half awake by then: the thought in his mind that it
couldn't be, that she was dead ... His eyes were open, and
focusing. Brain clearing too: registering, confirming it as
fact, *Nadia dead* ... The train had jerked convulsively —
again — but seemed now to be moving, and there was a
young woman in the doorway of the compartment, staring
at him. It was one of the two young nurses. Tousled light-
brown hair, turned-up nose, big teeth rather prominent at
the moment, as her mouth was open. Mary Pilkington.
One arm clutching an RAF greatcoat around her, the
other holding on to the door-jamb. He was reclining with
one leg up and one down and a rifle across his lap: he
remembered that he'd decided not to rig the plank-bunk
and turn in properly, only to snatch an hour or two's sleep

while Kinkead and company were making their preparations, and be available — as a sharpshooter, was the obvious thing — when he was needed, when they began the actual move. This was one of the two sniper's rifles — they were Mausers, with German-made telescopic sights. Schelokov had the other beside him on his bench.

Dead to the world still. So much for being available ...

They'd had supper, he remembered. *Farsh* with rice and beans. Delicious, absolutely. He'd woken Schelokov, who incredibly hadn't finished his, had fallen asleep again with the spoon still clutched in his hand. Bob remembered it all, now. He'd taken the spoon from him, and the plate, finished that up as well as his own, then lifted Schelokov's legs up on to that bench, spread the rug over him and put the rifle between him and the partition where it wouldn't fall off and damage the telescopic sight.

He swung his own other leg down, now, and sat up, moving the rifle to one side and massaging the knee, which had gone stiff. The train felt as if it was rattling along quite well — after that collision or whatever it had been. There must have been a fight, of sorts — the machine-gun, in his dream ...

He looked for the girl in the doorway, saw she was still there, gazing down at the blanket-covered, sleeping Tartar. He cleared his throat ... 'Hello, there. Miss — Pilkington, isn't it ... How are you — you and Miss — er — Reid?'

She swung round, stared at him.

'I don't *believe* it. I mean — we're very well, thank you, but — I honestly do *not* ... You, and — this — and—' she nodded towards Schelokov, the jutting grey beard — 'Boris Vasil'ich ... How can you *be* here?'

'Mary, what's going on? Who are you talking to — and what's—'

'Come here. Get out of bed and come *here*. And when you get here, don't you dare faint.' Her laugh was high and wild, slightly hysterical. 'If anyone's going to faint, *I* am, I was here first. Kate, hurry!'

'We're — *moving*, d'you realize?'

'Of *course*. And that, my dear, is only half of it. Are you *coming*, Kate?'

'Yes, yes ... Oh, my God, who's *this*?'

'How should I know? Ask *him*!'

Pointing at Bob, as the other joined her. The small, dark, pretty one. Katya, they'd called her. In the doorway beside the slightly larger, fairer one, her dark hair hanging loose in the soft light. She'd peered at Schelokov, started in surprise, was now gazing at Bob as if he was a burglar they'd caught prowling.

'Commander — Cowan?'

'Yes. And you're Katya. Look — both of you — I'm sorry you're seeing me — us — like this. We're badly in need of a good wash, change of clothes, shave and so forth. You see—'

Somewhere astern, one of the armourer's devices — a wagon-load of petrol, he guessed — exploded. It came from a long way back in a rolling, thunderous blast that lit the night outside the drawn blind on the window and sent coaches, box-cars and flat-cars ramming against each other in a ripple-effect that travelled up the length of the train and then back again.

Still on the rails, though. Picking up speed, in fact, by the sound and feel of it, getting into a rhythm not unlike that of a fast canter. Schelokov still snoring, and the two girls just inside the doorway with their arms round each other, Katya's pale-blue eyes fixed on Bob with that astonished and slightly accusing look, while her lips seemed to be trying to frame some question. He smiled at her, and told her — told *them* — 'I think we're going to be all right, now.'

Only minutes later he'd asked himself *Don't you ever learn?* Because they were *not* home and dry yet, not by a long chalk, and just a few hours before he'd been reminding himself that there was always the next hurdle — and the chance it would be the one where you came a cropper.

Even though things did seem to be on the up-and-up, at this time. The only losses to the train in the action on and around Debaltsevo station had been that two young soldier-railwaymen had deserted, vanished into the night. Probably seeing that the longer-term future was written on the wall in big *red* letters. And they were Ukrainian boys, Baibakov said, hadn't wanted to leave their home ground anyway. Good riddance to bad rubbish, had been his response: and three hours out of Debaltsevo the train steamed grandly into Korsun, displaying the Russian and Union flags side by side on the engine, and was greeted by cheers from soldiers on the crowded platforms. Most of them came from an armoured train in which, according to its Russian commander, they'd been about to launch a raid on Debaltsevo to rescue the gallant British aviators. In fact all the signs were that the train's purpose had been — still was — to evacuate the last of the Korsun garrison. So that if the RAF train had arrived a couple of hours later, they might well have found Korsun under Red occupation. It was in everyone's best interests to accept the story at its face value, however, and there was a great deal of mutual congratulation. More importantly, the RAF train now had a fully-manned armoured train as its escort to Taganrog and thence Rostov-on-Don.

Bob and Schelokov had spruced themselves up by this time. A bucket of hot water on the moving platform between two coaches served as a bath. You stood over it to wash yourself down, then sluiced off with a second bucketful. Bob had also shaved, while Schelokov had only trimmed his beard with a pair of scissors, and Mary Pilkington later cut Bob's hair for him, as a preliminary to cleaning and dressing the partly-healed lacerations on the back of his skull. Bob had had some clean shirts, underwear and socks in his holdall — which Leading Airman Pickerell had recovered from storage — and he gave Schelokov a shirt and other items. New outer clothing — breeches, sweaters and greatcoats — were provided from RAF stores, and everything the three of them had been wearing — except boots — went into the furnace.

Bob was still stiff and sore from those long days in the saddle, but apart from that felt almost like new, for being clean and shaved. Hot food and sound sleep helped too. Another factor was having the armoured train as escort, which provided a welcome and unusual sense of security.

There was also the pleasure of good company, including that of the two girls.

He asked them — while Mary was gently swabbing the back of his head — how they'd come to vanish from their nurses' training at the hospital at Simferopol, in the Crimea. He put the question in the first place because he'd genuinely wanted to know — after all, it was what had started this whole business — but also as a diversion from Mary's and Katya's questions about Nadia and Irina.

It was all right: he and Schelokov had agreed on what could and could not be told. But it was still preferable to say as little as possible. Ibraim would say nothing at all, would profess to speak no word of Russian and in particular not to react in any way to questions about *Mamasha* Solovyeva. He'd nodded: wooden-faced, impenetrable: he'd certainly be impenetrable to these girls, who in fact were the only ones likely to ask questions. While Bob and Schelokov's story was that Nadia had been killed by a shell at Bogodukhov — that story in as much detail as

Irina had provided — and that a former patient of the *letuchka*, a man named Maltsev, had told them that Irina had died of typhus. They'd found Maltsev in hiding at the farmstead, and he'd had Ibraim with him but hadn't known what had happened to the others, only that the *letuchka* had to all intents and purposes disintegrated. Ibraim had been left on his own, living like a wild beast, starving, until Maltsev had taken him under his wing.

Bob had given them the gist of this, commiserations and tears had followed, and then before the questions could become more detailed he'd changed the subject ... 'Tell *me* something now. When you were — or rather were *not* — at Simferopol, and we were all trying to find you — you'd skipped the training course, had you?'

'You've certainly every right to ask.' Katya changed her seat, to sit in front of him. With the other girl working on his head, until now he'd only been able to squint at her sideways. Katya — Katherine, or Kate — told him, 'If we'd known what trouble we'd be causing — well, we'd have still been there, I suppose. What an extraordinary thought.' Her light-blue eyes were very striking, in contrast to all that dark-brown hair framing a wide forehead and good cheek-bones. Very expressive eyes too: at this moment, troubled. 'Making you risk your neck for us. I feel so guilty — *and* so grateful. It's really incredible, what you've done for us.'

'Nonsense. It was really a bit of a jaunt, at first. Just happened that one thing led to another, then. Nothing to do with you that Boris Vasil'ich and I trekked up to Valki, for instance. By the way — I suppose you've had no news of Dr Markov?'

'No. But I don't know how we would have.'

'No. No ... Anyway, tell me how you came to vanish from Simferopol?'

'You tell it, Mary.'

'All right ... Sorry, did I snip your ear then?'

'Not that I noticed.'

'Must have leather ears ... Well — to start with, we were frightfully bored with the training. And some of the

senior staff were — well, in particular, we'd both taken a
terrific scunner of the matron. Stuffy old — besom ... We
weren't learning much by then anyway. And we knew they
were terribly short of nurses at the front, we were dying to
make ourselves useful — what we'd joined up for in the
first place.'

'So you skipped.'

'There was a doctor who'd come down with a trainload
of wounded from Ekaterinoslav. He told us how the *letuchki* were so short-handed that when they were really up
against it they couldn't cope. In the war against the
Germans, you see, a *letuchka* would have three or four
doctors and at least a dozen nurses. And masses of transport, of course. Whereas by now — well, anyway, we told
him how *we* felt, and he said why not go back with him.
Nobody was going to look gift-horses in the mouth, and
so on, and — that's what we did. We had a few days' leave
due to us, and never went back.'

'Never saw that doctor again, either, after we got there.'
Katya's eyes were on Mary, over Bob's head. 'Much to
somebody's disappointment. Heavens, what *misery*—'

'Kate — please—'

She winked at Bob. 'They'd packed the poor man off
heaven knows where. But he'd been right, nobody *did* ask
us any awkward questions. They either assumed we'd
completed our training, or turned blind eyes. And though
I say it myself, we *have* made ourselves quite useful, from
time to time.'

'Your parents are going to be enormously relieved to
hear you're safe. When we get to Novorossisk — to a ship,
get a signal off—'

'Oh, but they'll have heard already! General Holman
was going to get a message off to Constantinople — from
Novo Cherkassk. He went off in the same flying-machine
that you put us in. So by now — I certainly *hope*—'

'Well, that's capital. Of course, I'd forgotten Holman ...
But whether since then the War Office can have known
about this train being trapped — or let the news out even
if they have—'

'Let's hope *not*. Be a bit *too* much!'

He nodded. 'Major Kinkead's hoping to get a message off by land-line from Pokrovsk, he tells me. As long as the lines are open — as they're said to be.' The armoured train's commander had told Kinkead they were. 'So pretty soon your fathers'll be opening the champagne, even if they haven't yet — eh?'

'Well ...'

'*Might*, I suppose ...'

Smiling at each other ... Katya said, 'Once they get over being furious with us ...'

They were darned nice girls, he thought. Natural, and forthright, and as far as he could tell unmarked by their own experiences, which must at times have been fairly gruesome as well as frightening. Katya was the more sensitive of the two. For instance, she'd realized that Nadia must have meant a lot to him, and was touchingly sympathetic.

'She was really *lovely*, wasn't she?'

'I thought so.'

'Well, she was. And she was very kind to us, in that short time we were with them. Oh, Irina too, of course, but—'

'Yes.'

'This man who told you about them — you said he was in hiding actually *at* the farm there ... So was that where Irina died?'

'I think so. Yes, must've been.'

And that was no lie — geographically speaking. But there was absolutely no reason to burden these young girls with anything like the full story. In fact it would be a criminal act, he thought, to give them even a hint of it.

'The *letuchka* — just split up, you said. So the others—'

'Maltsev couldn't tell us. He was only really positive on the subject of Nadia's death. And about Irina, I suppose, but that could have been more like hearsay. I think he must have been discharged from the *letuchka* and come back to take refuge there when the front collapsed. So — as I say, it's rather vague. And there was no one else we could have talked to — fact is, we were lucky to come across *him*. Red cavalry were thick on the ground by that time, we weren't out to attract attention.'

'I'm sure *not!*'

Schelokov joined them then, and they switched into Russian. He'd been on the footplate, he told them, chatting with Baibakov, with whom he'd found common ground in their detestation of all Bolsheviks. Baibakov had had a son whom they'd hanged for trying to evade conscription into the Red Army, apparently. Schelokov smiled at Bob, murmured with no smile at all in his eyes, 'They have their endearing little ways, haven't they?'

Katya asked — still on the subject of their experiences at Valki — 'You brought the Tartar back with you, but for some reason not — er — Maltsev?'

'He's from Kiev. Wife and child there, I think he said. Anyway that's where he wanted to get to when he could. But Ibraim's home's somewhere on the western shore of the Caspian, so the idea is to take him along as far as Tikhoretsk.'

'Tikhoretsk ...'

'Hundred miles east of Rostov. Railway junction where — touch wood — we'll turn down for Novorossisk.'

Katya grimaced. 'Awful long way, still ...'

'Never mind. You'll have plain sailing now, you'll see ...' Schelokov had put himself down between the two girls. 'Let's talk about the future now. Will you continue as nurses when you get home to England?'

'Scotland.' Katya frowned at him. 'If you *please* ... No — not on your life!'

Bob asked Mary, 'Where's *your* home?'

'Norfolk. D'you know it?'

He shook his newly-trimmed head. 'I've heard it's cold. But then—' looking at Katya — 'so's Scotland ... Whereabouts in Scotland?'

'Lanarkshire. A place you wouldn't have heard of, called Lesmahagow.'

'Well, I think I may have *heard* of it ...'

'We have a farm there. My father's a doctor but he

inherited this place, and — we love it.' She shut her eyes, took a long breath. 'My, but it's going to be *wonderful* to see it again ...'

Scott broached the subject of the seven corpses they'd left in that other train. This conversation took place in the corridor on the first evening, with no one else in earshot except Ibraim, who'd taken up permanent residence outside their compartment. Bob had gone out there to smoke his pipe — out of consideration for the girls, who might not have appreciated the fumes of Navy-issue tobacco.

He'd left a tin of it in his holdall. Finding it still there had been like stumbling on buried treasure.

Scott said — glancing round first, and speaking quietly — 'They say the inside of that wagon was like a slaughter-house, Cowan.'

He nodded. 'I did suggest they should be warned.'

'But — the three of you did that — with *swords*?'

The light was fading, woods and snowfields merging into night, the train somewhere between Korsun and Pokrovsk at this stage. He glanced round at the Canadian. 'If you're passing some kind of judgement on us, Scott—'

'No. I'm not. But it's — kind of stunning ... Hell, in cold blood—'

'Would you rather this train was still stuck there, waiting to be attacked?'

'Of course not. Don't get me wrong, I'm not—'

'It would be if we hadn't done it. There was no other way, absolutely none. Unless we'd been little gentlemen and said oh, we couldn't have anything like *that* on our consciences — and ridden on, left you all — and those girls—'

'Cowan — hold on. I am completely in agreement. And grateful. *Deeply* so. I guess what stuns me is how you'd have — well, faced up to it. Even just the plain physical aspect of it, I mean. I'd have — run a mile ...'

'I wouldn't pretend the prospect exactly thrilled one. But we were saving our own skins too — don't forget that. First and foremost, that's what it was. When we were told this train was still there — good Lord, it felt like Christmas. A way *out* — which otherwise we were far from sure of. You don't have to be grateful, Sam.'

He found himself wondering — as they changed the subject, Scott describing the action on the station at Debaltsevo — how he'd have reacted to the story of the wolves, if he'd heard it.

But he wouldn't. Nobody would — ever.

It had been dark for an hour by the time the two trains pulled into Pokrovsk, and after Kinkead and the armoured train's CO had conferred with the local military commander it was decided to stay there for the night. There was fighting around Taganrog, apparently — about twenty miles down the line — and it was thought wiser to pass through that area in daylight. In fact the Taganrog marshalling yards were under attack when the train made a short stop there early next morning. Bodies of cavalry had been sighted from time to time; they were too far off to be identifiable, but the fact they kept their distance from the armoured train with its jutting gun-barrels suggested they might be Budyonny's men. A layer of smoke hung over the port area, and while the trains were at rest one could hear continuous rifle and machine-gun fire.

Schelokov commented, when they were on their way again — rumbling east, with the coast of the Sea of Azov on their right and Rostov-on-Don about forty-five miles ahead — 'You and I might still have been riding south, Robert Aleksandr'ich.' Pointing back towards Taganrog: 'Heading for *that* refuge — eh?'

He nodded. Catching a sight of muddy-looking sea, and thinking that it was only eleven or twelve days since he'd landed on this coast, from HMS *Terrapin* ... And from that thought, to the prospect of embarkation at Novorossisk in a few days' time, for passage first to the Horn and later — but please God not *much* later — to England.

Looking over at Schelokov. This would be as good a time as any to broach a subject that had been in his mind a lot, in the past twelve hours.

'Are you still set on leaving us at Rostov, Boris Vasil'ich?'

'Yes.' Schelokov put his hand on his mug of breakfast tea, then looked round for some sugar. Jim Davies passed it to him, and the Russian used one of the four or five English expressions that he had in his vocabulary: 'Senk you very moch.' Then to Bob: 'There's no other course for me. In my place you'd feel the same.'

'I've been doing some thinking, though ...'

'You're *very* thoughtful, Robert Aleksandr'ich. And very kind, and a good friend. *But*—'

'It could be a terrific thing, Boris Vasil'ich. I mean for me as well as you. Give me a chance to explain this — I *have* thought it out ... I mentioned to you that my father left me certain business interests — the business he built up? There are — substantial assets. Lawyers are looking after it all for me now, but it's there for me to take control of when I get back. Shipping would be a natural thing. With the war finished there'll be a lot of ships going cheap. But all sorts of opportunities, anyway. Exciting, really. And I'd be much easier in my mind if I had a partner. We'd go halves — or something like it — it'd be very much to my own advantage—'

'My dear Robert Aleksandr'ich.' Schelokov's eyes had been steadily widening. 'My *dear* fellow ...'

'I truly *am* thinking of my own advantage, as much as yours. Chance in a million — to have a partner I could trust like a brother—'

Scott pushed in, then, with Kinkead, shouting for Pickerell to bring them some breakfast. Kinkead nodded to Bob and to Schelokov as he sat down. 'Rostov by noon, eh.'

'I suppose so.'

'Just saying to Sam here, the likely thing is they'll divert us to Novo Cherkassk from there. To hand over our Camels to Denikin's chaps, you see. In which case I imagine you'll change trains. Might have to kick your heels for a while, but—'

'I may stay with you, Cowan—' Scott cut in —

'depending on whether "A" Flight's been shipped out yet. If not, they'll be at Novo Cherkassk too, I guess, so I'd go along.'

'Davies too?'

'If "A" Flight's gone, he'll stay with this crowd. Marcus is one pilot short. So—'

'What I was about to say—' Kinkead had frowned slightly at the interruption — 'is that our two young ladies will need escorting to Novorossisk.'

'Of course.' Bob nodded. 'I'd expect to anyway.' He asked Kinkead, 'The land-line was open from Pokrovsk, I take it?'

He'd meant to ask, and forgotten. Becoming too much of a passenger, he thought — leaving it all to others. Better watch that . . . Kinkead was saying, 'It was indeed. Got my report out, and a reply from Ray Collishaw crack of dawn this morning. They'd realized we were stuck but hadn't been able to get any hard facts anywhere. A certain degree of relief was evident — as you can imagine.'

'Can indeed.'

'You've been given the full credit, I may say. Naturally . . . But I can tell General Holman that you and Major Schelokov have taken the young ladies into your care and protection, can I?'

Schelokov had glanced up at the sound of his name. Bob told him in Russian, 'He's asking if you're coming to Novorossisk — since Katya and Maria will need to be escorted there. This train's likely to be sent up to Novo Cherkassk, apparently.'

The grey eyes held his, for a moment.

Then he'd taken a long breath, and nodded. 'Novo Cherkassk would be best for me too. Since headquarters are there. I'll get a regiment together, perhaps . . . It's what I *have* to do, Robert Aleksandr'ich. I'm grateful to you, and honoured, but—'

'All right.'

Schelokov looked at Kinkead, and pointed at himself. 'Novo Cherkassk, me.'

*

In the letter which she wrote two weeks later to her older sister, Kate Reid described the scene at the Rostov railway station as *even by current Russian standards, middling pandemonium...*

She wrote — at a desk in the captain's day-cabin in the destroyer *Mistral*—

We had a six-hour wait there. Mary and I, Commander Cowan, Major Scott and the Tartar they call Ibraim. A very strange individual, even in comparison with other Tartars whom one has known — although the commander (and for that matter Boris Schelokov) seemed to have great respect for him. This is a complicated story and none too clear in detail, but Ibraim was with the mobile field hospital which they went off to find, and seems to have been its sole survivor. He came back with them. In saying it's complicated what I mean is that I'm sure the full story has not yet been divulged. It is however a long way to Tipperary, and who knows what may yet emerge? Patience being a virtue, and curiosity never having come anywhere near killing this cat. Despite some overdoses — as I'm sure you're thinking as you read this! But here, for instance, is a sample of these still waters that seem to run so deep ... At Rostov, Major Schelokov left us, on his way to Novo Cherkassk with the RAF contingent. Novo Cherkassk is now the White headquarters, and Boris expects to obtain a cavalry command. Having — I quote him — 'Loafed about long enough'. He's a very determined, strong character, as well as a kind and gentle one. I hate to say this, but I very much doubt that any of us will ever see him again. It was therefore an emotional farewell — for all of us — and there was something I heard Boris say which has rung in my ears ever since: he said to Bob — very earnestly, as they were shaking hands — 'On the subject of Nadia Egorova — remember — when it's bad, my friend — remember how it could have been for her. And thank God.'

Kate sat back, glancing over what she'd just written and

wondering yet again what he could have meant. She hadn't asked Bob Cowan about it during their five days together in the train from Rostov to Novorossisk — via the railway junction at Tikhoretsk, where Ibraim had left them — (a) because Bob might have thought she'd been eavesdropping on that private conversation, and (b) because she'd very much doubted whether he'd have given her a straight answer anyway.

In any case, this wasn't by any means her only way of knowing — *knowing*, now, not guessing — that there was a lot more to the Valki story than had yet been told. Mary knew it too, since they'd shared the nursing and Bob had been in delirium for days and nights on end. None of it had made any sort of coherent sense, but there'd been an undercurrent of violence and terror which several times even *without* comprehension had chilled her to the bone. Irina's name had come into those parts of it quite often, but Nadia's had not. Nadia's had recurred constantly, though, in his quieter ramblings, when he'd been in the condition which the textbook referred to as Typhomania — a low, muttering delirium which sometimes lasted for hours at a time, the words barely audible and totally confused but that name, Nadia, as clear as anything, time and time again.

Perhaps because one had been listening for it.

Kate glanced out of the porthole — which these people called a scuttle for some reason — at the great rolling mass of white-streaked green out there. It was rougher than ever now, with a far more violent motion on the ship than there'd been in their first few days on board, when she, Mary and Sam Scott had all been as sick as dogs.

She picked up her pen and resumed the letter to her sister.

> *The six hours we spent on that platform were nothing compared to the discomfort that was to follow — five nights and four days in a train so crowded that one could hardly move a finger! We were lucky to have food and drink with us — by courtesy of the RAF — since many of*

our fellow passengers were really starving, hunting for food at every halt and either finding nothing or indescribably awful stuff at exorbitant prices. We saw some people exchanging items of jewellery, furs, etc. for nothing more than loaves of black bread. Of course we did what we could to help, but had to keep enough for ourselves — physical weakening is particularly undesirable in an area where typhus is now endemic. At least the stove in our carriage was kept burning, so we didn't freeze, and both Bob and Sam (Major Scott) went to enormous lengths to make us as comfortable as was possible. But the crowding, and the lack of air, and revoltingly inadequate facilities — not to mention the fact that our train was twice fired on by brigands or Bolsheviks — well, am I giving you some idea of the delights of long-distance travel in the Caucasus? Enough for the moment anyway. All good things come to an end, so they say — but what follows? In our case it was arrival at Novorossisk — where, if you'll believe this, the town was under attack by Bolshevik artillery, the train-driver could not or would not continue to the actual station and we were left — dumped — in a siding where there was no platform, no facilities of any kind, nobody from whom to ask directions, only this panic-stricken mob — and total darkness, the town's electricity supply had either failed or been switched off! Shells were exploding every few minutes — nowhere near us, thank heavens, but one never knows where the next might fall — and warships, British and French, lying in the bay, were firing back with their big guns at the Bolshevik artillery. The gun-flashes lit the sky like sheet lightning. Jean, my dear, I tell you honestly, I have never in my life been so ...

She'd stopped writing: glancing round as Mary burst into the cabin. Propping herself in the doorway while the ship flung over and the scuttle turned green again, another great weight of sea booming across the iron deck overhead, exploding around the torpedo-tubes and the after superstructure — which as well as supporting a searchlight housed the ladder down to this and other cabins and the wardroom . . .'

'Bouncy.' Mary shut the door, came across the cabin and flopped down on the Admiralty-issue, horsehair-stuffed sofa. 'Really, *quite* bouncy . . . Our patient sleeping?'

'Was, when last peeked at.' Kate blotted the page she'd been writing. 'And golly, Mary — I was just thinking, we are *so* lucky.'

'You mean *he* is.' Nodding towards the sleeping-cabin. 'But he's as strong as an ox, as well as lucky.'

'Personally, I'd say it's nurses' luck as well as patient's.'

Mary smiled, showing her big teeth. 'But that's an *entirely* personal view, isn't it? You might as well admit, Katey.'

'Nothing *to* admit.' She turned that page of her letter face-down. 'Anyway, what d'you mean, might admit?'

'Well, never mind.' Mary stretched, yawning. 'Time will tell . . .'

'Oh, I'm sure it *will*. But Mary, there is one thing I wanted to say. When we get to Constantinople—'

'Hang on — that's what I was supposed to tell *you*. It's now more likely to be the day after tomorrow than tomorrow night. Even if the weather does moderate tomorrow, as they expect. This is straight from the horse's mouth — namely that of Lieutenant Wells, the navigating officer. We've slowed right down, did you notice?'

'All to the good.' Kate nodded. 'Give him a bit more time. What I was saying, anyway — when we do get there, obviously he'll have to stay put for a while. Time to recuperate, but also you may remember he told us in the train he's going to apply for release from the Navy — which he's entitled to—'

'So?'

'Well, the red tape'll take a little time, one imagines. And the point is, I think I'll stay with him — if it can be arranged.'

'You mean if *he*—'

'He *will* need looking after, Mary.'

'Whether he wants it or not, you mean, you'll—'

'How *dare* you!' The blue eyes flashed at her. 'What a *horrible* thing to say!'

'Oh — go on with you.' Mary laughed. 'I was only teasing. Come on, don't be so touchy! Of *course* he'll need looking after. Good heavens, he hasn't even got out of bed, yet ...' She came over to the desk, stooped to kiss Kate's forehead. 'But, Katey, I'm *extremely* fond of you — even if you do have a tendency to fly off the handle — and I'd hate to see you — well, let down. Seriously — reading between the lines of all that raving, for instance—'

'Nadia Solovyeva.'

'Well, yes ...'

'Two things. One, she was married to someone else. Two, she's dead.'

'As long as he can get that into his head — really accept it. Because otherwise—'

'I know, Mary. I'm not a *complete* idiot, you know.'

Bob lay drowsily with their low voices in his ears. Too low to hear anything they said: not that he'd have wanted to. Memory was patchy still and he wasn't fighting it, he was content to let his mind drift while bits and pieces fell into place in their own time. This destroyer, for instance, HMS *Mistral — Lightfoot*-class, built as a flotilla leader, as was obvious from this cabin layout. It was accommodation for a senior officer, not for your common-or-garden destroyer skipper. He'd mentioned this to Katya a few hours ago — or last night, whenever they'd last chatted. Intervals of time were vague, to say the least ... Anyway, while she'd pretended to be interested, she obviously hadn't been, not in the least; those light-blue eyes miles away, reflecting whatever she *was* thinking so hard about.

Getting home to Mummy and Daddy, probably.

Very nice kid, anyway. Efficient nurse, too. He probably owed her his life. Katherine Reid. A little jingle surfaced in memory: *Mary Pilkington and Katherine Reid* ...

Scott, and the Welshman, in the train to Kupyansk. The flavour of malt whisky, and the train's wheels beating out their rhythm: biddle-de-dum, biddle-de-dum, biddle-de-dum ... Then the same rhythm — different train — and Ibraim, at Tikhoretsk. That impassive face, as if carved crudely from mahogany, with tears gleaming in its slanting eyes. One hand raised, the figure dwindling and as unmoving as a statue as the train curved around the long bend to head south-west and its rear carriages shut off one's view of the platform. Schelokov's mutter in the dark: *By God, I'm glad Ibraim's on* our *side ...*

He thought of the wolves. Not, strangely enough, with any great sense of horror. Unlike another image which only flashed into mind for a split second, and was gone.

Mercifully. But the threat of it would always be there. Like a malarial infection that could flare at any time.

The girls' conversation had been interrupted by a telephone call from the bridge, the captain enquiring about their patient's progress. Resting quietly, Kate was telling him, and she hoped he might manage a light meal later on.

'Well, that's splendid!'

'Yes. And thank you *so* much—'

'None of that, now ... Are you two standing the weather all right? Back on *your* three square meals a day, I hope?'

Bridge and quarterdeck areas were virtually cut off from each other, that was the point. There was no way through a destroyer below decks, her centre part was all engine-room and boiler-rooms, with no through-connections. When the really big seas swept over, if you happened to be on her upper deck you needed to be quick on your feet, have all your wits about you *and* both hands for hanging on with. Life-lines had been rigged for this purpose but it was still a gauntlet to run. Despite which the captain — a lieutenant-commander by name of Claverhouse — told her before he rang off that Major Scott wanted them to know he'd be paying them a visit shortly.

She hung up. Mary said, glancing up from a book which the first lieutenant had lent her — a new novel by Somerset Maugham entitled *The Moon and Sixpence* — 'He's changed his tune a bit, hasn't he!'

'We did rather take advantage of him. I think considering everything he's been marvellous.'

Claverhouse hadn't known he was getting a passenger who had typhus. Hadn't *wanted* any passengers at all, let alone that kind.

Kate returned to her letter. Pausing in thought for a moment, she put the last page aside and started a new one, giving it a heading: JEAN. PRIVATE NOTE!

I'll continue with my narrative of events later. Just for now and while it's in my mind I want to explain why I'm writing all this when you might think that being on my way home I could as well wait and tell it to you. Well, to start with, I'll probably be stopping off for a while at Constantinople, in order to continue looking after Bob Cowan, who has been extremely ill — in fact might easily have died — as most typhus patients do. Yes, it was typhus, and he's on the mend now, but he's going to need quite a bit more looking after and it really is my responsibility. After that, with any luck we may be able to travel on home in the same ship — a hospital ship, perhaps, in which case I might be able to 'work my passage'. But Jean, this is strictly between us — I don't believe he has any home or family in Britain, but he will want to come to Scotland, as he has connections of some kind I believe in Glasgow, and it might be a good idea for him to come to us. After all, there's masses of room, and the peace and quiet would do him good. Do me good too — I'm dying to get home. And — again, strictly between ourselves — I think he and Father would 'hit it off' very well. To be perfectly frank, I can't imagine any normal person not liking him. Which I suppose must give you an idea how I feel about him, dear Jeannie.

Now destroy this, please — and be a darling, see if you can prepare the ground a little?

He'd been thinking about Colonel Temple and the report he'd have to make to him. It had seemed tricky at first, but he'd got it straight now and it was actually very simple. He'd put the girls in the observer's cockpit in Scott's DH9 because that had been the only sure way to get them out. Having then to get out himself, his best bet had seemed to be to team up with this Major Schelokov, who'd been hoping to find and bring out with him the personnel of another *letuchka*, then supposedly in the same area. They'd failed in this, had had several brushes with Red cavalry units and been on their way south with horses acquired in one of those actions when they'd heard about the train.

In other words one would tell the truth, except for saying nothing of having had any personal interest in that *letuchka*.

He heard the door slide open, slide shut again. Then Katya's whisper: 'Are you awake, Bob?'

'Hello, Katya.'

'Are you always going to call me that?'

'Shouldn't I?'

'Oh — I don't mind. Only at home I've always been called Kate. Or Katherine when I've misbehaved.'

'Misbehave often, do you?'

'Hah. That's a matter of opinion.' She was beside his bunk; the distance to it from the sliding door was only about three feet. The sleeping-cabin was really a sort of closet with this bunk in it, drawers under the bunk, a hanging-cupboard at one end and a scuttle in the ship's side at the other. Green water was flooding up over it at this moment: as the ship rolled he was looking down at it, past his feet at that end of the bunk.

He told her — with a picture in his mind of exactly how the ship and her surroundings would be looking at this moment from her bridge — 'Katya's a pretty name.'

'Well, if you think so ...' She was straightening the bedclothes. 'Bob, I came to tell you that Sam Scott's here. D'you feel up to receiving visitors?'

'Receive that one, certainly. And don't you go.'

She'd smiled as if that had pleased her. 'Mary's here too. But perhaps—'

'More the merrier. Let's have a party!'

'Well — no parties *quite* yet ...' She slid the door back. 'Sam, come on in. You too, Mary, if you like.'

Scott loomed over him. 'Say, *this* is how the other half lives!'

'Us Grand Dukes, you mean.'

'Ah. Remember *that* nonsense, do you ... How's your Highness feeling?'

'Not nearly as low as he was, thank God. Or rather thanks to these girls. But I believe I owe *you* for the fact we got here at all.'

'Bob, old chap, in present circumstances just about everyone owes just about everyone else. But you surely did pick a peach of a time to do it!'

'I'd felt bloody awful all that day. I think I'd passed out once or twice in the train.'

'Didn't think of mentioning it.'

'What could anyone have done?'

'You have a point ... Did you think then it might be typhus?'

'All I remember is hoping to God we'd make it to the port before I keeled over altogether. Tell me your side of it, Sam?'

'They've said I mustn't tire you out—'

'Go on. I'm nothing *like* tired out.'

'Well. We got out into the road — from where the train gave up on us. Remember? No, I suppose you wouldn't. You'd gone flat on your face once, pretended you'd tripped. I didn't guess the truth, but Kate here did. Well, both you girls did — eh?'

'Had a suspicion.' Mary shrugged. 'Said a prayer or two.'

'And Kate grabbed my arm, hissed at me we had to get you aboard some ship double-quick no matter what. She has a way with her, you know, this half-pint one here.'

'Hasn't she, though ...'

'We were something like four miles from the port, in a mob of about four thousand other people all with the same idea. Bloody chaos, I tell you — sorry ladies, but the language is well justified, as you know ... Then this motor came along, big old Ford hooting and waving through the peasantry, you could be damn sure *someone* was going to stop it before it got much further and I thought it might as well be me. So I did. Driver tried to circle around us, I got up on the running-board, put my revolver against his head, and he stopped. We had to be quick then — 3,996 other people saw *their* chance too. There was this fat Russian in the Ford, making an awful song and dance — politician of some kind making a run for it, I'd guess, or an oil nabob from Baku. Something of that sort. Ground-length sable coat, big fur hat, face like a blancmange. I hauled him out, pushed you in with the girls each side of you — should've mentioned, you'd passed out again, I'd had you over my shoulder the last hundred yards or so, I tipped you in and got in with the driver myself, told him to take us to the docks or I'd blow his brains out.'

Mary said, 'Literally. Revolver against the poor man's ear, cocked. Actually he'd cocked it when he intimidated some others who tried to cram in with us.'

'And he drove us to the docks?'

'Wasn't easy. Roads full of people, wrecked motors, dead horses, smashed-up carts — oh, *and* shell-holes — the railway station and the docks were being shelled, did I mention that? Some Bolshevik horse-artillery that had broken through — so they told us when we got on board here. And ships outside the port shooting back at 'em — ranging on the flashes maybe, I don't know. Battleships. The word is chaos — real, total—'

Katya interrupted: 'This ship was alongside one of the quays, and easy to spot because it was the only one.'

'Right. With a guard of bluejackets with fixed bayonets on the quay, a searchlight and machine-guns manned on deck. We'd crashed through a barrier, and damn near went into the basin at one point, incidentally. They were taking in oil-fuel and fresh water, from an oiler and a water-boat on the quay close by. Hoses still connected, but as soon as they'd filled her tanks she was going to push off. The one and only chance we had, I tell you — every other ship that had been in port had cleared off to escape the shelling. And this one was not about to embark refugees, let me tell you, she was sailing for the Kerch peninsula — east side of the Crimea, right?'

'Right. But—'

'I got on board. Pulling rank like I was at least a general — and briefed by guess-who. *This* one. You'd come back to life temporarily, in the motor, she'd asked you did you have a rash of a certain kind, you said you surely did, and described it — no recollection I suppose—'

'None at all.'

'Well, these two knew for sure then. Kate also guessed that the chances of any ship welcoming a typhus case on board weren't all that good. So she told me it was your head wound, nothing else, delayed concussion that had caught up with you. So, I told this guy — very snooty, unfriendly second-in-command — first lieutenant, right? First thing he said was' — Scott put on a plummy pseudo-English voice — "Kindly get off this ship, sir, we're about to sail" — Captain Bligh in person, whom we now know as Charlie Dimmock, as nice a guy as ever walked the plank — I told him who I was, pointed out that I had with me two British nurses who'd escaped from the Bolsheviks by the skin of their lovely teeth, and last but far from least Lieutenant-Commander Robert Cowan from the Commander-in-Chief's staff at the Horn, suffering from a head wound and in urgent need of treatment which he couldn't get on a dockside under shellfire. "Ah, but we have no doctor," Dimmock tried to tell me—'

'Why is that?'

'Seems they lent him to some hospital ship that was in dire straits for lack of them.'

'Lucky, then. If there *had* been—'

'Wouldn't've made an ounce of difference. They couldn't have checked you out on that quayside, and by the time we had you on board the ship was sailing. I stayed where I was, in case they tried to pull a fast one, two sailors carried you up and the girls came up with you. The gangway was being taken off then, but also the skipper'd joined us, got an eyeful of these two and started Oh by Jove, we could use his quarters here, what?'

'Sam, that's *nonsense!*'

'It's God's truth. But he has a little sea-cabin behind the bridge, uh? So then his steward was rushing around scooping up his gear, and — oh, general haste and confusion, no one had time to think about *you* any more. Gangway gone — ropes away — propellers churning. Then of course Nurses Reid and Pilkington discovered the whole truth — brown rash, when they were stripping you.'

'Stripping me.'

'Sure. I helped them. You're no featherweight, you know.'

'He is now. He's lost a couple of stone, I should guess.' Katya nodded. 'Reminds me, Bob. Lunch. You could have chicken broth — with toast, I suppose — or a poached egg—'

'This is where I came in.' Scott checked the time. 'How the other half lives ... Better leave you now, Bob. Five minutes, I was told.'

'Thanks anyway, Sam. For lugging me on board, and—'

'Forget it. Glad you decided to stick around, that's all. Oh, listen. Skipper asked me to tell you he's had a signal from Constantinople saying they're glad too. He'll be down to see you when the weather eases, show it to you then.'

He'd had the broth *and* an egg, and slept again. Wide awake then after an hour or so, he decided to try his legs out. He'd had enough of bed-pans anyway, felt sure *they* must have too.

Embarrassing. And stripping him, for God's sake. They weren't real nurses, they were young girls he'd been on a train with. He sat up, swung his legs off the bunk, and slid down. Careful at first, getting used to the ship's movement as well as to being upright. There was slight dizziness to start with, but it soon passed, and so far he felt no worse than he had lying down.

No worse than Dr Markov had looked standing up, as

he remembered him. And Markov had been setting off to trek about a hundred and fifty miles to Debaltsevo.

Probably never got there. Might have, but one's instincts told one he probably had not. There'd been just him and the matron and that other nurse, and only one able-bodied male with them — the Tartar driver. Not all Tartars were of Ibraim's calibre.

All right. Reasonably steady on the pins: and decently covered, in someone's striped pyjamas. He slid the door back.

'*Bob!*'

Katya was on duty again. She seemed to have been taking the lion's share of it. At the desk, writing a letter, but starting up now, pushing the chair back ... 'Bob, you should *not*—'

'Don't worry. Trying it out — so far so good — and a brief trip to the heads. No, I know where it is. Anyhow, if we're going to be at the Horn tomorrow—'

'Day after, now. We've had to slow down.' She came across the cabin to help him, but he warded her off, assured her, 'I'm all right. Truly.' A big sea smacked down overhead at that moment, and his eyes went to the scuttle, the stream of brilliant white as the ship threw herself the other way. He was holding the back of the sofa for support: glancing at Katya again now. 'How long have we been on board?'

'Just over a week. They were patrolling off Kerch — inside the Sea of Azov?'

'Keeping the Bolsheviks out of the Crimea. More vital than ever now.'

'I suppose so. We went into Kerch itself twice, then this last time into Theodosia, to refuel. Must be nine days we've been on board.'

'And you've been cooped up down here all that time.'

'Oh — not *all* the time. Anyway, it's—'

She'd cut that short. He guessed she'd been going to say 'it's my job'. She was pointing at the deckhead: 'I wouldn't want to be up *there*, anyway!'

'Not at this moment, perhaps.' He'd come round the

end of the sofa, thinking he might sit for a few minutes.
Picking up Mary's novel, glancing at its spine. 'Maugham
... Tell me, what's for supper?'

'Are you feeling *that* well?'

'Not bad at all. Thanks to you.' He let himself flop
down. Pointing at a camp-bed that was folded and lying
against the bulkhead near the desk. 'Is that what you sleep
on?'

'No. Where you're sitting.'

'On this?'

'Mary's too long for it, she has the camp-bed ... Bob,
d'you think Colonel Temple will want to keep you long in
Constantinople?'

'He'll want to be rid of me as soon as possible, I'd
imagine.'

'Seriously. Because you'll need — oh, at least two or
three weeks, to get your strength back.'

'They'll keep me *that* long, I dare say.' He nodded.
'Probably a bit of work to clear up, anyway. And getting
my papers through. A few weeks, I'd guess.'

'The thing is, Bob — someone ought to keep an eye on
you, for a while. And if I did — well, there's sure to be a
nurses' hostel or somewhere where I could put up. Then
we could travel on home together, you see—'

'Katya—' he was shaking his head — 'from my own
point of view it would be lovely — of course — but—'

'You won't be really fit at least for—'

'I'm sure I will be. Admittedly I'm feeling a bit weak
now, but — well, look, Katya, first of all this is *very* kind
of you — and I appreciate it very much — but—'

'Not *kind*, at all!'

'*I* think it is. But it would also be very *un*kind to your
parents. Secondly — as I say, I'll be right as rain in a
matter of a day or two, and third, I'll most likely get a
berth home in one of HM ships. Keep a watch, earn my
pay. I won't actually be released until I get to England,
you see. So really that's not very practical. It *is* sweet of
you to offer, but—'

'I'd *like* to stay with you, Bob.'

She was standing facing him with her hands behind her gripping the edge of the desk, and looking — he saw it in that moment — quite desperately anxious.

'My parents will know I'm on the way. I've been writing a long letter home, explaining ... They won't be worrying now, Bob. So *you* don't have to. And it's not kindness, it's what I *want* — don't you understand, I—'

'But — here's another thing now, Katya.' He pushed himself up. Hardly believing this, but having to, and realizing in the same breath how important it was that she shouldn't see his understanding of it. Having to act and speak casually, and not look at her more than he had to ... Telling her — on his way over to the scuttle — 'They're bound to have passages arranged for you both. Right away. Absolutely sure to. After all, when I was sent to find you they were all screaming blue murder to know where you'd got to and get you packed off home. This came through the Admiralty, let me tell you — political strings, see? Oh, you can bet on it — you'll be shipped off long before *I* will ...' At the scuttle, with his back to her, gazing out at the wilderness of sea through the distorting effect of streaming-wet thick glass ... 'Heavens. *What* a sight this is ...'

God, he thought, but I can be slow in the bloody uptake, when I try.

Early morning now: he was wide awake after a long, dreamless sleep. On his back in the narrow bunk, recalling with shame how damnably slow he'd been to catch on.

He hoped it was going to be all right. That she'd believe he'd meant all along to get in touch with her when they were home, not just dredged it up on the spur of the moment — as he had ... Then he'd gone from the day-cabin to the heads, and back to his bunk as expeditiously as he could have done without making the escape seem too obvious, and he hadn't seen her since. Mary had brought him his supper. Corned beef hash — a reminder of cruder versions of the same dish prepared by Boris Schelokov in those snowbound forests.

Mary might well have a good idea of how the wind had been blowing, he thought. She had a shrewd head on her shoulders, that one. Not that Katya was anything like stupid ...

He *would* see her. At least, write to her, ask to see her.

He thought the weather might have begun to moderate a little, by the feel of it. *Might* have ...

Get up there — out of this damn cupboard?

The suddenness and strength of the urge bewildered him.

Hearing the storm up there: even if it *had* moderated — a little ... Lying still and listening to it, as it were sending his mind up there ahead of him. Asking himself, *Crazy?*

Shut in, here. Claustrophobic. And having begun to think about it made it worse. For 'cupboard', read 'coffin'. As it might well have been, at that ... Well, God, why *not* ... sliding his weight off the bunk. No more thinking to be done: except the problem of getting out through the day-cabin without waking them. Once outside — well, there'd be oilskins hanging in the wardroom flat, for instance. There always were. Men came off watch, had to hang the things somewhere. He found a sweater in one of the drawers, too. Not a watchkeeper's sweater, more the sort a cricketer might wear, with the Royal Navy colours knitted into its 'V' neck. He pulled it on over his pyjamas and wrapped a towel around his neck to fill the 'V'. Looking for footwear then, he found nothing he could get his feet into — except for the boots he'd acquired at Valki, and they'd have filled with water in the first minute he was on deck. Therefore, no point in borrowing any of the skipper's socks either.

He slid the door back very, very cautiously — about one centimetre at a time. Expecting a squawk at any moment ... Although there was more than enough ship-noise and weather-noise to drown any small sounds he might make. The influx of light from the cabin flat when he opened the outer door might be the main danger. But it wasn't a bright light: it showed through the air-slots in the top of the door, not much more than the glow you'd get from a night-light in a nursery. He crept around the back of the sofa — aware of the small figure humped under blankets, moving on past without glancing down again. He'd seen the camp-bed's oblong against the bulkhead too, hoped *she* was as sound asleep. Reaching the door now, turning the handle slowly, then opening it no further than he had to, to slide out into the flat.

He'd escaped. Could breathe now.

As he'd expected, there were wet oilskins on the hooks below the steel ladderway. There was also one pair of seaboots; but they wouldn't have fitted, and his feet had been wet and cold so often in the Ukrainian snow he didn't think one more time would hurt. He took down an 'oily' that looked bigger than the others, and under it on the same hook was a pair of baggy waterproof trousers with a draw-string waistband. So-called waterproof — he knew them of old — but they'd be a lot better than nothing. He pulled them on over the pyjama trousers, buttoned the coat and went up the ladder.

The watertight door in the caboosh at the top was held shut by only one clip — as he'd have expected. He stepped out over the high sill, and put the same clip back on the door, all in one swift motion while the ship was on a more or less even keel.

The twenty-inch searchlight was mounted on this structure: a barrel-shaped object, black against the night sky. Wind screaming and buffeting and the air wet with continuous icy spray ... He found the life-lines — steel-wire rope set up taut on both sides of the foremost pair of torpedo-tubes, between them and the ship's sides. Sea racing by close on his left, coming closer every second as she rolled and a mound of it lifted — mountainous, threatening ...

Swamping over — *now*. He was holding with both hands to the jackstay as the torrent swept around him waist-deep. She'd been bow-down and leaning hard to port — *this* way — and now there was a second rush of sea behind the first, pouring over the fo'c'sl break, seething like a mill-race around the funnels and the mounting of the four-inch gun there. He was on the move again as it leaked away — she'd come soaring up, then her stern dropped as a valley opened under her quarter, and she was rolling hard to starboard. Bow still well up — for the moment ... He'd passed one funnel, and that gun-mounting, was between the middle funnel and a seaboat in its davits when the forepart began its powerful downward lunge, sea flying white like a shroud back over her whole length. He covered the last few yards at a run — bare feet had something to be said for them — guessing there'd be a big one coming in about five seconds. Past the foremost funnel — narrower than the other two, almost stovepipe-like in comparison — and the foot of the mast, and he was on the ladder, climbing, as that next one rushed aft, slamming against the front of the bridge — he didn't see that, only heard and felt it through the steel rungs and handrails — then flooding over the ladders port and starboard, deluging down into the waist. If he'd been slower he'd have had that lot on top of him.

The first level of the bridge structure — it was actually fo'c'sl deck level — housed the wireless office, skipper's sea-cabin and chartroom. One level higher — the physical effort was telling on him more than he'd realized, he might even have accepted at this stage that he'd been less than sensible to have left the cabin — this next level now was the after end of the bridge, the signal deck, and he was hauling himself into it. Breathless, heart hammering, and that dizziness again ... But he was off the ladder: among signal-lockers, a central structure with another searchlight on it, a proliferation of cleated halyards slanting up to the yard and masthead, and other signal paraphernalia. In the bridge itself — there was a step up into that forward section — he could see three dark figures hunched, two at its forefront and one — the helmsman — at the binnacle behind them. It wasn't likely they'd notice him: they had their work cut out with keeping a lookout ahead and steering a more or less straight course, without worrying about some outsize passenger lurking in the background.

He was feeling better now. The dizzy spell had passed, and his heart wasn't pounding as it had been. More cure than kill, perhaps: two minutes ago he wouldn't have put money on it. Jamming himself into the starboard after corner — hanging on, as the bow came down like an axe-head to split an oncoming mass of sea, the ship's frames shuddering from the impact and displaced water leaping like a geyser, black fringed with white, a few tons of it lifting on the wind to sheet solidly over the bridge's fore-front. He was in the way of some of that: spitting out salt water, and the pyjama-top and sweater not much drier now than the pyjama trousers.

But it was fine here in this corner, with one arm locked around the top rail and the other shoulder hard up against the metal side of a signal-locker. The rails had splinter-mattresses lashed outside them. Starboard side rolling down, the ship jolting as she leant *her* shoulder into a lifting, oncoming mound of sea. When she listed this hard, in his railed corner he was out over the sea itself, that seething whiteness directly under him until she began to come back and eventually the dark curve of the ship's side broke up through it. Rolling hard to port now, and bow-down, burying her snout deep and a mass of black water thundering up over her fo'c'sl, drowning the gun down there — he guessed, couldn't see it from this position — then almost literally exploding — sound and impact like a collision or a shellburst, the ship feeling it so drastically that it had almost stopped her: and again, an avalanche of solid water cascading over into the bridge. Not a shell-burst, he thought — as she recovered, her forepart breaking out of the welter of engulfing sea — a *chemodan*, that one. If that had been snow instead of foam, and laced with scarlet. Not that there'd have been any such traces for a long time now, under the snowfalls of recent weeks. No trace at all — except in memory, and dreams of what might have been. He spat salt down-wind again. Feeling much stronger now, and thinking that if they continued to leave him to himself he'd stay up here and see the dawn.

HISTORICAL NOTE

'B' flight of 47 Squadron RAF were stranded at Kupyansk for only three days — from 3rd to 6th December 1919 — after the engine of their train had been stolen. Encirclement by Red cavalry was very much on the cards; the airmen were issued with rifles and prepared to fight. But on the 6th their CO (Lt.Col. Raymond Collishaw, a Canadian whose personal score of 'kills' on the Western Front had been sixty-eight) and General Holman arrived with an engine, and the long haul to Novorossisk via Debaltsevo began. Taganrog was under attack when they passed through, the train itself was attacked near Rostov, and the situation in Novorossisk was a great deal worse than my fictional Sam Scott's rather flippant description might suggest. Nor was it a brief ordeal, as Odessa's had been. Refugees continued to flood into the town from December until the end of March, during which time British and French ships struggled to maintain a shuttle service to the Crimea. Ashore, thousands died — of starvation, typhus and the intense cold — and the evacuation was hampered by icing in the port. The end — for those left behind, as the last ships pulled out on the night of 27th March and Budyonny's formations swept down from the hills, is sickening to imagine.

There was a young RN officer by name of Peter Ashmore billeted at the Kist Hotel in Sevastopol in the latter part of 1919. He was later to become an admiral but at that time he was working for Colonel Temple, RM, chief of naval intelligence in Constantinople. My descriptions of the Kist Hotel, Captain Kotter with his Lewis gun set up in the foyer, and of the French treatment of refugees in Sevastopol are drawn from Ashmore's own notes which are embodied in a typescript now in the Ministry of Defence's naval library. It may be of interest that part of his brief was to (a) find, (b) arrange repatriation for, English women who had formerly been employed as governesses in Russian households in the Crimea.

Warner now offers an exciting range of quality titles by both established and new authors. All of the books in this series are available from:
Little, Brown and Company (UK) Limited,
Cash Sales Department,
P.O. Box 11,
Falmouth,
Cornwall TR10 9EN.

Alternatively you may fax your order to the above address. Fax No. 0326 376423.

Payments can be made as follows: Cheque, postal order (payable to Little, Brown and Company) or by credit cards, Visa/Access. Do not send cash or currency. UK customers: and B.F.P.O.: please send a cheque or postal order (no currency) and allow £1.00 for postage and packing for the first book, plus 50p for the second book, plus 30p for each additional book up to a maximum charge of £3.00 (7 books plus).

Overseas customers including Ireland, please allow £2.00 for postage and packing for the first book, plus £1.00 for the second book, plus 50p for each additional book.

NAME (Block Letters) ....

ADDRESS...

....

☐ I enclose my remittance for _____

☐ I wish to pay by Access/Visa Card

Number ⬚⬚⬚⬚⬚⬚⬚⬚⬚⬚⬚⬚⬚⬚⬚⬚

Card Expiry Date ⬚⬚⬚⬚